Finding It All

A Finding Happiness In
Harmony Novel

STACEY KOMOSINSKI

Finding It All

Join the mailing list for updates and follow Stacey here:
https://msha.ke/staceyakomosinski/

Dedication

For Ruth Smullin

Twenty-seven years have passed since I last hugged you and not one day goes by that I don't think of you. My most vivid memory of you is when you sat at the kitchen table with your cup of tea reading a romance novel.

A childhood with you taught me a lifetime of lessons …
Love like today was your last day, make family the most important part of your life, and remember that money can't buy you either.

I miss you.

Chapter 1

Chloe Larson listened to Gaby babble on and on, thinking, *Wow, can this girl talk!* Her best friend was never quiet. It was easy to see why people flocked to her, with her bubbly personality and long wavy dark hair that seemed to bounce everywhere when she spoke. Chloe admired her animation and energy. With how close they were, one would think they had been childhood friends, but it had only been seven years.

They had met the first week of their freshman year in college when a fire alarm went off late one night. While waiting in the grassy quad to go back to the dorms, getting eaten alive by mosquitoes, Gabriella Rodriguez leaned over to Chloe and said, "Thank God we're in an all-girls dorm! I'm not wearing a bra and, believe me, I need one. God did not bless me with that kind of perkiness!" She easily made Chloe laugh, and they had been best friends since.

They met their other roommate and best friend, Jessica Taylor, later that same year. Chloe and Gaby had joined Jess one day for lunch in the cafeteria, and the three of them clicked.

While Jess might have been a bit reserved at first, it didn't take long for her sarcastic side to show. This, she later told Gaby and Chloe, she blamed entirely on their encouraging natures and relentlessly infectious personalities. Chloe and Gaby could see, even from that first day, that Jess fit in well with her sharp and witty comments.

Chloe knew she was lucky to have found them. Growing up had been lonely, and these two amazing women had filled an emptiness she'd carried for years. She couldn't imagine going through life without them.

Now, standing in their kitchen as Gaby continued her talking rampage, Chloe gathered her things for work. She usually brought breakfast and lunch with her and ate while she multitasked at her desk. Most days, she grabbed an apple and a snack too, just in case she had to stay late or head out to get a story near the end of the day.

Jess walked through the doorway and gave Chloe a sideways look as she twisted her hand in a gesture that said: *wind her up and watch her go.*

1

Chloe tipped her head up and smiled.

Luckily, Chloe and Jess were the listening type and didn't mind Gaby's love of talking or overall excited nature.

Instead of packing up her things too, Gaby waved her hands around, illustrating the crazy dream she'd had the night before—which featured a gorgeous man leading her through a sensual Latin dance.

She put her arms up, showing off a tango hold. "He was so close I could feel his breath and the warm skin of his bare chest! So sexy."

Chloe didn't share the same energy Gaby had in the morning, so she wasn't processing every word her friend said. Instead, she focused on getting out of the house and to work on time, waiting for the right moment to cut in and tell Gaby to get a move on.

Finally, Gaby's story died down and she stared off, lost in her dream. Chloe seized her opportunity. "Gaby, we need to get going or we'll be late. I can't miss today's morning meeting."

Ever since Gaby's car died a few weeks ago, Chloe had let her share her car. It was the least she could do; after all, Gaby had driven Chloe around all through college. Conveniently, Gaby didn't work far from Chloe either.

Chloe focused on Gaby. "Who's driving today?"

Gaby took a breath, having finally finished recounting her dream. She answered Chloe with a shrug. "I am good either way. I plan to go out at lunch, but I can walk. Do you remember that guy I met last week at the farmers market? Rob. He asked me to meet him for coffee today around the corner from the hospital. So, you can just drop me off, that way you don't have to drive the news van if you need to go out."

Chloe nodded. "Oh yeah? Coffee? That's great!" She made a move toward the door. "I'll start carrying my stuff out to the car."

Chloe walked out to the curb, where her little white car waited. The sun already shone bright overhead, and Chloe could tell that it would be another hot July day in Texas. She opened the back door and put down her bags, then returned to the driver's side to start up the engine. She made sure to crank the air so the car would start to cool down.

Heading back inside the house, she smoothed her low ponytail, a perfect style for a low-maintenance Friday in the office.

The cute townhouse the three girls shared sat on a quiet street in a safe neighborhood near the outskirts of Galorston. The friends had found the place right after graduation three years ago. They all decided to stay in the city where they went to college. Chloe had no interest in going back to Pennsylvania where she grew up—too many bad memories. Jess was in a similar situation; she didn't want to go back to Oklahoma to live with her crazy mom.

Gaby, on the other hand, loved the place she grew up and wanted to live close to home. Of course, she loved it, her mom was amazing. Plus, she came to visit every couple of weeks. In return, the girls visited "Momma R." often and saw her every holiday. Gaby's mom acted as a surrogate to all of them, loving each as if they were her own.

Once back inside, Chloe could see that her nudge was successful. Gaby quickly gathered the last of her things and headed for the door. Jess also looked ready to head out. Her sunglasses sat on top of her head and her bags waited by the door.

Jess was the most efficient person Chloe knew. She was quick to make decisions, quick to get things done, and quick to accomplish anything she put her mind to. It was these characteristics that helped drive Jess to early success in her career as a programmer. She'd started out writing code to develop statistical programs for an IT firm. She did so well that she soon climbed the ranks and now ran a project for one of the firm's larger customers. Chloe could see Jess running her own company one day.

Chloe grabbed the last of her stuff and smiled at Jess. "When will you be home tonight?"

Jess smirked. "It's the end of the week, so I will try to be home at the regular time or even earlier if I can manage it."

Gaby opened the front door for Chloe and added over her shoulder, "I sure hope so since I have a new recipe I'm trying out tonight!"

"I can't wait! You know I live for Friday nights with your cooking and Chloe's desserts!"

Chloe smiled as they made their way to the car, admiring Gaby's dress. "Is that the new one you ordered on Monday? It's so cute on you!" To herself she added, *With Gaby's curves and dark brown curly hair, anything looks good on this girl!*

Trim and of average height, Chloe stood a bit taller than Gaby and was less curvy, but still had them in all the right spots.

Gaby smiled back. "I bought this and a jumpsuit but decided this was more appropriate for a dietitian to wear to work. Since it's strapless, I'll save the jumpsuit for going out tomorrow night."

Chloe got in the driver's seat and looked at Gaby. "Jess and I should get something new for tomorrow night too. Maybe we can run to that new shopping area that recently opened on Strayer Street. I heard good things about it from Mya at work."

Gaby got that same excited look in her eyes she always did anytime someone mentioned shopping. Glancing at her phone, she scrolled for some music to play. "Yeah, we'll head there tomorrow morning. We can stop after class."

Gaby taught Latin hip-hop dance classes Saturday mornings and usually managed to drag Chloe and Jess with her. Neither girl thought of it as dragging, though—maybe just a drag to get moving early on a Saturday.

Gaby's classes were a lot of fun because she was a great teacher. She kept the steps simple for those who just wanted to have fun but added in some spicy moves for anyone who wanted more of a challenge. Gaby taught other classes for more advanced dancers during the week around her hours at the hospital, but this one was more for fun, exercise, and laughter.

Gaby chose a song with a salsa flair.

Out of the corner of her eye, Chloe saw her friend counting the beat aloud and tapping her feet. "Is this song for tomorrow?" she asked as she drove.

Gaby nodded. "Yeah, I've come up with some really good moves to this next part where the refrain comes in … wait for it … good stuff, right?"

Chloe agreed. "It's awesome! Are the moves anything like last week?"

"Hell naw, totally different! I can't stand repeating the same stuff! So boring!" Gaby's amazing imagination was just one more thing that made her so good at dancing.

It didn't take them long to pull up to the employee entrance of the hospital. Gaby grabbed her purse and lunch from the back seat. Before she closed the door, she said, "I'll text you later and give you at least a thirty-minute warning."

Chloe laughed. "I'm good with that. Pray for me that today is a quiet day. I'm not in the mood for a busy Friday!"

Gaby smiled in agreement. "Pray for me that this guy I'm meeting for coffee doesn't turn out to be a creep like every other guy recently!"

Chloe shook her head. "Already done. We can't take too many more of them! All right, I gotta run. Talk later." Chloe waved as Gaby shut the door and each went their separate ways.

~~~~~

Chloe's day passed as she'd hoped—quietly. No lectures from Lou, her boss, since she made the meeting on time. He didn't assign her any breaking news stories, which kept it a mild day. Working at the Local 9 News meant some days got crazy while others seemed lifeless. Chloe liked both atmospheres, as long as there weren't too many of the same right in a row. Too many crazy days left her exhausted, and too many quiet days made her think she could die of boredom. Variability made the job interesting.

Getting the job right after graduating college, she'd at first assumed it would just pay the bills, but over the years, she'd started to like the place. They liked her too and had promoted her to field reporter a few months ago.

However, writing fiction made Chloe feel alive. Something kept drawing her back to it. It was lonely growing up without any brothers or sisters. Friends were scarce for her too. There had been her neighbor Jeremy when she was young, but he'd faded away in middle school. From then until college, stories became Chloe's escape.

Now, Chloe still loved using her imagination. She'd turned her love of writing into a career but writing about current events wasn't the same as writing short stories. At home, she wrote as much as she could and always kept a book on her nightstand. Eventually, she planned to try her hand at writing a novel, but for now she needed a paycheck, and writing news stories provided that. Sometimes, though, she imagined getting a PhD in literature or teaching college writing classes. Someday …

Today, Chloe stayed in the office and worked on a few feature ideas. One of them involved the new shopping center that she and the girls planned to hit off tomorrow—part of the Strayer Street Shoppes, located in an area of the city slowly being revived. Untouched since the 1970s, a new developer had come to town late last year and made remodeling the area—shops included—his big project. The entire shopping center had just opened a few weeks ago. Stopping there tomorrow would give Chloe some perspective for the article. It would also be fun to see the area come alive. The girls couldn't wait to try out all the new places that had opened. They already had their favorite haunts around town but enjoyed adding a few new ones to the list every now and then.

Chloe really liked being with her friends out on the town. Most Saturday nights they either went dancing at a club, to a bar with a live band, or to a coffee shop—which was why she needed something new to wear. She thought back over the last few months and realized she hadn't bought anything new in quite a while. It was time to put an end to it. She grabbed her phone to text Jess.

Chloe: *I'm jealous over Gab's new clothes. Shopping tomorrow?*
Jess: *Definitely, but I'm not buying a jumpsuit like Gaby's. I couldn't pull that off.*
Chloe: *You can too*
Jess: *Ehhh*
Chloe: *How about the new Strayer Street Shoppes?*
Jess: *Yup*

Things have seemed a bit mundane lately, Chloe thought. Her job offered excitement sometimes, but her personal life could do with a kick. Maybe she needed more than new clothes. She thought about a trip to the Gulf Coast. *That could be fun.* She and the girls had spent a few summers there in college, renting a house near the beach. Maybe they could find a small place for a few days in August.

They could also visit Gaby's mom. She lived in a quaint little town outside Galorston called Harmony. The town consisted of a couple streets where you could find all the basics for the local folks before the land opened to ranches. Chloe always found it so relaxing there.

Back to work, Chloe, she told herself, snapping out of her daydream. She wanted to submit at least one of her articles from earlier in the week. All ideas about escaping for a few days would have to wait. She'd talk to her friends later and see what they thought of taking a quick trip together before summer ended.

Once she buckled down, it didn't take long before she completed one of her articles. Right as she finished, a text came in from Gaby.

Gaby: *Hey, I'll be ready on time at 4:30. Does that work for you?*
Chloe: *Yup, I should be done by then too.*
Chloe: *Do you need any ingredients for dinner tonight?*
Gaby: *No, I picked up a few things yesterday, so I'm good. Do you need anything?*
Gaby: *What are you making tonight? Give me something to dream about as I count down the minutes to the weekend :)*
Chloe: *Not positive. I have what I need to invent something with chocolate and peanut butter.*
Gaby: *Mmmmm*

~~~~~

Once Chloe and Gaby walked through the door, a huge sigh escaped both. They looked to each other and Chloe said, "Oh yeah, Friday night!"

Gaby yelled, "Jess! We're home! Where are you?"

They'd seen Jess's car out front, so they knew she was there somewhere.

Jess came down the stairs. She'd already changed into comfy shorts and a T-shirt.

"How long have you been home?" Chloe asked.

"Only fifteen minutes, just enough time to forget the week and think ahead to the next two days of no work! Do you guys want anything to drink? Wine or something?" She turned to Gaby. "What would go with dinner tonight?"

Gaby raised her eyebrows and smirked. "Sangria, of course!"

Chloe headed into the kitchen and grabbed a cutting board and a knife. "I'll start cutting the fruit."

Jess was already heading to get the sangria and the pitcher.

While they mixed the sangria and fruit, Chloe asked, "So, how was the coffee date, Gaby?"

"We need all the juicy details!" Jess added.

Gaby looked down at the fruit she helped Chloe cut, smiling. "So, I walked there. I figured even though it was a hot one, it was just around the corner. But darn, it was hot! I was sweaty by the time I got there. Luckily Rob didn't seem to notice when he leaned in for a quick hug and hello!" She laughed.

"He seemed really sweet, a gentleman," she continued. "He held the door for me, pulled out my chair, bought my coffee, and listened to me talk." Jess and Chloe shared a look. "He seemed genuinely interested in me. He asked me about work, y'all, my family, and lots of other stuff. Most guys I date spend seventy-five percent of the time talking about themselves, making sure I know how much money they earn or how much they can bench press. Rob didn't do that, though, and the conversation flowed smoothly. It didn't take work to keep it going."

Jess laughed and said, "He must have a sister. Guys with sisters are always nicer."

Chloe agreed. "It does seem that way."

Gaby laughed at that. "He does actually—two of them, both older."

Chloe felt her friend's excitement. "You really like him. You deserve a good guy after control-freak Kirk."

Gaby agreed. "God, yes. He suffocated me. Last I heard he took a job in Louisiana."

Although Gaby's first impression of Rob seemed like a good one, secretly Chloe wondered if he was too good to be true.

Growing up, Chloe had a keen intuition and an ability to sense things before they happened. Sometimes, she saw events play out in her mind, a film reel flickering across her vision. Other times a strong sense of foreboding overwhelmed her. However, after an accident several years ago, her "gift" vanished. Only a minute amount of intuition remained. At times she would catch hints of things—flashes of a shadow or a face—however, they didn't always make sense or lead to any actual event.

Chloe's intuition toward Rob left her with a muted ache in her gut, but she decided to keep her feelings to herself for now. The last thing she wanted was to intrude on something that could be great for her friend. The girls continued to chat away about him and finished making the sangria.

After putting it in the fridge to set, Chloe and Gaby ran upstairs to change.

Meanwhile, Jess found a good country song list to play. All three girls loved country music, so they could never go wrong in choosing to blast it through their Bluetooth speakers. Jess chose a mix of classics and new songs, singing along while preparing the chicken and vegetables for the meal.

The girls started their Friday night with a great dinner, washed it down with sangria and topped off with some rich cake concoction Chloe created. Then they moved to the couch to digest and veg.

Draining the last of her glass, Jess got up, announcing, "I need one more piece of that cake! Either of you want one?"

Gaby said with a sigh, "I'll come out and get a forkful since we are going to sweat it off at class in the morning. But I can't eat an entire piece. Not all of us have the metabolism of a toddler!"

Jess was willowy, all legs and arms. She called herself a stick, but that wasn't how her friends saw her. She had killer long legs and a delicate look about her—almost ballerina-like. Her metabolism made other women envious and allowed her to eat close to anything she wanted without gaining weight.

Jess smiled. "One day it will catch up with me, so don't let the hatred linger too long!"

They headed to the kitchen, and Gaby grabbed another forkful of cake. After one bite, she sighed. "This really is delicious, Chloe. You should think about writing up some of your recipes. It could be your first hit seller."

Chloe considered Gaby's words as she wandered to the counter and swiped another forkful too. "You're right," she admitted, chewing. "This *is* good. Women all over the world should get to experience this decadence! I'll think about it. I did write this one down, so I could repeat it if I wanted to."

Jess swiped her own forkful. She tipped her head back to keep cake from falling out of her stuffed mouth and managed to add, "You have to!"

Chloe added the recipe to the binder of "best bakes" she'd been creating over the past few years. For some reason, baking came easy to her. She loved it almost as much as writing. It also offered opportunities to create and entertain others.

She laughed after a time. "Actually, I'm not sure my waistline could sustain writing a baking cookbook since I'd have to bake everything to get pictures of the finished products. That would be a lot of eating!"

Jess snorted. "Not a problem!" She raised her hand. "I volunteer to be the official taste tester. You go ahead and bake all you want, and if I can't consume all of it, I'll take the leftovers to work. Considering the number of single geeks I work with; I am sure the extras wouldn't last long in the break room!"

"Don't go giving all the extras away," Gaby whined. "I'm gonna need to taste everything too." Drilling her finger into Jess's shoulder, she added, "And why aren't you talking to any of those girlfriend-less geeks? I bet they all drool over you!"

Jess shook her head while swallowing another bite. "Maybe they do, but there isn't anyone who really grabs my attention. I need a guy who can carry a conversation. Some of them are so antisocial, I can't imagine trying to go out to coffee with them and have a good conversation like you had with Rob today. But I'll keep my eyes open."

"You better. I hear geeks run the world."

~~~~~

Chloe watched her best friend yell instructions from the front of the room. Gaby seemed like a natural there, completely in her element. The room thumped with the force of the music, creating an irresistible pull to dance.

Gaby wore a crop tank and leggings, which Chloe noticed showed off her curves. Strands of her curly dark hair fell out of a messy bun. The wall mirrors all around the room allowed Chloe to see every angle of her best friend, and she was a real beauty.

Chloe sometimes wished she was shorter and curvier like Gaby. Deep down, she knew it really wasn't height or shape that bugged her, but her own insecurity. She had worked hard over the past few years to feel more secure, allowing herself small treats such as new hairstyles and outfits that reinforced she was worth the effort. Her confidence had been a work in progress since childhood, although she hadn't made any real strides until seven years ago when she left her hometown.

Back then, her confidence had taken several big hits, the last one after the car accident six years ago. Gaby and Jess had been there for her through that time, and while it had been a low point for her, there had also been some positive outcomes. When she was in the hospital, she met Jake, the first man to make her blush. In addition, the support Gaby and Jess gave her brought the three of them even closer together.

Chloe saw Jess out of the corner of her eye click her fingers and mouth, "Snap out of it."

Chloe shook her head and focused on the activity around her, noticing she'd missed the new sequence Gaby had added on to their dance.

Seeing her friend's distress, Gaby shimmied over to her and shouted above the music, "You okay?"

Chloe shook her head again. "Sorry, my mind started wandering."

"That's the price you pay for high intelligence. Here, follow my steps." Gaby repeated the moves several times next to her friend, until Chloe mimicked her almost perfectly, then she made her way back to the front. Soon Chloe moved like the best of Latin dancers.

As class came to an end, the girls gave a quick clap and complimented Gaby on another great class. Chloe knew it made her friend happy to hear that her students enjoyed themselves. She walked up to the front to join her friends and gave Gaby a huge smile. "Now, that was good. I think I burned off our Friday night indulgences!"

Jess slid a bag over her shoulder. "Yeah, great class," she agreed. "But now … it's time to shop!"

The friends exchanged goodbyes with the other women and made their way to the Shoppes in Jess's car. While they drove, Gaby's phone dinged.

"Rob?" Chloe asked.

Gaby nodded, then read the message out loud. "Hi Gaby, it was great to see you yesterday. Are you heading out tonight? Meet for a drink?"

Chloe and Jess ooo'd.

Gaby grinned, then asked with a hint of giddiness, "Where are we going tonight?"

Chloe thought about it. "I'm feeling like some music, and a little dancing maybe. Should we head over to Harry's for the band on the patio?"

"That's good for me."

Jess nodded.

"Do you guys care if he stops by?" Gaby's words tumbled quickly from her mouth.

She must really like him, Chloe thought.

"Chloe, you can read him and tell me if he's a good guy."

She nodded. "Fine for me. I'd like to meet him. I'm not sure how successful I'll be at reading him since my radar has been off."

Jess spoke up. "That's not true. You've been right on about a few things lately. Remember last week you called it when that woman in the grocery store was going to ram into another cart around the corner?"

Chloe shrugged. "It seems like it's hit or miss, though. Whatever. You should tell him to come, Gabs."

Gaby murmured her response as she wrote back, "We're heading to Harry's tonight. Stop by."

Jess pulled the car into a spot in the new parking garage. "Fancy," she said.

They then headed toward the elevator and down to street level. A clothing shop beckoned from across the street, but before the girls crossed, they admired the area. None of them had been there since construction had finished. Now, covered sidewalks kept the sun off the shoppers, while planters and pretty flowers lined the curb. Good music piped in over the loudspeakers. The newly renovated downtown area felt alive.

Jess whistled, looking around. "It's looking really good down here now. It will be cool if they extend this to the next block up and add in a couple more late-night hangout spots and restaurants." She pointed across the street. "The one over there looks good."

Gaby laughed. "Look who has food on their mind?"

"Of course, I do! I just burned off everything I ate in the last forty-eight hours during the ninety-minute class that you ran like a drill sergeant!"

Gaby smiled. "I do what I can!"

The girls crossed the street laughing and ducked into the new clothing store. Instant drooling started the minute they saw the clothing racks—and three stories to explore.

Chloe looked up; her mouth wide. "Oh my God. I think I might be in love! This place has three floors! And I am *loving* everything I see!"

Gaby didn't even make it ten feet into the store before she started piling her arms with things to try on. Jess stopped at a rack next to Gaby while Chloe headed upstairs.

After an hour of hunting, they each tried on several outfits and picked out a few to buy.

Chloe was first to check out. "You guys really have a lot of great pieces here," she said to the cashier. "I had to put several things back so I could still pay rent!"

The woman gave her a big smile. "Oh, I know! Try working here and seeing everything new as it comes in. I spend more than I make!"

A little retail therapy was just what the girls needed. They laughed and smiled as they returned to Jess's car. They headed home to recharge in the air conditioning and possibly catch a short nap after lunch.

~~~~~

Later in the evening the sun started to set, and the girls started to prepare for a night out. By the time the Uber arrived, the heat wasn't as intense as it had been earlier. Chloe thought tonight would be a perfect summer evening to listen to music and unwind.

Chloe hopped out of the car first and waited for the others to join her. They looked great in some of their new clothes. Jess wore ripped jean shorts with her boots and a new tank top. Gaby had on her jumpsuit and new open-toed heels, and Chloe wore a cute strapless dress she'd purchased at the Shoppes, along with a pair of strappy sandals. They looked perfect for a summer night at one of their favorite hangouts.

Tonight's band, which they'd seen advertised on Twitter, was one they'd heard before. Not only would the band play some of their own music, but they would also cover other country bands. *Just the right mix to dance and listen to,* thought Chloe.

The girls entered Harry's through the open patio along the side of the main building. While Gaby and Jess stopped to talk to a few people they knew, Chloe looked around. She felt like someone was watching her. Then she spotted him. *Kirk.*

Chloe turned to the group and leaned in. "I spotted Kirk at the bar."

Gaby gasped and whirled her eyes toward the bar, looking over her shoulder, and found her ex-boyfriend's unmistakable smirk coming their way. Turning back around, her eyes wide, she whispered, "What is he doing here?"

He sauntered up next to Gaby and leaned down. Chloe could hear him whisper, "Hey, Gaby. How are you doing?"

Gaby tried to shrug him off. "Hi. You're blocking my view."

He didn't move. "You're more beautiful than the last time I saw you."

Gaby scoffed and shifted away from him. Kirk laughed.

He must have felt Jess breathing down his back then, because he swiveled his head in her direction. "Don't get all huffy, Momma Bear. I'm leaving."

He gave Gaby's upper arm a squeeze and a half smile then headed toward the exit.

When he was out of sight, Gaby let out a long breath. "Oh God. What is he doing in town?"

A chill ran down Chloe's spine. "What a creep."

Jess rubbed her friend's arm. "I'll do some research, see what I can find. Maybe he did take that job over in Louisiana but is just here for the weekend."

Gaby frowned. Kirk had really done a number on her a few months ago. She told the girls stories about how he'd acted the perfect boyfriend at first, then something in him snapped, and he started getting creepy—showing up at the same places as her, unexpected and unwanted; wanting her to spend all her free time with him. Chloe remembered the several times he'd had the nerve to come to their house late at night and bang on the front door. Finally breaking it off was the right decision, they all agreed.

Chloe knew Gaby loved spending time with her friends and needed to be with a guy secure enough to give her the time and space she needed in a relationship. Unfortunately, she seemed to find men who didn't get that and needed way more attention than she was willing to give. Chloe hoped that Rob was different, for Gaby's sake.

Sighing, she went up to the bar and ordered a round of drinks. The music was about to begin, and Chloe hurried back to her friends to enjoy the tunes.

They all turned their attention to the singer, who announced that they would start with some acoustic music. Chloe watched, hoping the songs and drinks would take the edge off and push the night's rocky start far back into their minds.

Jess wound her arm around Gaby, and Chloe smiled at her friends. "We'll be dancing soon, ladies," she said.

By the end of the night, all three felt much better, having danced without sleazy men in sight and laughed over bad work stories. Rob hadn't shown up, nor did he text Gaby to say why. But Chloe was relieved he didn't show. Without him, the girls enjoyed their night just the three of them, as always, and she didn't get another bad feeling in her stomach.

~~~~~

Chapter 2

On Monday morning, as usual, Chloe dropped Gaby off at the hospital and then made her way into the station. She thought it had been a good weekend, minus the drama for Gaby. The rest of the time they'd managed to relax.

Chloe hadn't experienced dating disasters like Gaby. The truth was she hadn't had any real dating experiences, thanks to Jeremy.

Chloe thought she had been lucky growing up next door to her best friend. They spent summers playing outside until dark, and winters featured snowball fights and lots of sledding. Jeremy was a great ally to have in school too. When kids would tease Chloe about her premonitions, he came to her defense. Still, it didn't stop everything, and all throughout her schooling people bullied her if they found out about her "gift." It'd taken her a long time to come to terms with it, and to recover from her past.

Back then, her premonitions could be anything from a vague feeling, or hunch, to a detailed vision. Things came easy to her in school since she often knew what the teacher would assign next and what material would likely be on the tests. Her classmates didn't understand how she knew the things she did. Some called her a witch, or worse.

Chloe struggled at home too. Her father was angry a good deal of the time, though to this day Chloe didn't know why. He punished her often. Chloe hated that her mother never challenged him or stood up for her daughter.

The only person who seemed to appreciate her was Jeremy. They remained close through elementary school; however, that changed in middle school. Girls started to notice Jeremy, and he noticed them. He began hanging with the "cool" crowd too. Chloe didn't like that she was losing her best friend. She felt she could never compete with the popular kids for his attention. He drifted away completely the year before high school.

During school, she sometimes caught glimpses of him, but there was no interaction. At home, she would see his friends pick him up for either football or baseball practice, but he never gave her a nod, wave, or hello.

While Jeremy went out every weekend, Chloe stayed home and kept to herself. She went to the library a lot to borrow books and study.

Even with her struggles, high school went by quickly. She kept to herself and did her work, getting good grades, but not making any true friends. She couldn't wait for graduation so she could leave her town and start a new life somewhere else.

One day in March of her senior year, Chloe came home late from the library. She didn't see Jeremy waiting outside her house. He caught her off guard when she walked up the front path. She knew he was drunk by the way he stumbled and slurred his words.

"Hi, Jeremy," Chloe said cautiously.

He muttered something in reply, then came at her.

Before she understood what was happening, Jeremy started kissing her and touching her in places she didn't want him to. He mumbled, "Come on. Let's hang out. It will be fun."

Chloe's mind screamed. *No. Stop. I don't want this! You're hurting me!*

She couldn't form the words she wanted desperately to spit out at him. Instead, she put all her effort into physically trying to make him stop. She tried to push him away, but the strap of her bag had trapped one of her arms. She tried to use her other arm, but he had a vice grip on it. She felt tears spring to her eyes.

They had never hung out like this before. He had never touched her this way! What was he thinking?

This was the first time anyone had kissed her, and she didn't like it.

Chloe continued to struggle against him and almost screamed out when the porch light came on. Her father's head peered from behind the front door and he yelled to Chloe, "Get in the house!"

Chloe breathed a sigh of relief and darted inside. Her dad had saved her.

But then she heard the door slam and her dad shout, "What were you thinking, acting like that? Are you going to fool around with any boy who gives you a second look?" He pointed toward the stairs. "Get up there. I can't even look at you!"

Chloe turned and climbed the stairs two at a time. She didn't look back.

Alone in her room, she locked the door and sank to the floor. Her tears fell freely there. She felt so violated and disgusted. She wondered what hurt more, the groping Jeremy did or her dad thinking she would want Jeremy to do that?

What upset her worse than her father's words was the fact that her premonitions had failed her. She'd had a vague worried feeling earlier in the day, but it hadn't given her any clear details.

That night stuck with her for a long time, leaving her closed off to relationships with men. However, over time and with the help of a counselor in school, she redirected the blame to Jeremy and her dad. While she never found a man she clicked with, she built friendships successfully, preventing her from being emotionally stunted.

Okay. Think happy thoughts now, Chloe, she coached, burying the memories as she headed into work.

After Chloe walked through the front entrance to the building, she waved hello to Eve, the receptionist. Eve was a friendly lady in her fifties with short hair and a kind smile. And she had a soft spot for Chloe, bringing her treats on her birthday and little gifts for holidays. Chloe enjoyed the doting Eve did, especially since she didn't have a relationship with her own mom. Of course, Gaby's mom helped fill that role too.

Thinking of Gaby's mom reminded Chloe that she had never mentioned her idea of a summer getaway to Gaby and Jess. She made a mental note to text them once she got to her desk.

Chloe continued past Eve and down a hall toward the main work room. Framed news clippings and pictures hung on the walls. Fresh flowers, courtesy of Eve, brightened common areas sprinkled throughout the open space. All around, cubicles peppered the floor. Along one of the walls giant windows let in the Texas sunlight.

Chloe's desk sat near the windows. Looking out, she could see a courtyard that catered to the entire building and often provided inspiration while she worked. Caddy corner to her desk loomed Lou's office space. A glass wall separated it from the open area.

As soon as she set her things down, she grabbed her phone and sent a group text to Jess and Gaby.

Chloe: *I was thinking we should get away for a few days before summer is over. Gabs, do you think your mom would want company? My other idea was the beach…*
Gaby: *I'll ask her, I'm sure she'd love a visit*
Gaby: *Beach would be fine too, but it has been months since we went to see her.*
Gaby: *When?*
Chloe: *Sometime in August or Labor Day weekend*
Gaby: *Ok, Labor Day in Harmony can be fun. There is a town celebration.*
Chloe: *Jess?*

When Jess didn't respond instantly, Chloe put her phone down and started writing her next article. This one centered on the city's education system. Chloe had blocked out some time today to collect a statement from one of the high school principals, but that wasn't scheduled for a few hours yet. For now, she decided to research the history of the school district.

When Lou gave her the assignment, she felt disappointed. With her recent promotion, she thought she would have more complex and exciting assignments. But all of those were being thrown to her coworker, Mya, lately. She wondered, *Should I talk to Lou about it? I don't want to sound demanding or petty, but I want the additional responsibility promised with my promotion.*

Her phone buzzed, interrupting her thoughts. *Jess.*

Jess: *It sounds like fun. August is going to be busy for me with this client.*
Jess: *Labor Day would work great.*
Chloe: *That works for me!*
Gaby: *Me too, I'll just check with Momma*

Turning back to her computer, Chloe tried to focus on work. She shook her head to clear the disappointed thoughts from her mind. *Later.*

Surprisingly, researching the school district's history made the morning go by quickly. She grabbed her bag then stuck her head into Lou's office. "I'm going to head over to the high school to conduct the interview for my article."

Lou looked up. "Sure, sure. Go ahead. Do you need the van?"

Chloe shook her keys. "Nope, I have my car today."

"All right, then. See you, in—what? —two hours?"

Chloe pursed her lips and tilted her head, thinking. "Probably, maybe a bit more. So, like three?"

Lou waved two fingers in salute and went back to work.

"Bye!" Chloe called over her shoulder.

Out in the hot midday sun, Chloe started her car and rolled down the windows. *Man*, she thought. She hated suffocating in this heat until the air conditioning kicked in. It was nothing like the summers she'd experienced as a kid in Pennsylvania, but she'd adjusted. The hot summers seemed a small price to pay for the mild temperatures the remainder of the year. That was what made her happiest about her move here. She could be outdoors almost any time she wanted, regardless of the season.

Chloe made it to the high school and got out of her car. Even with her sunglasses on, she squinted in the bright sun. Gathering her things and making sure she had her tablet and recorder, Chloe headed to the front door. As she hit the buzzer outside, Chloe's heart skipped a beat.

"Ringing a buzzer shouldn't make me this excited," she murmured as she waited.

Over the intercom, a woman's voice sounded. "May I help you?"

Chloe leaned in closer. "Hello, I'm Chloe Larson with Local 9 News. I'm here to interview Mr. Sherman."

The lock clicked to open, and Chloe stepped inside. She walked to an open vestibule area where a window resembling a movie theater's ticket window sat. Stopping before it, she saw a woman sitting at a desk in the office area beyond.

The woman came up to the window moments later. "Could I see I.D., please?"

Chloe pulled out her employee badge and held it up to the glass.

The woman nodded then pointed to a door nearby. "You can come in through there."

Chloe put her badge around her neck—the station required reporters to wear it at all functions—and then found a seat just inside the office. Moments later, the woman started talking again. "I'm Marion, by the way. Can I get you a bottle of water? It sure is a hot one today!"

Chloe returned her smile. "You're right, it is! Oh, that would be great. Thank you."

Marion handed her a chilly water bottle. "Oh, you're very welcome. Mr. Sherman will be right out. I already let him know you're here."

Chloe smiled. Not long after she started working on her article again, the sound of footsteps told her someone was headed her way.

The man who greeted her was tall with dark brown hair like her own. He wore a golf shirt and khakis—a more relaxed look since school was not in session, Chloe guessed. The way his hair swept over his forehead gave him a boyish appearance, but Chloe thought him a few years older than her, probably in his early thirties. She liked his smile, and the fact that he looked a little bit like a celebrity. *Maybe a little too much like a celebrity*, she said to herself as he drew closer.

"Hi, Mr. Sherman?" Chloe asked, getting to her feet.

His bright blue eyes met hers, and she felt her heart pick up its pace as he reached for her hand. *Wow, he is good looking!*

"Yes, but please call me Chris." His hand felt strong and a bit rough—nothing like what she thought a school principal's hand would feel like. Shyly, her eyes swept over the hand at his side. She noticed he didn't wear a ring.

The longer their eyes held, the more Chloe's palm sweated. Her stomach did a flip. "I'm Chloe Larson."

Chris let her hand slide out of his. "Nice to meet you, Ms. Larson. We can go to my office. It's this way."

Chloe grabbed her bag and water bottle before following him. Watching him walk, she could make out the shape of strong leg muscles. *I wonder if he works out,* she thought. *He must, with a body like this.* Finally, she remembered to respond. "Great. Thank you for taking the time to meet with me. I'd like to get some firsthand information and statements for my article. I understand there have been significant upgrades to the school building, added technology, and a change to the structure of the class schedule?"

Chris led her in through a door at the end of the hall. "Yes, we have been working hard the last few years to make huge strides in both physical renovations and educational advancements. It is our goal to improve not just the education of the students, but also the experience."

Chloe pulled out her recorder. "Do you mind if I record our discussion? I will of course send the article to you for review prior to publication."

Chris directed her to a chair. "Recording the interview would be fine. And yes, I'd like to sign off on the article before you print it. We have to be very careful that what we say is not misconstrued in any way."

Chloe studied his chin. She wondered what it would be like to kiss him with those dark whiskers starting to show. *Whoa, where is that coming from? And crap, I'm staring! I hope he didn't notice!*

Nodding quickly, she said, "Of course, Mr. Sherman. I completely understand."

"It's Chris."

Lowering her lashes, she said, "Oh, I'm sorry, you did say that. My apologies. *Chris.*" His name felt foreign on her tongue.

He smiled and studied her with those bright eyes again. The intensity in them made her feel a little nervous and giddy. God, she hoped she could be professional and keep it together for this interview.

Luckily, the interview went well, and Chloe soon launched into full reporter mode rather than flirtatious schoolgirl. At the end, Chloe turned off her recorder and collected her things. "I'd really like to thank you again for your time today," she said. "I hope I haven't taken up too much of it. I know you must be busy being a school principal."

Chris stood up. "No worries. You picked a good time for your article. Summer isn't anywhere near as busy as it is during the school year. Plus, I am glad to share all the great changes we have been making here."

Chloe put out her hand to shake his in gratitude. "It is a very nice school you have here, and the district is lucky to have you."

"Thank you. I appreciate that." His demeanor was calm and his voice firm. Chloe liked how he spoke with confidence and intelligence. He took her hand once more.

He has great hands, she admitted with a blush. She bravely met his eyes and smiled. "Of course. It was great to meet you today. You've made this assignment an easy one."

"It was nice to meet you too." He paused and his eyes trailed over his desk, as though searching for something. "So, how long have you been with the station?"

Butterflies flitted in her stomach as she let her hand drop. "For three years now, right after school. A journalism major needs to take what they can find. I needed to make some money. Local 9 fit the bill."

Chris laughed. "Yeah, I know what you mean."

"Have you worked here long?"

Still laughing, he said, "For a few years now. I started here as a teacher eight years ago. During my first year, I started the extra classes I needed to become a principal."

"Nice," she said.

His eyes rested on her face and his lips curled in a small smile. "Is Galorston your hometown?"

This man is a dream, Chloe thought as she shook her head. "A transplant from the northeast. Pennsylvania. You?"

"Born here in the great state of Texas, in a smaller town about an hour west."

Chloe smiled. He was nice to look at.

He grinned. "You should visit some time. It … uh … has great state parks at Lake Whitney. Might be a good story."

Chloe stilled, repeating his words in her mind. *Is he trying to … flirt with me?*

His next words carried a more casual tone. "So, when will I hear from you again?"

Her eyes focused on his mouth, and all thoughts flew out of her head. Shaking her head, she uttered, "Uh," then recovered. "Within a few days. I'll work on the piece today and tomorrow. Then I'll need my manager's approval before I send it to you for review."

He nodded. "I look forward to it."

Chloe wasn't sure if he meant he was looking forward to reading the article or to hearing from her. She hoped both. "Great. Here's my card for when you've finished it, or if you need anything in the meantime."

He took it. "Sure thing. Thanks."

Chris reached past Chloe to open the door for her. As she stepped into the hallway, Chloe could feel his eyes on her. She gave a small nod as she walked away.

"Hey."

Chloe turned around; her eyebrows raised. Chris stood just beyond his door, hand against the wall.

"Yes?" Chloe asked, her heart pounding as she waited.

He ran a hand through his hair. "Do you … ever go out for drinks?"

She raised a brow. "Sure. I do."

He nodded. "Ah." Then he sighed. "Thanks again. Uh, have a good day, Ms. Larson."

She couldn't help laughing as she gave a small wave.

"You can call me Chloe," she said, then headed toward the front office. *Maybe he was flirting with me.*

Marion stood up from her desk when Chloe approached. "You have a safe drive now and stay cool."

Chloe smiled. "I will. Have a good afternoon."

Once out in the parking lot, Chloe let out a long breath. *Oh wow, I'm glad I didn't try to bail on this assignment.* Her heart beat fast. She knew the heat radiating in her face was not from the hot sun, but the blush that reached all the way to her ears. She pulled out her phone. She had to tell Gaby and Jess about this.

Chloe: *I think a cute guy was just flirting with me! I didn't know what to say or do! But OMG he was CUTE!!!!!*

Jess: *I'm sure you did just fine!*

Jess: *Can't wait to hear all about it tonight!*

Five minutes later, her phone dinged. It was Gaby saying, *Oh baby! Juice tonight!*

Chloe started making her way back to work. She let the hot air hit her face and swirl her hair around. She couldn't help but smile. She'd had very few experiences like this, and she had to admit, it felt exhilarating!

Chloe headed downtown, avoiding looking as she passed "The Exit" where the serious accident happened six years ago. It was that accident that led to her meeting Jake, her hero and one-time love interest. No one she had met since made her feel how he had, until maybe today.

~~~~~

After Chloe left, Chris sat in his office staring at his computer and thinking of anything but work. He winced as he remembered his last words to her. He shook his head. *Of course she goes out for drinks! What kind of loser are you?*

But God, she was beautiful. Her thin shoulders, defined collarbones, and toned legs drove him crazy. He'd caught a sweet, delicate scent whenever she'd tossed her hair or pulled her bag's shoulder strap higher on her arm. It clouded his thoughts and teased him, threatening the loss of his professionalism. He held onto it by a thread.

Those dark chocolate eyes and pink lips almost made him forget the words spilling out of his mouth. He must've pulled something off, though, since she'd laughed as she walked away. She'd also mentioned earlier how much she enjoyed hearing about the school. He took those as wins.

But now, waiting a few days to hear her voice again would be tough.

He liked the way she'd greeted him with her high cheekbones flushed from the heat and her windblown hair spilling over her shoulders. His last girlfriend had been so neat and proper, with never a hair out of place. She wore perfectly pressed suits, spoke in perfect English, and sat as straight as a rail. She cared too much about what people thought. Chris couldn't live in her perfect world and didn't want to. He broke it off back in January after the holidays. Chris knew he wanted something else, but he hadn't known exactly what—until today.

It wasn't just the way Chloe carried herself or how beautiful she was that attracted him. She was articulate, professional, and had an innocent sweetness that captivated him. He wanted to see her again, not just talk on the phone. *But how?*

He spun her card in between his fingers, deciding he would send her an email asking her to meet him for a drink or lunch. *But was sending an email an hour after their meeting too soon?*

~~~~~

Chapter 3

That night the girls settled into a dinner of barbecued chicken, rice, and broccoli made by Gaby.

"Sooo?" asked Jess. "Do tell!"

Chloe bounced up a bit in her chair and washed down with water the bite she had just taken. "Well, I ran out to Galorston City High School today to do an interview. They have made a lot of changes in the school, adding new programs and renovating. They've done this to several schools in the district, but the high school's projects are the most advanced. I had been in touch with the administrative associate at the district office and she arranged for me to meet with one of the high school principals, Chris Sherman, to get his insight into it all."

"How big is that school that they have more than one principal?" Jess asked with surprise. "Back in Oklahoma, there were only two schools, one for kindergarten through seventh grade, and then another for eighth through twelfth! Only one principal for each!"

Chloe agreed. "I know. I went to a small school too. This one is huge, though. They have associate principals and senior principals." Shrugging, she added, "It's what you need when you are in a city."

Gaby laughed. "Get to it! I want to hear about Mr. Sherrrrrman!"

"Well, he came out from his office to meet me in the waiting area. When I looked up, our eyes met. I know it sounds corny, but it's what happened. It was like we were the only two in the room, even though his assistant was right there. He held onto my hand just a second longer when we shook, and his smile would give a young Tom Cruise competition."

Gaby giggled.

Chloe continued, "We went back to his office and even though my stomach was in knots, I kept it professional. At the end he was doing this thing with his eyes—looking deep and sexy." She leaned back in her chair. "To think I didn't want this assignment!"

Jess blinked a few times. "Why?"

"It sounded boring. I thought this would just be another mundane one from Lou, like the majority has been lately. But I'm sure glad he gave it to me!"

"Us too," said Gaby. "Seems like Mr. Sherrrrman will give you so much to write about—and not just for your work." She winked.

Chloe gave Gaby a gentle shove. "Does it sound weird for me to say that the way he looked at me made me feel powerful, like a goddess? He asked when he would hear from me again, like he would be waiting! Then, kind of randomly, he asked me if I go out for drinks. Is that … Do you think he is interested?"

Gaby looked at her with big eyes. "Are you serious, Chloe? He is so into you! What are you going to do?"

Chloe studied her friends. "It depends on him. I don't think I'd ever gain the courage to ask him out."

"I think he'll come to you," Gaby smirked. "Remember, you're a goddess!"

~~~~~

The next night, Chloe and Jess leaned back in their chairs. They had eaten out on the back deck, enjoying the nice evening, and now took advantage of the cooling air to sit awhile and talk. Today hadn't been as hot as yesterday, Chloe realized, thankful for a slight reprieve from the constant heat.

Now she just wanted Gaby to come home. "What time is it?" she said, stretching. "I can't wait much longer for her to get here!"

Jess laughed. "Yeah, there's a lot to talk about for a Tuesday night." She looked down at her watch. "It's almost eight. She should be here soon. Come on. Let's go make her a plate and clean up."

Chloe and Jess headed in through the double glass sliding doors that led into the kitchen. The kitchen table sat right next to the doors, and usually resulted in one of them banging their hip or knee against it if they weren't careful as they entered. It was just big enough for four people and the plant centerpiece. The kitchen had needed mild updating when they'd first moved in. They'd started by painting all the walls a pale-yellow Gaby had recommended. They'd also added shelving for more storage and organization. Chloe had been thankful the design of the kitchen had ample counter space, which worked well for the trio. All three could work there at the same time. Now, Chloe loved its cheeriness.

Down the hallway toward the front door, archways led into the living room and study areas. Chloe enjoyed using the study for its oversized chair. It was the perfect place to curl up and read a good book. When she worked evenings or weekends, Jess used the simple desk facing the wall opposite the archway for her workspace.

The living room was comfy with a homey feel. That was likely why Gaby was most drawn to it. She could be found relaxing on one of the two couches or the lounge chair. Additional furniture was set up around the room, creating a great place for watching TV or simply hanging out. On the walls hung a few paintings made by Gaby's mom, which enhanced the room's comforting ambiance.

While Chloe and Jess cleaned up, they chatted about other things that happened during the day. Jess had another successful client meeting, and Chloe had worked on her articles for the Galorston school district and the Strayer Street revival. She also researched a few new topics to present at the weekly ideas meeting Lou held. There they would all brainstorm new story topics. Lou would take the ideas he liked and assign them to people on the team for that week.

Putting the last of the dishes away, Jess checked her watch again. "Geeze! She is *late* tonight. It must have been a really good class." Chloe was agreeing when they heard keys jingling at the front door.

Chloe was first to talk as Gaby walked into the kitchen. "It's about time! What took you so long? We have so much to tell you!"

Gaby smiled. "Y'all could've just texted me!"

Jess took the plate they'd made her and put it in the microwave while Chloe grabbed a glass of ice water.

"Good class tonight?" Chloe asked as she set the water down by her.

Gaby nodded, taking a big gulp of water. "Yeah, but class ended on time. I got held up afterward talking with some of the girls. Jenny found a guy lurking around her car after our last dance class. Unfortunately, she didn't get a good view of his face so she couldn't give any details to the police. It had us a bit creeped out. We decided none of us should walk alone to our cars anymore."

Jess commented, "Wow, that's a bummer! Good thinking, though."

"Yeah. We'll be more careful now," Gaby assured them.

She took the plate Jess offered her, her eyes growing as she saw the pile of food. "Oh, wow. This looks great! Thanks. I'm starved!" In between a mouthful of food, she said, "So, let's hear this news y'all got."

Chloe and Jess exchanged glances, but Chloe's mouth was already open. Jess nodded. "You go."

"This morning I got into work and saw an email from Chris, A.K.A. Mr. Hottie-Sherman, as you like to call him, Gabs!"

Gaby ooo'd.

Chloe smiled. "Yeah, I was definitely surprised to see it. Yesterday, I had let him know that I would be in touch in a few days with the article for his review. He sent the email last night, just a few hours after I left!"

Gaby swallowed. "Oh. My. God. What did he say?"

Chloe knew her cheeks were turning pink by the warmth she felt in her face. Looking down, she pulled out her phone and opened the email thread. "He said, *Hi Chloe, it was great to meet you. I enjoyed talking with you very much. I'd like to see you again. If you'd like to meet for coffee, drinks, or dinner sometime, let me know. Chris.*"

Jess's eyes went wide. "Ohhh … That's so cute! What did you do? Did you write him back already?"

Chloe bobbed her head slightly. "Yes. I wrote, *Hi Chris, I agree, very nice to meet you. I will be ready with the article for you to review on Thursday. Instead of emailing it to you, we could meet for a drink and I can bring a copy for you to read. Would that work?*"

Gaby and Jess grinned.

Chloe continued, "*Then* he responded about ten minutes later. He said, *Hi Chloe, that would be perfect. Do you know The Charcoal Pit downtown? It's a nice bar and grill if you want to grab something to eat too.*"

Gaby whooped.

"I wrote back," Chloe added.

"You bet you did!" Jess shouted.

"*Hi Chris,*" Chloe read. "*Yes, I was there once before. Good choice. Does seven work?* We each wrote back one more time confirming it worked and I'd meet him there." She took a big breath. "I know it doesn't sound super flirty, but do you think it's okay?"

Jess pointed at Chloe. "It's great. Stop worrying."

"Jess is right, Chloe. It's time for you to get out there and date. We're so happy for you. Enjoy every second of the attention he gives you. And we want to hear all of it!" She raised her eyebrows several times. "Well, at least everything you want to tell us."

Chloe nodded, laughing. "I know. It's just hard. I don't have much experience with this sort of thing. And the only guy I have ever felt this way about was Jake. I'm pretty sure I made that to be something more than it ever was for him—if he felt the same then he wouldn't have let our email exchange die off after a year." Chloe's shoulders slumped and her gaze drifted to her lap. "I've let my imagination run for years with what could have been. I've created such a fantasy with him as my leading man."

Gaby patted her hand. "Honey, it is great to have fantasies, but the real thing is even better."

Chloe agreed with them. "I know. I am going to try. So, changing the subject, I asked Lou today if he had any passes to concerts coming up."

In unison, Gaby and Jess said, "And …"

Chloe smiled. "He has tickets to the festival over in Round Valley in October. Backstage passes, baby!" The three girls all shrieked and did a little dance.

"Oh. My. God," said Jess. "We have to find the lineup! I am sure it's gonna be big names. Last year's fest was off the charts awesome!"

Gaby yelled, "This is the best night!"

Chloe agreed. "It really is!"

Gaby took her empty plate to the sink. "Thanks for dinner—a tasty meal and tasty talk! Jess, you're next. What's up?"

Jess stopped smiling. "Unfortunately, my news isn't as fun as Chloe's. I did a little sleuthing on Kirk."

Gaby rolled her eyes. "Please tell me he was just here for the weekend and really does live out of state?"

Jess nodded. "I think so. I was able to find out that he has an apartment registered in his name over in Shreveport and has Louisiana plates for his car. However, it is quick for him to get here. So, we should probably start mixing up the places we go so we aren't so predictable. We don't want any more surprise run-ins!"

Gaby let out a breath. "Thank the Lord. I was hoping you would say that. How did you find that stuff out?"

With a mischievous gleam in her eye, Jess said, "Never underestimate a computer geek."

Gaby hugged her. "You are an evil genius!"

"I know," Jess said, smiling.

Chloe focused on Gaby. "Did you ever find out what happened to Rob? Why didn't he show up Saturday?"

"He texted me on Sunday and said he ran into some friends he hadn't seen in a while, then he lost track of time. I was kinda glad he didn't make it. After running into Kirk, I felt off. I agreed to meet up with Rob this Saturday afternoon instead."

Chloe sighed. Her friend lost some of the sparkle in her eyes when Rob's name was mentioned.

"Do you want me to do any digging on him?" Jess asked.

Gaby shook her head. "No. It seems wrong to distrust him until he's given me a real reason to."

"I can see that. But if you change your mind ..."

Gaby laughed. "Oh, I know. You're there for me!" Looking at both friends, she yawned. "Well, I'm beat and need to shower yet."

Chloe and Jess nodded.

She grabbed her gym bag and headed upstairs. Getting to the top step, she yelled, "Oh! I talked to Momma. She'd love to have us Labor Day weekend!"

Chloe beamed at Jess. She called out to Gaby, "Great!"

Jess grinned. "A visit to Harmony is what we all need for a quick recharge! Good idea, Chloe."

"Yes. I figured we could all use a getaway!"

Jess leaned in to give Chloe a hug. "I'm going to head up too."

Chloe stifled a yawn. "I'll be up soon. Good night."

After Jess left, Chloe stood in the kitchen, deep in thought. She missed her keen intuition at times like these—with it, she knew she could try to keep the people she loved safe. On the flip side, always knowing what would happen ruined the element of surprise. Today would not have been as exhilarating if she had known it was going to happen. Still, her sharp intuition had been useful in the past, helping her survive school bullies, jerky neighbors, or accidents. Without it as strong since the accident, she didn't feel whole.

Chloe thought back to the summer that changed everything. She'd just finished her first year of college and planned to head home to Pennsylvania.

She had tried her best while at school to stay in touch with her parents, calling them every few weeks to say hello to her mom and exchange some words with her dad. The calls never lasted more than five minutes and usually consisted of small talk, which was good and bad. It meant they knew she was still alive, but also that the strained relationship with them persisted. Sometimes she wondered if they cared at all.

Still, she had thought she should see them. After all, she had few other options for where to spend the summer months and decided she might as well wander familiar streets. Once finals ended, Chloe packed her things, said goodbye to friends, and then took a taxi to the airport.

Traffic swarmed on the highway, and the taxi driver wove in and out of the lanes, making the most of any gaps he could find. Last minute he cut across three lanes, trying to reach the exit. Chloe remembered hanging on to the car door, watching them travel across the dashed lines. One, two, three …

Suddenly, a feeling of blackness overcame her. Her skin prickled and everything grew quiet. A flash of a car flipping warned her just before impact. Seconds later, the crunch of bending metal and screeching tires screamed in her ears. The taxi skidded from the road and down an embankment on the far side of the exit. Chloe learned later that she'd hit her head and blacked out before the car stopped moving.

When Chloe woke, she saw the white walls of a hospital room and heard a monitor beeping from somewhere behind her. She called, "Hello?" but her voice came out in a crackly whisper. She looked down and saw a cast on one arm and bandages on the other. Everything else appeared normal.

Chloe lifted her bandaged arm and gently touched her face. A bandage also covered the side of her head and forehead, the same side as the casted arm.

She closed her eyes and tried to remember the events leading up to the accident. She remembered being on the highway in a taxi on her way to the airport and getting her premonition. She couldn't recall anything after.

"Hello," a voice sounded from the door.

Chloe opened her eyes and saw a young man in scrubs standing there. *Is he the doctor?* She whispered, "Hi."

Looking at his face, she felt familiarity and instant calm.

"I'm Jake, a nurse's aide. I'm glad to see you awake finally. You've been here for two days."

Two days? Are my parents here?

He entered the room and checked her vitals. "How are you feeling?"

"I feel okay but kind of weak."

"You'll regain strength quickly," Jake reassured her. "You are lucky. No major injuries. I'll go call the doctor so he can have a look at you."

Thinking back now, Chloe had indeed been lucky. She escaped with only a broken arm, a few stitches by her hairline, and mild scrapes and bruises. Her driver wasn't as lucky.

Every day after, Jake would visit her, help her get ready for the day, and talk with her, mostly about places he wanted to visit. While Chloe never gave traveling outside the United States much thought, Jake "wanted to see it all!"

"Like where?" she remembered asking him.

"Everywhere. Deserts, rain forests, cities. I want to meet the people. Their lives are so different from ours. Don't you ever wonder what it would be like to live in another part of the world?"

"I don't know," Chloe answered after a pause. "I spent most of my time focused on just getting out of my hometown, but not really planning much on where I would end up. I came here because it was far away from everything I knew. I've started over here."

Jake's eyes studied her. "Why did you want to get out so bad?"

"It wasn't a good fit, I guess." Even though those were the words that came out of her mouth, she hadn't felt like they were the right ones. Chloe couldn't tell him everything, so she settled on the usual story she ran by strangers, "I had a rough time growing up. Kids teased me a lot and my parents punished me for it instead of helping me."

"I'm sorry. Why would kids tease you? I think you are amazing." He patted her hand, and something inside her came alight.

She began to look at him differently after that day, sneaking more glances than usual at him whenever he walked into or out of the room. She even toyed with pushing her call button just to see his face when she was bored.

He talked to her often, but after that first incident, he kept things professional. Still, by the time she was discharged, Chloe wanted more. He'd become a constant in her life, and she wanted it to stay that way.

"I'll miss seeing you," she said, finally bold enough to express her thoughts aloud.

He smiled. "I'm glad you're feeling well enough to go home."

"Will I ever see you again?"

He frowned. "Not likely. I am enlisting in the army in the next few months. I finally get to travel!"

Chloe's heart dropped. He never mentioned joining the army in any of their conversations. "That's nice."

"Actually … maybe we could write. I'll give you my email address. I can tell you about the places I see."

She felt a light go back on inside her. *He does want to stay in touch!* "I'd like that!"

Later that day, after she left the hospital, Chloe thought about her visits with Jake, and the other times she was alone in her room. She hadn't had one feeling of impending sadness or disappointment or glee or sensed anything at all. Things just felt … unexpected. Come to think of it, the last time she had a premonition was the day of the accident.

Had she lost her gift completely? It made her uncomfortable thinking she might have to permanently face the unknown. Without her sharp intuition and premonitions, she would have to live in the world like everyone else, not knowing what was coming next. Everything would be a surprise.

As the months turned to years, Chloe realized her gift hadn't left her entirely. She still felt things, but not in the same way, and not all the time. She wondered if she'd ever fully gain her gift back, and what it would take for it to happen.

~~~~~

Chapter 4

Why is today taking forever? Chloe asked herself, eager to get out of work and to her date that night with Chris. She hadn't heard from him since Tuesday, which made her feel anxious. She hoped he hadn't changed his mind and that he'd be at the restaurant at seven as planned.

What if he stands me up? No, don't think like that!

Eventually, the clock moved to five and Chloe headed toward the office door, her bag swung over her shoulder, the article safely tucked inside.

"Bye," she said to Eve, who was also finishing up for the day.

"Oh, Chloe. I'm glad I'm running into you now. You looked so serious all day. Is something eating at you?"

Chloe stopped in front of Eve's desk. "Yes, but nothing bad. I'm excited—well, nervous. I have a date tonight."

Eve clapped her hands and patted Chloe's arm. They started walking toward the front door. "Well now, that is exciting! How did you meet?"

"I interviewed him for an article I'm writing on the Galorston school district. I went to the high school on Monday to get some details and quotes."

Eve smiled, her eyebrows raising. "And he asked you out then?"

"Oh, not then—he sent me an email later. It seemed like he was interested while I was there, though. And I guess he was." She shrugged and grinned.

"Oh, sweetie," said Eve, giving her a quick hug, "I hope you have a great time tonight. Give me a thumbs-up when you walk by my desk tomorrow morning so I know it was as good as I expect it will be."

"All right, I will. You have a good night!"

Eve winked and turned to walk toward the parking lot. "Good night then! See you tomorrow!"

Chloe found Gaby waiting for her near the curb. Hopping in, Chloe greeted her. "Hey, how was your day?"

Gaby waved. "My day was fine. But the bigger question is, how was yours? Did it take forever to pass?"

"My God, yes! Longer than forever!"

"When's the date again?"

"Seven!"

Gaby glanced at the car clock. "Well, I'll have you home super quick. What are you wearing?"

"I think the pink dress I picked up last Saturday." She had a lot of time to consider her options today and liked the sound of that one.

"Good choice. Pink looks great on you. Perfect for tonight."

Chloe smiled but said little the rest of the trip home.

After the girls pulled up to their house, Gaby shut off the car and turned to Chloe. "Are you just nervous or is something wrong?"

Chloe sighed. "I don't know. I really do like Chris and I know it is time for me to get out there. It just seems like I am leaving a comfy space by going out tonight and that's a little scary."

"Of course, it is! Leaving your comfort zone is never easy." Gaby put a hand on her arm. "I really do think everything will be fine. Jess and I will be here for you every step of the way, as much as you need. Hell, we'll even follow you there for backup."

Chloe snorted then let out a deep sigh and rested her head against the dashboard. "Argh. Why is change so hard?"

"Girl, you can do this." Gaby waved her along. "Come on, let's go get you ready. Want me to do that cute updo that looks so great on you?"

Chloe nodded. "Sure, thanks, but I'll run up and change first."

When they got inside, Chloe turned to her friend. "You're right. Tonight will be fun. Thanks for the pep talk. Come up in ten minutes!"

~~~~~

A few minutes before seven, Chris walked into The Charcoal Pit and chose a tall table in the bar area as his lookout until Chloe arrived. He thought back to their first meeting, wondering if she'd come through the door of this place looking flushed and windswept as she had that day. He smiled at the memory.

Over the past few days, he'd thought several times about emailing her, but he didn't want to seem too pushy. He'd get to know her better tonight and judge from there what type of relationship she was looking for.

Relationship. The word seemed more exciting now, thinking about her.

He stared at the entrance, and as if on cue, there she was, walking his way. She looked better than windblown. Wearing a pink dress and tall heels, the outfit showed off her long legs and accented her figure. Her hair was piled on top of her head, drawing his eyes to her elegant neck and face.

He stood up as she approached the table and surprised her by bypassing the hand she extended and leaned in for a brief hug instead. "It's good to see you, Chloe. You look great." He hoped he didn't blow it just now by hugging her.

Her eyes swept over him. "You too, Chris. Thanks for inviting me."

Chris gestured toward the opposite chair. "Do you want to sit here, or would you like to get a table for dinner?"

She tucked a loose strand of hair behind her ear. Chris noticed her earrings sparkled and glinted in the light. "If it's okay with you, I'd like to get some food. I didn't get a chance to eat anything in between work and coming here."

Chris nodded. "Definitely," he said, finding the courage to put his hand on the small of her back and guide her to the host desk. He sighed in relief when she didn't tell him to stop.

"A table for two, please."

They ended up at a table on the second floor. Chris pulled out Chloe's chair and then sat down next to her. He hoped that was okay. Again, she didn't say anything, so he took that as a good sign.

The hostess handed each a menu and listed off the specials, then left them to their server.

Next to Chris, Chloe wasn't sure she could eat after all. She had been hungry on the drive here, but now butterflies warred inside her stomach and she didn't feel so hungry anymore. Chris's hug left her mind racing and his touch on her back sent tingles through her body. Food was the last thing on her mind. Still, she glanced through the menu to find something small to pick at.

While Chris studied the menu, he asked, "Would you like an appetizer first?"

"That would be nice. What do you like here? I haven't tried any of their starters. I'm sure it's all delicious, though."

Chloe met Chris's eyes, and she instantly blushed. She'd forgotten how blue they were. He smiled, and Chloe thought of a celebrity again. *Please pinch me!* she thought. *How is this happening to me?*

"It is. I've been here a few times and I've yet to have anything bad. Pick whatever you'd like," Chris said, his eyes twinkling.

Chloe stared at the table, a light smile on her lips. She tried swallowing the lump that had formed in her throat and murmured, "Okay." *Relax, Chloe. You've got this. You can do this.* She gripped the menu tighter, her eyes flickering over its contents as the server appeared.

"What can I get you?" the server asked.

"Um," began Chloe. "I'll have the chicken tortilla soup to start."

"Great! You know what you'd like to drink?"

"A half glass of white wine, please."

The server then turned to Chris, who ordered his appetizer and drink.

Chloe hoped her nervousness wasn't showing. If only she could get it together, she might be able to pull this off.

Chris turned his attention to Chloe once the server left and asked, "How was your day? Were you busy?"

Taking a breath to steady herself, she said, "No, not too bad. I haven't had too many new stories this week. My boss, Lou, knows I have several in progress and wants me to close them out. My coworker Mya caught some of the busy, exciting ones instead."

"What kind of stories are exciting around here?"

Chloe's eyes sparkled. "Things like crime or accidents. Those tend to get a lot of attention. We must turn those articles around quickly, which is why we get busy with them. This week has been quiet for me. I've spent most days at my desk writing and finalizing the articles I am working on."

"Are you allowed to talk about the articles you're writing? Or will I have to wait until they come out?"

This made Chloe smile. "They aren't classified."

Chris gazed at Chloe. Her shoulders had dropped, and her eyes seemed more focused rather than darting around the room whenever she spoke. She grabbed his attention with everything she did, especially the more she bit her lower lip. God, it was driving him crazy. *What is it about this woman?*

He focused on her words as she spoke, trying to distract his mind.

"Would you like to see the article on the school while we wait, or you could take it with you?"

"Is waiting until tomorrow is okay? I don't want you to miss a deadline."

"Oh no, that's okay. I don't have a strict deadline on this."

"Great. I'll have a look at it tomorrow morning then and let you know."

"Perfect. I'll give it to you when we head out," Chloe said. She studied her fingers then, searching for more to say. *What! Don't look down! Talk to him! Remember, you liked talking to him? Talk!* When she raised her eyes, she noticed him watching her. Heat warmed her cheeks.

He opened his mouth to speak and then closed it. Chloe looked away again.

Is this it? We have nothing to say after a few minutes? Chloe sighed. She'd felt such a connection that first day. *Why is it so tough now?*

Chris started, "I have to admit. I'm nervous around you."

Chloe's eyes widened. *He feels the same way?* "Really? Why?"

"Because I'm trying to make a great impression on you."

Chloe was surprised at his admission. "I'm very nervous," she said. "I don't go out on many dates."

"What? A woman as beautiful as you? I'm surprised you're not turning men down left and right."

Chloe laughed. "Hardly but thank you. That's a very nice compliment."

"It's the truth. I was very happy when you agreed to meet me tonight."

Chloe felt her cheeks get warmer. "I hoped you would ask."

Chris grinned. "Is there anything I can do to ease your nervousness?"

"You are already doing it. Just talking makes a difference," Chloe said as she sipped on the wine delivered to their table. It soothed her dry throat.

"Okay, good. I want you to be yourself. I really enjoyed talking with you on Monday. Let's recreate the ease we felt then. Okay?"

Chloe nodded. "Yes. So, tell me a bit about you."

Chris leaned back in his chair. "As I mentioned on Monday, I'm from a place about an hour west of here. My parents are still there. But my sister and brother have both moved. My sister Briana lives up in Kansas City with her husband and one kid. My brother lives here in Galorston and is my roommate. We get along well. You know, we keep our slobbish ways to a minimum." He winked. "It works out pretty well."

Chloe giggled. "What does he do for a job?"

"He's a civil engineer. Todd designs roadways, bridges—that sort of thing. He's good at it. It's cool to drive on his work when he's done and know that it was his design that made it a good, safe road."

Chloe leaned forward. "Has he built anything around here that I would know?"

"His most recent project was the new bridge on I-695 where I-40 runs under."

"Neat! I've seen that bridge and it is impressive. Very cool."

"Yeah, I think so too."

The server brought the appetizers and took their meal orders.

"What about you? Do you live in the city? Have roommates?" he asked.

Chloe smiled and seemed to relax even more at this question. "Yes, I have two roommates. The three of us became friends in the first year of college. Jess builds code for an IT firm here in Galorston. Gaby is my other roommate. She works at St. Mary's Hospital. She also teaches fitness classes and dance classes. Jess and I both go to Gaby's Saturday morning class. She teaches it more like a fitness class, so you don't have to be too skilled."

"Interesting! Did you take dance classes when you were younger?"

Chloe shook her head. "Oh no, not until I met Gaby. I had a boring childhood. I spent a lot of time with my nose in a book. I was a regular at the library." She laughed. "I guess that isn't something I should admit, should I?

Basically, tell you I'm a complete geek."

"You're talking to a school principal. I also read a lot and spent a lot of time in the library studying."

Chloe didn't think there was one geeky thing about him. If anything, she would've pegged him as a former varsity athlete with his strong body and chiseled face. He was a very handsome man. Chloe could look at him all day.

She was smiling now. "So, how do you spend your time out of work, besides with a book?"

A wide smile formed on Chris's face. "I play some basketball and baseball for fun. Todd and I are on a few different teams. In the winter we don't play as much, but we do head to the gym a few nights a week. On the weekends, I do typical stuff around the house—cooking and cleaning. I go for runs in the morning before it gets too hot. And we go out sometimes to grab drinks."

Chloe smirked. "Wait, go back. You cook? I'm going to need to hear more about that."

Chris clutched his heart in mock hurt. "What? A man can cook!"

"Oh, I know they can. I just have never met one in person!"

"Really? Well, I've been on my own a long time now and I'd have either starved or got fat off fast food if I didn't cook for myself. It was something my mom made sure I knew how to do before I left for college. She also made sure I knew how to do my own laundry. She wasn't allowing me to come home on weekends with it all for her to do!"

"Sounds like you have a good mom. Do you still see her often?"

"I do see her pretty often. She either comes to see us or has us come home. How about you?"

Chloe hesitated. "I haven't stayed in touch with my parents much—long story." She shook her head then smiled. "I am close to Gaby's mom. We're all planning to go see her over Labor Day weekend. She lives in Harmony. Have you heard of it?"

"Yeah, I have. It is the next town over from Riverbend, where I grew up. I didn't go there much other than when we faced them during football games."

Chloe nodded.

The rest of the conversation revolved around college stories, favorite sports teams, best coffee shops for book lovers, and more work talk. Through it all, Chloe couldn't believe how lucky she was sitting across from such an incredible man.

~~~~~

On her way home, Chloe thought about her date with Chris. *Not a complete failure,* she admitted. She hated that the nerves never did go away completely, but at least she'd managed to make a bit of conversation. He even laughed! Her favorite part was when he said he was just as nervous as she was.

When they had walked out of the restaurant, he had put his hand on her back again. She had no idea why, but that made her shudder each time he did it. Geeze, who was she kidding? His look alone could do that to her. He had walked her out to her car and gave her his number. He asked her to text him when she got home so he knew she had made it safely.

At her car, he leaned in and gave her a hug. "I'd really like to take you out again, Chloe. Let me know, okay?"

She responded almost instantly, her heart swelling, "Thank you for tonight. I'd like that."

At this, he had squeezed her in another hug and then released her. He smiled at her. "I'll talk to you later. Drive safe."

Twenty minutes later, Chloe pulled in front of the townhouse. She sat there, smiling and hugging herself. *You did it, Chloe. You went on a date! And it was fun.*

Before she walked inside, she texted Chris.

Chloe: *Thank you again for dinner tonight. I had a really nice time.*
Chris: *It was a great dinner. Thank you for coming out.*
Chloe: *Talk to you tomorrow.*
Chris: *I'll call after I read the article.*

Chloe headed up the front walk, but before she reached the porch steps, the door opened. Out popped her best friends' enthusiastic faces. "So?" they asked.

Chloe smiled. "It was amazing. I can't wait to tell you all about it."

~~~~~

Chapter 5

As promised, when Chloe walked by Eve's desk the next morning, she gave her an enthusiastic thumbs-up. Eve offered Chloe a huge smile. "Yay!" she mouthed, raising her arms in a silent cheer.

Once at her desk, Chloe didn't want to admit to herself that she was watching her phone. *What will he think of the article? Will he still want to see me?* Most of all, she couldn't wait to hear his voice again.

By mid-morning Chloe had filled Eve in on her date and managed to get some work done. She had finally stopped watching her phone. *He'll call when he's ready*, she told herself.

Right before lunchtime, her phone rang. It was Chris! "Hi, Chloe. How's your day?"

"It's good." She wondered if he could hear the happiness in her voice. "Nothing special. How about you?"

"Same old too. By the way, the article is great! I like the style of your writing."

"Thanks." Her whole day seemed brighter now. "Do you have any changes or corrections?"

"Just two minor things. I will email them to you." He paused. "Do you have any free time this weekend to meet me?"

"I think I can manage that," she answered with a playful grin. "What did you have in mind?"

"How about I pick you up tomorrow at one?"

Chloe laughed. "Okay, but are you going to tell me where you're taking me?"

"Is it okay if I keep it a surprise?"

"Yes, of course. I love surprises. Well, I have to get lunch and then finish up my other article. Thanks for calling, though, and have a good day!"

"You too, Chloe. Bye."

Setting down her phone, Chloe felt like all smiles on the inside. Hearing his voice gave her butterflies, and now knowing he wanted to go on another date only added to her excitement. *But where is he planning to take me?*

She wracked her brain for ideas. There were a lot of different events happening in the area this weekend—festivals, markets, and even a guided hike. It could be anything. She just hoped it wouldn't be the dirt bike rally she'd heard Lou go on about earlier. That screamed anything but romantic to her. Regardless, it would be hard to concentrate this afternoon. She'd been thinking about him a lot lately, and now she had an excuse to keep doing so.

Turning back to her computer, Chloe yawned. *Better get some sleep tonight, or you'll get dark circles again,* she admonished, thinking of the restless nights she'd had since she had met him. A happy mind is a sleepless mind, apparently.

Thank God it was Friday. She could relax after work and then wind her night down early. There was a book she wanted to start reading, and tonight seemed like a good time to do that. Hopefully it would distract her so she could doze off.

Wanting to stretch her legs, Chloe stood up from her desk and wandered to the break room for some tea, a pick-me-up to get through the rest of the afternoon.

By the end of the day, Chloe had made the small corrections Chris had sent over and finished the Strayer Street article. That's one thing she enjoyed about her job, the chance to write about a little of everything. While this week allowed her to catch up on several loose ends, she hoped next week held more exciting stories and trips out of the office to where the action happened.

~~~~~

Friday nights were always the girls' favorite part of the week. All three enjoyed being home together, unwinding with delicious food, yummy treats, and uninterrupted girl talk.

"Gaby and Chloe, you really outdid yourselves," Jess said as she chewed the last of her meal. "It's just what I needed after the week I've had."

Chloe nodded in understanding. "That client still giving you a headache?"

Jess rolled her head back and sighed. "Oh, you know, they've just requested several significant changes to the program I am designing for them, due the start of next week. I know it's my job to deliver what they want, but they threw me for a loop this week. This program is for a team of statisticians in California. The time zone difference has had me working late hours so I can be there for web meetings with them, which means I have to start early each morning to do the actual work. Ugh. I also heard that I will have to go there in a few weeks to meet the team. Ladies, I love a challenge, but this project feels like something else!"

Chloe remembered Jess saying she'd spent several nights that week slaving away in front of her computer. She was always the last to go to sleep and the first around the coffee pot in the morning.

"I just hope it pays off!" Jess said.

"The way you're working you should get a bonus!" Gaby said, raising a fist and shaking it with a menacing glint in her eye. Chloe laughed, thinking she looked like an old lady telling off some naughty kids.

Jess laughed too. "I'll take it, but I'm unlikely to get more than recognition at this point."

Jess often told the story of how she'd started tinkering with computers in high school. Her family had been poor, and she could only gain access to a computer while at the public library. Jess would go there most days after school and on Saturdays. Mrs. Snyder, the reference desk librarian, was a kind, older woman who had lost her daughter at a young age and took an interest in helping some of the local underprivileged girls. She recognized in Jess a real knack for computers and would let her sit at the main desk sometimes to use the programs on her personal computer.

Mrs. Snyder had helped Jess apply to college and obtain a full scholarship. They had stayed in touch by emailing each other every few weeks. Often, Mrs. Snyder gave her updates on the girls that she helped and told her what was going on in the town. Occasionally, she'd update Jess on some of her old classmates too. It was nice to hear about the people she liked and cared for in the town where she grew up. She still had some nostalgia for the place, even if she wasn't rushing back there anytime soon.

Honestly, Jess kept away more because of her family rather than her hometown. Growing up in Oklahoma, she was the oldest of four kids, with two younger brothers and a younger sister. Her mother expected Jess to do everything around the house, taking advantage of Jess's good and helpful nature every chance she could. Jess knew what was happening, but she felt like she had no choice. With her dad always working, doing whatever job he could find, and her mother claiming to be sick, Jess knew her siblings would suffer if she didn't help them. Now, she stayed in touch with her dad, but didn't deal with her mother unless she had to.

Standing at the sink, Jess told the girls, "My dad is coming through town next week to see me."

"That's great," said Chloe. "It's been a while, right? He's still out on the road?"

Jess nodded.

All throughout Jess's life, her dad had done odd jobs—everything from going out for weeks to months at sea on a fishing boat to running pipe for petroleum. Right now, he was working in Texas on a new oil field, drilling and installing equipment.

Jess and her dad had a strong bond that only seemed to get stronger with age. He always wanted what was best for her, even if it meant Jess leaving to live her own life away from home. She'd never forget the day before she left for college. Her dad had given her an envelope of cash. "I've been saving some extra money for you," he'd said, "so you could get your start in Texas."

"Aw," said Chloe, breaking Jess's thoughts. "That is sweet. When was the last time you saw him?"

"It was last year about this time. He had been driving up from the gulf after finishing a fishing job there. I can't wait to see him. I really miss him."

"Will you have him over to the house? We'd love to see him too," said Gaby.

"He's coming through on Tuesday. I am trying to get him to stay over one night, and I'll take off Wednesday to spend with him. He's not sure he can, though. You know, Mom *needs* him." She rolled her eyes.

For as long as Jess could remember, her mother had mastered the art of drama. Seldom a day went by when she wasn't complaining about something. Jess had seen it all—mono, cancer, and anything in between. When her dad was home, he was kind and giving, and her mother took advantage of him too. Jess thought the only way her parents stayed together was by Dad constantly avoiding seeing her mom.

"If you can convince him to stay, he has to stay here," said Gaby. "I have class Tuesday night but can make sure I am home on time. We could have a late dinner with him."

"I can cook it," offered Chloe.

"Oh, you guys are great. I'll call him tomorrow and see what he can do. Unfortunately, my younger brother is now taking care of everything since Seth left for the marines last year. Marisa, my baby sister, has started down a bad path. She has some terrible friends she hangs around. Johnny told me he found some drugs in her bag a few weeks ago. He confronted her about it, but she denied knowing what they were. My dad was heartbroken to hear it." Jess shook her head. "So was I."

"So, it's not just your mom he has to watch now," said Chloe. "I'm so sorry. That must be really hard on everyone."

Jess nodded. "I know I should go home to visit her to see if there is anything I can do to change her attitude, but she was so young when I left, I doubt she'd care what I thought or said. I think she resents me for leaving her. I'm lucky Seth and Johnny don't. They will at least talk to me when given the chance."

"Are you afraid of seeing your mom?" Chloe asked.

Jess scowled. "Not as much as I used to be. Funny thing is, though, after all this time I still let her get to me. She has an excellent method for guilt tripping me. I'm going to see how work goes for the next few weeks. I don't think I could get many days off right now. I am way too busy. But maybe if things calm down after this client I could."

Waving her hands in the air, Jess added, "Some good news is that the California trip isn't until the week after the music fest. I would die if I had to miss that!"

"Oh, thank God," Chloe exclaimed. "You have to be there!"

Gaby held her phone out to Chloe and Gaby and pointed. "Unbelievable. Look who's thinking of me."

Chloe gasped as she read, *I've missed you these past few months. Reconsider and call me?* At the top of the message read Kirk's name. "Oh my God!" she said loudly. "He clearly did not get the hint the other night!"

"What are you going to do?" Jess asked.

Gaby shook her head. "Nothing. Nothing at all." Then her eyes grew round as they scrolled over her phone screen. "Oh God, there's a text here from Rob too. I blew him off for tomorrow."

Chloe drew her brows together. "Why?"

Gaby shrugged. "I've lost interest. He's not as different as I thought he would be. Anyway, what do we have going on this weekend?" She turned her head to Chloe. "Any plans with Mr. Hottie-Sherman?"

Chloe felt her face glowing at the mere mention of him. "Yes. But I want to know why you're losing interest in Rob. You seemed to really like him when you met for coffee."

Gaby tossed her hair back. "I know, but I haven't seen him since, and he seems to play games. Some days he'll text me a slew of times then I won't hear from him for two or three days. Sometimes the texts come at weird hours too, like late at night."

Chloe rolled this over in her mind. Maybe there was something to that feeling she had when she first heard about him … *too good to be true.*

"Enough about that pain in the ass, though. What about Chris?"

A smile peeled across Chloe's face. "I will see him tomorrow. He asked if he could pick me up at one. I don't know what he has in mind, but I'm interested to find out."

Jess raised her eyebrows. "Are you nervous to see him again?"

"Not nervous, more like excited. I haven't been able to think about much more than him all week. Do you think that will slow down or stop?"

"If it does, then you probably shouldn't be in a relationship with him," said Gaby. "I think if you're right for each other, you should always have that special person on your mind."

"I agree," added Jess. "I think it's really sweet that you're so excited. I can see how happy you are just by looking at you. Is he picking you up here?"

"Yeah, I will send him our address."

Gaby waved her hand. "What are you going to wear, if you don't know what you'll be doing?"

Chloe shrugged. "I'd like to think he'd tell me if we were going hiking or something, and since he hasn't said anything about that, I might wear a sundress and those flat sandals I just got."

Gaby nodded. "That will work. You'll look really cute."

"I hope he'll think that too!"

"How could he not?" Jess exclaimed. "You are freaking beautiful!"

Chloe looked away. "Oh, please."

"Yes, you are, Chloe!" Gaby exclaimed.

Admitting defeat, Chloe said, "Thank you."

Later, Chloe sat on her bed and read a text from Chris:

Hey you, I hope your Friday night was good. Tomorrow can't come fast enough for me. Send me your address later. Good night

Chloe wrote him back:

Hey you too. My Friday was good, fun. I'm excited to see where you are taking me. I'll send you a Map link. Good night

~~~~~

In the morning Chloe found herself lying on her book with the light still on. She lifted her head and felt a crick in her neck. *Great.* Sitting up, she stretched, hoping that would help ease some of the tension. She grabbed her phone and saw a few texts from Chris:

Chris: *I fell asleep after I texted you last night.*
Chris: *My night was good. Two of our friends stopped by to hang out.*
Chris: *Looking forward to seeing you soon!*

A smile played on her lips, and she fired a message back to him.

Chloe: *Good morning, you're up early! Heading to the gym or out running?*
Chris: *Running off my crazy ;)*

After Chloe got ready for class, she walked to the kitchen. No one was down yet, so she had a few minutes to clear her head. She grabbed some ice water and a slice of wheat toast—she had baked a loaf earlier in the week. After smearing some butter on it, she stood at the sink blankly staring out the window, taking small nibbles. *This really is good*, she admitted. *Maybe good enough to add it to my recipe binder.*

Hearing footsteps, Chloe turned to see Jess walk into the kitchen, with her gym clothes on and her hair pulled into a ponytail.

Jess joined her at the sink. "Hey, sunshine, how are you? Sleep better?"

She rubbed her neck. "Oh, yes! Fell asleep on the book I was reading." She laughed. "Wonky neck today, but at least I finally got a good night's sleep. How about you? You didn't do any work, did you?"

Jess shook her head. "No way, Friday nights are off limits. I will do some this afternoon, though. It can't wait until Monday."

"What can't wait until Monday?" Gaby asked, sliding into the kitchen.

"Work," said Jess with a sigh.

"Ugh, that sucks. Are you staying home or going into the office?"

"Staying home. I want to meet Mr. Sherman!" Jess placed a hand on Chloe's shoulder.

Gaby's eyes lit up. "Ooo, yeah! What time did you say he's coming?"

Chloe slyly smiled. "About one. So, should I have him come in then?"

"Uh, yeah! That's a dumb thing to ask. Of course! We want to meet him," said Jess.

"Okay, okay. I'll have him come in," Chloe said with a giggle. "God, I'm acting like a teenage girl!"

"Enjoy it, honey," replied Gaby as she gave Chloe a hug. "This is the fun part!" Clapping her hands, she continued, "Okay, let's head out, girls. No being late for my class!"

~~~~~

Chapter 6

The doorbell rang as Chloe took one last look in the mirror. She had put on a little makeup and had styled her hair in a twist with some loose tendrils. *Classy yet comfortable*, she told herself.

She grabbed her sandals and ran down the steps. *Here we go.* After taking a deep breath, she opened the door.

Chris smiled when he saw her. God, he was attractive. His grin made his eyes dance and shot darts right through her.

Chloe dared herself to look down at the rest of him: the thin T-shirt he wore clung to his muscles in all the right places, and his shorts hugged his slim waist. She started picturing his arms wrapped around her in a tight embrace.

Getting a grip on herself, Chloe leaned in and stood on her tiptoes to give him a quick hug. "Hi. Did you find our place okay?"

Still smiling, he said, "Yup, no problem. It was only twenty minutes. Pretty quick."

She filed that bit of information away for later. "Great. Come on in."

Chloe started walking toward the study, where Jess sat working. "Chris, this Jess. She's the smart one," Chloe said with a big smile.

Chris leaned in to shake her hand. "It's nice to meet you. I hope you have some fun plans later today and aren't planning to spend all of it working."

"Oh no," Jess answered. "Just a few hours this afternoon. If the others are up to it, we'll head out for a drink later tonight."

"Good to hear. It was nice to meet you. I'll let you get back to it."

Next, Chloe took him to the living room, where Gaby was. She turned around to make sure he followed. Sure enough, he was close behind, staring at her with a goofy look.

"What?" she asked.

Chris shook his head. "You bounce when you walk."

Chloe grinned. "I'm happy."

"Me too."

"This is Gaby," Chloe said, stretching her hand to her friend. "She's the fun one."

"Hi, Gaby. It's great to meet you. I'm Chris."

Gaby stood and shook his hand. "Well, hello! I've heard some good things about you." She grinned at Chloe.

Chloe touched her flushed cheeks with her fingertips. She looked to Chris, who winked at her.

"That's good," he said with a chuckle. "I've also heard great things about you—well, both of you." He gestured toward the study.

"Our little Chloe is so quick to compliment everyone," Gaby said. This caused Chloe's cheeks to turn an even darker shade of pink.

Chloe had to quickly end this banter, or she'd become permanently embarrassed for the day. She gave Gaby a quick hug and said, "We're heading out. I'll see you."

"See you!" Gaby replied, squeezing her arm.

Not waiting to hear Gaby say anything else, Chloe grabbed Chris's hand and shuffled him past the study. "See you later, Jess."

"Later!" Jess called.

At the front door Chris watched as Chloe leaned over to slip on her sandals. She seemed so graceful. He opened the door for her and called out to both Jess and Gaby, "Nice to meet you. Hope to see you again soon!"

They reached Chris's car moments later, and he opened the door for her. "After you," he said.

Her dress pulled some as she slid in, Chris catching sight of her long, toned thigh. She smiled on the inside. *Take it easy, Chloe!*

"So, where are you taking me?" she asked as he slid behind the wheel.

"The farmers market over by Big Red River. Have you ever been there? They have a lot to do there on Saturdays."

Chloe nodded. "I was there once a few years ago. I remember liking it."

"They have added even more things to do there in the past two years. They bring in animals to pet and ride. There are more vendors with food, and they set up pop-up stores that showcase local artists."

Chloe looked over to smile at him. "It sounds fun. I love to see local artwork. Do you do anything artistic?"

Chris laughed. "No, not at all. I never did too well in art class. I was more the reader and writer. Those classes and math I did well in. What about you?"

Chloe shook her head. "No, me neither. I actually like drawing; I'm just not any good at it."

"You'll have to show me some time," Chris said as put the windows down. "It's a great day."

The breeze blew through the windows as they reached the edge of town and the land opened up. Chloe looked over at him and met his smile.

He leaned in to turn on the radio. "You can't live in Texas and not love country music."

"You've got that right," Chloe agreed as she tucked a blowing wisp of hair behind her ear. "We listen to country all the time at home. Gaby and Jess are also big fans."

Chris raised his eyebrows. "Really ... a big fan?"

"Oh, I love it."

"Any favorite artists?"

She listed off a few of the more modern ones.

"I'm more of a classics guy, but the newer stuff is still really great."

The back of his hand brushed her thumb as he let his wrist rest next to hers, sending sparks flying through her and making her dizzy. He looked over and smiled at her. "I noticed you called Jess the smart one and Gaby the fun one. Which one are you?"

Chloe pursed her lips as she considered his question. "I never really thought about it. Who do you think I am?" She bit her lip and leaned closer to him. She saw Chris stare at her and wondered if he was thinking about kissing her now. Flirting was turning out to be more fun than she realized.

The smile he gave her said it all. "Hmm, I think you're both smart and fun."

Chloe laughed, batting her eyelashes. "Is that right? Maybe I am."

Not much later, they arrived at the Big Red River market. Chris pulled into a parking spot on the grass then came around to Chloe's side and opened the door.

"So chivalrous," Chloe said.

Chris smiled. "I do my best to impress."

"I'm a fan," Chloe encouraged.

"Where do you want to go first?" Chris asked, holding out a hand. She took it.

"How about we just walk around and go with whatever strikes our interest?"

"Sounds good to me." Together they walked toward the stands.

Chloe saw a band playing by the river. There were a few people dancing and singing along. "You're right," she said. "There is so much more going on here than the last time I visited."

After some wandering, they headed toward the local crafters and artist vendors. Chloe enjoyed seeing how much talent this one part of the world could produce. Everything was on display, it seemed—rugs, paintings, pottery, photography, and quilts. She enjoyed the different acrylic paint artists best. Their style reminded her of Momma R.'s paintings.

By then, the sun was beaming down on them. Chris looked at Chloe. "Do you want some ice cream?"

"Yes, please. It seems hotter now," she said fanning her face.

Chris took Chloe's hand and headed toward the concessions area. While Chloe studied the ice cream flavors, Chris picked up two large ice waters and passed one to her. She sighed with satisfaction after taking a large gulp. "Thank you."

"No problem! Did you choose yet?"

"I'm eyeing up the graham slam cone. What are you going to get?" Chloe asked.

"I'm a fan of the chocolate peanut butter cup, though I've heard graham slam is also good. What size do you want?"

"How about large?"

He laughed. "You've got it."

While Chris went up to order, Chloe sipped on the ice water and looked around. It was hot with the sun shining, but there was a small breeze coming off the river. A few trees down by the water gave some shade. Chloe saw an empty bench and motioned to Chris, as if to say, "I'm going to go grab that empty bench."

Chris nodded to her, then watched her head toward the water. He loved the way she swayed just a little bit when she walked.

Chris joined her soon after and handed her the large graham slam cone. Its chocolate scoops teemed with fudge, marshmallows, and graham crackers.

Chloe's eyes widened. "Wow!" She dug right in. "Oh my God, this is heaven! You have to try it."

She held it out to him. "Here, have a bite."

Chris held out his cone too.

"Oh God," Chloe said. "That is good too!"

The two weren't far from one of the stages where a band played, and they started to listen to the music more closely.

"I really like it here," said Chloe after a while. "The band is actually really good too."

"Yeah, they are. Do you dance?" he asked.

"Sure, I like to. Do you?" She turned her face toward his, a playful challenge in her eyes.

"Sometimes I can be persuaded, especially by a beautiful woman." He grinned.

"You know what?" Chloe asked feeling bold.

"What?"

"You're sweet."

Chris smiled.

Chloe had just taken another bite of her ice cream, but taking advantage of the courage she felt, she closed the short distance and delivered a sloppy kiss. Chris laughed as she came in for it and after she pulled away.

Chocolate ice cream dripped down her chin, which Chris wiped away with a thumb. She smiled. "Sorry. I couldn't resist. All this flirting got to me," she whispered near his ear.

"Me too," he said with a devilish smile that ran right through her.

Once they finished their ice cream, Chris took her hand and pulled her in the direction of the band. He looked over his shoulder at her with a twinkle. "Since you're beautiful and you like to dance …"

He twirled her once before putting one arm around her waist and holding her other hand in his. "What do you say?"

Chloe giggled and nodded, completely lost in the rush of emotions flooding her then. He was so suave and sexy. He made her feel alive, fun.

The two of them fell in line with the other dancers. Chloe whooped as they moved quickly to the beat of the folk song the band played. Every now and then she'd cast glances at Chris, and he would always greet her with a grin. She couldn't get enough of his smile.

While Chris led her around the open space, Chloe noticed how relaxed she felt today compared to the case of nerves she'd been on their first date. *It's nice not to overthink every word I say or every action I make*, she thought. Here, in his arms, she felt more confident, accepted. She didn't shy away when his face came close to hers either.

After a few songs, they walked to the river and sat on a large rock by the edge to catch their breath.

Chloe put her hand to her head. "Wow, that was fun! One more spin and I might have gone down!"

"No way would I have let you fall."

"You're a pretty good dancer, Chris. Are you persuaded by beautiful women often?"

Chris paused before responding.

Chloe winced. *Am I prying too much?* She couldn't deny her curiosity about his prior relationships. He was a catch if she ever saw one and couldn't fathom why no one had snatched him up yet.

Chris shook his head. "Don't be fooled. I'm not that good. And no, I'm not persuaded often."

"You don't have to spare my ego." Chloe poked his shoulder. "I bet you are!"

His eyes flickered over her face, her mouth. "The last time I danced was probably a few years ago at my sister's wedding. I'm usually at sports bars—no dancing there."

Chloe let the conversation stop there. He'd talk about his past when he was ready. Although that didn't mean her curiosity would vanish.

Chloe inwardly sighed and leaned her head on his shoulder. They sat there for a while and cooled off in the shade, listening to the water run over the rocks and the band play.

Beside her, Chris thought about how long it had been since he felt this content. It was nice to be close to a woman who made him comfortable.

~~~~~

Once back at home, Chloe was on cloud nine. It seemed like she just floated from room to room. For the first five minutes after Chloe arrived, Jess and Gaby looked from one another and back to their friend. Chloe couldn't stop smiling. Happiness rolled off her in waves.

"So, today went that well?" Jess dared to ask.

Chloe flopped on the couch with a contented sigh. "It was just amazing, an absolutely perfect day. Once he started flirting, I returned the playfulness and couldn't stop. I was a flirting machine! I was so forward that I kissed him!"

"Oh my God! Really? Chloe, you had your first kiss!" Gaby cheered.

"I'm not sure it really counts. It was more like a lip smack. It was a messy ice cream kiss." Chloe said with a giggle. "I'm still waiting for my first real kiss. The kind of steamy kiss that makes my toes curl. When he does *really* kiss me do you think he'll be able to tell how inexperienced I am? That I've never been kissed for real before? I don't want him to think I'm pathetic."

Jess cocked an eyebrow. "I highly doubt he will notice or think that! He'll just be happy he's kissing you."

Gaby nodded. "It's true."

Squeezing her eyes shut, Chloe ventured, "I wonder how much dating he does?"

Gaby shook her head. "I don't think he's a serial dater. You have nothing to be insecure about. If he was dating anyone when he met you, he ended it. I saw how he looked at you. The man is seriously into you!"

"For sure, Chloe," added Jess. "He looks at you as if you are long-lost treasure."

"I hope you're right."

"We are." Jess answered for both Gaby and herself.

"I don't think I can wait a few days to see him again. God, how do you do this dating thing, Gaby? It's torture—wonderful, but torture!" Chloe had her fists near her face, but her voice was loud with excitement.

"Oh, sweetie, it's only torture when it's this good! Tell him to meet us tonight to have a drink," Gaby suggested.

"Hmm, I just may."

~~~~~

It was a few hours after Chris had dropped Chloe off at her house, and he couldn't stop thinking about her. Todd caught him spacing out a few times. He couldn't help it; she consumed his thoughts. He was thinking about the sweet kiss she had given him at the market. He had been tempted more than once after that to give her a longer, deeper kiss, but he thought that might be moving too fast.

When he walked her to her door, he gave her a hug and had looked into those large brown doe eyes. He was lost. *Patience, Chris, patience,* he told himself. *One step at a time. Let her take the lead.*

To burn off some energy, Chris had gone for a second run of the day when he had gotten home. Two runs in one day left him starving by dinnertime. Luckily, Todd had some chicken and vegetables cooking on the grill. One of their friends was coming over. They would probably watch sports and drink a few beers.

Chris took a quick shower and then sat on the couch, flipping through TV channels. Settling on some college game, he grabbed his phone, thinking he would text Chloe. He smiled when he looked at the screen.

Chloe: *Hey you, I'm heading over to Greene's. Stop by if you want another dance with a beautiful woman :)*

Chloe: *Bring your brother and friends if you want.*

He couldn't pass this offer. He turned to his brother, who sat on the chair opposite the couch. "Hey, Todd, you want to meet Chloe? She asked us to come out tonight."

"Hell yeah, I need to meet her. I'm sure Rex would get a kick out of this too." Todd had a wicked smile on his face. A lesser man would have been concerned his buddies were going to wreck him with teasing. Not Chris, though.

He was happy to show off this cute girl.

When Chris walked in, he scanned the crowd. It didn't take him long to find Chloe since he knew to look for her by the band. He leaned over to Todd. "She's over there. The one in the silver dress."

Todd looked toward the stage and saw a couple of girls—all very cute, he noted. He focused on the slender brunette in a short dress. *Chloe.* He understood why his brother was drawn to her. Her big smile could make any man weak and judging by the amount of laughing she was doing, he guessed she liked to have fun. He noticed a few guys watching her and her friends. They hovered in between the bar and stage, throwing glances their way but getting nowhere.

Todd smirked and studied his brother. Based on the scowl on his face, he was pretty sure Chris didn't like those guys watching his girl, but he knew Chris was a cool one. He wouldn't let that get him hot headed.

Rex elbowed Todd and nodded toward the bar. "I'll go get us a few drinks." Todd gave him a thumbs-up then watched him disappear into the crowd. He followed his brother to the trio of women, keeping his eyes on the guys nearby too. *Let's see how they handle this.*

Chris walked up behind Chloe and made eye contact with Gaby. She smiled wide and waved. Sensing his presence, Chloe turned and leaned into him winding her arms around his neck. He wrapped his arms around her waist and lifted her a few inches off the floor.

"You made it," Chloe whispered into his ear.

Just hearing her voice made him feel better. She slid down the length of him and pressed in close. "I'm glad you're here."

Chris's eyes swept over the guys. "I see y'all are being ogled," he said in her ear so she would hear him over the music.

She nodded. "Yeah, it's annoying."

He kept his hands tight on her waist and started moving with her to the music. He couldn't help but smile as the lurkers started turning toward other groups of ladies on the dance floor. *That's right. Nothing for you here.*

Remembering Todd, he paused long enough to introduce his brother, then went right back to gazing at Chloe. "Hi."

Chloe reached up and gave him a quick kiss on the cheek. "Hi."

He slid his hands up and down her sides and swayed with her again. He knew he was taking a chance by being this forward, but she didn't seem to mind at all. In fact, he thought she liked it.

Moments later, Rex came over and handed a beer to Chris, and then leaned into Chloe. "So, you are the one?"

Chloe dropped her gaze and smiled. She shrugged in response, but to herself she admitted she hoped she was. *Chris is really special.*

Shaking out of her thoughts, she turned toward the group and introduced her friends. She noted with a thankful sigh that the guys watching them had slunk back now that Chris, his brother, and friend were around. She was glad for that. Maybe the girls could enjoy themselves a bit more now.

For the rest of the night, Chris didn't take his eyes—or hands—off Chloe. He couldn't remember a time when he had danced to a band this long, but he didn't mind.

Eventually, he leaned down to whisper, "You look tired. As much as I have loved dancing with you tonight, I think it's time to get home. What do you say?"

"Aw," Chloe whined. "The night can't be over yet!" She reached her arms up around his neck like they were alone. "One more dance?"

Chris's lips brushed her forehead and he held her close. "Okay."

Once the dance had finished, Chris decided to really make his exit. This time, Chloe agreed to wind down the night.

"It was a fun evening," Chris told her, their hands laced together as they stood, taking each other in. "I'm glad I could be here."

Chloe enthusiastically nodded in agreement. "Me too." She then turned to her friends. They were huddled together, laughing about some joke Rex had told. They really had fun tonight letting loose after a long week.

She gave her friends a head nod toward the exit and mouthed the words, "Are you ready?"

They nodded and started trailing through the crowd to the parking lot. As they left, Chris walked behind Chloe, keeping one hand on her back—mostly to touch her again, and partly to not lose her.

Chloe grinned as she walked, enjoying the feel of Chris's fingers grazing her back. *What is it about this move that makes my skin feel on fire?*

The guys walked them to Jess's car, then Rex and Todd sauntered off toward their cars. After a brief goodbye, Gaby and Jess climbed into the vehicle, leaving Chris and Chloe alone.

Chloe buried herself into Chris's chest and lingered there for a minute. She loved the smell of him, his warmth, the way his arms made her feel safe.

"I'm really glad you came out tonight. I had a lot of fun dancing," she said.

"Surprisingly, I had a lot of fun dancing too," Chris murmured into her hair.

"Is it really that surprising?" she asked, giving him a look.

"No, you are beautiful, after all," he said, adjusting her so he could see her face. Then he swallowed, and his eyes searched hers. *Don't just stand there. Ask her.* He'd been wanting to do this since he first saw her on the dance floor tonight. His words escaped him with a little catch that made him sound like the adolescent he felt right now. "Would you like to come over for dinner some time? I'll cook for you."

Her heart fluttered in her chest. *He wants to cook for me.* "I would love that," she said with a flirty smile. Then her hands slid over his shoulders and she leaned closer. He watched as she stood on her toes and gave him a light kiss. "Good night."

"Goodnight," he managed back at her, the corners of his mouth curling into his usual Chloe-induced grin.

Although her lips lingered on his for only a few seconds, the promise the moment held said so much more.

~~~~~

Chapter 7

Traffic wasn't too bad for a Monday morning, Chloe noted as she zipped along the freeway toward the east part of town. Lou had sent her a text earlier in the morning asking her to cover a fire at a car manufacturing plant that had started just before six a.m. This is what she had been hoping for—an exciting field assignment!

Chloe turned in to the parking lot, getting as close as she could to the scene. Smoke billowed into the air. Fire trucks were parked before the burning building, and firefighters were lined up in front of the blaze actively using water cannons and water hoses to pump water as fast as they could to the plant. Other law enforcement and medical personnel also milled around. A medical tent treated several workers nearby. Reporters from other news channels rattled into their microphones.

You can do this, Chloe, she coached, taking a steadying breath. Then she said out loud, "Why do I feel so nervous? I've covered fires before." She knew the answer, though: she'd done all of it away from a camera. This time, she really had a chance to impress Lou, the station, her coworkers, and even herself, and prove to everyone that she deserved the promotion given to her.

As she twisted to grab her camera bag from the backseat, one of her heels slid off her foot. *Darn,* she thought. *I'm a mess!* She shook her head, focusing on reaching the camera. *Just a little farther.* She sighed, reminding herself not to toss her stuff this far next time, and stretched. Just then, a pain jolted from her foot. She'd stubbed her toe on the bottom of the steering column. She muttered under her breath as the sting sent shocks through her system.

There! Finally, she grabbed the camera and pulled it forward. Then she rubbed the spot on her toe. *Get it together*, she mouthed to her reflection in the rearview mirror as she slid her shoe back on. The sting faded quickly.

Upon exiting her car, she noticed her film crew was nowhere in sight. *Great.* Things were happening and she couldn't wait for them. She decided to go out on her own until they arrived.

Quickly walking to the makeshift triage area, she put on her press pass and scanned the scene. Two men stood off to the side with only a few scrapes and bandages.

Waving with one hand and extending the other, Chloe introduced herself. "Hi, I'm Chloe Larson with Local 9 News. Would you be willing to answer a few questions?"

The younger man with shaggy dark hair shook her hand and shrugged. "Sure."

"Great, thank you." She wasted no time turning her recorder to them and firing off her first question. "Are you an employee of the plant?"

"Yes, ma'am. Ernie Anderson's my name. I've been working here for nine years. I work the night shift, eleven to seven."

Chloe felt energy flow through her as her familiar on-scene confidence started to take over. "When did you notice something was wrong?"

Ernie sighed and scratched his cheek. "That's just it: there was no warning. It was a regular night, nothing out of the ordinary. I run the press on the far end of the building." He pointed to the side opposite the fire. "I had just finished my last break and was walking back on the floor when the fire alarm went off. The automated warning came on, ordering us to evacuate."

He pointed to the man next to him. "My buddy here, Steve, walked off the floor with me. Neither of us knew what was going on. We made our way to the stairwell. Hearing noise behind us, we turned to see a few guys come running through the connecting doors to the riveting area. Smoke dusted their faces. They waved their hands and shouted that the building was on fire." Taking a breath, he continued, "We moved and made our way to the exit with the rest of the guys."

"How many people work on your floor?"

Ernie paused. "Geeze, I'm not sure. There's about twenty in the press area, but I don't know about the other areas. Behind the riveting areas is the assembly room. There's probably fifty more back there. What do you think, Steve?

Steve twisted his face. "Yeah, probably. So, eighty or ninety of us on the floor, I'd reckon."

The questions poured from Chloe now. She was grateful she had found such easy talkers. "Was the fire in the riveting area then?"

Ernie shook his head. "I heard someone say it came from the casting and welding room."

Chloe squinted and cocked her head to one side. "Do you think a faulty machine could have been the culprit?"

"I don't think so. They take safety real serious here. All of us have checks we have to do every time we go to turn something on. Before you put power to something, you have to make sure it's going to work right."

"I see. And how long did it take you to evacuate?"

Steve leaned forward. "It was pretty quick. About five minutes."

Ernie nodded. "Yeah, but a lot can happen in five minutes. That's how I got these scrapes, see." He spread his hands wide and gestured to his palms and face, which were slightly cut up. "More guys came running into the stairwell from the floors below us. They were freaking out, not doing it orderly like my team was. I got shoved in the commotion."

Chloe's eyes widened. "Oh no! Were others hurt in the stairs during the evacuation?"

Steve shifted, drawing Chloe's attention downward. He twisted his leg to the side. His pants were ripped down the length with raw scrapes underneath. "A couple of us were. Nothing real serious, though."

Ernie added, "Yeah, nobody meant any harm. They let fear get to 'em."

Chloe hit the off button. "I think that will do it. Do you mind if I get a picture to go along with the interview?"

They agreed.

Once she snapped a photo she was happy with, Chloe turned to them again. "Thank you both. I really appreciate you talking to me and providing details. Feel better and stay safe!"

The men muttered thanks and began to talk among themselves once more.

Stepping off to one side, Chloe pulled out her phone and told it to call the station. "Hey, Lou," she said when he picked up, "which crew did you send? I'm here. Just wrapped up an interview using my recorder, but I want to check in with them."

Lou sighed into the phone. "Too bad you didn't find them before you interviewed. But it's Max's team. They are there somewhere. Call Max."

"Will do. Thanks, Lou." As she hung up, Chloe started to second-guess her actions. Should she have found her film team first, and then visited the tent? She was so used to going out on her own, and given the situation, she had wanted to act fast, but now she had a sinking feeling she should have waited. Her assignment was supposed to be on camera, after all.

Just as Chloe was about to call Max, a loud bang sounded behind her. She jumped but didn't have time to do much else. Within seconds, heat rushed over every inch of her skin. She wasn't thrown, but the smoke that came with the heat billowed around her, pushing her forward. Coughing and swiping at her eyes, she struggled to open them. The smoke was so thick it hung like a curtain all around her, drowning out the sun. *Shit*, she thought as she fought for breath. *This is bad.*

Although her lungs and eyes burned, Chloe forced herself to walk in the opposite direction of the blast. Getting a safe enough distance away, Chloe knew she had to capture this moment as it unfolded. *Lou loves this kind of real-life drama.* She set up her camera at the very edge of the smoke cloud; however, a survivor stumbling past her urged her to move farther ahead. "Get outta here," he coughed.

"I just need this one shot," she said back to him, holding her ground.

Several people filed past her, sputtering and searching for help. *This is what I need everyone to see back at home*, she thought. She pulled the collar of her shirt up around her nose in an attempt to filter the smoke. She clicked and clicked and clicked. Then, when the smoke became too intense, she headed for clearer air.

Tears streamed down her cheeks and soaked her shirt as she walked. During the few scary moments it took to emerge from the smoke cloud, thoughts scrolled through her head. *Will I make it out of here? What about everyone inside the building? How many are hurt? Trapped? Dead? What if the smoke damaged the pictures I took? Are the pictures enough to make up for my off-screen interview mess-up?*

Her vision blurred and she began to lose track of her steps. Was she moving away from the scene or toward it? She couldn't remember. The smoke followed at her heels. A few cautious steps later, her toe caught on something, making her lose her balance. "Ahh," she moaned, landing hard on the ground. She stayed down for a moment to gain her bearings and try to let the pain pass.

Pulling from her inner strength, she positioned her feet to stand but realized her body was much weaker than her mind. A man's voice came from behind her and she felt a light touch on her elbow. "Are you okay?"

He sounded far away.

"Miss, are you okay?" He repeated when she didn't answer him.

Chloe's eyes swiveled toward his face. She squeaked when she realized he practically stood next to her. "I think so."

"Here, lean on me. I'm Danny. I'll walk with you."

She weakly answered, "Thank you. I'm Chloe."

Holding onto his arm, she followed him to an ambulance. "You're in good hands now, Chloe," he said as he left her to be examined.

"Thank you." Her voice crackled. "I appreciate your help."

After a cursory assessment, the paramedic determined her eyes should be flushed.

He had her sit down and tilt her head upward. "This may sting some, but you will feel relief soon after."

Chloe braced herself. "Okay."

The first few moments of the flushing increased the burning sensation, causing her to wince. "Ouch," she murmured through clenched teeth.

"It's almost over. Hang in there a few more seconds."

A loud sigh of relief escaped Chloe's mouth when the flushing stopped. "I'm glad that's over." She blinked several times and dabbed her eyes with the clean gauze the paramedic handed her.

Assuring the paramedics she was much better, Chloe stepped away so others could receive medical attention. She headed toward an open area where bystanders gathered, cursing as she realized the rubbing and flushing of her eyes had made her lose her contacts.

Looking around with blurred vision, she observed the chaos around her. The fire trucks had moved back, and more fire engines were pouring onto the site. Ambulances wailed in the distance, and people kept creeping from the shadow of smoke that loomed ahead. *It's like a war zone.*

A woman came into view then. "I see you're with Local 9 News. I'm Clare with GBC. You were caught up in the blast, right? How are you feeling? Are you willing to do a live interview?"

The questions swirled around Chloe's head, but she focused on the last one. *Here's my chance!* "Yes, I think I can do that." A wry smile swept over her lips.

After blinking to get her bearings and adjust to her contact-less existence, she positioned herself so the scene was behind her.

Clare wasted no time beginning the report. After an introduction, she asked Chloe, "How close were you to the building?"

In a scratchy voice, Chloe responded, "Too close. I had been in the original triage area close to the building. After I had interviewed a few of the injured for News 9, I moved off to the side. I heard a loud bang behind me, and within moments I was surrounded by smoke. It looked like a curtain hung all around me."

"How long were you stuck in the smoke?"

"It felt like hours, but it must've been only minutes. It was so hard to breathe, and my eyes stung. I tripped, losing my balance and falling to my knees." Remembering her throbbing toe brought another thought to Chloe's mind … *When I stubbed my toe in my car, was that a premonition?*

Turning her head to hide her revelation, she studied the area around them. "It's devastating. There are so many injured."

"It really is," Clare conceded. "But tell me, how did you get to safety?"

Chloe's head ached. "With help. A man walked with me to an ambulance. It's times like these you see there is still a lot of goodness in the world."

Clare turned her attention from Chloe to the cameraman. "I couldn't have said it better myself. Well, that is the latest here at the Tri-County Automotive Plant in East Galorston. Local 9 News Chloe Larson and I signing off for now.

Back to the station."

Once the camera stopped rolling, Clare handed Chloe her card. "That was great. Thanks. Here's my card. Stay in touch."

~~~~~

Across town in the Galorston City High School office, Marion scrolled through the news on her computer. The latest breaking story was about a fire at the car manufacturing plant. Marion had been following it closely since she got to work. *Oh my*, she thought, seeing there was another update. She clicked. Now there had been an explosion! She started a video included at the bottom of the article.

Marion gasped, and instantly called for her boss. "Mr. Sherman, come see this! There was a second explosion at Tri-County Automotive!"

Chris came out from his office and quickly joined Marion in front of her computer.

Marion's mouth was still hanging open. Then she squinted at one of the reporters on the scene. "Isn't that the journalist girl who was here last week?"

"Yes. Yes, it is."

Marion gasped then turned her head at the sound of Mr. Sherman dashing to his office. He called over his shoulder as he resurfaced moments later and raced to the front door. "I need to run an errand. I probably won't be back today."

Marion watched as the door closed behind him. *Geeze*, she thought. *What was that about? He flew out of here like he had been touched by the devil's firebrand.* Then she paused. "Oh yes," she muttered. "The journalist. I did see some chemistry between those two last week." A slow smile formed across her face.

~~~~~

Chris sped down the freeway as his mind raced. All he could focus on was finding Chloe. *I have to make sure she's okay. Hold her. Take care of her.*

Arriving at the scene ten minutes later, he hit Chloe's name on his phone and dialed her number. No answer.

There were people everywhere. Noise and smoke filled the air. Chris first went near the triage tents then circled around to the where the news reporters congregated. No luck.

Calling her name would be useless given all the noise. He decided to keep walking, checking any brown-haired reporter-type woman he met. Each blank stare left him feeling deflated but not defeated. Finally, approaching an open grassy area, he saw her at the edge of a small group. His heart pounded. *Chloe.*

Almost as if she knew he was behind her, Chloe turned her head as he approached. She squinted and strained to see his features, but she could sense it was him.

The pounding of his heart increased when he saw how swollen and red her face was. *She looks even worse than in the video.* Then he felt sick.

He reached for her as he called her name. "Chloe!"

"Chris? It is you!" she said. Her voice sounded as scratchy as sandpaper.

"Yes. I was worried. Marion showed a video of you here. I couldn't sit in the office and wait to hear from you."

Chloe slumped against him. Sliding his arm down, he made to pick her up. "No," she whispered. "I can walk."

He stepped aside and wrapped an arm around her waist.

Chloe leaned on him. "I'm glad you came."

~~~~~

Later at the Emergicenter, Chris sat in the waiting room looking out the window. Deep in thought, he pictured Chloe's pretty face and their sweet first kiss. Then he remembered her soiled clothes, her bewildered look as he'd escorted her from the automotive plant to this place. He ached to see her in pain. *How can she mean this much to me already? Have I fallen for her? Whoa, slow down!*

The door opened, breaking his musings. He stood as Chloe walked his way. In a light whisper she said, "The doctor said I'm fine. No contacts, lots of fluids, and major rest. My voice should be better in a day or two."

Chris took her hand and squeezed. Then he laced his fingers with hers. "That's a relief," he said. "I'll take you home. We'll figure out how to get your car later."

~~~~~

Once Chloe was home, she left Chris in the kitchen and slipped into her room. Needing a minute to collect her thoughts, she leaned back in her chair. The quiet of the room gave her time to just breathe.

I'm so glad to be home. Today was scary, but also exciting. The worst part of the incident was the fall while trying to get out of the smoke. She looked down and saw a small tear in her pants and some dried blood. It wasn't the bit of pain she experienced on her foot or her hands that had scared her, but the fear of the unknown. *Would there be another explosion? Would she suffocate from the smoke? Would she die?*

She wondered what Lou would say when he saw the pictures she'd taken. He was probably doing that right now, along with listening to the interview she'd done when she first reached the scene. She sighed, wishing she could've connected with Max to really hit this assignment out of the park. *I hope Lou'll still think I can handle this job.*

After showering and dressing in leggings and a T-shirt, she headed downstairs to find Chris. Walking through the hallway, she smiled at the thought that he had dropped everything to find her today. And now he was in her kitchen.

Chris looked up as Chloe padded barefoot toward him. She saw steam wafting from the corner of the room. Tea steeped in a large mug on the table. A soft fruit cup sat beside it.

Smiling, Chris moved to her, taking both of her hands. "Better?"

Her eyelashes flitted as she lightly returned the smile. To avoid using her voice, she mouthed, "Much."

Chris guided her over to the chair. "Do you want anything else?"

Chloe shook her head.

Still holding his hand, Chloe rested her head on Chris's cheek. His free hand swept up her back to the nape of her neck. He inhaled. "Mmm, coconut."

She pulled back from him and looked into his eyes. He tucked a strand of damp hair behind her ear. "You should sit and drink this. It's chamomile with honey," he said, sliding the mug toward her. She took a few tentative sips and smiled again.

The warm liquid soothed her scratchy throat and calmed her nerves. After a few bites of fruit and more sips of tea, her eyelids started to droop.

Chris reached out to stroke her cheek. Her eyes fluttered open at his touch, and her heart beat faster. "You're falling asleep as you sit here," he said.

She shrugged, then loosed a silent shriek as he gathered her in his arms and picked her up. "Allow me to escort you to your bed, ma'am."

Chloe stared at him, a playful expression on her face. He cradled her as he paraded through the house and toward the stairs. Chloe loved this, and almost told him so, but she decided to see how things played out instead. She directed him to her room with a few moves of her hands.

Laying her down on top of the covers, Chris pulled a throw blanket from the bottom of her bed and covered her.

Chloe's eyes lowered. She thought, *maybe he'll join me*, as sleep pulled her closer. She sighed as he touched her forehead.

Chris stood there a few moments to be sure she settled into a deep sleep. He leaned down and gave her another kiss, this time on her cheek, then brushed her jawline with his fingers. She breathed against his hand, telling him she really was asleep.

Downstairs, Chris searched the refrigerator for soup ingredients. *No time like the present to help a lady out.* Besides, everyone he knew raved over his vegetable soup. Now he would see what Chloe thought. After grabbing the vegetables he found in the fridge and a chopping board, he went to work.

The soup had just started to boil when Gaby and Jess walked in.

"Hi there," Gaby said, a little surprised.

"Hey." Chris set the knife down. "Chloe's sleeping."

"How is she?" asked Jess.

Chris nodded toward the steps. "I took her up about thirty minutes ago. She was exhausted."

"Aw," they said in unison.

He waved his hand toward the stove. "I hope you don't mind that I helped myself to ingredients from your fridge. I made soup."

"Chloe mentioned you cook," Jess said as she peered into the pot brewing on the stovetop. "And there's enough for all of us, I see. Great. You're welcome to stick around until she wakes. I'm sure she would want to see you again."

"I'd like that."

Gaby looked in the pot too. "Mmm. It looks delicious. Perfect for her throat."

"Thoughtful of you," Jess agreed, smiling.

Chris felt his ears reddening. "I'll let you know when it's ready." Gesturing toward the living room, he said, "Mind if I watch a little TV while I wait?"

"Not at all. Go ahead," said Jess. "I'll be in the study if you need anything. Feel free to help yourself."

Gaby nodded.

"Thanks." Chris headed there, leaving Jess and Gaby to exchange smiles. Gaby wiggled her eyebrows. "He's head over heels."

"I like him. He's good for her."

~~~~~

Upstairs, an oncoming cough woke Chloe. *Oh right,* she thought as she tried to get her bearings. *That happened.* The events of the day played through her mind. Then her thoughts settled on Chris. *I wonder if he's still here. He carried me upstairs. So romantic! That's a first!*

She pulled off her throw and sat up. Even though she blinked several times and slid her glasses on, Chloe's vision was still blurred. She started down the stairs, holding onto the railing to steady herself. She could make out Jess sitting at the desk in the study.

As soon as Jess heard her, she stood and came to hug Chloe. "Oh, sweetie. I'm so happy to see you are okay! Gaby and I felt sick when we heard you were there when the explosion happened. How are you feeling?"

Chloe whispered, "Okay, I guess. Taking in copious amounts of smoke has left my throat, lungs, eyes, and nose constantly burning. The doctor says I'll be fine in a few days, though."

"Oh, thank God. Chris is waiting over in the living room for you."

"Where's Gabs?" Chloe's voice was barely a whisper.

"She's upstairs, I think. She and I will go pick up your car later," Jess told her.

"That would be great, thanks."

Chloe headed into the living room and found Chris stretched out on the couch. The stress of the day must have zapped his energy too. She slid next to him and nuzzled into the crook of his arm. He stirred and looked at her. It felt so natural to cozy up to him. He pulled her in tighter and closed his eyes again, content to lay there holding her.

Chloe whispered, "Thank you for everything today."

Chris opened his eyes and said, "I was happy to help. How are you feeling? Better, I hope?"

"Some," she rasped.

"Are you hungry? I made some soup. Or if you aren't hungry yet, can I get you something to drink?" He smoothed her hair back from her face.

"I'm a little hungry. Soup sounds good." She reluctantly sat up and leaned on her elbow. "I must look horrific."

"I've never seen you look more beautiful," Chris said very seriously.

"Oh please!" she snickered.

"Naw, I'm serious. I love your glasses." He gave her a quick peck on the lips. "I'll go get you some of the soup. Don't get up."

Chloe felt the warmth of his lips linger on hers. She lifted her fingers to touch them and found they were still quite swollen, and her cheeks still warm from earlier in the day. She sat up fully and crossed her legs to wait. Picking up the remote, she turned the volume up on the TV. Chris had channel nine on. She saw they were providing a full recap of the coverage of the fire. The camera swung from the top of the building and across the scene to focus on Shondra, who'd stood in for Chloe after she left. She gave a run-down of the events and a short interview with a few bystanders.

Chloe smiled as the photos she had sent Lou from the edge of the smoke cloud flashed across the screen. *So he had liked them enough to use them!* She pointed at the TV as Chris walked in holding two bowls of soup. "Those are pictures I took!"

Chris's eyes focused on the TV. "That's awesome! They're really good." Slowly, he eased back next to Chloe.

"I'm so glad that they got to use them. I have the interview I can use to write up a nice piece for tomorrow's edition too." Chloe tapped the side of her face. "Hmm. I could do a first-person's point of view too."

Chris nodded. "You should. People love that sort of thing." He handed her a bowl. She gladly took it and the spoon he offered her. After a spoonful, she realized just how hungry she was. She whispered to him, "This is really good!"

He smiled. "I'm glad you like it. Eat up. You had a long day." He put his hand on her leg and gave it a squeeze. Then he left it there to rest.

Chloe liked the way the palm of his hand tingled her leg as it sat there. She had never felt so appreciated before. *Please let him be the real deal and not like one of Gaby's exes*, she prayed.

~~~~~

Later that night after Chloe had said goodbye to Chris and good night to the girls, she lay down in bed and thought through the day. So much had happened, but strangest of all was the stubbing of her toe and when Chris appeared. *It was the exact toe that tripped later. And I knew with certainty that Chris was standing behind me before he said a word. Are my premonitions back now?* She hoped so.

Feeling tired, Chloe rolled over and soon sunk into a deep sleep. All of her dreams swirled around her growing relationship with Chris. She wondered what it would be like to touch—really touch—him. Romantically. She was excited to see where it would go. It felt right and good.

~~~~~

Chapter 8

The next morning Chloe woke up able to see and breathe easier, even though she'd had a few coughing spells during the night. She grabbed her glasses and phone before heading downstairs. As she walked, she flipped to her email and saw one new one from Lou:

Great photos, Chloe. Eager to see what your next article will look like. Rest up now and speak soon, Lou.

Chloe couldn't hide the grin from her face as she rounded the corner into the kitchen. To her surprise, Jess stood at the counter, mixing fruit into her yogurt. "What are you still doing here?" Chloe asked. "It's after nine."

"I stayed up late last night so decided to sleep in. I'm making today a short day and leaving at three to meet my dad."

Chloe walked to the cabinet to grab a mug. "Oh, right. That's today!" She'd forgotten about it after yesterday's rollercoaster of events. "Will he stay overnight?"

Jess nodded with a smile. "Yes, he will. It will be too late for him to drive the rest of the way to Oklahoma, so I told him to stay on our couch tonight."

"That's wonderful. I can still cook something for us," offered Chloe as she poured some hot water over a tea bag.

"No, no, you can't do that. You shouldn't do too much today. I'll pick up some takeout for all of us."

"I really don't mind. I will make something simple, like pasta and sauce. There are some meatballs in the freezer I can defrost. It really isn't a problem," Chloe reassured.

Jess shot her a look. "Okay. Well, as long as it is really, really simple, I'll allow it." She studied her friend's face. "The swelling has gone down. How do you feel?"

"Way better! I can see and breathe!" Chloe said, sighing for emphasis.

"That's great. You sound better too. Not as scratchy." Jess shook her pointer finger at Chloe. "You still need to take it easy, though."

"I won't do much. I plan to draft an article on the explosion. I'll sit outside and sip water all day, I promise," Chloe said with her hand up. "I give you my pledge."

"You better!" Jess gave her a side hug. "I'll see you in a few hours."

After Jess left, Chloe took her tea into the study and sat on the oversized chair. She looked at her phone and saw missed messages from Chris and Gaby. Chloe read Gaby's message first and saw her friend was just checking on her.

Chloe took a sip of tea and rested her eyes. She still wasn't at a hundred percent, despite how enthusiastic she'd seemed to Jess. Looking down at her phone again, she read Chris's texts.

Chris: *Good morning beautiful*
Chris: *How are you feeling?*

Aw, he called me beautiful, she thought. Smiling, she typed a response.

Chloe: *Hi there*
Chloe: *I feel way better this morning. Not fabulous yet, but better.*
Chris: *That's great, what are you going to do today?*
Chloe: *I think I'll sit outside and write.*
Chris: *Great, keep feeling better :)*

She wondered what he was up to, how he'd been since they'd seen each other last night. She remembered his arms around her, the way he took care of her and made soup for everyone. *A real nice guy.*

Her mind drifted then to her article. Lou wanted it as soon as possible but reassured her if it took longer given the circumstances, that would be okay. She wanted to impress him, though, and not make him regret his decision to have given her a new role at the station. After taking another sip of tea to bolster her, she set down her mug and started her story.

By noon, a solid draft had come together. Chloe tapped Lou's name on her phone.

"Hey, Lou. It's Chloe."

"Hey, how are you?" He seemed relieved to hear from her. "We've all been thinking about you."

"I'm doing better," Chloe replied. "I'll be back to as good as new in a few days."

"Good to hear," he said.

"I sent over the article I wrote about the Tri-County plant fire for you to review."

"Yeah. I just saw the email pop up." She imagined him downloading the file and scanning its contents as they spoke. "Oh, and thanks again for the photos last night. Great moment you caught."

Chloe grinned. "I'm glad you liked them."

"They worked really well with Shondra's piece. Good stuff." He paused. "You know, we all caught your interview on GBD. That was some real nice work you did with them. I've got to say, Chloe, I'm really impressed with the initiative I see you taking. And your quick hustle and commitment to the job in the face of your own discomfort is commendable. It's got me thinking of more assignments we could use your eye and determination on. But for now, I'm looking forward to reading this. I'll get back to you shortly."

Feeling pride well up inside her, Chloe bit her lip and smiled. "Thanks, Lou. That means a lot to me. I'll talk to you soon."

She gave a fist pump as the call ended then set her laptop aside and basked in her happiness. She'd worked hard to get that article finished, and she hoped he'd like it as much as he liked the photos. The words he'd said bounced around in her head, and her mind raced with thoughts of what would be in her future at Local 9 News.

Chloe's stomach growled. *Time for lunch.* She heated a bowl of leftover soup, smiling to herself as she remembered who made it. She couldn't wait to tell Chris about her work call. She poured a glass of iced tea and plopped down on a chair under the umbrella on the deck.

While taking small bites, Chloe examined the small flower garden growing by the back fence. It teemed with color, and even had a bird feeder hanging from one of the trees. Insects and birds now explored petals, pistils, and pollen with gusto. *I don't get to watch this that much, at least not until later in the day*, Chloe noted. *It's soothing, watching nature in our backyard.*

Soon, Chloe's eyelids flickered, and her head bobbed. Soup slopped on her leggings. *Darn it!* The afternoon was getting hot, even with the shade from the trees overhead. *I can't stand these things anyway*, she complained, moving to shed her leggings. She pulled her long t-shirt down, so she didn't worry about the neighbors getting a show and sat back down. *Much better.* She rested her legs on a chair nearby and closed her eyes. The sun felt good shining on her skin. She was out within minutes.

~~~~~

At work, Chris had Chloe on his mind, as usual. He couldn't focus on anything he needed to get done. When he had come in that morning, he told Marion where he had gone yesterday. She was very polite, asking only a few questions then letting him go about his day.

Now, sitting at his desk, he felt irritable not knowing when he would see her again. They hadn't planned a time when Chloe would come for dinner yet, but last night had felt so natural, so comfortable. He wanted that feeling again as soon as possible.

He picked up his phone then put it back on his desk. *No, don't send another text. Buy her flowers and deliver them!* It was almost lunchtime—the perfect time to leave the office for an errand.

Chris found a florist on his way to Chloe's house and picked out a bright and colorful arrangement. *This one has Chloe's name all over it,* he thought while handing his credit card to the cashier.

On the drive over, he couldn't stop thinking about how it'd feel to see her again. To hold her. To make her happy.

He parked in front of the townhouse and decided to walk around back instead of going to the front door remembering she had mentioned sitting outside to write. He walked down the small path around the house and opened the gate leading to the yard. He felt sweaty and nervous as he stepped inside. *Come on, Chris. Snap out of it.*

He stopped midstride when his eyes landed on her. Her hair hung behind her chair in waves, and her face was peaceful. Her feet were propped up on another chair, and her head rolled toward one shoulder. *She's stunning even when she's dreaming.* Then he wondered, *is it creepy that I'm watching her?* He tried to move, but his feet wouldn't budge; it was like they were trapped in cement.

His eyes traveled from her face down to her sexy legs. Her T-shirt stopped at the top of her thighs, showcasing their length. She had her bare feet crossed at the ankle.

He stared for a few minutes longer at the sight of her in the sunlight. It took his breath away. Forcing himself to move quietly, Chris walked to the deck's bottom steps.

"Chloe," he whispered. No movement. "Chloe," he repeated, a bit louder this time.

This time her eyelids fluttered and once her eyes regained focus, she saw him. "Chris?" she asked, squinting.

Chris climbed the deck's three steps to her. "It's me," he said as she put on her glasses and smiled in recognition.

"Hey, you," she said. "What are you doing here? You caught me napping." She looked down. "And without pants!" She stood up and pulled her T-shirt down a bit more.

"Okay by me," Chris said with a wink. He saw her cheeks turn a dark shade of pink, but she still smiled.

His face grew more serious as he focused on her eyes. They weren't as puffy or as red today. Only inches from her now, he asked, "How do your eyes feel?"

"A million times better. Less burning. Thank God."

Chris reached a hand forward to brush her cheek with his fingertips. "I hope it's okay that I just stopped by. I brought you these." He set the flowers on the table. "Plus, I wanted to see you."

"Aw, these are beautiful. And yes, it's okay. I wanted to see you too." Chloe reached up to give him a brief kiss on the cheek and then leaned in for a hug. "I am glad you came."

Chris smiled. "I've been thinking."

Chloe eyed him. *About what?*

He placed his hands on either side of her waist and looked into her eyes. Chloe felt something shift between them, a deeper understanding growing like a flower in the garden. Her heartbeat quickened.

Chris took a breath. "I'd really like to kiss you. May I?"

"Yes," she said, shivers suddenly running over her arms. Her heart swelled. *This is it.*

Meanwhile, Chris could feel his own heart start to pound against his chest. "You're so beautiful," he said quietly as he lowered his mouth to hers.

He brushed his lips against hers and felt them open slightly. Tilting his head, he started to kiss her more deeply. She pressed her body into his and rested her hands on his shoulders. His hands loosened on her waist and slowly moved up to rest on the small of her back.

He used his left hand to pull her snugly to him while his right hand rubbed down her side to the hem of her T-shirt. Pulling it up slightly, he ran his fingers across her thigh. Still holding her pressed up against him, he continued kissing her slowly and deeply. She moaned and ran her hands down his arms to his waist.

Chris relaxed his grip on her back and released her mouth from his. Her eyes danced open and he could see the passion in them. They were both breathing more quickly now.

"Are you okay?" Chris asked her.

Swallowing hard, Chloe said, "Yes, that was amazing. Is it always like that?"

"What? Kissing?" he asked, his eyebrows drawn together.

Still breathing heavily, she said, "Yeah. Is kissing always that intense?"

Realization dawned. "Was this your first kiss?"

"Yes, and it was amazing," she said, shifting her gaze downward.

"It was. I never experienced anything that intense."

Looking up to meet his eyes, she asked, "Really? Are you just saying that?"

Chris touched her cheek softly and responded, "I can assure you that was unlike any other kiss I've had."

Chloe smiled. "Good." She leaned closer and waited. Chris touched his lips to hers again and pulled her closer.

After several minutes of more slow, deep kisses, Chloe leisurely pulled back. "Still intense?" she asked.

"Even more," he said. Her head tipped back, and she let out a shy giggle.

"I like your smile," he muttered close to her ear. He mused, *So sweet, so innocent, so perfect.* He held her close, hugging and swaying slightly.

"I like your kisses," Chloe replied.

"Thank you," he said.

She tilted her head and bit her lip. "For what?"

"Allowing me to be your first kiss."

Chloe leaned forward once more fitting her lips to his. A small sigh escaped her as he took his time smoothing his hands over her back and using his tongue to taste her mouth.

After Chris left, Chloe went to sit on the couch and write. Lou had sent through another assignment after approving her plant fire piece. With one eyebrow cocked, Chloe reread the brief—a story exploring the recent speculation of scandal in the mayor's office. However, even with the promise of an exciting assignment, she couldn't manage to type anything. Her mind raced and her stomach flitted at the memory of Chris's kisses. She looked to the flowers he brought her, now tucked into a vase on their coffee table. They were so beautiful and thoughtful.

Today was full of firsts for her. Her first kiss. Her first bouquet from a man. A shiver ran through her. Chloe wanted to see him again, and soon.

~~~~~

Jess arrived with her dad later that afternoon. She smiled when she walked in the living room, catching sight of the bouquet. "I bet I know where those came from."

Still on the couch, Chloe jumped. "You scared me!"

"How long have you been sitting here staring? Minutes or hours?" Jess teased.

Chloe had her hand on her chest, trying to catch her breath. "I didn't hear you come in. I was in another world."

Jess's dad cleared his throat, drawing Chloe's attention to him. "It's so good to see you, Mr. Taylor. It has been so long!" She stood up and gave him a hug.

"Hi there, honey. It has been too long. I heard what happened," he said, looking her over. "I am glad nothing serious happened."

"Me too," Chloe said.

"Okay, stop evading my question. When was Chris here?" Jess asked.

"At lunch." Her eyes glittered as they rested on the flowers again. "They're so beautiful. It was thoughtful of him, wasn't it?"

"That is how a woman should be treated. Don't ever settle for less than that, girls," Mr. Taylor said sternly.

"We know, Daddy," said Jess. She then motioned her father toward the kitchen. "Come on. Let's sit outside and leave Chloe to stare at her flowers."

Out on the deck, Jess's dad asked, "How's my girl doing these days? You look great. Happy."

Jess smiled. "I feel great. And I am happy. I have two amazing friends; my career is growing … The last few months have been rewarding with a new project, as well as tough. But you know what you always say—"

"Ain't nothing makes you tougher than tough stuff," they answered in unison.

Jess smiled then continued, "The additional responsibility at work is bolstering my confidence. And at home, the girls have helped so much in improving how I feel about myself."

Soon after Jess started her job and had some money to spend on herself, Gaby introduced her to makeup and skin-care products. And she went along with Chloe to the salon. The waves that used to be unruly curls were tame now. All of this helped her redefine herself and gain a better understanding of what it truly meant to be Jessica Taylor, IT professional.

Her dad squeezed her hand. "They are so good for you. That Chloe looks to be in love. When is a nice boy going to come along and make you see stars like that?"

Sighing deeply, Jess said, "It's not because I haven't been looking. I have been out on a few dates, but none of those worked out. I want what Chloe has, but no one has made me feel that way yet. I'll know it when I find it."

"That you will, sugar snap. You'll feel all gooey inside and you'll know he's worth your time. He's going to have to be pretty special to be worth it, because you are pretty special."

"I know I am," she said, touched by her dad's pride in her. She continued, "Work has been crazy busy, which also leaves no time for dating, really. I am working with a client in California building code for a statistical program. Right now, they are hitting me left and right with changes. I'll travel there in a few weeks to present the final draft and make any last-minute tweaks."

"Now, that's my smart girl. I bet you will blow them away."

Jess sighed and thought to herself, *it's going to be a busy few weeks until the trip.* She left out the fact that she might have to go back a second time or possibly stay there for an extended period to provide training on the program.

"It's a great experience," she admitted. "But enough about me. How are you? I worry."

Her dad shook his head. "Oh, you know, I'm tired from all the manual labor and travel. It's hard being away so much. I guess you heard Marisa has been getting herself into trouble?"

Jess nodded.

"Last week the police brought her home. They found her behind the liquor store. She wasn't drinking, at least from what they could tell, but the twenty-year-old boys she was with were." Her dad sighed. "I just don't know what to do. You know your mother doesn't pay attention, and Johnny is a seventeen-year-old boy who has already done more than he should. I need to find work closer to home. The paint factory may be hiring; however, that wouldn't cover the bills for long."

"Oh, Dad. I'm so sorry things are so rough. I can help you. Nobody needs to know. I owe you, after all; you helped me get here." Jess really admired her dad for working so hard to take care of everyone else. He always put his family first. It was time someone took care of him.

Her dad snorted. "I wouldn't dream of taking your money. That's yours. You worked hard for it and hard to get where you are today. You did that, not me. But thank you, honey. I'll find a way."

Jess's shoulders dropped. "I wish I could help."

"I know you do."

"How's Johnny doing?" Jess asked. "Is he still working at the Ice Cream Palace?"

"Johnny is fine. He is still working and mostly keeping out of trouble. There was a girl that had been hanging around, but I haven't heard much about her lately."

"I hope he can get through one more year. Is he still talking about joining the marines?"

Her dad nodded. "That's still his plan."

"What about Seth? Have you heard from him recently? It has been at least two months since I last heard from him. I tried about three weeks ago, but I haven't heard back."

"I caught up with him a few weeks ago. He said he was expecting to have several missions that would keep him from being in touch for a while. The marines keep him busy." Jess's dad shook his head. "You never stop worrying about your kids, no matter how old they are."

"I worry about all of you. I don't like that you travel all over and work so hard. I don't like that Seth could be in danger. Then there is Marisa and Johnny. Who knows what Marisa is going to get into next, and Johnny has to be worn out from her and Mom." Jess was exhausted just thinking about it.

She slouched and leaned her head back to look up and see the setting sun. Jess always loved watching a good sunset. A good sunrise too. It reminded her that everything had an end and something new was around the corner. She found it inspiring. Things for her family would hopefully turn around soon.

She looked back to her dad and broached a topic she didn't know if she wanted to hear about. "How is Mom? We've never talked much about her, but do you think there has ever been any truth to her complaints? After I left, I used to lie awake at night thinking about her and feeling guilty. I never believed anything she complained about. Maybe that's why she complained so much, because no one would believe her."

Her dad was quiet for a moment, his own internal turmoil twisting across his face. "Your mom was legitimately sick before Johnny was born. You and Seth were five and three, so you wouldn't remember any of this. She experienced abdominal pain sometimes. A doctor at the walk-in clinic found a mass that required surgery. We didn't have health insurance at the time, so she had to wait a few weeks until I found a job that had it as a benefit. That was when I was working at the grocery store in the back room unloading deliveries. The mass was luckily benign, and no long-term issues were expected."

Her dad paused, his eyes closing as he remembered. "I felt horrible making her wait like that, being in so much pain, but there was no way we could afford all of that out of pocket. I guess that is when she started to develop feelings of paranoia and I spiraled with guilt. I overcompensated. I took her to the doctor several times, and each time he found nothing. On the last visit, he told her she had hypochondriasis—an illness where the person is always afraid they'll get sick or are getting sick. She was angry that he thought she was making it all up. She became depressed and said she would never go back to the doctor again. The doctor explained there were treatments to help her anxiety, but she refused to hear it." His tone grew solemn, sad.

That must have been the point of no return for Mom, thought Jess. She recalled her mom laying in the dark for hours a day and losing a lot of weight. Other times she would binge and gain a lot of weight. It was a vicious cycle.

Jess moved over to sit on her dad's lap, just like she did when she was a kid. "I wish there was help we could get her. I hate to say it, but is there a clinic we could check her into to get help? Maybe once they stabilize her, she will realize for herself that there is a way out."

He hugged her close. "I would have to take her to a facility against her will with a court order since she refuses help. I am not sure I can do that to her. And I think she is too far gone into this dark hole she created to come out on her own."

Jess frowned. "It is for her benefit long term, though. I can help with the legal stuff. Make a few calls, see what would need to be done. We could just collect some information then make a decision."

"Oh, sugar snap, I know you want to help. If it would make you feel better to investigate it, that is fine. But please no action until I can hear the details and think it over. She may be challenging to deal with, but she is sick, and she is my wife. I'm not sure you can understand it, but I love her so much. The thought of putting her in a facility … just breaks my heart."

Sniffling, Jess said, "I never thought about it being a mental illness. I want to make some calls and do some research. I am hopeful there is something we can do."

She stood up, took her dad's hand, and pulled him to his feet. Then she gave him a huge hug and led him to the sliding glass door. "Daddy, I love you. I'm sorry if I haven't always been there for you. I should have never left like I did."

He stopped her. "I won't have you feeling guilty too. You were a child and you deserved to build your own life."

"Well, I'm going to help now that I am old enough to understand the truth of what's going on," Jess said as she walked into the kitchen.

As they entered, Chloe looked up from the tray of cheese, crackers, and veggies she was arranging. "I thought I would get something out for us to snack on while we wait for Gaby."

"You read my mind." Jess said with a smile. "We need something to hold us over."

Mr. Taylor moved through the kitchen after his daughter, heading toward the hallway. "I'll be right back."

"Okay, Dad."

Jess turned to Chloe. "Are you sure you're up to making dinner?"

Chloe smiled. "I really am fine, I promise. I napped while you and your dad were out back. How is he?"

"Good," Jess said. "It was great to talk and catch up."

Moments later, her dad walked in carrying a small gift bag. Setting it down, he said, "That's for later. A little surprise for when Gaby gets home."

"Aw, Dad!" Jess said, whining.

After returning Jess's grin, Mr. Taylor turned his attention to Chloe. "Tell me about this special man that makes you smile from ear to ear."

Chloe took a deep breath before diving in. There was nothing she liked talking about more now than Chris. "I interviewed him for an article on the city school system and we hit it off. It hasn't been that long yet, but so far everything has been going well. He's been treating me very well."

"Good! Make sure he keeps doing that. The second he doesn't, kick him to the curb!"

Chloe laughed. "I will!"

"Dad, you're so protective!"

Chloe's phone dinged. "Oh, goodie. Gaby says she is out a little earlier tonight and will be leaving soon. I'll start heating dinner."

After a filling meal of spaghetti and meatballs followed by some cookies Gaby had picked up at the bakery near work, the four of them sat back and sighed.

"Mr. Taylor, is there anything else I can get you?" Chloe asked.

"No, no. Now, you stay seated. You cook, I clean." Grabbing a stack of dishes, he winked at the three of them. "Then, I have a little something for you all."

"For all of us?" Gaby exclaimed.

"You're too much!" Chloe added.

"Well, it's just something small, but when I saw them, I knew they were perfect for you three."

He grabbed the gift bag on his way back to the table and pulled out three small boxes, each tied with a little pink bow. Handing one to each of them, he said, "I found these at a store near the work site. I couldn't resist."

Jess pulled the lid off first and exclaimed, "Aw, Dad. It's beautiful! I love it!"

Gaby and Chloe said at the same time, "Oh my God!"

Jess added, "You are so right, these are perfect!"

Dangling from each of their fingers was a long silver chain. A peapod charm twirled in the center. Inside the charm glistened three pearls.

"You are my three little peas in a pod," he said.

Jess went around the table to hug her dad, and Gaby and Chloe quickly followed, making it a group hug. Jess's grin spread from ear to ear. "I'm so lucky to have a dad like you!

~~~~~

Chapter 9

What a nice day, Chloe thought as she lay in bed the following night. It had been another day to recover at home, and she was starting to feel like herself again. Lou had suggested she work remotely the remainder of the week but expected her back in the office Monday for their weekly ideas meeting. That morning, she had worked on her laptop, toying with a few topics to run by him. In the afternoon she had been able to fit in a nap and a walk at the park. Dinner was calming too, since the meal was a quick and easy prep, leaving room for lots of talking out on the deck.

Even when the sun had started to go down, Gaby, Jess, and Chloe stayed out longer. The smoke from the chiminea kept the bugs away. Chloe found watching flames to be comforting.

They talked about Jess's visit with her dad and the latest with Gaby and Rob. It turned out that Gaby hadn't spoken to him in a few days, and she had blown off hanging out with him again. Now she said he didn't interest her. "He's likely a dud, just like the rest of them."

Jess spoke of the visit with her dad. "He's doing well, but he wants to get work closer to home to help my mom. He told me she'd been sick many years ago and even though she had been treated and cured, she developed anxiety and later depression. She never received treatment. I didn't put it together that she had a mental illness. I feel horrible. I had only seen her as *crazy* and dramatic."

Chloe patted Jess's shoulder. "Don't be so hard on yourself. No one told you about her condition, so that is how it appeared to you."

Jess balled her hands into fists and narrowed her eyes. "Now that I understand the underlying problem, I'm determined to help. I'm going to see what I can dig up about her condition and try to find a way to persuade her to get the help she really needs."

Gaby offered to talk to a few doctors at the hospital, and Chloe said she'd help research.

Jess couldn't contain her gratitude for these women. "I'm glad I have you both as I go through this. It's not easy, but knowing you are there for me makes things better. Thank you."

Chloe examined the three pearls on her necklace then looked back at her friends. "We're always here for each other."

Now, lying in bed, Chloe nestled under the covers. A text had come through. *Chris.*

Chris: *Ready for sleep?*

She nodded, as though he could see her. *Yes,* she texted back. A sleepy emoticon followed her words.

Chris: *Sweet dreams! :) Oh, and are you up for dinner tomorrow?*

Chloe grinned. *I never thought you'd ask me,* she replied.

After a few more goodnight texts, she set the phone down, feeling bad they hadn't talked much today. She'd gotten sucked into her latest assignment on the mayor's office scandal and the ideas task, and then dinner happened. She lost track of time. Still, knowing he cared enough to send a goodnight message meant a lot to her. She remembered the feel of his lips on hers, and excitement twittered in her stomach. She couldn't stop herself from enjoying the thought that they'd be together again soon. She fell asleep thinking of his hugs and the heat he sent coursing through her every time they touched.

~~~~~

Chloe woke to her phone ringing. Blinking a few times, she groaned ... *It's morning already?* She grabbed her phone and squinted at the name. Momma R. Clearing her throat, she hoped she sounded more awake and back to normal. "Hey, Momma R. How are you?"

Gaby's mom's familiar voice made Chloe smile. "I am wonderful, but I am more interested in how you are! I heard what happened and saw the news that night. I was so scared for you, Chloe."

"I'm back to normal—almost. Did Gaby tell you Chris came to find me at the fire and brought me flowers the next day?"

"She did mention that your new man helped. I didn't hear about the flowers, though! That is great! He sounds very nice."

Chloe sat up in bed, patting the covers around her and running a hand through her hair. "He really is very thoughtful. He invited me to his house for dinner tonight. I'm excited to go."

"I bet."

"Oh, and Mr. Taylor dropped by for a visit on Tuesday. He brought us the cutest necklaces."

"Aw," Momma R. said. "That was nice of him."

"He is the sweetest man." Chloe thought about how much he meant to her, and how much of a role model he'd been to her over the years. *A lot like Momma R.* The two of them were so different from her parents. They'd helped shape her into who she was now, encouraging her toward healthy relationships. She made sure to cherish the warmth she shared with them always.

As though reading her thoughts, Momma R. replied, "And he is the perfect father figure to have."

"You're certainly right. I'd be lost without both of you."

"We are all so lucky, aren't we?"

"Very!" Chloe switched the phone to her other ear. "So, tell me about you. What's new?"

Chloe envisioned the short and vibrant middle-aged woman sitting in her small kitchen. "Oh, I've been busy preparing for the new school year. The end of summer always means a new group of fourth graders. But I love it and wouldn't have it any other way."

Chloe and Momma R. continued chatting away, catching up on other gossip and enjoying each other's company. Chloe loved how easy it was to confide in her.

After some time, Momma R. exclaimed, "Oh my gosh! When did it get to be this late? I have to run over to the school and start setting up my classroom. I'll talk to you soon!"

"Okay. Thank you for calling. Bye!"

"Chao!"

Chloe made her way to the kitchen and poured herself some coffee, then positioned herself in the study with her computer to start researching Mrs. Taylor's illness. Before long, she was buried in online videos, testimonials, clinical studies, and blog posts discussing the ins and outs of this particular condition and other related mental struggles.

The more she dug, the more inspiration hit her. She knew she had to do more than just research and print out articles to show to Gaby and Jess. She wanted to *write.* An idea sprouted then. *Why don't I pitch to Lou a series of educational articles on mental illnesses? It could lead to a lot of growth—through social media, expert interviews, exclusive features, and maybe even a podcast.* She thought it was worth a try. No one else in the area was doing anything like this. Besides, there was so much more that could be done to help raise awareness of the many mental illnesses in society today. She wrote the topic down and promised to pitch it on Monday. If nothing else, it might spark ideas for other assignments.

~~~~~

Later in the day, Chloe stood in her closet wondering what a girl should wear to a guy's house for the first time. *I already went with a pretty in pink look for dinner and a cute and casual look for our Saturday afternoon date, so what's left? Mmm ... sexy and sultry!*

Sliding a few hangers to the side, she found a white tank with lace trim and a deep V neckline. She paired it with her favorite jeans and wedge sandals. *Perfect*, she said to herself as she looked in the mirror. *Next, hair and makeup.* She added some loose curls at the ends of her hair so it would fall around her shoulders in soft waves. She opted for smoky eyes, aiming for a captivating, irresistible look. Both her hair and makeup complimented her outfit well.

As Chloe made her way out the door, Jess popped her head out of the study. "Whoa, hold up, you little vixen! Where did you get that top?"

Chloe paused and met her friend's gaze. "Ha! A few months ago when we visited the big mall in Dallas."

"Oh right! Well, you look H-O-T in it. Mr. Sherman will be drooling the whole night!" Jess had her phone in hand. "Let's send Gaby a pic! Pose!"

Chloe gave a little pout. Jess snapped a photo. "Let me see." Chloe leaned over Jess's shoulder. "Oh, that's pretty good." Laughing, she said. "Send that to me. I do look hot!"

Jess did as Chloe asked, then followed her to the door. "Have a great time. I expect a full run down!"

"Thanks, girl. I'll see you soon. Bye!" Chloe called as she turned and headed to her car.

She didn't have any trouble finding Chris's place. His neighborhood resembled Chloe's, with its mix of townhouses and family homes, although the style was more modern with concrete and neutral colors. Chloe found an open spot to park on the street then walked toward the front door. She could hear music coming from inside. She knocked twice, her familiar nerves invading as she waited.

In a minute the door opened, and Chris appeared, looking sexy as ever. He started to say, "Hey, I was—" then his sentence fizzled as his eyes darted over Chloe.

Chloe smiled, watching him. His mouth hung open just a bit, and his eyes looked a little glossed over. She felt beautiful in that moment, knowing that she had such an impact on him.

"May I come in?" Chloe asked, cutting into his stare.

Stuttering, Chris said, "Yes, yes. Umm, yes, come in."

She walked through the door and leaned in to put a light kiss on his cheek. "Hi." As she wandered farther into the house, he grabbed her around the waist and pulled her in close.

"Not so fast," he said, his breath hot on her cheek. Without questioning, he brought his mouth over hers, his lips moving in fast, needy motions. His tongue licked her lips and slid smoothly into her mouth.

Taken back, Chloe stilled for a moment, her thoughts racing. *Oh my God! This is different than last time. I don't know how to kiss passionately like this! Wait. I'm already doing it. Oh, wow! He is good!*

Chris wrapped his arms tighter around her and picked her up. Twisting, he kicked the door closed behind him with one foot. Then he set her back on her feet, his arms loosening and his hands skimming over her waist. She thought he'd say something now, but without another word, he pulled her tight against him again. His mouth dipped to find hers, moving feverishly and making her dizzy.

Slowing his movements and urgency, Chris let a little space come between them. He touched his forehead to hers. "Are you okay? Was that too much?"

It was her turn to stutter. "No, no, it's … it's okay … I'm okay."

"I didn't mean to come on so strongly. Your beauty draws me in and stirs me into this crazy turmoil."

Bringing her fingertips to his lips, she traced the outline of his mouth, enjoying the curves, the lines and the smile that he gave her as she did this. Then she said, "That was different than our first kisses. Did I do it right?"

Chris leaned in and scooped her mouth in his again, lighter, gentler, and much shorter this time. "Yes, you were perfect." Smiling, he added, "You are so sweet. It's one of the things I admire most about you."

Chloe tilted her head to one side. "Why?"

"You are humble and thoughtful of others—that's attractive to me."

"Good answer." Chloe said teasingly.

"Good, my goal is to always impress you," Chris said as he took her elbow and guided her to the living room. "Here, let me give you a tour."

The living room décor was different compared to that of Chloe and her friends'. For one thing, it was very modern. The TV hung on the wall as a centerpiece, an altar by which Chris, Todd, and his friends worshipped the gods of different sports every week. The furniture was dark leather and arranged around a glass coffee table. Silver-framed art took up space on the other walls, and glass and silver shelves finished off the look.

Chloe turned to Chris. "It's very male. Very dark and modern. I like it."

Chris laughed. "Yeah, I guess it is. Most of the furniture here is Todd's. I moved in with him after he had been living here for a few years."

Chloe swept her eyes around the room again. "Where is Todd? Will he eat with us?"

"No, I kicked him out. At least for a few hours anyway."

"Well, I'm happy to have a private dinner, but you don't have to kick him out. I like him and wouldn't mind getting to know him better."

"That's nice of you to offer, but I am more focused on getting to know *you* better," Chris said, raising his eyebrows.

Chloe returned the flirty banter. "Well, it would benefit me to have him around so I can get some dirt on you."

"Ohhh, is that right?" Chris grabbed her and twirled her around.

Giggling, Chloe held on to his shoulders while he spun her. She never knew that dating could be this fun. It felt amazing to get this kind of attention and have someone to be physically close with.

Setting her down, Chris continued the tour of the house. Chloe followed him into the kitchen, gawking at all it had to offer. It was easily twice the size of her kitchen, she realized. A mixer, smoothie maker, food processor, and many other appliances sat on a large shelf that lined the wall. *I could bake for days in this place!*

"It's very nice," she said. "A lot of space. I love it." She then ran her fingertips along the shelf. "Do you use all of these gadgets?"

"Yup, all of them. Both of us like to cook."

"That's cool." Chloe's eyes ran along the long breakfast bar, then focused on a big gas stove and all that counter space again. Like the living room, with its dark and silver furniture, the kitchen was mostly black and chrome. Also decorated in a modern style with drop lights hanging over the breakfast bar and the corner table.

Chloe met his eyes and smiled. "It feels formal yet comfortable."

"Come, let's sit down." Chris took her hand and led her toward the corner table that had already been set. A candle glowed in the middle.

"Wow, you did all this for me?"

"I wanted it to be a cozy dinner for two."

She sighed, feeling so special. *No one has ever done this for me.* Her eyes gazed at the pots and plates on the table. "So, what do we have here?" She pulled up a lid to peek. The smell that wafted from the dish was spicy.

"That is barbecue pulled chicken. It has a little kick to it. I hope you like your barbecue a little hot," Chris said.

Chloe nodded. "I've lived in Texas long enough to adjust my taste buds to handle heat."

"Great!" He gestured for her to sit, then started serving.

Chloe's mouth watered as Chris piled food on her plate. "It looks amazing!" she said. On her first bite, she knew she was absolutely right. Everything was perfectly cooked.

"Would you like a glass of white wine?"

"Yes, please."

Dinner went well and the conversation flowed, just like their first one at Galorston City High. Chloe didn't think it was possible to like him any more than she already did, but he constantly surprised her. By the end of their conversation, she knew without a doubt she was getting in deep with Chris Sherman.

After taking her last bite, Chloe leaned back in her chair. "That was great!"

Chris slid his chair sideways and covered her hand as it rested on the table. "You're very welcome. I'm glad to have you over. I missed seeing you the last two days."

Smiling, Chloe stood and slid onto his lap. "You missed me?"

"Yes, I missed seeing your face." He reached one hand to trace her cheek with his fingertips. His palm then glided along her jawline until his fingers laced into her hair at the base of her neck.

Chloe expected him to pull her to him and kiss her. Instead, several moments passed where he looked into her eyes. She said in a breathy whisper, "Well, are you going to kiss me?"

"Yes, in a minute. When you kiss, your eyes close and I want to look at your beautiful face with them open."

The anticipation was killing Chloe. When she couldn't take the intense, sensual trance any longer, she moved in. She intended to kiss him gently, with the same tenderness they had shown with their first kiss, but she felt impatient. She moved her mouth over his, letting her tongue lick and taste him. His tongue flickered back. A small moan escaped her throat as her insides turned molten.

Chris released his hand from around her neck and pulled back. The corners of his mouth creased in a smirk. "You drive me crazy, Chloe ... in the best way possible."

"Well, you make my insides turn gooey."

He laughed. "Gooey, huh?"

"Oh yes, very gooey!"

Still smiling, his gaze shifted down. "I like your necklace. Three peas in a pod. I am guessing it is to represent you, Gaby, and Jess?"

Chloe reached up to touch the pendant. She smiled, breathing heavier with his touch. "Yes, Jess's dad got us each one. He gave them to us the other night when he visited."

"You three must be pretty tight if her dad thinks of you that way."

"We really are. I guess we connect so well because we each had struggles with our parents as kids." Chloe inwardly winced. *Did I just open a door for Chris to ask me about my parents?*

"Is there a mom in the picture for Jess?"

Chloe's shoulders relaxed as she answered, "Her parents are still married. Her mom hasn't been well for a long time, though. Jess grew up as the caregiver for her mom and siblings. Her dad always traveled a lot for work. And Gaby's dad died when she was little. She doesn't have any brothers or sisters, so she grew up with only her mom."

"That does sound hard."

Chloe hesitated, feeling uncomfortable with the way this was going. She worried he would feel sorry for her, like people usually did. She didn't need pity or sympathy, just someone to listen.

Tilting his head, studying her, he asked, "Where in Pennsylvania did you grow up?"

Chloe took breath. *Here we go.* "A small town outside of Pittsburgh. No one's ever heard of it."

The light in his eyes dimmed a bit. "Oh, okay."

She decided to volunteer more information to save her from talking about everything all at once. "I'm an only child. I lost touch with my parents soon after I moved here." *Please don't ask anything more. Please let this be enough for right now.* She'd shout those words if she could.

Chris surprised her by moving on. "Do you stay in touch with anyone else from your family? Cousins, grandparents?"

Thank God. "I don't know if I have any extended family. We aren't really the talking kind. Never have been. My parents kept to themselves." Chloe dropped her hands from his shoulders and stood. "I'll help with these." She began stacking the plates—*anything to stop talking about my life before Galorston*—and carried them to the sink.

Chris followed her lead, carrying more to the sink and loading the dishwasher after her. *Can he sense my unease?*

Leaning against the counter, Chloe said, "Everything was very good. I appreciate you making all this and decorating it so special."

Chris turned his head from the sink, fixing her with those eyes she loved to lose herself in. "You don't have to thank me. I'm glad you liked it. Was it good enough that you would come again?"

"Of course I would! I'll bring dessert next time." Already recipes started flipping through her mind.

"That would be great!" Hanging up the towel, Chris took her hand and led her back to the living room. "Want to sit down for a bit?"

"Sure."

In the living room, they sat on the couch. Chris put on the news. "Do you watch the news, or do you avoid it since you work in the field?"

Chloe snuggled in close and put her head on his shoulder. "I do watch sometimes. I usually read it on my tablet at night before bed."

Taking her hand in his, Chris held it on his lap and rubbed his thumb across her knuckles. "I like cuddling with you."

"Me too." Content, Chloe snuggled closer, thinking, *Yes, I would be very happy to do this again.*

~~~~~

Chloe startled when she heard a door close. Blinking several times, she focused on Chris next to her. They had dozed off. She picked up her phone. "Wow! Ten already?"

Todd walked into the living room. "Hi, Chloe. How are ya? Did he feed you well?"

Smiling, Chloe said, "Yup, he did. Real good."

"Leftovers?" Todd asked, staring at his brother with one eyebrow arched. "I need something after playing all night."

"Fridge," Chris said quickly, stretching.

"What did you play?" Chloe asked.

"Just a friendly game of basketball. Not even enough for full teams," Todd explained as he headed into the kitchen.

Chloe leaned in to Chris and whispered, "I should get going. I may not have to go into work tomorrow, but you do." She gave him a quick kiss on the cheek.

Standing and following Todd, they walked into the kitchen.

"I have to get going, but it was good to see you." She waved.

"Yeah, see you soon," Todd responded. Chloe smirked, realizing he was about to stuff his mouth with chicken. She then headed for the front door, with Chris close behind. "I'll see you out," he said.

He held her hand as they walked to her car. "I meant to tell you earlier that you looked beautiful tonight."

"Thank you." Chloe still felt awkward around compliments, but she was starting to believe the ones Chris told her.

When they reached her car door, Chris touched some of the lace near her neck. Her skin radiated shivers in all directions. He leaned closer to her and mouthed the word "sexy" as he brushed his lips across hers. She blushed.

"When can I see you again?" he asked, leaving just a few inches between their faces but not letting her go. His one hand was tangled in her hair and his other was wrapped around her, holding her close to him.

Chloe copied his move. She moved in closer and mouthed "soon" as her lips flickered across his. Backing a few inches from his face, she added, "Very soon."

"God," Chris said. "I want to crush your lips with mine. You drive me crazy." Chloe could feel his warm breath against her cheek as he bent to give her neck a nuzzle.

"Next time. Soon," Chloe said as she tilted her head toward his neighbors.

"You promise?" He gave her one more soft kiss.

Chloe could barely breathe, much less talk at this point. She managed a whisper, "Oh yes."

Chris opened the door for her then leaned in after she put the window down and brushed his knuckles across her cheek. All he wanted to do was keep touching her. "You are okay with all this? I don't scare you by coming on too strong?"

Chloe laughed, shaking her head. "I'm fine. I promise." Absently touching her fingers to her lips, she added, "It's exciting."

Chris grinned. "Just checking. Let me know when you get home. Okay?"

"I will."

Aw, he worries about me. He cares. I don't know what the future holds. But God, it's going to be a fun ride finding out!

Pulling out from the curb she called, "Bye!" She could see him standing in her side view mirror, watching her drive away. *God, he is sexy.*

~~~~~

Later that night, lying in bed, Chris wondered if Chloe was able to fall asleep. He had been tossing and turning for over an hour with no luck. Her face was permanently fixed in his mind. Over and over, he relived the kisses they'd shared and was driven mad by the thought of her in his arms. There was some kind of magnetism she held over him. He couldn't get enough.

He sent her a quick text. *Thinking of you …*

After a few seconds, he saw the bubbles, indicating a response.

Chloe: *I can't sleep… you're on my mind.*

Chris: *Can I see you tomorrow for lunch?*
Chloe: *Yes, I can pick you up. Time?*
Chris: *11:45.*
Chloe: *Perfect. I'm going to try to fall asleep again.*
Chris: *Me too, Gnite Beautiful*
Chloe: *Gnite, Mr. Sherman*

Tossing his phone aside and rolling over, he thought, she *drives me crazy! I'll never fall asleep tonight ... or any night again as long as she's in my life.* He grinned wide. *I sure as hell hope I never sleep again.*

~~~~~

Chapter 10

After Saturday morning dance class, Gaby looked in the mirror to see the reflection of her regulars. She was partial to this class, since it was filled with a fun group of women—Jess and Chloe included. Cheers, laughing, and clapping were common throughout it. Now, looking at their smiling, flushed faces, Gaby experienced fulfillment. There was nothing more rewarding than helping her students feel physically and emotionally charged.

Gaby shut off the music and grabbed her water bottle. When she joined the group, she heard Jenny say, "The police don't have any leads yet on the guy I saw lurking around my car last week. Without a witness, pictures, or video, it's unlikely they'll find him."

Jess placed her hands on her hips. "Has anyone been giving you any trouble? Anyone from work or other places you go?"

Jenny shook her head. "I have no clue. I have been wracking my brain trying to figure it out. I can't think of anyone who I might've bothered or upset—or attracted, even." She laughed at that. "The best the police and I can come up with is that it was random. A few kids were messing around."

"And there was no sign of anyone trying to break into your car? I heard thieves will target the parking lots around fitness places because people often leave valuables in their car while inside."

"No, no sign of a break-in. That's sad."

Jess nodded, catching Gaby's concerned look.

Most of the group decided to head to the smoothie shop down the street for their post-workout "debriefing," as they liked to call it. Gaby knew it was a cover for getting breakfast after their class. She, Jess, and Chloe joined them today, a rarity now that Chloe was dating Chris and Jess's work kept burying her.

Gaby slid in line behind Chloe and glanced at the other customers as she waited. Most here were families or couples. Many wore workout gear or running shoes. Then her gaze narrowed as it caught the unmistakable sight of Kirk paying at the register. "Why is he here?"

"Not sure but looks like we'll find out soon. Here he comes," said Jess.

Sure enough, Kirk walked over, all swagger and sweat, just like he had at Harry's. Gaby wanted to smack the smug look off his face.

"I hoped your schedule was still the same," he said. "I decided to visit here this weekend and thought maybe I'd see you here after class. Can we catch up?"

Gaby put up an arm as he leaned closer. "No thanks. I came to get a drink with the girls." She dug in her bag for her wallet, hoping he'd take the hint and go away.

"Here, I'll get it for you. What do you want?" Kirk waved his wallet in her face.

"No, I got it." She pulled her wallet free from the bottom of her bag.

Chloe stepped closer to her, and Jess looked like she was ready to punch him. She gave them a look. *I can handle it.* Then she fixed him with steel in her eyes.

He seemed not to notice. "So, it's Saturday ... Where are you planning to hang out tonight? Harry's again?" Kirk asked. Was it Gaby's imagination, or was he starting to sound a little desperate?

"Yeah, I think so," she lied.

"Great." Kirk leaned in again. This time, Gaby couldn't dodge him as expertly as she had before. His hand landed a little too low on her hip for her liking.

"Hey," Jess said, unable to stay quiet anymore. Kirk pulled back like someone had fired a gun. "Geeze," he responded. "She's *my* ex. I thought it was okay."

Gaby rolled her eyes.

"Well, it's not. So just move along now." Jess was not having it.

Gaby waved him off. "See you, Kirk," then she walked farther up in line. "God." She breathed as he vanished from the shop. "He's such a creep. Why did I let myself date him?"

"We aren't sure, but we got your back, Gaby," said Jess.

"Put that away," Chloe ordered, pointing to Gaby's wallet. "It's my turn." She waved to the woman behind the counter. "Add whatever she wants to my order, please."

In a few minutes they all had their smoothies. Gaby took a deep drink and smiled at her friends. *They're the best,* she thought. *Every girl should be this lucky.*

~~~~~

Chloe walked into work Monday morning and instantly made eye contact with Eve. She stood up from her desk and waved Chloe over. "I am so glad to see you! How are you feeling?"

"I'm good, actually. All back to normal."

"I'm so glad to hear that. I was worried about you!"

"Aw. Thanks, Eve."

The phone on Eve's desk beeped. "I have a call coming in. I'll catch up more with you later. Okay?"

Chloe waved and chuckled as she headed toward her desk. *She is the sweetest woman.* Plopping her stuff down, she saw it was almost nine. She glanced in the direction of Lou's office. He wasn't there. She turned around and saw Mya walking her way.

"Hey! You doing okay?" she asked, handing Chloe a coffee cup.

Chloe took it, grateful for the warm beverage. "I was fine before, but even better now!"

"I thought you could use a little something to start the week off. We're all so glad you're okay!"

"Thank you," Chloe said as she raised her cup.

Mya nodded toward the conference room. "Lou moved up the ideas meeting—last minute, as usual. You made it just in time, though."

"Oh, thanks for the warning." Chloe picked up her laptop and headed to the conference room. *Note to self: always check work email before coming in to work.* Entering the space, she slid into the chair next to Lou.

"Chloe, good to see you. Feeling better?"

Chloe put on her best early morning smile. "Much!"

"Good," he said, nodding. His eyes flickered to the clock then around the room. "Looks like we have our full crew." He turned to his left. "Do you mind starting us off, Darren?"

After Darren recapped last week's meeting, the team went around the table and each pitched their new ideas.

"And last but not least, what ya got, Chloe?" Lou asked.

Chloe took a breath. She'd practiced her pitch in her head several times while the team members made their way around the table. At the sound of her name, she stopped twisting her fingers and looked up. "How about a series of educational articles on mental illness? I'm thinking there is a lot we can do with this."

"Like what?" Lou asked. Chloe thought she detected skepticism in his voice.

She swallowed. "We could include things like expert interviews and exclusive features—profiles, dramatizations, on-air polling, or something. Then push the growth with social media and a podcast." Making eye contact with him then, she added, "We can put the series out, one piece a day, during Mental Illness Awareness Week in October. It's fresh. None of our competitors are doing anything like this. And we could bring more awareness to the topic. Help stop stigma while giving people answers."

Mya leaned forward in her seat. "I like it. It's original, kinda trendy, and does have a lot of potential for growth."

Lou nodded. "Okay then. Let's run with it. See how it goes." Pointing two fingers at Chloe and Mya, he continued, "You two flush out the details."

Chloe's shoulders dropped and wind rushed out of her lungs. Beside her, Mya gave her a nudge. "Hey, great suggestion."

Chloe offered a weak smile. *Is she trying to be supportive or a thief? I don't want this to be a joint assignment. I can carry this one to the end on my own.* She studied her lap, blinking several times to hold back the tears that threatened to fall.

"We can meet later if you have time," Mya said, rising from the table.

"Sure." Chloe answered softly. She headed straight to the bathroom. Locking herself in a stall, tears clouded her vision and started to trickle down her cheeks. *I don't understand! Just last week Lou was praising me. Now he's giving me assignments with Mya. What can I do to prove to him I can do all these things alone?* She wiped her face and shook her head. *This is going to be one a hell of a week.*

~~~~~

The following Saturday, Chloe pulled into the parking garage off Strayer Street. After staying in the prior weekend and focusing on work all week, the girls were itching to get out. They made reservations at a new restaurant, Relish the Taste.

They found an open spot in the nearby parking garage. *Great*, thought Chloe. *Not too far of a walk to the restaurant this way.*

Climbing out of the back seat, she paused. The hairs on the back of her neck prickled and she picked up a faint floral scent. She turned and swept her eyes across the full lot of cars. Nothing seemed out of place. Only Gaby and Jess were around.

Chloe shook her head. *Must be Jess's perfume.* She quickly left the car, heard the locks click, and raced to catch up with Jess and Gaby at the stairwell.

The girls sat on a bench outside the restaurant for only a few minutes when they called Jess's name. Entering the open reception area, all three gasped, taken in by the beauty of the place. Overhead lights swept from the ceiling. All were dimmed to provide an intimate setting, and muted colors splashed over the room's walls, adding to the elegant yet comfy feel.

Off to the right was the bar. Some people waited for their tables while others had chosen that space to eat and socialize. Large-screen TVs were tucked into each corner, each featuring a different sports game or news briefing. A couple of tall tables lined the wall opposite the bar, and several booths filled space by the big picture windows near the entrance.

The women followed the host up the stairs to the dining area on the second floor. It boasted a similar décor and ambiance to the bar. Here, there were fairy lights and candles. Each of the round dining tables had high-backed benches surrounding them. The patrons could enjoy privacy and a quiet atmosphere.

On their way to the back corner of the room, Gaby leaned over to Chloe and Jess and whispered, "Gosh, this is the perfect place for a date! You could make out and no one would see!"

This made Chloe slyly smile. She'd already planned to take Chris here someday. She leaned back and said, "Don't get any ideas. We aren't a thruple!"

The host stifled a laugh. The girls burst into giggles.

The host rattled off the specials then left them at their table. Gaby turned her head to watch him walk away. "Did anyone else think he had a nice butt?"

The girls laughed harder.

"Oh my God. What are we? Sixteen?" Chloe said, breathless.

Jess jumped in, her eyes shining. "Yes, we are sixteen, and yes, agreed; there was a nice view on our way up the stairs." Thankful that the high-backed benches acted as sound barriers, they continued snickering.

Coming back to reality, Gaby wiped her eyes and took a breath. "Woo! I needed that. I haven't laughed like that in a while."

Chloe nodded. Her thoughts flipped to the Mental Illness Awareness Week assignment that she was now sharing instead of leading solo. "It has been a long week. This was much needed."

The waitress eventually brought water glasses and a bottle of wine no one had ordered. Catching their curious looks, she explained, "Courtesy of a gentleman admirer. Would you each like a glass?"

Chloe drew her brows together. *Who could've sent them wine?* "Yes, please." The others nodded too.

"Of course." The waitress poured each a glass and left the bottle in the center of the table. "Enjoy."

Jess's eyes grew round as she grabbed the bottle and scanned the label into an app on her phone. "Holy crap! This is a good one! Do you think it was from the host?"

Gaby leaned in, smiling. "It must be. Who else?"

Jess pointed at Chloe. "Did you tell Chris you were coming here tonight?"

"I did. Do you think he called to have it sent?" She pulled her phone out of her purse. "I'm going to ask him." Talking out loud, she typed: *Hey, did you send a bottle of wine to our table?*

She set her phone down, and they each picked up a glass.

"To a tough week behind us!" Gaby said.

"And to us, the best girlfriends ever!" Jess cheered.

They clinked their glasses and sipped.

As Chloe brought the glass to her lips, she caught a whiff of a pungent odor. Eyeing her friends over the rim, she saw them each drinking without any concern. She looked down at her own glass, and for a split second it appeared too red to be wine. *That's weird.*

Gaby sighed. "Wow, this *is* really good!"

Jess agreed as she looked at Chloe. "If we have too much, we can call a rideshare to take us home." Then she tilted her head, studying her friend. The face Chloe made caused Jess to raise an eyebrow. "You didn't like it?"

Chloe shook her head and met Jess's gaze. "No, it's fine. I'm just a little off tonight." Pausing, she added, "It was a tense week at work. Lou decided to have Mya partner with me on the mental illness series. I feel like she is stealing my thunder."

"I've had stuff like that happen at work too," Jess sympathized. "Try not to take it too personal. You don't want to look like you aren't a team player. That was the mistake I made."

Chloe nodded. "You're right, of course." She took a small sip of wine, and a bitter taste clouded her tongue. *Yuck.*

Chloe felt her phone vibrate. Her eyes widened, reading Chris's message. "It wasn't from him. He said, *Unfortunately, I didn't think of that. Should I be worried?*" She looked at her friends. "It must be from the host. Who else?"

Gaby giggled, straightening on her seat. "He did seem to like us."

"He might be interested in a quadruple!" Jess said, laughing in between each word.

Gaby looked at Jess and shook her head. "You're going to pee yourself if you keep laughing like this."

Jess twisted her face into a look of mock hurt. "It was one time. *One time!* And I had been the champion of a beer pong tournament. That's too much for any bladder!"

Chloe found herself deep in thought while Gaby and Jess continued bantering. *The red wine looked like blood. I feel sick. This has to be a premonition.* She studied her friends. They were completely oblivious. She sighed to herself. *I'll ruin tonight if I convince them to leave early. No, I have to keep these thoughts to myself and hope my mind is just playing tricks on me. Premonitions don't happen anymore, remember?*

She looked at her phone, trying to compose herself. Staring at Chris's text, she thought, *I don't want him to worry, or to be a girlfriend with drama. Whoa! Did I just call myself his girlfriend? Think about that later.*

To him she typed: *Gosh no. We made the host laugh earlier. It must be him. I'll call you later :)*

Putting her phone back in her purse, Chloe watched as tears ran down her friends' faces now.

"You two are too much!" Chloe said, hoping she sounded more relaxed than she felt.

Both Gaby and Jess took some deep breaths and tried to make serious faces. It didn't work. Eventually, Gaby asked, "Did you smooth it over with Mr. Sherman, so he isn't jealous?"

"Oh, I don't think he's jealous. Just curious. By now he knows that you bring this kind of attention everywhere we go!" Chloe teased.

"Yeah, yeah, yeah. I hear it all the time from you. I bet he's jealous and it's because *you* are beautiful. There is an equal chance the host is as into you as he is into Jess or me, so don't give me that crap!" Gaby reached over and squeezed Chloe's arm. "Give yourself more credit!"

"I do." Chloe said. "I'm working on it, anyway."

Looking down at her lap, Chloe decided to broach another topic that was bothering her. "Speaking of jealousy, I've been obsessing over how good a kisser Chris is. He's so good he seems like a pro! I wonder how many different women he's kissed. I feel like I must suck at it since I've had zero experience and most of the time all I do is make a fishy face and hope he takes care of everything else."

Jess shook her finger. "We've gone over this, Chloe! You're going to drive yourself nuts!"

Gaby poured herself another glass of wine and gave Chloe a pointed stare. "He's into you. No question. How can I tell? It's how he looks at you, deep and long. You can see a twinkle in his eyes. Trust me: you are the only one he is thinking about. The kissing matters, but it's not everything. And who cares if he's the only guy your lips have wrestled with? He wouldn't want to go near you if you were bad."

Chloe drew her eyebrows together and tilted her head. "It's just that he's so good at kissing. He's had to have had a lot of practice!"

"Whatever his history is, it brought him to you now. Focus on the here and now. Enjoy that the kissing is that good!" Gaby said, a crooked smile playing on her lips.

"Yeah," Jess echoed. "Stop beating yourself up or overanalyzing and know that you've got something he really likes!"

Chloe held her hands up. "All right! I'm going to try." Changing subjects once more, mostly thanks to her rumbling stomach, she said, "Okay, so what are we ordering? Are we sharing plates or each getting full meals?"

"Let's see what they got," Gaby replied.

After studying the menu for a few minutes, the girls decided on a few plates to share. Chloe also ordered a different drink, not willing to go back to the glass of wine she'd barely touched since they got there. Before long, steaming plates of food sat in front of them, warming their hearts and their stomachs in no time. After the meal, they stared wide eyed at each other, leaning back.

"Good Lord, what did we do? I'm stuffed!" Chloe declared.

Gaby groaned. "I should have stopped ten minutes ago!"

Jess tipped the last of the wine into Gaby's and her glasses. Chloe was relieved neither friend cared she had ordered something different. They sat nursing their drinks until the waitress asked if they wanted dessert.

"Oh no!" Gaby sighed.

"If I eat any more, I'll burst!" said Jess.

"No thank you," Chloe replied. "Just the check, please."

Gaby asked as they walked toward the steps. "Why don't we stop down at the bar for a little bit and check it out?" She gave a little shrug. "And we could thank the host for his generosity."

"I'm game," said Jess with a smile.

Both of her friends' eyes rested on Chloe, waiting.

"You're crazy," she said, "but sure. Let's see what the vibe is there. We may want to come back another time for just drinks."

Back on the first floor, they spied the host desk, but to Gaby's disappointment, he wasn't around. Slowly they made their way to an open booth by the front window. The place had gotten even more crowded since earlier, Chloe noted. *I can't blame them. They do have great food and dedicated staff.*

"I like what they did down here," she said to Jess and Gaby. "Not just the restaurant, but all of it." Chloe examined the outside nightlife as she spoke, watching people pass by and shops close for the evening. Since she had written about the Strayer Street renovation project, she knew some of the area's history. "Across the street used to be an old textile mill." She pointed to the small independent stores there. "And down the street was a meat packing and distribution center. This building was a bar and restaurant—go figure. I heard they had to gut the original place, but the layout is still mostly the same."

Gaby and Jess nodded; their eyes still focused on the host desk. "He must've left," Jess said eventually.

"Yeah," Gaby replied with a sigh. "Darn."

Catching a shift in priorities, Chloe jumped on the chance to discuss their plans for Labor Day weekend in Harmony. "So. Labor Day. Does your mom care when we come, Gaby? I am thinking of taking off that Friday for sure, and maybe Thursday too. We can leave at any point, though."

"I can swing taking off Friday and probably Thursday too. I have a lot of comp time saved up," Jess said.

Gaby shook her head. "Of course Mom doesn't care when we come. If we came for a week, she'd be in heaven. I can also swing a day or two. So, let's leave sometime Thursday then."

"Where are we going?" Teased a voice.

Their attention shifted, and Gaby honed in on a man leaning casually against the bar. She waved, her lips curving into a smile. "Hi."

Chloe exchanged looks with Jess. *Maybe this is why I've been feeling the way I have tonight.* She regarded the man with caution and glanced at her phone, wondering how long it would take for Chris to get here if she asked him. She watched as the man neared their table. He had a friendly smile and gelled sandy hair, but he was too gangly for Gaby. Chloe's eyes narrowed. *How does she know him?*

The man paused when he reached them, and Gaby finally introduced him. "Rob, this is Chloe and Jess. Girls, Rob."

He nodded at them, then sidled up next to Gaby on the bench. "Where have you been? I never heard back from you."

Gaby cleared her throat and looked away. "Oh, just busy."

Chloe smirked. *She hasn't told him she's not interested.*

Rob shrugged. "Okay." He started to slide away from Gaby. "Well, if you ever find you have some free time and—"

That was all he got out before he was ripped from the seat. Roses were simultaneously thrown on the table and petals scattered.

The girls watched in horror as Kirk grabbed Rob and asked through gritted teeth, "Who the hell are you?" He used his forearm to pin him up against the wall.

Gaby yelled. "Stop it! Kirk, stop!"

But Rob had successfully evaded Kirk's clutches and fought back. People stepped aside to watch the two men batter each other. Rob shoved Kirk to the ground and punched him. Kirk growled and wiggled in an attempt to get away.

Rob roared and delivered another blow to Kirk's face. "You messed with the wrong guy, dude!"

Blood started to spray from Kirk's nose then. Chloe hid her face in her hands. *I can't watch.* Gaby threw her arms in the air. "Stop, Rob! His nose is broken! You've done enough!"

Kirk twisted and dodged another hit. He grabbed Rob's shirt and brought him forward. The two men rolled across the floor. A woman at the bar quickly vacated her stool as they tumbled toward her. Others backed away, giving them space.

The fight escalated when Kirk got Rob into a wrestling position that had his arm at an unnatural angle and his face pressed against the floor. "Who's stronger now?"

The bar went silent as Kirk partly stood and kicked Rob in the stomach. "Take that, you son of a bitch!"

From the back of the room a man rushed forward and yanked Kirk back, tossing him sideways. Rob scrambled to his knees, his eyes brands that burned into Kirk's weaselly form. "Screw you! Prick!"

Kirk had suddenly lost his machismo, and a groan escaped him. He looked like he was going to be sick, and he clearly needed help getting his bleeding nose under control. Chloe gasped as he tilted face-first into the bar. His head bounced as it hit the ground, and a few bloody teeth flew out. *God!*

As Kirk slumped to the floor, sirens could be heard.

The police walked into a gruesome scene. Kirk was laid out on the floor, not moving. Rob was hunched over moaning. Overturned tables and chairs littered the floor. Mostly everyone in the bar had gone into the street, to their cars, or into the main restaurant on the second floor. However, Chloe, Gaby, and Jess huddled in a corner by the bar, not sure what to do. It seemed like they were to blame for all of this, and yet not at fault at all.

The officer pushed a button on his radio. "I'm going to need an ambulance at the corner of thirty-third and Strayer."

Two policemen moved forward and positioned Rob and Kirk on the floor, separating them by a good distance.

The first officer then turned to the three friends, noting Gaby's panting breaths. "Do you know these guys?"

Gaby nodded; her voice shaky. "Yes."

"Okay, could you come outside with me?"

Another officer approached Chloe and Jess, waving for them to follow him.

Chloe turned to Jess. Jess looked like she felt—scared, silent, and very pale. Chloe had never witnessed a fight like this before. Even the violence she experienced with her dad wasn't that bad.

They followed the officer through the front door. Gaby stood away from them, on the other side of the entrance. Chloe saw she had her arms wrapped around her.

The officer looked at Chloe and Jess, a pad of paper in hand. "Do you think you can answer some questions?"

"Yes, we can try," said Jess. She sighed. "That was …" She shook her head and closed her eyes.

The policeman stopped writing. "I know that was upsetting to witness. Do you know either of them?"

"Not well. They had both dated our friend Gaby." Jess nodded in Gaby's direction. "They went out at different times. Kirk, the one with the broken nose, she dated last year. The other one was more recent. That was the first time we met him."

Hearing some movement near the front entrance, all three turned their heads. They watched as the paramedics brought Kirk and Rob out to the ambulance. Their clothes were torn, and blood splattered. It made Chloe's stomach churn. *Now I understand why the wine was red. It was blood. I had a premonition!* She took a few steps away from Jess and the policeman and leaned over, putting one hand on the side of the building to steady her. *I think I'm going to be sick.* She turned her head and retched.

Chloe's eyes swiveled to Jess as she wiped her mouth with the back of her hand and stood up. "Sorry. It's just ... I think I'm going to sit."

"Good idea," said the policeman. He offered to send a medic over, but Chloe refused. "I'm fine. Really."

Jess continued speaking to the officer, but Chloe didn't listen. She was lost in her own thoughts. *I should have trusted my gut. I knew something bad was possible tonight, but I ignored it. Why? I should have asked Gaby and Jess to leave earlier.* A few tears rolled down her cheeks. *This is my fault.*

She thought about calling Chris, but the sight of Jess and Gaby coming to join her on the curb made her stop.

"Are you okay? You're shaking." Jess wrapped an arm around Chloe.

"I'm fine," she whispered. "I'm just processing everything that happened tonight."

Chloe looked up at Gaby as she sat down. "How are you?"

"I'm shaken, but okay. That was crazy! Correction, Kirk is crazy. I feel bad for Rob."

Jess sighed, "This sucks."

"Yeah," murmured Chloe.

An hour later, the girls walked into their house like zombies. It was after midnight and exhaustion was setting in. They called for an Uber, since all three had been drinking before Rob and Kirk appeared.

Gaby had texted her mom on the drive. She was already on her way to their house, insisting on being with the three of them after a crazy night.

The girls sat down at the kitchen table and stared at one another. No one wanted to talk anymore about their evening. They needed space away from it.

The three of them stayed huddled in the kitchen, saying little, until Gaby's mom arrived, practically flying through the door. She wrapped her arms around Jess and Chloe as Gaby made her way around the table.

After a comforting group hug, Momma R. started boiling water for tea. Gaby and Jess scattered to settle in for the night. Chloe picked up her phone. As she thought there would be, several messages from Chris flashed across her screen, all asking about her night. A small smile flickered over her face. *It is nice to have someone care about me.* She texted him back.

Chloe: *Unfortunately, we had a very drama filled evening.*
Chloe: *We are all okay though*

Chloe walked over to help Momma R. She reached for Chloe as she came around the counter. "How are you feeling?"

"I'm still a little shaken up. That was a nasty fight."

Momma R. sighed. "I have only seen a fight once. It was when I was still in school. Two boys got into it. From what you describe, what you saw was way worse."

Chloe laid her head on Momma R.'s shoulder. "Why do some men get so obsessive and angry?"

Rubbing Chloe's back, Momma R. said, "I don't know what crosses their minds. You certainly have had your run-ins with bad men, but I promise you, there are some good guys out there. I know you girls will find them. It's only a matter of time."

She smiled, her heart leaping at the thought of one good man she knew. "Chris seems to be one of the good ones I think."

"Honey, if you think he is a good guy, I am sure he is. Remember, you all knew there was something wrong with Kirk. Trust yourself."

~~~~~

On the other end of Galorston, Chris waited for Chloe to call him.

Todd noticed how unsettled his brother was. He watched Chris check his phone every five minutes and sit on the couch only to move and pace around their living room seconds later.

"What gives, Chris?"

His brother sighed. "Chloe mentioned something about a mysterious bottle of wine delivered to the table and I haven't heard from her since."

Todd frowned. "Ease up a little. I'm sure she'll get in touch eventually. She's with Gaby and Jess, right?"

Chris nodded.

"Nothing to worry about then."

But worry he did. He had the feeling whoever had sent the wine wouldn't just have it delivered and leave. Now he laid sprawled on his bed, sleeping in fitful increments. Waiting.

Finally, around three o'clock his phone buzzed. "Hello?"

"Hello, Chris."

A huge tide of relief washed over him at the sound of Chloe's voice. Chloe told him all about their night, which led Chris right back to worrying, and anger. *What an asshole thing to fight in a bar over a woman. And poor Chloe for having to watch that.*

It bothered him to hear she was so upset that she had thrown up, but he was glad that she didn't try to drive home. "If you wanted, I would've come got you all," he said.

Chloe grinned. "It's okay. The police made sure we got into an Uber instead of driving after drinking, and now Momma R.—Gaby's mom—is here."

"That's nice of her to be there."

"She likes taking care of us."

Chris heard Chloe yawn. "It's late. I don't want to keep you up. You should go to sleep." The truth was, he wanted to stay on the phone all night, but he knew he had to let her go.

In a hushed voice, Chloe agreed. "I'm sorry about tonight."

Why is she apologizing? "It was a horrible night for you. I'm just glad to hear from you."

"It certainly didn't go as planned." She let out a small laugh.

After saying goodnight, Chris tossed and turned, mulling their conversation over in his mind. Her fear seemed excessive. *Why had Jess and Gaby both talked to the police afterward, but she didn't? And why throw up? Hmm?*

~~~~~

Chapter 11

Chloe slept better than she thought she would. After saying goodnight to Chris, she passed out. It was now almost ten o'clock the following morning and she still didn't hear anyone moving around the house. She flopped over and decided to lie there a bit longer. She faded in and out for about a half hour until she heard some whispers and decided to wander downstairs. Sitting at the kitchen table were Jess and Momma R.

"Is Gaby still sleeping?" Chloe said from the doorway.

Momma R. smiled, stood up, and went around the counter to pour Chloe a cup of tea. She gestured to her vacant chair. "Sit, sit. Yes, she was the last I checked on her."

Jess fiddled with her spoon as she stirred her tea. Chloe knew Jess took her tea black, no reason to stir. *Nerves?*

Chloe sat next to her friend. "How did you sleep?"

"Not good. I had flashbacks of it all. Replayed it over and over in my head. I wonder if they are going to be okay. Don't get me wrong, I don't want to see them ever again, but I don't want anyone to be hurt either."

"I know what you mean. I hate what happened, but I still can't wish either of them harm." Chloe shivered as she remembered Kirk and Rob's fight. It'd been so fast and so brutal. *If only I'd insisted we leave, none of it would've happened.*

"That's because you all have good hearts," Momma R. chimed, bringing a mug over to Chloe and then turning back to the counter. "I think we should call the police today and see about getting a restraining order in place. I don't want to worry any more about you three than I already do."

Chloe sipped her tea. It was steamy but steeped just right. She liked it hot, so it soothed her throat on the way down. She needed a lot of soothing today. "I think that's a good idea, Momma R."

Gaby's mom had always been motherly toward Chloe and Jess. They came up with the nickname Momma R. soon after the three of them became friends. She was a warm woman who included everyone in everything she did and went to great lengths to make people feel comfortable, so Chloe and Jess found it easy to love her. The girls would do anything for her. It wasn't just because she had done a lot for them, but because she was amazing and resilient. Momma R. kept it together after Gaby's dad passed away. She worked hard and was a great mom. She was a very easy woman to admire.

The women sat together sipping their tea, enjoying the comfort and security of their own home.

Eventually, Gaby appeared in the doorway. She looked surprisingly refreshed and curiously happy. "Good morning."

"How do you look so good?" Jess scowled.

"I don't know how I look, but for some reason I feel pretty good. I guess it sounds crazy, but I was able to sleep last night. I don't like what we saw, but you know what it made me realize? I have no interest in wasting my time on guys. I am declaring myself guy-free for a year. If I find one worth my time, I guess I'll reconsider, but that is the plan right now. I fully anticipate sticking to it too."

Gaby walked to her mom and gave her a kiss on the cheek. "Mornin', Momma."

"Baby, don't you think it's a little much to have a plan to stave off men?"

Gaby crossed her arms. "Mom, I'm tired of it. I know men are attracted to me and that is flattering, but it's always the wrong kind of men. It's always self-absorbed jerks who pursue me. I'm taking back control. I will decide who when I am ready. I'm the one calling the shots. No more being a pushover!"

Chloe and Jess raised their eyebrows and exchanged looks. *This is new.*

Momma R. put her arm across Gaby's shoulders. "I don't see anything wrong with you being selective and taking your time choosing who you want to spend time with. Just be careful not to shut yourself off. You might miss out on something great if you put up walls. Not all men are bad."

"I'll know if I see something great, but until then …" Gaby waved her hands in front of her. "This is off limits."

The women shared a small laugh over Gaby's proclamation.

"Here, sit down and have some sustenance," Momma R. said, gesturing to the biscuits waiting on the kitchen table.

"I will. Let me grab a mug first."

Once Gaby joined them, all four dug in and ate like they hadn't eaten in days. The only thing that could be heard for the first five minutes was chewing. It was Chloe who broke the silence first. "So, Gaby, your mom mentioned looking into a restraining order against Kirk."

Gaby's eyes flew to her mom's face. "You think so?"

Momma R. nodded, wiping her mouth with a napkin. "The way he's been acting and what happened last night makes me think it's a good idea to look into."

"Great," Gaby sighed. "Now we have a huge mess on our hands."

Momma R. reached for Gaby's hand. "Sweetheart, you can't predict these things. Even if you could, you can't blame yourself. That man has a lot of issues and I am sure he was like this long before he met you. Now we just have to keep him away from you and make sure you're safe."

Chloe repeated what Momma R. said in her head. *You can't blame yourself for what happened.* But in her mind, she did blame herself. She could have prevented the fight if she'd taken the visions seriously. The prickles on her neck and the flower scent in the parking lot, along with the wine, all made sense now that she looked back. Those were premonitions. With what happened at the fire and now last night, Chloe wanted to believe her premonitions were returning. But if they were coming back, maybe they were changing, just like she had over the years without them.

She shook her head. *Shouldn't that be the pattern? I have a vision then I have time to react. I must stop thinking I can prevent everything. It isn't healthy or reality.* The visions she'd seen lately, however, made her think harder. Maybe she had never been able to prevent anything, good or bad, from happening. Maybe the premonitions were to prepare her for the aftermath, not help her alter them. She sighed. *Maybe I'll never really understand them.*

"Earth to Chloe."

Chloe startled. "I'm sorry."

"Are you okay?" Jess asked.

"Of course. I'm going to go shower."

Still looking like she was a million miles away, Chloe took her dishes to the sink and left the kitchen.

Gaby leaned in. "Do you think she's okay? She looks so distant and foggy."

"I'm worried about her," said Jess. "You know she threw up last night while the police questioned us?" Gaby nodded.

Momma R. gasped and shook her head.

"I'm thinking it's because of her history with her dad and Jeremy. All those bad memories."

Gaby's mom headed to the sink with more dishes in her arms. She tutted as she said, "The explosion couldn't have helped either."

Gaby swiveled her head in her mom's direction. "We can finish that up later, Mom."

The doorbell rang before Momma R. could reply. She wandered to the door and peeked out the window. Her voice echoed back to them. "Girls, the police are here."

Opening the door, she greeted them. "Hello, officers."

"Hi, ma'am," said the taller of the two. "We're looking for Jessica Taylor, Chloe Larson, and Gabriella Rodriguez."

"Of course. Please come in. I am Gabriella's mother, Louisa Rodriguez." She took them into the kitchen to wait.

Gaby recognized the taller officer as the one who interviewed her last night. "Hi. We met last night. Gabriella."

"Hi there, and yes. Officer Thatcher, and this is my partner, Officer Price. We thought we would come to you to share some information and ask a few questions."

Gaby bowed her head. "We appreciate that. Last night was disturbing for us."

They all gathered around the kitchen counter. Chloe joined them soon after donning her robe.

Officer Thatcher started. "We questioned both men last night and found Kirk Abrams had been following you."

Gaby bristled at that. *That's why I kept running into him.* Shivers ran down her body and her heart thundered. She caught Jess's and Chloe's eyes narrow. "Following me? How? Like sitting outside the house and watching us?"

Officer Thatcher shook his head. "He admitted to putting a tracker on Chloe's car about two weeks ago. He's been following both of you for some time now. He also had put a tracker on the car of one of your friends first, Jenny Fitzpatrick. He had been following her with the hopes of seeing you. That is how he knew where you would be last night. He waited for you outside the restaurant and became infuriated when he saw Rob Livingston talking to you."

"Oh God," Gaby gasped. She wrapped her arms around her middle. "So creepy."

"Yes, very unsettling, I'm sure," murmured Officer Thatcher. He jotted something in a notepad then continued, "Rob Livingston's friend corroborated his story that he coincidentally was there. He'd seen you enter and sent you a bottle of wine."

That solves that question, thought Chloe, shifting as her mind remembered the blood red drink.

Office Thatcher pulled out a folder. He took out a form and looked up to Gaby and her mom. "Okay, just a few more questions. Let's see what events occurred leading up to last night."

Taking out his pen, Officer Thatcher started with how Gaby had met Kirk. He questioned her on the number of times and places she saw him and collected any other details she could think of. He asked for text message exchanges, emails, voicemails, or any other evidence she might have showing contact between them.

Next, he questioned Jess and Chloe on any interactions they had with Kirk. The officers also had looked Chloe's car over and found the tracking device Kirk had installed. They documented it then removed it. They would also enter that into evidence.

Although the tracking device demonstrated a privacy violation, no verbal or physical threats were delivered. The case for a restraining order against Kirk would be weak without such direct evidence of threats.

Even though the police warned him to stop, Gaby knew him well enough to know he wouldn't. She could only hope the warning jarred him enough so that it wouldn't escalate to something more serious.

Gaby slumped back in her chair, defeated. "Where do we go from here? This all feels so depressing. We'll never stop looking over our shoulders."

Officer Thatcher disagreed. "There are some things you can do. You can call the police anytime you see him or feel threatened. If you see him sitting outside your house or at your work, then call. Tell the dispatcher that you see someone suspicious watching you. We never get tired of responding to calls; however, he may get tired of being questioned. Let's hope we can tire him out and scare him off."

Gaby sighed. "That sounds like a long and tedious process that may not even be successful."

Officer Thatcher put his paperwork away and collected his things. "You can learn what to look for and how to protect yourself. There are classes you can take and techniques you can learn to feel empowered and better prepared."

Officer Price handed Gaby a card. "This is the contact information of a retired officer who runs such a class. I highly recommend you call him. He has a lot of experience helping victims of stalking and harassment."

Gaby took the card. "Thank you for coming. I don't mean to come across as anything but grateful for your help and advice." She held out her hand. "Thank you for all you are doing."

Chloe and Jess thanked them too, then Momma R. walked them to the door. "We are appreciative. I know you are doing all you can. You have a nice day."

~~~~~

Later in the day, after Chloe had a chance to visit a bit more with Momma R., she laid around in her room. The book she was reading did little to distract her. She turned on the TV, but that wasn't any better.

Finally, she picked up her phone. She hadn't spoken to Chris since last night.

For some reason, she couldn't quite bring herself to text him. She hated that in the few weeks she had known him she'd been involved in two dramatic events. He had comforted her in the first situation, and she wanted the same now. However, she didn't want to come across as too needy or demanding of his time.

Instead, she wandered downstairs to see what everyone else was up to. Momma R. was in the kitchen cooking casseroles for the girls to freeze. She didn't see Jess or Gaby, though.

Chloe smiled when she saw Momma R. "Thank you for everything you're doing."

"Of course! Anything for my girls."

"And I'm glad you can stay for dinner." She peered over Momma R.'s shoulder. "Can I help with anything?"

"Oh no, mi amor. I am almost done."

Momma R. put her hand under Chloe's chin and tilted her head up gently. "Why the long face, beautiful?"

"I miss Chris. I want to see him, but I'm afraid of being too needy."

"Oh, sweetheart. I don't get that feeling at all from what you have told me of him. I bet you he is waiting to hear from you and dying to see you. Men like him want to take care of the people in their life. Give him a call. Tell him to come for dinner."

Chloe looked away. "Maybe."

"No *maybe*. You stop thinking so much and call him. It will make you feel better and him happy."

Momma R. took Chloe's wrist and held her phone up to her ear. "Call him. If you didn't want to, you wouldn't be carrying your phone around with you."

Chloe smiled. "Am I that transparent?"

"Yes. Call."

Chloe beamed. "Okay, I will."

Chloe stepped out onto the deck and sat on one of the chairs under the umbrella. *Okay*, she coached, taking a breath. *Just call him. You talked last night no problem. Why would he mind if you called today too?* Before she could talk herself out of it, she pulled up Chris's number and pressed "Call."

"Hey, it's Chloe."

She could almost hear the smile in his voice. "Hey, how are you today?"

Relaxing back into the chair, she answered, "Okay, I guess. Hanging in there. How are you?"

"I'm good. Out running some errands."

"Oh yeah? Like what?"

"Groceries and some other little stuff."

"If now isn't a good time, I can call later."

Chris laughed. "Now is a great time. I am just getting to my car."

"Oh, okay." Chloe paused for a few moments, hemming and hawing over whether to ask him to dinner or not. Then, she decided she would never hear the end of it from Momma R. if she didn't. "Would you want to come over for dinner tonight? Gaby's mom is still here. She is the one cooking, so the food will be really good."

Chris chuckled. "You don't have to try to lure me into coming."

She smiled and kicked her feet up onto another chair. "Okay. I guess I am having trouble telling you that I'd like to see you tonight."

"Aw, well, all you had to do was ask. I'd like to see you too. I've missed not seeing you for the past few days." The prior week had slipped by with only one night working for them to spend together. It would be good to have time together again. "And after what happened last night, I'd like to give you a hug and see your pretty face."

She blushed at that. "Only if you are sure."

"I am positive. I want to see you and hold you—that is, if we can sneak off to be alone."

Chloe's smile deepened, and she felt a wave of excitement wash over her. "That would be nice. Dinner is around six, but you can come anytime you want. We are just hanging out."

"Great! I'll be there in a bit."

"Great. See you soon."

After hanging up the phone, Chloe walked down the steps and out to the edge of the yard. The conversation with the officers floated through her mind. *What improvements could we make out here to help us feel safer?*

She walked along the side of the house, eventually reaching the gate. Anyone could probably hop over or open it, she admitted. It didn't even latch right. *Maybe these are the things that Officer Thatcher was talking about.* They could get their gate latch fixed and maybe a motion detector to pick up any movement on the side of the house.

She turned and headed back into the house. Momma R. looked at her expectantly. "He's coming," Chloe said, a wide smile spreading over her face. "Maybe I should go change."

"No, no, eres muy bonita! Besides, he's coming to see you, not your clothes."

"I know but looking cute doesn't hurt."

As Chloe walked out, Momma R. shook her head and mumbled, "If only that girl knew."

Upstairs, Chloe stared into the full-length mirror on the back of her closet door. Maybe Momma R. was right. She didn't look that bad. Still, she could use a different tank top and a pair of earrings.

Once she moved to the bathroom, she decided her hair could use some attention too. She threw it into a loose braid, then added to her ears the small silver hoops she liked wearing for special occasions. After applying a little mascara, the look was complete.

Not sure what to do until Chris got there, she plopped down on the end of her bed and checked her email. She opened one from Lou. *More assignments. His mind must never stop working.* She shook her head and took a few notes, then got back to her feet. *No working right now. Chris is on his way.*

The sound of a car passing by made her look out. She watched Chris get out of the car and pull a few bags along with him. *What did he bring?*

She tossed her phone aside and went down the steps quickly, unable to wait for him to get there. Before he had made it up the walkway, she opened the door. "Hey!" She went down the few stairs to meet him and gave him a quick kiss. She knew it must look like her eyes were dancing, because her stomach certainly was. She flicked her gaze at the bags. "What did you bring?"

"I have a surprise for you." Smiling, he put his one free arm around her and brought her close again, nuzzling her nose with his. "It isn't too exciting, so don't get your hopes up too much."

Chloe fake grabbed at one of the bags. "Show me!"

Chris held it out of reach, laughing. "I can't yet. It's for all of you."

Fake shock and hurt played out on Chloe's face. "You bought my friends things? What kind of boyfriend are you?"

Chloe instantly reddened and dropped her eyes. *Oh no, I just called him my boyfriend.* She started stuttering. "I-I don't know why I said that."

Chris put his fingertips below her chin and tilted her face up. "Because it's true. I want to be your boyfriend." His eyes grew serious as they locked with hers. "Chloe, will you be my girlfriend?"

Chloe felt like she'd burst with happiness. "Really? You want that?"

"I knew I wanted to be your boyfriend when I walked out of my office to meet you that first time."

Chloe was speechless. Instead of trying to find words to express herself, she wrapped both arms around his waist and pulled him very close. Staring up at him, her eyes searched his. Then, in a rush, she laid on him a deep kiss.

Chris raised his head, breaking the kiss. "You're not worried the neighbors might see?"

"Rational thinking goes out the window when it comes to you and kissing. I want to do it again, anywhere."

Chris chuckled. "Oh, we will. You can count on it. But for now, let's head in so I can show you what I brought."

Grabbing his free hand, she led him into the house and back to the kitchen where she heard voices. Gaby and Jess were sitting at stools opposite Momma R. at the counter.

All three heads turned when they walked In. "Well, hello there. I'm Gaby's mom. The girls call me Momma R. and you may too." She came around the counter and reached out her hand. "So very nice meet you. I have heard some very good things about you. I believe something about flowers and cooking."

Chris shook her hand and shrugged. "Guilty. I have brought her flowers and cooked for her."

Momma R. laughed. "Well now! I'm guilty of being impressed!"

Chris smiled ear to ear. Then he nodded to Gaby and Jess. "How are you doing? I'm sorry to hear about last night."

"Yeah, the end of the night definitely sucked," Jess said first.

Gaby agreed. "Big time. It was unsettling."

"I brought a few things that I thought might help." Chris set the bags on the counter and started pulling out an assortment of pepper spray, whistles, alarms, key chains, and other self-defense gadgets.

The girls picked up a few of the items. Gaby had a key chain in her hand. "How would you use this?"

Jess had two different pepper spray cans. "These are awesome. This one here says it can shoot as far thirty-five feet! It could stop a bear!"

"Where did you get all of this stuff?" Chloe asked.

"I know a guy." He said with a big smile.

Chloe put her hands on her hips. "You didn't have to get all this!"

"I wanted you to be able to choose what would work for each of you. You can keep all of it or none of it."

Momma R. patted his shoulder. "This is very thoughtful of you."

~~~~~

Sometime later, Chloe and Chris managed to escape up to her room. Chris saw this as a good time to bring up a few things he'd been thinking about. He sat on the oversized chair in her room and pulled her onto his lap. "I was worried about you last night when I didn't hear from you. I hope you know how much I care about you. I really like you."

"I really like you too."

He wrapped her into the nook of his shoulder. "It especially worried me how upset you were. So upset that you threw up."

"Yeah, it was really disturbing. So much anger."

"Is that what scared you so much, the anger?"

Chloe nodded. "I don't like violence. I never understood it. There was so much blood. It splattered everywhere."

"What about the stalking? That scared you a lot too?"

"Well, yeah. Kirk followed us around. He's been so weird ever since he and Gaby broke up. I didn't get a chance to tell you … the police were here today. They told us that Kirk put a tracker on my car. They located it when they were here and removed it."

Chris breathed out heavily, taking this all in. Chloe had been targeted specifically because she and Gaby shared a car. If he ever met this Kirk guy, he didn't know what he would do to make him pay for upsetting everyone.

Still, it seemed like there was something more bothering Chloe. Chris had seen students have similar reactions to traumatic events. *Could Chloe have gone through something else before?*

"Has anyone ever hurt you?" he asked.

Chloe stilled. "What do you mean, hurt me?"

"Has anyone ever stalked you or physically tried to hurt you?"

She was quiet for a few moments, hesitating.

Chris decided to try a softer approach. "I could be wrong here, but I'm going to guess something upsetting has once happened to you."

Chloe stared at the floor; her eyes narrowed. "It's really hard for me to talk about."

Chris took hold of one of her hands and pulled her in a little closer. "See if you can try. If it's too difficult, you can stop."

Chloe sighed. She'd wanted to tell him everything, but her fear of facing the past overwhelmed her. She hadn't thought much about Jeremy or her dad. She tried to put that behind her and let ghosts lie. But she wanted Chris to trust her, and her to trust him. "It was a neighbor. He and I were friends when we were young, but as we got older, we drifted apart. One night, about a month before high school graduation, he stopped me on my way home. He was drunk and started putting his hands on me."

Chris felt anger start to build up inside him. He brushed his chin across her forehead, thinking her soft skin would calm him. It only marginally worked. He kept listening.

"I wanted him to stop, but he kept trying to get under my clothes. He kissed me. Kissed me hard. I didn't like it." Chloe peeked up at him. "Until you, I didn't want anyone to get close."

Chris rubbed her shoulder, thinking back on her story. *Did he rape her? Don't push. She'll tell the rest of her story when she's ready.*

Chloe continued, "There have been a few dates over the years, but I always kept my distance. Some thought of me as cold or bitchy, and others thought I just wasn't interested."

Chris hated that this beautiful woman had been sexually harassed and mistreated, leaving her scared and insecure in relationships. He wanted more than ever to treat her right and show her how a real man treated a woman. "Well, those others missed out big time."

Chloe offered him a timid smile. "Thank you. Still, it felt horrible that night. It sometimes haunts me." Her voice trembled as she tried to steady her emotions. "I worry that the obsession Kirk has for Gaby could end for her like it did for me. No one should feel that way."

Chris shook his head. "Yes, that is terrible. I hope Gaby and all of you can take precautions and get rid of the jerk. And I'm sorry you went through that, Chloe."

Chloe touched Chris's cheek. "I hope you understand now why I am so nervous around you. I have no experience in relationships or the physical stuff that happens. I hope it doesn't bother you that I don't know what I am doing."

He kissed her forehead, the anger leaving him as quickly as it had started. "You don't ever have to worry about that. There isn't much to know. Just be yourself. You'll never be wrong if you just do what feels right." She moved her head to his shoulder. "I want you to be honest with me at all times. If I ever do anything you don't feel ready for or that makes you uncomfortable, you have to say something immediately. Can you promise me that?"

She turned her head in closer to his neck and nuzzled him. "Yes, I promise." Then her lips quirked into a smile. "Is it okay if I tell you I missed you and would really like for you to kiss me now?"

Chris was happy Chloe had confided in him today. It showed trust. That was important to him—correction, that was critical to him.

Chris slid out a bit from under her and tucked her under him in the oversized chair. "It is more than okay. I missed you too."

He leaned in, hovering just above her. He was so close he could feel her breath on his face. This woman turned him inside out. Her sweet innocence was so appealing to him, it physically made him feel hot everywhere.

Right before he brought his face to meet hers, he whispered, "I think about you all the time."

Trying to control himself, Chris barely touched his lips to hers. He moved them lightly, soft like feathers over her lips. He kept his eyes slightly open to see her reaction. He wanted to pay close attention to all her subtle cues, so he would know just what she wanted and needed. Or if she wanted him to stop.

Her beautiful brown eyes were mostly closed, her eyelashes fluttering. He felt her shift her hips closer to him and move her hand up his back. She dug the fingers of her other hand into his hair. He knew she would be receptive to him kissing her deeper but wanted to keep it slow and controlled.

Pulling her in just a bit closer and holding her tighter, she responded by parting her lips, and her breathing quickened. She was having a powerful effect on him too. His heart pounded in his ears.

Chris moved his free hand farther down, off her waist and under her, twisting her hips closer to him. She weaved her hand deeper in his hair and pulled back a bit to nibble his lips in small bites. He groaned in response. *Easy, easy. She's new to this. But she's so good too!* She trailed her other hand up and down his back, to his side and then under his shirt.

She didn't know she was doing it, but she was also reading cues. His cues. Chloe felt him shiver, just a tiny shiver, when she touched his skin. His reaction told her he liked her touching him and he wanted more.

She was amazed at how powerful this was making her feel. With just her fingers brushing gently over his back, she was making him shutter. His skin was smooth, but hard muscle rippled underneath. Over the years she imagined what it would feel like to touch a man and recently imagined what it would feel like to touch Chris. She knew it would feel good but had no idea it would feel this incredible.

Touching him was doing things to her. She felt herself respond to his kisses and yearn for him. It felt as though her body had disconnected from her brain and was reacting to him the way it wanted. Her skin tightened and prickled with goose bumps, and everything inside her went hot and molten.

Chris inwardly growled. The hell with the controlled plan. He couldn't think anymore. He couldn't continue at that slow, torturous pace. He quickened his kisses and tightened his hold on her. Even with a faster pace, he was still being tortured.

Then he felt the fissures of electricity when she reached under his shirt to touch his back. She surprised him with her boldness.

Fighting to gain the ability to think, he forced himself to determine how far this should go.

But God, it felt so good to have her body pressing into his. He wanted to keep kissing her and touching her. He stopped himself before he reached under her shirt. He knew he would be sunk if he touched the skin of her stomach, or more.

Chloe ached for him to touch her. She wanted his hands on her, all over her. She needed more. Pushing her body even tighter to his, she expected him to react. He surprised her when he raised his head and started to pull away.

Her breathing was heavy when she opened her eyes. "What's wrong? Did I do something? Did I push too hard on you?" She gestured in the direction of his lap, which she was still partially on top of.

This made him smile. *God, she is so cute.* "You didn't do anything wrong. Actually, the problem is you did everything right."

She laughed. "Then why did you stop? I want you to touch me."

Chris stopped her hand from reaching out to him again. "I want to, but what I want more is for you to emotionally want this. You're physically ready, and that is awesome. But I need to make sure all of you is ready." He lightly tapped her forehead. "We should talk about what you want and how far you want to take things. Tell me as we go."

Disappointed, she sighed. "You're right. And I will. I guess I got caught up in how amazing it felt to be so close to you. I like the way you excite me." She felt embarrassed that he had to be so cautious with her. "I'm sorry."

"Why? You said you were sorry last night on the phone too. You don't have anything to be sorry about, Chloe." Chris stroked her face. He couldn't make himself let her go just yet.

"Well," Chloe closed her eyes tight then opened them to look into his clear blue ones. "I feel like you'll get annoyed or tired of having to treat me like I am fragile. That you won't want to wait for me." She shrugged. "I kind of feel pathetic."

"You are not pathetic. I think you're beautiful, both outside and inside. I will wait if that is what you need. I promise I am not going anywhere."

Chris noticed her eyes start to get a little glassy with tears. He pulled her to his chest and held her there, hugging her.

She rested her hands on his arms, basking in the moment. Her body still felt a rush of energy just sitting near him. After a few moments she whispered, "You have nice shoulders. I like how strong your arms are and how you make me feel in them."

Chris chuckled. She had a powerful effect on him, and if he was being honest with himself, he wanted more. He would need to dig deep if he wanted to uphold his end of this arrangement and wait for her to tell him she was ready.

"Your legs are what get my attention," he said, letting his fingers trail along her thigh. "So long, so perfect. Your eyes drew me in the first time we met. But it was the time I found you in just a T-shirt on the deck that your legs had me. While I'm being honest, your toes too. So damn cute. I haven't been able to stop checking out your legs and toes since."

She laughed. "For me it was when we shook hands the first time. I liked how you held my hand."

Chris kissed the tip of her nose and caressed her cheek with a finger. "Should we go visit with Gaby's mom? I'd like to get to know her better."

"Yes, that would be good. Let's go."

Chloe slid off his lap to let him stand. She fixed her tank top and turned to him. Pressing herself into him after he stood, she gave him a hug. "Is it okay if I hug you whenever I want? Before you answer, you should know it could be a lot."

"Anytime you want. Seriously, *anytime*."

Chloe grinned. "Thank you for making me feel important."

He squeezed her. "You are very important to me, Chloe."

~~~~~

Chapter 12

The following morning, Chris struggled to pull himself out of bed. He'd stayed over at Chloe's until almost ten, and by the time he climbed into bed, it was late and he should have been tired. Instead, he'd laid there for quite a while with her on his mind. He'd willed himself to stop getting aroused every time he thought about her, but nothing seemed to work. Hell, even a cold shower hadn't done the trick. It seemed that rather than her inexperience taming his desire, it only fueled it further.

Todd hypothesized it was because Chris had to tell himself to keep it slow and controlled. Almost like the forbidden fruit, he wanted what he couldn't have. That wasn't how Chris saw it, though. Chloe may be inexperienced and naive when it came to romantic relationships, but she threw off sexy vibes that pierced through him.

Their make-out session in her room had been intense. If he hadn't stopped before he touched her stomach, he would have carried her over to the bed. She wasn't ready for that, but he couldn't stop himself from thinking about what it would be like when she was ready. He could picture her gorgeous body squirming under him and kissing her beautiful face.

Exercise would have to be an outlet for how much she revved him up. He would increase his runs from three times a week to five. If he had to, he'd go to the gym every day too. Anything to expel his excess energy and decrease his sexual frustration.

Staring at the clock, he forced himself up and out of bed to start one of those additional runs. He grabbed his sneakers and headed downstairs.

Todd was already up. He had a work project that needed the final touches done, and the deadline was right around the corner.

Chris grabbed water from the fridge. "How long have you been awake?"

"Since five-thirty." Todd looked his brother over and pointed to his running shoes. "You're going running? You never run on a Monday."

"I woke early, so I thought I'd fit an extra one in."

He knew he wasn't fooling Todd. Nobody knew him like he did. Bracing for the teasing that was about to start, Chris turned and fully faced his brother. "Let's have it."

"Have what? You want me to state the obvious?"

Chris squinted and hardened his face, knowing his brother was dying to do just that. "Give it."

"Naw, you're tired and sexually frustrated. It would be dangerous for me to say anything."

After taking another swig of water, Chris put the bottle on the counter and walked toward the door.

"Look at it this way," Todd's voice followed him. "You're going to be in the best shape of your life until you finally seal the deal."

Chris whipped around, and in two strides he was up in his brother's face. "It's not like that. I'm not trying to 'seal the deal.' With her, it's a whole hell of a lot more than a roll in the sheets." He leaned closer. "I'll destroy you if you talk like she's someone I'm just trying to get off with."

Todd put up his hands. "Jesus, take it easy. I was trying to keep it light."

"Whatever. What would you know about anything serious anyway?"

After Chris strode out, Todd turned back to his coffee and reasoned with himself. *Okay, I was being a prick, I wanted a reaction out of Chris. But hot damn, I wasn't expecting a reaction like that.*

Starting his run at a fast clip, Chris thought about his past relationships. He never thought of himself as a one-night stand kind of guy, but he did have a few of those experiences. Before his last serious girlfriend, Beth, he had made a series of poor choices. Todd had convinced him to try a dating app. It had been exciting at first with numerous flirty messages and interest to meet. However, that wore off quickly when he found none of the women he met actually wanted more than sex. After the fourth woman he'd slept with ghosted him, he deleted his account.

Chris was very interested in a serious relationship since he met Chloe. He wanted her physically, that was true, but he also wanted so much more. She made him smile, and he could make her laugh.

They were working on building a relationship based on trust and comfort, and that took time. Chris wanted to know everything about her. She opened up to him some yesterday, but he knew there was still work to do. That was expected, though. Just a month ago they were strangers meeting through work. He couldn't demand she confide everything in him in that short time. Now that he was her boyfriend officially, though, he hoped she'd come to realize she could.

In between his heavy breathing, he smiled when he thought, *Wow, a month.*

Was that all? It seemed like it had been much longer.

Once back at home and showered, Chris grabbed his stuff for work. The school year would be starting soon, and that would help keep his mind busy. The few weeks leading up to the first day of school and the few weeks after were always very hectic. He'd bury himself in those activities to keep his sexual frustration at bay.

On the drive there, he dialed his mom. "Hey, Mom. How are you?"

"Hi, honey. What's wrong?"

Chris scoffed. "Why would anything be wrong?"

His mother saw right through him, as usual. "Chris, it's not even eight in the morning. You never call me this early."

"I don't? Well, maybe I should start. I'm on my way into work and thought I'd see what was new at home."

She hesitated. "Okaaay. Well, I'm going to let it slide for now, only because I'm glad you called."

Chris chuckled. "Wow, thanks for the pardon."

"Not much is really that new," she said. Your father is busy doing yard work. He's hell bent on that garden this year. Claims he will win the pumpkin contest at the East Texas Fair this year too. You are lucky to not be witness to his craziness. He treats those pumpkins with more tenderness than he does me."

"I'll be sure to be there this year. I wouldn't want to miss the blue-ribbon ceremony if Dad gets it."

"You are required to attend. And what about this new girl?"

Chris rolled his eyes. "Todd's got a big mouth, huh?"

"I hear she's a cute little thing. Is it serious?"

"I want it to be serious. It's kind of early, though, so don't start planning on grandbabies."

"Yeah, yeah. Well, a mom can dream, can't she?"

Chris laughed. "Well, keep your dreams to yourself, especially when you meet her."

"Oh, you're going to let me meet her?"

"Yes. I want her to see how great you are. She isn't in contact with her mom and could use someone like you. She has her best friend's mom, but I think she would really take to you."

"Aw, well that is probably the nicest compliment you have given me in a long time! I wouldn't mind another young woman to spoil since Briana is so far away."

"I figured, and I think you'll adore her."

On the other end of the phone, Chris's mom raised her brows and smirked. "I can't wait," she told him. "You just tell me when you're coming."

"I'll let you know. I haven't mentioned it to her yet. Maybe in a few weeks." He sighed. "All right, I'm pulling into the parking lot, so gotta run. Love ya."

"Love you and call me any time!"

~~~~~

Chris wasn't the only one who struggled with sleep and frustration. Chloe never had urges before. Sure, she thought guys were cute and thought about kissing, but God, she felt like an animal around Chris. Her brain didn't work, but her body did. God, did she grind her hips into his? Yes, she most definitely did, and even more surprisingly, she wanted to do it again.

Lying in bed after only a few hours of sleep, she was tortured with thoughts of what he would look like without his shirt on. She had wanted to rip it off him yesterday when they made out. She thought about doing a lot more than that too.

Ugh, she had to stop this torture. What could she do? She decided to get out of bed and do something, anything.

She went downstairs and grabbed her computer. *Now was as good a time as any to start writing that cookbook. I will bake my way through this.*

She pulled out her binder of recipes and started sorting through them to see how she could group them. She could organize them by type—cakes, muffins, breads—or by the meal each paired best with—breakfast, lunch, dinner. *Which would work better for a reader?* She thought back on all the cookbooks or recipes she'd turned to when she was first learning to bake. Most had been separated by type. Chloe shrugged. *I think breakfast, lunch, and dinner works best while I figure out which recipes, I want to put in it. I can switch to type after.*

She saw her favorite chocolate oat muffin recipe and decided she would surprise Gaby and Jess. A warm muffin would be a good way to start a Monday.

After sticking the muffin tray in the oven and cleaning off the counter, she typed up her recipe and put it under the "Breakfast" category.

Soon after, the timer rang, and she peeked in the oven to see if they had risen and looked just right. *Perfect,* she cheered silently, admiring their dark-brown deliciousness. Chloe put them on a cooling rack and went to get dressed for work.

Jess walked into the hall as Chloe reached the stairs. She had a questioning look on her face. "How long have you been up that you had time to bake?"

Chloe rolled her eyes. "Unfortunately, longer than I would have liked, but fortunately for you, I used my time to make muffins."

Jess shot her arm up. "Yes! I really didn't feel like having cereal this morning and that is all I had time for."

Seeing Jess already had her purse, it looked like she was heading out right away. "Another busy day?"

Jess stuck her tongue out the corner of her mouth. "Every day is a busy day. It will be that way for a while."

"Well, grab some muffins to take with you." Chloe headed up the stairs.

Jess was packing up two muffins when Gaby sauntered in. "Looks like our little Chloe was up early. I guess she didn't sleep well."

"I'm thinking you are right. She's falling big time. I can see why, though. I really like him."

"Chris is really different from the guys I have met. I think he'll treat our girl right. My mom was really impressed with him."

"I think it's because he is older. Guys in their twenties are so immature."

Gaby rolled her eyes. "Tell me about it. They're too busy playing games and looking to get laid."

"So true. Well, at least we don't have to worry about how he will treat her."

Gaby took a small bite of a muffin. "I think our biggest worry is going to be helping her figure out the fooling around part."

Jess shook her head. "Don't look at me. Derek only got as far as under my shirt. I got nothing to offer the girl. That's all you."

Gaby smirked. "You make it sound like I have all this experience. It was only one guy, one time, and it wasn't that good."

Jess let out a breath. "Crap. We're a hopeless lot, aren't we?"

Gaby just rolled her eyes and sat down to breakfast. "Yeah, I guess. Full disclosure here, but I'm kind of jealous of Chloe. Chris looks at her like she is the only girl in the room and is the only girl he has ever seen or will want to see."

"Oh my God, I know!

"We'll get our turn. Someday. I hope, anyway." Gaby took a big bite of muffin. "Until then, we have each other—and food."

"Cheers to that." Jess raised her breakfast container in a toasting gesture and headed out.

~~~~~

Chloe dreaded her walk into work. Not only was she exhausted from lack of sleep, but she had to face Mya for what would be a second week of uncomfortable silences and forced, tense interactions. She tried last week to not let the fact that she had to share her idea of the mental illness awareness series with someone bother her. But it did. A lot.

As luck would have it, when she turned the corner into the office area, her eyes made contact with Mya. Chloe slapped a fake smile on her face and trudged to her desk. She shook her head and rolled her neck out as her computer started up. *How will I get through today, let alone another week of this! I need to talk to Lou.* She stole a glance in his direction and saw he had his office to himself. Before she lost her nerve, she walked to his door.

"Come in," he called out after hearing her knock.

She wasted no time entering.

Hearing her quick walk, Lou glanced up and pushed his laptop to the side. "What's up?"

Chloe closed the door behind her. "I came to ask your perspective on why you thought the mental illness series was a joint assignment. I had hoped to carry it out solo."

Lou gestured toward the chair in front of his desk. "I thought Mya would be good to partner with for a few reasons. First, I think it's going to be a big job. I want to split the workload to keep some of your time free. The series is a great idea, but it's not field reporting. You really shined at the Tri-County fire and I want to keep you going in that direction."

A smile spread across Chloe's face. The thought never crossed her mind that he would want her to focus on something else simultaneously. "I'd like that."

"I thought you would." Catching Chloe's reaction, he continued, "You're really going places Chloe, and I think Mya could push you to explore some other views that would fully develop the series. And you could learn a lot from her on the social media aspect. She's strong in that space."

Chloe nodded. "She is really good at it."

"Yeah, she is." Lou tilted his head. "But you're strong in research, and your insight is killer. It would be good if you could share some techniques with her. Trust me, you two will crush it together."

"I appreciate the perspective. I never wanted to come across as anything but a team player."

"Naw." He dismissed the notion with a wave.

"I held on to this idea a little tighter than I should have. You're right. Two heads are going to be better than one."

"I am glad you see it too."

Chloe stood, feeling relieved. "I do. Thanks."

Closing the door after her, she looked in the direction of Mya's desk and felt hopeful this would be an opportunity to learn and grow rather than hate. *Maybe this will be a better week than I thought.*

~~~~~

And a good week it had been. After Chloe patched things up with Mya, the course of her week improved a thousand-fold. Monday night the girls had a good dinner together and laughed out on the deck. Tuesday night Jess and Chloe got in a good workout at the gym while Gaby taught a class. They dropped her off and picked her up, so Gaby didn't have to walk to the car in the dark.

Wednesday night Chloe went to Chris's for dinner. Todd was around, so the three of them hung out. It was probably best because Chloe wasn't quite sure she trusted herself alone with Chris. She might be too tempted to let her hormones take over.

Thursday night the girls went to buy some used gym equipment to put together their own at-home gym so they could still workout when they didn't have a buddy to go with. They arranged to have it delivered Saturday.

And their sacred Friday night was starting off well. The girls didn't want to go out for a while, so they made margaritas and had their own backyard happy hour. Gaby hung string lights and lit some tiki torches. Chloe hung some bright streamers, making their deck look very festive.

They were feeling good. Lots of nachos were crunched and margaritas guzzled. Gaby had just posted some good selfies of them when Chloe brought up a new topic. "Okay." She took a breath. "What do you guys know about sex? I need to hear some firsthand experience!"

Jess started laughing so hard she almost fell off her chair. "You can't seriously think I have any firsthand experience to give, do you?" She stilled for a minute. Then, looking very serious, she said, "Well, I do have some *hand* experience!"

Gaby choked on her margarita and sprayed it all over the table. This sent Jess and Chloe roaring. Jess grabbed some napkins and pointed at Gaby at the same time. "She's the only one that can give any advice."

Gaby rolled her eyes as she cleaned herself up. "Trust me. I don't have any good advice to give either, because I never had good sex."

"Wait, James from senior year wasn't good?"

"Hell no. He was selfish. It was one time and it was over in two minutes. Did nothing for me."

Chloe looked serious. "What's it supposed to *do for you*?" She burst out laughing when Gaby's eyes grew wide.

It was Jess's turn to spew margarita then. "Oh my God. She's messing with you."

Chloe shook her head. "Got you!"

Gaby threw her crumpled napkins at Chloe. "Oh my God!"

"I know what it's supposed to do for you. Okay, so if it didn't do it for you with James, were you with anyone else that *did it for you* but without actually having sex?"

"There was Stephen two years ago. Some heavy petting was involved there that worked for me."

Chloe shrieked. "Heavy petting? Under clothes or over?"

Gaby could barely get out the words she was laughing so hard. "It was over!"

Jess just stared at her. "And that worked? Like, you were grinding up on him and that just did it?"

"Well, yeah! I don't know. I guess I was extra horny or something!"

Chloe shrilled. "I guess I got all the information I can from you two!"

Not laughing quite as hard, Gaby looked at her friends. "I know guys seem to flock to me. I don't always acknowledge it when you say it, but I know. It's just strange and uncomfortable for me to think or talk about."

Chloe spoke for both her and Jess. "We know, Gaby."

Gaby continued, "What I hate most about it is that getting noticed so much gives the impression that I know a lot about men. But I really don't. Because it's always the wrong kind of guys, it never goes far." Her shoulders slumped. "I've never been in love."

Jess rubbed Gaby's arm. "Gabs, first of all, we know you don't do anything wrong. You're a naturally beautiful person, and people can't help noticing that."

"And second of all," Chloe jumped in, "no one has the impression you are some kind of slut. I knew you were only ever with James. I didn't know that you didn't really like it, though."

Gaby shrugged shyly. "I was too embarrassed to tell you I let him go all the way with me and it didn't mean anything. My mom always told me it should mean something. I wasn't too proud of myself."

Jess assured her, "Everyone does things they aren't proud of sometimes. Think of James as a learning experience. All the men in our lives up to this point have been for purposes of learning, since we haven't met 'the one' yet. Well, except for you!" Her eyes shined toward Chloe.

In reply, Chloe smiled. "To be honest, girls, I feel like he could be 'the one.' Is that crazy, though? That my first boyfriend would be my last boyfriend?"

"No way," said Jess. "It's completely incredible, and also annoyingly adorable!"

Chloe laughed.

Then Gaby picked up her margarita glass and raised it in a toast. "Here's to

Chris being Chloe's first boyfriend, only boyfriend, and last boyfriend!"

"Here, here!"

~~~~~

Across town, Chris met some friends out for beer and pre-football talk. To grow up in Texas and not be a football fan was sacrilege. Chris was a huge fan, but mostly a sideline fan now. He had played on both his high school and college football teams. Occasionally he would start and had held his own, but he hadn't been good enough to make it a career. Now he just lived to watch the game and goof around with his friends every now and then.

The beginning of August meant training camp and interviews to see how this year's pro teams were going to shape up. His friends often met up at a bar downtown where the barbecue was hot and the beer was cold.

After work, Chris had gone to the gym and taken a cold shower. In fact, he had taken a cold shower every day this week, sometimes twice. But nothing helped. Thoughts of Chloe still kept driving him crazy.

Tomorrow he would go over to help with their gym equipment delivery. He was glad she asked him to come over for the day. Having only seen her once that week, he missed her. They had stayed in touch, texting or talking every day. They had even exchanged some flirty texts that Chloe initiated. Chris tried to keep his responses mild, but the truth was, he really wanted to write every thought that came into his head when she was on his mind.

Meeting friends out tonight kept him from sitting home and torturing himself thinking about her, but she was still in the forefront of his thoughts.

Chris went straight from the gym to the bar. He had eaten lunch early and was starving now. Entering the familiar restaurant, he saw an open seat at the bar and went for it. Not long after he sat down, a cold beer was in front of him. *The perks of knowing the bartender.*

The touch of a delicate hand on his shoulder grabbed his attention. Standing there was Sandy, a woman he went on a few dates with in the spring. She seemed pristinely pampered, as usual, wearing an orange dress and tall heels.

In his mind, they never really clicked. He knew she felt differently, though. Ever since they had called it off, she had been trying to get back with him. Why she still wanted his attention after he dumped her, he didn't know. He had been very clear that he wasn't interested in her that way.

What made things worse was that she was friends with one of his buddies' girlfriends, so she sometimes came to these group get-togethers.

"Hey, Sandy. How are you?"

She kept her hand on his shoulder a little too long. "Oh good, real good. It's been weeks since I've seen you. How are you?"

"Yeah, just busy. Not up to much." He hunched his shoulders and turned back to his beer, hoping she'd get the hint.

"Oh, come on. Something has to be going on." She reached out her hand to run her fingers down his arm.

He flicked her hand off as soon as it touched him and said sharply, "I'm not interested." If she didn't listen to his words, which sometimes she didn't, maybe she'd listen to his tone.

She tossed her hair behind her shoulders, steeling herself against his anger. "Oh, well, I'm sorry for being friendly and bothering you."

He was sure she expected him to apologize, but he wasn't in the mood to deal with the "poor me" routine he knew she often put on. Instead, he said nothing. Time ticked by as she stood there, waiting.

"Fine," she puffed, and with a click of her heels she stormed off.

Good riddance. He was not in the mood to placate her.

He took a swig of his beer and picked up his phone. No texts from Chloe. He figured he probably wouldn't hear from her since Friday night was girls' night, but he couldn't help still looking. They had texted earlier. She told him they were having their own backyard happy hour since they temporarily put themselves on house arrest.

After another swig of beer, his barbecue arrived. He was ravenous, and the sandwich didn't stand a chance. As he pushed the plate back, a few of his friends and Todd arrived.

"Yo, dude. How long have you been here?" Josh said, gesturing toward his empty plate.

"Not that long. I was starved."

Todd smirked. "It's all the extra workouts and runs he's been putting in this week."

Chris shoved his brother. "Screw you."

Josh looked confused. "What did I miss?"

Chris muttered, "Nothing, just Todd being an asshole."

"What's new there?" Josh said sarcastically, and smacked Todd on the back.

Smirking, Chris turned back to the bar and motioned to the bartender that he was moving. He laid a twenty out and stood up. Grabbing his phone, he headed over to a bigger table that could accommodate him and his friends.

Chris sat opposite his brother. He didn't want to deal with his teasing tonight. It didn't work, though. Within five minutes, Todd was passing his phone around, showing a picture that Gaby posted of Chloe at their backyard fiesta. He heard a lot of muttering from the guys: *Cute. Hot. Sexy. Which one? Are the other two single?*

He wanted to tell Todd to go screw himself but decided against it. He'd get even another time. Instead he just nodded and agreed. She had looked hot in that picture. Tomorrow couldn't come fast enough. That woman was going to have to beat him off with a stick or he'd devour her.

~~~~~

When the doorbell rang, Chloe ran down the stairs, whipped open the door, grabbed Chris by his shirt, and pulled him inside. Knowing Gaby and Jess were back in the spare room, Chloe wanted to get Chris all alone as quickly as possible. She pushed him against the door and pressed herself into him. "I missed you," she murmured against his lips.

He took this as an invitation to ravish her mouth. He wrapped his arms around her and crushed his lips to hers, using his tongue to plunder her mouth. God, she could destroy him. He thought he would be the one to devour her, but right now it felt like the opposite. Chris lost all ability to think.

In one motion he picked her up, and she instinctively wrapped her legs around his waist. He carried her up the stairs, not missing a beat with their feverish kissing.

Kicking the door closed behind him, he sat on the bed with her still wrapped around him. It was almost more than he could take, having his hips fit between her legs. The tight leggings and cropped tank she wore didn't cover as much as he needed in order to be a good church boy.

She didn't have the good church girl persona now either, though. She slid her hands down his torso and rolled up his shirt, separating their lips for only a second to pull the shirt over his head. It crumpled to the floor. She wrapped her arms around his body and used her hands to knead the muscles of his back.

Moving her hands forward, she slowed her touch when they found his chest. Her lips stalled and her eyes flicked open. He saw surprise there.

Shit, what did I do? Panting, he asked her, "What's wrong?"

Chloe stared more, her chest rising and falling, breathing deeply. Stammering, she whispered, "I never touched a man before." She let her hands fall from his chest then moved from his arms to stand in front of him. Her breathing was heavy and her stance shaky.

"I'm not going to hurt you. I won't even touch you." Chris was now feeling disgusted with himself for letting it get out of hand. He grabbed his shirt and pulled it hastily back on. "I'm so sorry I let it go this far. I shouldn't have carried you up here."

"No, no. It's not that you did that. It's the feel of your chest. It caught me off guard. I don't even know what I expected, but it felt so intimate touching you there." Chloe dropped to the floor and buried her face in her hands. "I'm mortified."

"Why? No, don't be. There is nothing to be mortified over."

"I'm so pathetic. I'm a twenty-five-year-old who has never touched a man. And here is a wonderful, patient guy who I dream of touching." Lowering her voice to a whisper, she continued, "Of who I dream of making love to but am terrified of being close to."

Chris couldn't see her eyes, but he heard her start to cry. He kneeled in front of her, a rush of emotions hitting him. "It's okay, baby. This is all very confusing for you. I understand, and I am not upset by it. I don't want you to be embarrassed with me. Ever." He took her hands in his.

She looked up at him, her eyes glassy. "I want to touch you, feel you touch me, and do all the things a couple does when they are intimate with one another. But I can't, not yet. Will you wait for me to be ready?"

"I would wait an eternity for you. I promise that we will take this at whatever pace you need it to be. You are the one in the lead. I follow you. I won't touch you unless you allow me to."

Chloe's tears fell harder after hearing that. "Hug me?"

Chris leaned back on his heels, taking her with him. They sat for a long time.

Once Chloe's breathing slowed and her tears stopped, Chris started, "You know what I think? I think we have some damn good chemistry. I have never felt electricity like this before."

Chloe lifted her head to look into his eyes. "Really?"

"Yes, really. It's putting you at a disadvantage. For most people, the first few people they date are real duds and neither knows what they are doing, so it's lame." He put his hand to her cheek and brushed his thumb against her lips. "But with us? It's all sparks. I have experience and I can't control myself."

Chloe looked down at their twisting hands. "Can I ask ... how much experience you have?"

Chris studied the ceiling. "Well, I've had a few girlfriends over the years."

Drawing circles with her finger on his arm, she ventured, "How many is a few?"

"I dated in high school, and two or three girls in college, but my first serious girlfriend was in my early twenties. After we broke up, I dated some, and then my last relationship ended back in January. That is when I moved in with Todd."

"Oh. So you've kissed a lot, been with a few women ... and lived with one?"

He nodded. "Yes, I have. But it's not like I am drawing any comparisons. It's you I think about, you I want."

She bobbed her head. "Mmm, okay," she whispered.

"Did you know all week I have been moody and agitated? I came close to pounding on Todd several times for just looking at me wrong. I have been exercising like a fiend and have never had so many cold showers in my life."

Chloe laughed. "I was doing the same. I have been up early every day this week baking. I decided to start writing a cookbook."

"I didn't know you wanted to write a cookbook. That's cool."

"I've been toying with the idea for a while. It seemed like a good time to start. I need something to focus on or I'll die of torture thinking about you."

"I feel the exact same way. You know you can tell me anything, anytime? You can call me in the middle of the night if you can't sleep and tell me you're thinking of me. You can text me in the middle of the day to say you're anxious. I want to know what you are thinking. I genuinely like hearing from you." He pointed to her forehead then to her heart. "And I like knowing how you are feeling. I don't want to just be physical with you. I am not just thinking of you here." He squeezed her hip.

Chloe leaned into Chris, feeling his warmth. "Thank you for telling me. I want to know what you are thinking too. I wish I had known you were on edge all week. Maybe I could have done something to help, or we could have seen each other more?"

"Seeing a bit more of you would have helped. I know you need time to do your own things, so there is no obligation. But if you find yourself wanting to see me, tell me."

Chloe gently kissed him. "I will, and you too. I am sorry for today. It is my fault. I did start it."

Chris smiled devilishly and returned the kiss. "Yeah, you did, ripping me through the door and pushing yourself up on me like that. Don't be sorry. Truth is, I liked it. A lot."

Chloe tipped her head back and laughed. Chris saw the length of her neck. Between that sexy neck and contagious giggle, he was so gone.

He stood up and righted her on her feet. "Okay, let's go see if your friends need any help."

~~~~~

Chapter 13

Chloe jabbed at the mitt Jess held up. "Harder!" Jess yelled.

"Oof! Oof!" Chloe gasped with each punch.

The self-defense class they all decided to join met two times a week at a gym. Gaby had taken the advice of Officer Price and called last week to sign them up. Today marked their third class, and already the girls were feeling tougher. The first class was about recognizing risks and prevention. The second class explained how to face an attacker and take them down quickly with a strategic hit. This class focused on practicing how to make hits count.

Chloe stood next to her friends, practicing jabs with one of the other women. Soon they would switch boxing gloves and mitts. Ed, the instructor, walked by. "Nice form, Chloe. Put more shoulder and body into it!"

He sounded tough as he critiqued her, but Chloe knew he was a nice man. He reminded her of a grandpa—of course, one tough, kick-ass grandpa. Ed was a retired police officer. He had worked with victims of stalking and harassment for years on the police force. He offered this class to anyone who wanted to sign up; however, mostly women attended. Chloe watched as Ed and two helpers showed them how to punch. She had never hit anyone and hoped she would never have to. But if she ever did, she wasn't going down without a fight. This class was empowering, she had to admit.

She liked that it wasn't just about physical actions, but also believing in yourself and having the strength to fight back and not let yourself be the victim. It also helped her feel better about going out alone, but more importantly, it had a surprising effect on her confidence.

Chloe was tired of being the victim. Spending her childhood as a target of abuse and harassment had led her to play her early adult years carefully. She was a planner, not a risk taker. However, this class helped her overcome some of that, to live in the moment and take life in her own hands.

In the last class, Ed had explained, "There are verbal responses you can use to let the attacker know you won't be a willing victim. Instead of rewarding the attacker by pleading or being emotional, let them know you are in control."

Chloe had even been part of the demonstration that followed, which added to her growing confidence. The group had stood in a horseshoe shape around Ed and the helpers. His eyes focused on Chloe, and he waved her toward him. "Come on up. Let's act this out to show the group."

Ignoring her pounding heart and sweaty hands, Chloe forced herself to overcome her nerves and stand beside Ed.

He continued, "Verbal de-escalation is most effective before physical threat is imminent. Let's say Chloe is alone at a bar, standing near the wall. Her friend left early, and she is finishing her drink." Ed waved one of the helpers over. "This guy moves toward her, stands close, and partially boxes her in."

The helper sauntered up to her and put his arm on the wall behind them. Leaning in, he said, "I've never seen you here before."

Ed watched Chloe start to cower and go pale. "Chloe, stand up straight and don't let him know he's making you nervous. What can you say to tell him you aren't interested?"

Swallowing the large lump in her throat, she mumbled, "Back off."

Ed looked to the group. "That's a great answer." He looked back at Chloe. "But you have to say it like you mean it."

Chloe straightened her shoulders. "Back off," she said louder.

"Better. Say it again, louder and with more confidence."

Chloe stuck out her chin. "Back. Off."

"That was excellent. You said it firmly and clearly. Plus, you stood tall and defiant."

That small scene had encouraged her and resonated with her now.

Focusing back on tonight's class, Chloe let another punch fly to hit the mitt of her partner.

"Good job," Ed said. Chloe smiled. She hadn't known he was watching her. Then Ed turned to the group. "Now, switch it up!"

Chloe walked toward a woman a few years older than her, who had introduced herself the first night as a single mom of one daughter and an executive director at a large pharmaceutical company. Chloe admired her. She was strikingly beautiful with dark hair and sharp green eyes. She radiated power. It eluded Chloe how she could be a victim of anything.

The woman held out her hand. "Hiya. I'm Cher."

Chloe nodded. "Chloe. I saw your jabs with your last partner. You look pretty good at this!"

"I've taken some boxing classes before, but this is better. I'm learning a lot here."

There wasn't enough time for the exchange of anymore niceties, however, as

Ed's blow of the whistle indicated the start of the next round.

Chloe held the mitts, bracing for impact. *I was right,* she thought as the first punches rolled. *Cher has a strong arm on her.* Chloe could see a flicker of anger in Cher's eyes every time she hit. *She seems nice. I wonder what she's gone through to get her so fired up. It must be significant.*

The whistle sounded again. This time it meant the end of class. Everyone stopped, wiping the sweat from their foreheads and smiling to their partners.

Cher turned to Chloe, saying in between breaths, "Hope I wasn't too hard on ya. I just have something inside me I have to prove. These classes always make me go for it."

Chloe offered a smile. "You're not alone."

The women nodded to each other, then Chloe turned to find Gaby and Jess. She located them over by the wall, next to the lockers. They were busy chugging down water and trying to breathe again.

Upon seeing Chloe, Gaby huffed. "I wasn't expecting this to also be a workout class!"

Chloe laughed. "Tell me about it."

Just then, Ed walked up to them. He made a point to chat regularly with all his clients. "How are y'all feelin'? Because you're doing great!"

"Thanks, Ed," Jess said.

"Great class today," Gaby followed.

Ed beamed. "Wonderful. I love to hear that! Keep up the awesome work."

Smiles and thanks were shared before Ed continued on his rounds.

Chloe looked at the time. It was only seven-thirty. *Still early enough to drop in to see Chris.*

Chloe thought back to the weekend, when she'd last seen him. On Saturday, when the delivery men brought their gym equipment, Chris and Todd supervised the entire time. Then they did some work on the townhouse. They installed extra latches, deadbolts, and motion detectors. "All to keep the crazy guys out and the crazy ladies safe," Todd joked.

Afterward, the girls invited them to stay for dinner, which they had readily accepted. Gaby had made some fajitas, and Chloe threw together a quick cinnamon crumb cake. They didn't stay too long after that, however, which left Chloe disappointed. Still, she admitted, it had been a fun night while it lasted, all of them laughing and chatting.

On Sunday, Chloe called Chris and invited him to the park. They went for a long walk on the shady paths and then got Italian ice nearby. It had been a nice weekend with him.

Now it was Wednesday, and she hadn't seen him since. Busy schedules were to blame. Ramping up for the beginning of the school year started for Chris, leaving him in the office for longer hours. Chloe was also staying at the office later than usual to meet with Mya, planning out their work for the article series. They made great headway with the planning portion but completing the interviews and research would be even more time consuming. Chloe wanted to make the most of the free time she had.

"Girls, I'm thinking of making a stop at Chris's house."

Gaby looked at Chloe. "Go get him, girl. I'll hitch a ride with Jess. Say hi to the guys for us."

She called out over her shoulder. "I will. I'll be home around ten."

~~~~~

Chris's face broke into a huge smile when he opened the door. "Hey, you!" He grabbed Chloe and pulled her into a big hug. Chloe noticed he was in workout clothes. Chris smiled, following her gaze. "I just got back from a run. How bad am I?"

Pretending to sniff his neck, she said, smirking, "Slightly ripe! But I am too. It cancels out."

He laughed. "Good. How was class?"

"Really good. We learned how to throw a good punch tonight. Ed said I had to put more body into it. Did you ever punch anybody?"

Chris chuckled. "Todd. *A lot.*"

"I bet you got a lot back," she said, laughing too.

"Yeah, true enough."

"Seriously, can you throw a good punch?"

Chris shrugged. "Not bad, I guess. I was never into boxing or anything. But I grew up with a brother who pissed me off a lot and played football with a bunch of hot heads. Nothing ever crazy or serious, though. Just guys blowing off steam." Chris watched her as he spoke. The last thing he wanted was for her to think he was a fighter, but he didn't want to lie either.

She didn't seem upset, only curious. "I'll never understand how fighting is just blowing off steam to guys." Chloe shook her head, then put her hands on his cheeks and looked into his blue eyes, her face losing its playful appearance. "I have a huge favor to ask of you."

Chris raised his eyebrows. "What?"

She gave him a quick peck on the lips. "Do you have any food? Starving." She patted her stomach. "Absolutely starving."

He grinned and returned her kiss. "Yeah, come on out. We'll wrangle something up."

Chloe felt better after having some of the guys' leftovers. Tasty grilled chicken and potatoes left her impressed. "Really good. Who was the cook?"

Todd yelled from the living room, "That would be me."

"Very good," she responded as the two of them came to join him. "Thanks for sharing. I wasn't going to make it home."

He gave them room beside him. "Don't mention it. So, what's new? You girls kicking ass and taking numbers at that class?"

Chloe laughed. "Hardly, but it is really good."

"What are they teaching you?"

Chris smiled to himself. Todd seemed to be warming up to Chloe very well.

"I'll show you," Chloe said, rising from the couch. She gestured for Chris to stand too then moved around the coffee table, positioning him in front of her. "For demonstration purposes only."

Chris couldn't help smiling at that grin she wore. He put up his hands in surrender. "Don't hurt me."

Chloe nudged him. "Wouldn't dream of it."

She first directed Chris to come at her from the front, then from behind. These different scenarios let her demonstrate the best reactions to fit each situation. Finally, she ended with her attempt at a punch. It stopped just short of Chris's jaw.

Todd shook his head. "Only problem I see with it is that you aren't following through."

Chris barked out a laugh. "Okay, tough guy. Come up here so I can show her how to follow through!"

Todd's eyes gleamed. "Naw, I don't want to embarrass you in front of your girl." Slowly, he eased himself up from the couch. "I'm heading up anyway. I have an early morning." He went over to Chloe and gave her a side hug. "See ya soon."

After Todd left, Chris turned to Chloe. "Does this mean you're going too?"

Chloe's gaze met his. "I can stay a bit longer. I didn't get a proper boyfriend kiss."

"What's a boyfriend kiss?" He asked with a devilish smile.

"I'll demonstrate. This, of course, is a proper girlfriend kiss." Chloe wrapped one arm around his neck and guided his head down to hers. The other arm she rested on his chest. She pressed her lips to his and used her tongue to gently part his mouth. His body relaxed as she continued the kiss, burying her fingers into his hair and stroking his arm.

Her version of a proper girlfriend kiss tortured him.

He murmured against her, "Well, now that I know …" He brought his hands up to her waist. "I will give you a proper boyfriend kiss in return."

Chris slowly stepped closer to her, remembering not to let it get too hot. So, he held her just a little tighter and let her set the pace. *Slow and steady*, he reminded himself. Their lips lingered and danced as the kiss grew deeper, but he wouldn't let it push him over the edge. Before it got too intense, he lifted his head. "I like your proper kiss idea. I think we'll need more demonstrations soon."

Chloe beamed, tempted to pull him back to her for just a little more. *He's stopping for you, though, so don't tease.* "Definitely," she said breathlessly. "What are you doing this weekend?"

The answer came easily. "Seeing you, when you tell me you're free."

She stood on her tiptoes to give him a soft kiss and smiled against his lips. "All day Saturday."

Chris pretended to gasp in surprise. "I get you all day?" Chloe nodded. "Hmm, I can work with that."

An eyebrow lifted. "I'm intrigued."

Chris smiled. "I'm glad. I like to keep things interesting." He sighed then, staring at his watch and pulling her in for a tight hug. "I guess it's getting late."

Chloe studied her feet. "Yeah. I should get going."

He nodded, escorting her to her car as usual. "Text me when you get home?"

"Of course, Mr. Sherman."

~~~~~

Chapter 14

Chloe finished off her week later than she wanted but made it home in time to enjoy the sacred Friday night dinner with Gaby and Jess.

Gaby turned from washing dishes at the kitchen sink. "I barely saw you this week, Chloe. How have things been going with Mya and the project?"

"They're fine. I'm still harboring some bitterness about sharing. I should let it go."

"Easier said than done sometimes," Jess commented with a shrug as she entered the kitchen from the living room.

"It is, which is why it is still lingering," Chloe said. "I want to let it go, but I can't seem to shake it. It fades more each day, so I am hoping by the time the articles are published, I will have let it go completely."

Jess patted Chloe's shoulder then went to clean the counters. "I'm sure you will."

"Being so busy keeps me from thinking about it. This week Lou gave me three new assignments—and my live reporting debut."

"Wow! Exciting! Anything good?" Gaby asked.

"Yeah, the one is a continuation on the mayor's office scandal. The city council is going to vote next week on whether the mayor should be removed from office. Here." Chloe pulled up the Local 9 News website and passed her phone to Gaby. "I ran over there today for a story."

Gaby dried her hands and tossed the towel aside. "Oooh! Show us!"

Jess peered over Gaby's shoulder in time to see Chloe interviewing an older man in a suit.

Chloe's voice came in clear. "We're here at Galorston City Hall with council member Mr. Weisenberg. Mr. Weisenberg, thank you for joining me."

He gave a gruff nod.

"When is the vote scheduled to take place?" Chloe positioned the microphone in front of him.

"Next week. The committee reviewing the evidence will first present their findings to the council."

"It must be hard to keep things 'business as usual' around here. There is a rumor that everyone has chosen a side and is spreading any rumors they can on the other side."

The gentleman shook his head. "It is difficult, but don't believe everything you hear. The employees of city hall are professional and working hard to keep Galorston running smoothly."

"So, there is no indication how any of the council members will vote?"

"Well, like you said, there are rumors. But that is all there is. The committee has kept the evidence they are reviewing confidential."

Chloe reached in front of Jess and tapped the pause button. "He continued to dodge my questions … it didn't make for a very exciting interview, unfortunately, but it was so exciting to finally be on film!"

"You look so natural," Gaby said.

"Hardly! I was terrified. I guess I held myself together, though."

Jess nodded.

Then Chloe scrolled down. "And take a look at the comments."

Jess's eyes grew wide. "Wow. They are saying Mr. Weisenberg is just as guilty as the mayor."

Gaby added, "This comment says the mayor is actually covering for Mr. Weisenberg! That it is Mr. Weisenberg's longtime friend who owns the construction business they favor."

Jess looked at Chloe. "Juicy stuff. Lou must have liked this."

"He did. Loved it. I got an email from him soon after I left the office tonight."

Gaby squeezed Chloe's shoulder. "Good job, girl."

"Thanks," Chloe said, turning and stretching. "I'm really happy I finally got my chance in front of the camera. I feel like a real reporter now."

"You killed it," Gaby encouraged, "and I'm sure you'll have more opportunities soon."

She grinned. "I hope so." Then, stifling a yawn, she said, "Well, I should go grab a few things for tomorrow and turn in. Chris is picking me up right after dance class."

Chloe paused before leaving the kitchen. "He said I should wear jeans and bring a swimsuit."

"Interesting combination," Jess said, nodding. "Where do you think he's taking you?"

"Not a clue. Do I take a bikini or a one piece?"

Gaby shrugged. "Take both."

"True," Chloe agreed. "At least then I'm prepared."

Gaby skipped past Chloe to the hall closet. "Speaking of prepared—"

Chloe blushed. "Gaby, I'm not ready yet!"

"Sweetie, I'm talking about sunscreen!" Gaby tossed it to Chloe as she returned to the kitchen. "Girl, you got a one-track mind!"

Chloe scoffed, grinning all the while. "I do not!"

Jess smirked. "Either way, we're going to need a full run down tomorrow night."

~~~~~

The drive flew by as Chris told Chloe stories from his childhood. Already an hour had passed, and Chloe had laughed more times than she could count. Now she tried to catch her breath.

She managed to ask in between laughs, "How angry was she?"

"Oh, very angry. My plan worked. She had no clue I switched out the hard-boiled eggs with regular eggs. The problem was the mess it made. I should have thought ahead and realized I would have to clean it up."

"Sounds like you deserved that."

Chris nodded. "Oh yeah, and more. I did the dishes for a week. Painful for a twelve-year-old boy."

"I bet it was. Did you learn your lesson?"

He laughed. "Of course not. I pulled more pranks after that."

Chloe loved Chris's stories. However, listening to them made her ache for a normal childhood. She would have given her left arm to have had one like he described.

Chloe tried to picture Chris as a kid. "I'm going to need to see pictures of little Chris."

"I could show you some next Saturday at my parents' house, if you're free to meet them and have dinner." He had planned on asking her today and took the opportunity she offered now. He applauded himself at how smooth it was to fit in the invitation.

Chris's eyes darted to her. He hoped he hadn't scared her. Meeting the parents was usually a big deal, he knew. However, she seemed calm, and only hesitated a second.

"That would be nice," she said. "I'm free. You'll have to let me know if I can bring anything. Dessert, maybe?"

"You don't need to. My mom loves doing all of that."

Wow, Chloe thought. *An invitation to his parents' house. I hope they will like me, knowing what his family means to him.*

She saw how he was with Todd; how close they were even though they got angry with each other every now and then. She knew they would always have each other's back when things really mattered. She imagined that's how it was between him and his parents and sister too. *A family that cared.*

They soon pulled off onto an unpaved road, and Chloe gasped at the view before them. Ahead lay a deep valley peppered with lush green trees and brushed with wildflowers. Chloe drew her eyes from the valley to the road. There was a gate coming up. A sign on it said Havers. She turned to Chris. "Now can you finally tell me where we're going?"

"A friend of mine owns a ranch in the valley. He said I could come up and borrow two of his horses for a ride."

Chloe's heart pinched at his words. *He's done this all for me?* Once again, he'd completely surprised her.

From the corner of his eye, Chris watched as her face softened and the cute little crease lines of her smile appeared.

"Really?" she said. "Wow, I've never been horseback riding before. Well, I've been on a horse, but not for a ride on a ranch like this."

"Be prepared to be wowed. The views from his land are amazing."

"I bet!" The view of the hills and the vast expanse of sky took her breath away already. She couldn't imagine it could get prettier than this.

Watching out her window as the landscape rolled by, a picture of her and Chris standing atop rocks filled her mind. She shivered as the vision faded. *A premonition?*

Chloe stole a quick glance toward Chris. She hoped he hadn't seen the look of surprise on her face. Fidgeting with her fingers, she knew it was time to talk about her ability with someone. She couldn't keep it all to herself anymore, not now when her gift was resurfacing. Gaby and Jess would understand. Would Chris too? She studied him, enjoying the angles of his face and his easy smile. He was letting her into his life. Could she let him into hers? She sighed. No, not completely. Not yet.

Chloe scrambled out of the car as soon as Chris parked alongside the barn. Standing up, she took a deep breath to calm and center herself. The smell of farmland overwhelmed her, but she recovered. *Today is going to be great!* She snapped a pic for Gaby and Jess.

A man walked near the back gate leading to the barn. He motioned to them.

Chris steered Chloe in his direction. Reaching him, Chloe felt small beside his towering frame. She noticed he wore a large cowboy hat and steel-toed boots.

"Hey, man," said Chris. "It's been a long time." Chris leaned forward to grasp the man's hand then gave him a half hug and a slap on the back. "Chloe, this is Ben. We have been friends a long time."

Chloe smiled at the greeting. *It's interesting how men greet each other. Girls give full hugs, especially good friends. But not men. With them, it's a handshake or a "bro-hug."*

"Really nice to meet you, Ben," she replied, shaking his hand.

Ben smiled. "And really nice to meet you. I didn't get to hear much about you since Chris just called me the other day and left a message saying you guys were coming." He nudged Chris. "You should come up and say hi to my wife before you leave. She'll definitely want to meet you, Chloe."

She smiled. "I'd love to. Thanks for letting us come out."

"Yeah. No problem. Let's get you guys set up, then after your ride, y'all come up to the house."

Chris and Chloe nodded.

Ben turned on the heel of his boot and started wandering through the barn. "So, I hear you're gonna need an easy horse for a beginner?" His eyes fixed on Chloe.

"Yes, please," she answered. "I've been on a horse before, but just a short ride once at a fair."

Ben glanced over his shoulder while he walked. "You aren't originally from round here, are ya? I'm gonna guess you're a Yankee."

Chloe grinned. "I'm a convert. I came here for college and never left."

"Well, good. We need more good women like you here in Texas." He smirked toward Chris. "I see one man who's glad you stayed."

Chris had been quiet while the two talked, but at Ben's words he put his arm around Chloe and brought her toward him, planting a kiss on her cheek. "That obvious?"

"Very." Ben stopped before one of the stables and led a dappled gray horse out into the open. He handed Chloe the reigns. "Here you go. This here is Buttercup. She's a real sweetheart."

Chloe took the ropes in between her fingers and observed the horse, her eyes wide. "Am I holding this right?"

"Sure, sure. Just fine." He grinned. "Like a natural."

He moved to a stall on the other side of the barn. "And here we have Studdly. He's not what you think he might be, though. Unfortunately, all he has to show for that is his name."

The horse wasn't a thoroughbred with a shiny coat, but he was special. A few scars on his front legs and head indicated he might've had a sad past. His mane was full, however, ragged at the ends.

"He is beautiful," she murmured.

Chloe handed Chris Buttercup's reins and walked forward, mesmerized by the animal. She reached her hand out toward Studdly. While she spoke to Ben, she looked right at the horse. "May I?"

Ben and Chris exchanged a look. "Go for it. He's tame, even though he wasn't well cared for before I got him. Doesn't get too attached to humans, though. He doesn't trust many of 'em."

Chloe held out her hands and Studdly sniffed them. Studdly lowered his head.

Ben laughed. "Well, I'll be. He's taken with you! Chris, you've brought a horse whisperer to my barn. Well," he smiled to Chloe, "you better ride him then. I'll put Miss Buttercup back and get you another one, Chris."

He and Chris wandered farther down, leaving Chloe to bond with Studdly. "So, I thought you said she was just a *girl you were seeing*?" Ben raised his eyebrows at his friend.

"Did I say that?" Chris snickered. "Yeah, she might mean just a little bit more to me than that."

Moments later, Ben pulled a sleek black horse from the last bay. "This here is Fern. She's a little spunky, but you can handle her."

Ben pulled Fern next to Studdly. Then he put on the saddles and had Chris and Chloe get on. They spent a while out in the fields as Ben gave Chloe a short riding lesson. Before they left, he pointed to Chris. "You should be fine. Like riding a bike, right?"

Chris laughed. "Exactly like that!"

The two of them then headed out past the tree line, riding side by side. As far as Chris could tell, Chloe seemed comfortable, remembering all of Ben's advice. He hoped she was enjoying herself.

Eventually, they turned onto a trail. Chloe steered Studdly behind Fern, since the path wasn't wide enough for both, keeping her eyes on Chris. He seemed like a pro, of course. She wondered how long it'd been since he rode a horse.

Chris turned around to check on Chloe often, and Chloe couldn't help but smile. She kept reassuring him. "I'm fine, really. Ben taught me well, and Studdly is a gentleman."

Twenty minutes later, the trail ended at a clearing. Next to it was a river with a dam blocking the flow and forming a swimming hole.

Chloe gasped, taking in the scenery. "Wow, it's gorgeous here. Did Ben build the damn?"

Chris tilted his head. "Sorta. Beavers started it, but Ben made it bigger over time."

"How long has he lived here?"

"He grew up on this land. I spent a lot of time here as a kid in the summer."

"Huh. I didn't realize we were so close to where you grew up."

"Yeah, my parents are west of here, another fifteen minutes or so. Mom would drop me off on her way to work. I'd help out in the barn in the morning, then in the fields in the afternoon."

Chloe narrowed her eyes slightly. "I'm envious of you."

"Why? You always wanted to spend time on a ranch?"

Chris slid off Fern and tied her close enough to the water for her to drink. Then he did the same for Studdly. Finally, he turned to Chloe and held out his arms. She kicked one leg around and lowered into Chris's hands.

"Well, yeah," Chloe admitted. "That is something to be envious of, but more because you have a lot of friends and family. I can tell they really care about one another, and you about them."

Chris let his hands slide off Chloe's waist. "Yeah, I suppose I am lucky that way." His voice lowered then. "It must be hard not seeing your parents or knowing your family."

Inwardly, Chloe cringed. *You don't know the half of it.* She shrugged and simply said, "I have Jess and Gaby. They're my family."

Chris sighed. "They are great. I agree." He took her hand in his. *I wish you'd let me in.*

Chloe bit her lip. "It's hard to talk about."

He squeezed her fingers gently. "While I'd love for you to confide in me, baby, I can wait."

"That is very sweet." She scanned his face. *But what if I did tell you?*

They wandered a bit alongside the river, heading in the direction of the swimming hole. Chloe nodded to the water and the rocks above them. She recognized them as the rocks from her vision earlier. "How deep is that? Deep enough to jump from the rocks there, I guess?"

"You got it. That was a summer project of ours when we were about fourteen. We dredged the bottom out to make it deeper so we could dive off those rocks."

Chloe pinched his cheek and smiled up at him. "So little Chris spent a lot of time here? Cute."

Her smile started to fade, but she kept her eyes on his. Taking a deep breath to steady herself, she opened up. "I didn't have it as good as you. There are very few childhood memories that I want to actually remember."

Chris heard her voice quake. He rested a hand on her arm.

"My memories included a very grouchy dad," Chloe continued as her courage mounted. "Sometimes he was very angry. Sometimes he would be angry enough to hit me. It was usually a spank when I was little and a face slap when I got older. Once I fell and hit my head, needing a few stitches."

Chris winced. Chloe bravely forged on. "My mom wasn't at all like my dad. She was quiet, never angry. I used to dream she would rescue me and together we'd leave my dad. She never did intervene. He probably would have hit her if she had. I never saw him hit her, but that doesn't mean he didn't."

Chris couldn't keep the growl from his voice. "What was his excuse for hitting you?"

Chloe reached for his hand, suddenly desiring his touch. "Random reasons. Sometimes I wasn't where he thought I was, or I didn't give him the answer he wanted. He always asked me, 'What were you thinking?' And tell me that he couldn't look at me."

Chris clenched his jaw. "I've seen children who have been abused before—unfortunately, more than a handful at my job. None of your teachers ever figured it out?"

"No." Her voice caught in her throat. "No one noticed."

Chris turned to her, bringing his forehead close to hers. He wove his fingers through her hair. His face softened. "I'm sorry you had to go through that."

Chloe swallowed the lump in her throat. "It's okay. I learned how to get by and it's over now. I used to have anxiety and bad dreams. In college I got help from a counselor. She taught me how to manage my anxiety and deal with my poor childhood. I'm okay now." Her gaze held his. *Did I really just tell him all of this? It feels like a blur. But good too.* "I wanted you to know about my past. I can still be a bit shy with confrontation and slow to trust."

He caressed her cheek. "It doesn't change how I feel about you. I still want to build a relationship with you."

"I didn't think it would. Everything until now—every action you've made, every word you have said—told me you aren't like them. You're honorable and kind."

"Thank you. I'm glad you trusted me to tell me."

"There's something about this place. Serene. I feel at peace here." Chloe held his stare and whispered, "you make me feel at peace."

"It makes me happy to hear you say that. I will always try to treat you the way you should be."

Placing both hands on his cheeks and rising on her tiptoes, Chloe brought her lips to his. She backed down flat on her feet after a few moments. "Well, you brought me here for fun, so show me some fun!"

Chris smiled. "No doubt! Swim or eat first?"

"Swim ... but how am I supposed to change?"

"Easy! Over there, behind the bushes. And I won't peek. I promise. Scout's honor!"

"Seriously, you won't?" She would never admit it to him, but she wouldn't mind if he did. Just a small peek, anyway.

"Man of my word! You can't peek either! I'm going over there." He pointed to a row of trees.

Chloe giggled. "Okay. You have my word too!"

Chloe got her bag from Studdly's saddle then glanced inside at her swimsuit options. *Better go with the one piece if we're diving off rocks.* "Be right back!" And she dashed behind the bushes.

As she changed, she yelled, "Am I going to get poison ivy being back here?"

Chuckling, Chris yelled back, "Probably! Why? Does that scare you?"

Chloe rolled her eyes. "It probably should. I never had it. Just heard it was bad."

"You heard right. It sucks!"

She emerged from the bushes as Chris finished pulling up his suit. Chloe grinned, catching a brief view of that tight butt she liked. *Hmm*, she thought, *not bad.* She walked back to Studdly and set the bag down again. When she turned back around, she noticed Chris looking at her. It made her feel good to have his eyes on her. She propped a hand up on her hip and grinned. "Disappointed?" She motioned behind her with her thumb. "Diving and bikinis don't work."

"Not disappointed in the least." He said the words slowly and drawn out, taking a long look over her. Head to toe and back again. "You're beautiful."

While she appreciated the attention, too much made her uncomfortable. She turned away, asking, "So how do we do this? Check the water out first for snakes, or jump right in?"

Snapping out of the trance she'd put him in, Chris studied the water. "We'll ease in over there." He pointed to an area where rocks stuck up above the mud and grasses. "Here, I brought you old sneakers to wear so you don't scratch your feet up." He handed her a pair about her size.

She wrinkled her nose. "Where'd these come from? Please don't tell me an ex-girlfriend."

Chris scoffed. "God, no! I don't have an ex-girlfriend that ever came here with me. They have all been too prissy."

Chloe laughed. "Well, that opens up a whole line of interesting questions, but I'll save those for later."

"I'm hoping you'll forget. Moving on … they are my mom's. She left them at my place and said we could take them."

Chloe leaned over and slipped them on. They were only a little bit bigger than her size, which made them good enough for swimming.

Chris took her hand and led her over the rocks and down toward the water hole. Wearing jeans on the horse ride had been hot, so it was good to get in the cool water. Chloe was surprised that she could see the bottom well. From farther back, the sunlight made the water look murky. But up close, she could see nearly everything.

They waded gently, checking if there was anything they needed to avoid. When they got to the deepest part of the water, Chris went under and examined the bottom. He'd wanted to be sure they wouldn't hit rocks while diving.

Resurfacing, he took a breath and treaded water. "I should have asked you if you can swim. I see you can, though."

Chloe was treading next to him. "We had swim class in high school." She left out the parts about not knowing how to swim until she was fourteen and the way her classmates made fun of her mercilessly while she learned. "I wasn't on the swim team but can stay afloat."

"Can you dive?"

"Kind of. You can give me some pointers."

He grabbed the hand closest to him and pulled her toward him, in the direction of the embankment. "This is the best place to get out. Ben and I set up the rocks like steps. See?" He helped her find her footing and had her get out first.

They then climbed up to the rocks above, which didn't look that high up until they were on them.

Chloe glanced over the edge and took a deep breath. "Higher than it looks from down there."

"Yeah, it's deceiving." He then motioned to the water and told her roughly where to aim when she jumped. "Feeling okay?"

She gave a shaky smile. "I think so."

"Great. We can jump together, if you want?"

Chloe nodded. "Just the first few times until I get used to it."

They walked to the end and peered down. Chloe felt Chris tighten his hold on her hand as he said, "On three. One … Two … Three!"

Chloe took a deep breath as her feet left the rocks and air rushed over her body. She fought the urge to shriek. The cool water enveloped her as her legs cut through the surface.

They came up together. He saw her start to grin. "So?" he asked.

"Good. I'm good."

Chris swam over to the rock steps and dove in while Chloe treaded. *He's good*, thought Chloe, watching as he arched his shoulders and ducked into the water with a small splash. When he came up, she asked, "Were you on the swim team?"

Chris shook his head, spraying her with water droplets. Chloe whooped but didn't object. "No, just years of summers here."

Chloe examined the rock again. She wanted to prove to herself, and to Chris, that she could face her fears. "Okay. My turn!" she said, scampering to the edge. "Don't laugh too hard—my ego is fragile."

Chloe put her hands above her head and took a deep breath again as she pushed off. Her face and torso hit the water at almost the same time as her arms. When she resurfaced, she saw Chris at the side waiting. He smiled but said nothing.

She moved closer to him. "I know—not good. I think that was more of a belly flop."

"Maybe, but you looked damn fine doing it!"

They continued jumping and diving until Chris realized he was getting hungry. "Want some lunch?"

"Yes, I'm starving!"

They made their way over to the horses. Chris pulled a towel out of his bag for Chloe and a blanket for them both to sit on. Then he grabbed the little cooler he'd packed and took another towel out to dry himself off.

Sitting down crossed-legged, Chloe wondered if this was what normal kids got to feel like in summertime, so carefree and happy. She took the water bottle and sandwich Chris offered her. After a few bites, she said, "You made this? So good, thank you."

"Yeah, this morning before I picked you up."

Chloe leaned back on her elbows and tilted her head toward the sun. "I love this place. It's so beautiful. And I can't believe you got to spend summers here."

"Yeah, it was lots of fun, but we never had hot girls like you here."

She gave him a sidelong glance and took the grapes he offered her. "I bet you did. You probably had Friday night parties here skinny dipping."

He laughed. "God, no. Ben's parents would have skinned us alive. Plus, it takes too long to get out here."

Chloe leaned back on one arm and munched on a grape. "You make me laugh. I like you."

Chris put down his water bottle and moved his face closer. She thought he was going to kiss her, but instead he moved to her neck. Chloe dropped her head back as his soft kisses peppered her collarbone. She had no idea the skin there was so sensitive. It sent shivers down her arms.

He raised his hand to her shoulder and used his fingertips to trace the top of her swimsuit, toward her cleavage and back again. Feeling her shift against him, he paused. "Is this okay?"

"Yes," she breathed out.

At the center he dipped a finger down her suit and traced the skin there. This time his finger brushed against her nipple, making it tighten and sending warm pinpricks to her core. He repeated this again and again while he continued to kiss her neck and collarbone. Daring to go a bit farther, he then licked her ear.

Chloe lay back on the blanket when her arm could no longer hold her up. The moment Chris's tongue touched her ear, she stifled a laugh, but quickly followed it with a sigh of contentment. *He really knows what he's doing.*

Chris swung a leg over both of hers and positioned himself to be partly on top of her. He met her gaze. "May I?" he asked as pulled the strap of her suit slightly down off her shoulder.

Chloe closed her eyes. "Mmm-hmm."

He pulled her suit further down and used that same gentle brushing motion with his fingers, teasing her body making it tense and tingle.

The kisses he had been lazily giving her neck became more desperate as he made his way up her chin. His tongue dove deep in her mouth with needy movements, making her blood boil. The gentle motions he had been using on her breast changed to his full hand grabbing and rubbing her.

Chloe's brain had long turned to mush and was so foggy with lust she found herself reaching for him. Her hand grasped his back then slid down to his waist. It was her turn to dip her fingers and touch him. She pulled the top of his suit down, exposing part of that tight butt she had seen earlier. She started with slow circling motions and became headier when he moved his mouth to her nipple.

She left out a moan and pulled his suit further down. Chris realized how far they were taking this. He slowed and brought his face back to hers. "If we go any further, I don't think I'll be able to stop."

Chloe was breathing fast and shallow. Her wild eyes searched his face, pleading for more. "I don't want to stop."

"Neither do I, but I think we should."

She let her hand fall from his hip, disappointed and relieved she hadn't made it fully around to the front. "You're probably right, but the pounding in my head and the burning in my belly is telling me to keep going. I want you."

Chris grinned at that. "You don't know how much I want you. I'm dying here, literally dying. Your body is so erotic."

"Erotic? Really?" She giggled.

"God, yes. You really don't know how unbelievably gorgeous and sexy you are, do you? You are blowing my mind."

Another giggle slipped out of her mouth as she pulled her suit back into place. "So what's next on the agenda?"

Reluctantly, Chris sat up and reached for her hand. "Well, I have some great views to show you. Then we'll head back and meet up with Ben and Shannon. How does that sound?"

Chloe smiled, feeling his fingers wrap around hers. "Cool. I like that plan."

~~~~~

Later, on their way home, Chloe leaned her head back. "Today was great. I loved everything about it—Studdly, riding, swimming, and your friends. I knew today would be fun, but I didn't expect it to be this much fun. Ben and Shannon are great. I hope they meant it when they said we are welcome anytime. I'd love to visit again!"

Chris smiled. "I'm glad you had such a great time. They wouldn't have said it if they didn't mean it. They told me when you stepped out how great they think you are."

"Aw. That's sweet."

Chris's mind started to wander as he focused on the road. *I wanted her today— bad. Patience. She needs time to acclimate to all of the new experiences. But God, she tasted so good today.* Her body was the right mix of soft and tight. She had long toned legs he wanted wrapped around his waist. He wanted more of those full breasts that fit perfectly in his hand. And that mouth, he wanted that mouth on him, all over him.

How he would continue to stay sane while he waited was unfathomable. It would take everything he had to not touch her more deeply. To not let her touch him.

Chris didn't realize how lost he was in his thoughts until he noticed how hard he was. He glanced in her direction, relieved to see her head leaning against the car window and eyes closed. He tried to focus on something else, but his eyes kept drifting back to her. *She's so perfect. Too perfect.*

And I think I'm in love with her.

~~~~~

It didn't take long to get back to her place. Traffic moved quickly, and adrenaline from the day with Chloe gave Chris a bit of a lead foot. After reaching her street and parking, he took a deep breath and leaned over to wake her.

Chloe hadn't realized she had dozed off. She felt something gently brushing her cheek, and she opened her eyes. Looking around, she noticed she was home and Chris was still there with her. "Long day," she mumbled, disentangling herself from the seatbelt.

"Yes, but it went fast. Time always does when I'm with you."

Chloe smiled and stretched. "Thanks for driving, and for the date."

Still caressing her cheek, Chris gave her a brief kiss. "It was so much fun. Here, let me walk you up."

They climbed out of the car and headed to the stoop. Standing on the bottom step, Chris handed her bag to her.

"Don't you want to come in?" The question Chloe asked caused Chris's head to spin with possibilities again.

"Not this time. We're both tired. But maybe see you tomorrow?"

Chloe reached out to give him a hug. "Okay. Call me."

Chris watched her walk in and wave before closing the door. Walking back to his car, he hoped someday he wouldn't be saying goodnight to her outside but staying the night and sleeping next to her.

Chloe dropped her stuff inside the door after she locked it. "Gaby! Jess! I'm back. Where are you?"

"In here," they called from the living room. Jess paused the movie they were watching when Chloe walked in.

Gaby noticed the stars in her best friend's eyes. "That great of a day?"

"It was so fun. I'm dying to tell you all of it, but I am so gross. I need a shower."

"How about in the morning?" Jess suggested. "I think you're going to be toast after a shower. We'll have Sunday morning story hour."

Chloe nodded, suddenly feeling the weight of sleep drape over her. "Perfect. Goodnight, girls."

~~~~~

Chapter 15

So, are you in love?"

Chloe raised an eyebrow at Gaby. She and her two friends were enjoying the blueberry crumb cake Chloe made and the mid-morning air on their deck as Chloe recounted yesterday's romantic date at the ranch for "Sunday morning story hour." Gaby and Jess sat quietly with their chins propped on their hands and their eyes wide. They didn't interrupt once, only letting out murmurs of jealousy and *awes*.

Chloe had given this exact question a lot of thought the night before. And the answer was clear. Leaning toward her friends and bringing her voice to a whisper, she said, "I think so!"

"I knew it!" Gaby pumped the air with her arm.

Chloe buried her cheeks in her hands. "I can't believe I just said that! Do you think it's too soon?"

Jess patted her arm. "It's how you feel. Trust yourself, Chloe. More importantly, don't overthink this."

"I'll try not to. I promise." Chloe patted both on the shoulders. Then she sighed. "Not trying to change the subject, because I have loved telling you about yesterday, but I have something I want to talk to you about. There's something that I haven't always been so open about with you both and it's been nagging at me lately."

Gaby and Jess exchanged a look. "Spill, girl," Gaby encouraged.

Chloe took a breath and steadied herself. *You can do it.* "It's not something that happened to me. It's more about who I am."

"Okay," said Jess, leaning forward.

Chloe shook her head. "Hearing me say that makes it sound like I've been living a lie. It's not like that. Maybe a better way of putting it is: what I am capable of."

Teetering on the edge of suspense, Jess blurted out, "Out with it already!"

"Sorry, sorry," Chloe said as she swept her hand through the air. "Before the accident, I used to have a very keen sense of intuition. Sometimes actual premonitions." Chloe looked into her friends' eyes. *Please don't think I'm weird.* But only confusion and shock registered there. "I'm sorry I never told you. Please don't hate me!"

Gaby moved her chair closer. "We could never hate you, Chloe. We love you. Please tell us more."

"Yeah," urged Jess.

"Well, I don't know if you really call it premonitions. I sometimes would get feelings or see visions. Other times I would have a physical reaction, like feeling pain or getting sick." She paused. A weight felt lifted from her shoulders. *I should've told them a long time ago.* "I would just know or sense things. It could be why my dad was always angry. He and my mom knew I could do it. I learned very quickly that the more I let on that I knew something, the more trouble I would be in. I always wondered if my mom also had this ability. We both were very quiet and kept to ourselves. It seemed to be the only way to survive living with my dad." She gave a sad smile. "Anyway, I could always sense both good and bad things. Sometimes clearly, and other times not so well. But after the accident, nothing was clear. My sense of intuition was significantly weakened, and I couldn't predict a thing. But recently, things have changed. I can feel things again. Visions are popping up randomly too."

She held up her hand. "One more thing. The night of the fight between Rob and Kirk, I felt sick when we found out the wine had not come from Chris. When I raised my glass to taste it, I saw blood and it had a pungent odor. I knew something was wrong, but I had no idea how or why it was wrong. When it all unfolded and I threw up outside, it wasn't just because of the terrible front-row view we had or my bad childhood memories. It was my physical reaction to the awareness in my body of something evil."

Gaby and Jess gasped. "Oh, that's horrible!"

Chloe nodded, remembering it all.

Gaby tilted her head, and her shoulders softened. "Oh, Chloe, you've been carrying this burden on your shoulders for so long and doing it all alone. I am so glad you told us now."

"Thank you, Gabs." Chloe sighed with relief. "I was scared I would see disgust in your eyes if I ever told you. I couldn't bear losing either of you, so that's why I've never said anything."

"Your family may have deserted you, but that's on them. We never will."

Jess shook her head. "Never. We could never look at you any other way than as our Chloe."

"Thank you." Her mind started drifting again. "I think I still have a lot more to learn about it. Now that I can admit to myself and you that I have this ability,

I wonder if I could strengthen it more. Maybe channel it in some way."

Jess looked between Gaby and Chloe. "So, the lottery. How do you feel about playing that?"

Chloe laughed. "It means the world to me to have you both."

Jess stood up and started collecting dishes. "Back at ya. So, changing the topic, if you don't mind … I have some good news and some interesting news."

"Oh?" This earned getting looks from Gaby and Chloe.

"I finally got in touch with Seth last night. I was so glad I finally heard from him. It had been months. I really miss him *and* my family."

"Great!" said Gaby. "I know you've been wondering about everyone since your dad's visit."

Jess nodded. "Seth's doing really well. He didn't complain as much as I would if I were living in the Middle East. He just said he was busy, tired, and dirty all the time. He will be coming back to the United States next year sometime. I am hoping I can see him."

Carrying dishes through the door, Chloe looked back over her shoulder. "That's awesome. Does this mean he will be staying?"

Jess followed Chloe in with an armful. "His tour will be up. He has to decide if he will re-up."

"I'd love to meet him sometime."

"Me too, Jess!" Gaby called out through the door. She had the last of the dishes.

"I talked to him about Dad's visit and what I learned about Mom. He feels like I do—bad. He might try to go see them. We discussed both timing a visit around then."

Jess started loading the dishwasher. "Next year is a long way off, though. It seems too long to wait. My sister and Mom are a mess, which is making things difficult for my dad and Johnny. I am thinking of going soon—like next week even—to visit them. I'd like to see if there is anything I can do."

Gaby touched Jess's arm. "Are you sure? It's been years."

"Yes, I'm sure. I probably can't do anything immediately, but I want to see if I can build some kind of relationship or fix the one I have with Mom and Marisa."

"If it makes you feel better, then it's the right decision," said Chloe. "I assume you'll go see Mrs. Snyder?" She raised a teapot. "Any takers for tea?"

Jess nodded. "Yes, please. I will definitely try to catch up with her. I am thinking of leaving here Friday afternoon and maybe catch her for a late dinner or for breakfast on Saturday."

Gaby took out three mugs. "Where will you stay?"

"A hotel. There is one not too far."

Chloe poured the hot water. "We're always here if you need us,"

Gaby grabbed her mug. "Definitely. Chloe will be meeting Chris's parents Saturday, but I'll be home all weekend." She shined a teasing smile in their direction.

~~~~~

Jess was able to get out of work at lunch on Friday. This allowed her enough time to make it to Oklahoma for dinner with Mrs. Snyder.

Around the time she crossed the border between Texas and Oklahoma, she tapped Chloe's name on her phone. "Hey, Chloe. Do you have a few minutes? I'm starting to get anxious. I can't believe I'm going this direction across the state lines."

"Of course I have time. I can only imagine what you must be feeling, I don't know if I could ever go home again. If I did, I couldn't go alone. You are so brave."

Jess let out a sigh of irritation. "Don't say never. That is when you jinx it. I swore when I crossed over into Texas I would never go back."

"Too late! I've already said it. So you're coming with me when I find myself going back." They shared a laugh. Then Chloe continued. "Let's focus on the good that will come out of this weekend. You'll be able to make it in time to see Mrs. Snyder tonight."

"Yeah," Jess said with lightness in her voice. "I am grateful for that. Even though we've stayed in touch, it has been years since I've seen her. We are going to meet at a little Italian restaurant near the library. And a block down from the restaurant is the ice cream parlor where Johnny works. Dad told me he was working until nine tonight."

On the other end of the phone, Chloe nodded. "It will be good for you to see them. Seven years is a long time."

"Very long. I wonder how much Marisa and Mom have changed. I haven't seen pictures of them in ages either. I see Johnny's posts, but Marisa didn't accept my request to follow her."

Chloe said, "I'm almost home. I have to run for now. Gaby and I are going to Chris and Todd's place for dinner and to watch football with some of their friends. Put aside thoughts about Marisa and your mom for now and listen to some country music. Focus on tonight. Call us later if you need us."

~~~~~

Out of all of Chris's friends, Chloe had only met Rex so far, but tonight there would be others there. She wanted to look good. "What about this?" she asked Gaby, striking a pose as she entered the doorway of her friend's bedroom.

Gaby scrunched up her nose. "No! The second one you had on is way better. The black one."

Chloe gave Gaby a thumbs-up. "Oh! Be right back." Gaby watched her disappear down the hall. Moments later, she returned, wearing the black shirt Gaby recommended and holding two pairs of heels. "Which ones?"

Gaby pointed to the silver-and-black strappy ones. "Those. They'll show off that great pedicure you got today."

"Great. Thanks!" Chloe dashed back down the hall again, yelling over her shoulder. "I only need five more minutes. You?"

"It's pushing it. My hair isn't behaving."

"I thought you looked great!"

It took them longer than five minutes to get out the door. There were several trays of food and bags they had to load in the trunk. When they pulled up to Chris's house, Chloe saw Rex walking with a few guys up to the door. They stopped and turned when the girls parked.

Rex came forward. "Hey, how are you?" He nodded to both. "Here, load me up." He stuck his arms out.

"We're good, thanks," Gaby answered as she reached in the trunk and pulled out a foil tray wrapped in a towel. "This one's probably still hot. I took it out of the oven right before we left." She handed it to him and put one more tray on top.

One of the other guys came over then. "Hey, I'm Eric."

Chloe stuck out her hand. "Hiya. I'm Chloe, and this is Gaby."

"Hey, Chloe and Gaby. Here, you can load me up too."

Chloe grabbed the cookie trays and balanced them on Eric's outstretched arms. "Thanks so much."

"Yeah, sure. Want me to come back?"

Chloe shook her head. "That's okay. We can get the rest."

Gaby and Chloe turned to head inside, bags of chips and more dessert in their arms.

Chris came out on the porch just as they were climbing the steps. "I heard two hotties are here." He snickered as he said it. "Here, let me take that."

"Oh, really? Is that what you heard?" Chloe gave him a peck on the cheek as he took the tray she was carrying.

"Word for word." He tossed a bag of chips Gaby had been carrying on top of the dessert tray.

"Thanks."

As Chris walked past her, Chloe couldn't help but check out his butt. *It looks so great in those jeans.*

Gaby elbowed her. "Busted."

Chloe laughed.

Chris glanced over his shoulder. "Did I just hear you giggle?"

Chloe beamed at him. "Maybe."

Chris introduced the girls to a couple of his friends as they walked in. Chloe felt their eyes cataloging them as they talked. *They're probably judging me as the new girlfriend and Gaby as the new girlfriend's single friend.*

Chris set the trays down next to others lining the kitchen bar. "Your stuff looks amazing! What is this one?" He pointed to one dish.

"It's my sweet potato salsa," Gaby answered. "You must have it with these chips, though. So good paired together."

"Awesome." He turned back around and now that his arms were free, reached for Chloe and pulled her in. "*You* also look and smell amazing!"

Chloe blushed. "So do you." She sidled closer, whispering, "I giggled earlier because Gaby caught me staring at your butt in those jeans."

He gave her a playful squeeze. "Mmm, is that right?"

"Definitely yes!"

Chris reluctantly let her go so he could finish introductions. After winding his way around the room, he reached a couple seated at the kitchen table. "And this is Shane and his girlfriend Belinda."

"Nice to meet you," Chloe said.

They waved. "Hey, Chloe."

Chloe's eyes swept over the rest of the room.

The game was already on, and most of the guys hovered around the big-screen TV. The few women there chatted in the kitchen. They were all very friendly. One of them, Sandy, was overly friendly to Chloe. Something about the fake-sounding, sugary-sweet way she talked and the exaggerated interest in her rattled her.

"How long have you been dating?' Sandy asked, her eyes falling on Chris.

Chloe looked around, searching for an out. Gaby had her back turned and Chris was talking to Todd. *No way to avoid her, I guess.* "A month or two."

Sandy raised her eyebrows. "Oh, I see."

Chloe shrugged, trying to show her disinterest.

"Well, tell me everything about how you met," Sandy asked as if they were best friends.

"Through work," Chloe said, keeping it simple.

Still eager for more, Sandy pursed her lips and continued. "So, who asked who out?"

Slightly smiling and reminding herself to be friendly, Chloe kept her voice steady. "Chris asked me."

Sandy slipped in quickly, "Oh yeah. Typical Chris. He asked me out too when we dated."

Chloe's stomach plummeted. She stammered. "Oh. That's nice."

Stealing a quick glance over her shoulder, she was able to make eye contact with Gaby, who had turned around. She widened her eyes, giving Gaby "the look." In a few quick strides, Gaby moved beside Chloe. "Hey there. Sandy, right?" Gaby put her hand out.

"Right."

"Sorry, I'm going to steal Chloe for a few minutes. We'll be right back." Gaby moved toward the back door and stepped outside. "What is her deal?"

Chloe shook her head and blurted. "Chris dated her!"

Gaby's shook her head in disbelief. "No way!"

"Yes way. She slipped that tidbit in there after she grilled me," Chloe said through gritted teeth.

"I'm having a hard time believing he dated such a busybody," Gaby said, pulling Chloe further into the backyard.

Chloe crossed her arms. "He had to have. I don't think she would lie about it."

Gaby rolled her eyes to the darkening sky. "She's just jealous."

"I guess so," Chloe said, feeling disheartened.

Gaby put her hands to Chloe's shoulders. "Don't give her a second thought. He's with you."

"I know …" Chloe lost her train of thought when she felt a prickle on her neck. She turned her head to the back door.

Sauntering up to them was one of Chris's friends she had met earlier. By now, she had forgotten his name. He asked, "Who moved the party out here?"

"Uh, hey," Chloe said. Next to her, she heard Gaby shift. *Is she nervous too?* Chloe started to feel sick to her stomach.

Clearly drunk, the guy didn't take the social cues and moved in quick. He put his arms around Gaby and Chloe. "Remember me?"

Chloe looked to Gaby then back at the man. "Actually, no. I can't think of your name."

"Rick." The way he annunciated the "k" sent spittle flying in their direction. "I came to see if you ladies were interested in having some fun?"

Chloe's mind shot back to the night of Jeremy's attack. *No. Not this time!* She thought of Ed then. What would he have said to the class if anyone was in this situation? She stood taller and raised her chin. "Back. Off. Rick."

"Naw, now come on," Rick slurred. As he pushed in closer to them, they could smell the alcohol on his breath.

He licked his lips. "I'd love to have two beautiful women like you in my bed at the same time. How 'bout it, huh? Let's get out of here."

Gaby tried to slink away, but Rick's hand grabbed her shoulder and held her in place. In reply, she shoved him. "Seriously. Back. Off."

Rick lost his balance and took an awkward step back. When he righted himself, his eyes focused on Chloe. He stepped forward, bringing his hands close to her waist.

"I don't think so," she said, and used the heel of her hand to give an upward jab to his nose. Grabbing his face, he yelled, "What the hell!"

Inside, the game went to commercial break. Todd came out to the kitchen and stopped to look out the sliding back door. When his eyes landed on the people in the yard, he muttered under his breath, "Shit."

"Rick!" he called as he made his way to them. He grabbed Rick by the arm and hefted him up. "Come on. You gotta go." Todd led him around the side of the house.

Chloe muttered, "What a friggin' jerk."

Inside, one of the girls yelled, "Hey Chris! Rick is acting up again!"

Chris jumped up and bolted to the kitchen. "Huh? What do you mean?"

"Todd just escorted him out front."

He didn't see Gaby and Chloe out back as he went through the hall and out the front door. Todd already had Rick sitting down.

In just a few strides, Chris made it to them, noting Rick's bloody nose. "What did he do?"

Todd looked at him with a blank stare.

Chris stared back, waiting. "What?"

"Shit, I don't want to be the one to say it!"

"You have to now. What?"

"Fine. He was hitting on Chloe and Gaby. He tried grabbing them—"

Chris snarled. "Dammit."

Chris focused on Rick and brought his face very close. "Listen, man. I don't want to see you again. Got it? You've reached a new low tonight and upset people I really care about. You're lucky I don't knock some sense into you. But I see someone already did that for me." He turned away then. "Come on, Todd. Leave him here."

They turned to walk inside and found they had quite the audience. The only ones he didn't see were Chloe and Gaby. He muttered under his breath. "Dammit." He was going to be seriously pissed if this completely ruined their night.

He strode past the crowd and found them in the kitchen. They were cleaning up the food trays and whispering.

Chloe looked up when she heard his footsteps. "Hey."

He headed straight toward her. "I heard what happened. Are you okay?"

"We're fine." Chloe bit her lip.

Chris's face hardened. "Todd said Rick had his hands on you."

Chloe shook her head. "Just on our shoulders. He was disgusting though and asked if we wanted a threesome."

Gaby smirked. "Chloe took care of him."

Chris stared at Chloe and remembered Rick's bloody nose. "Wow. Nice shot. And shit, I'm sorry it even had to happen. I didn't see him drinking so much."

"It's okay. You shouldn't have to babysit him." Chloe licked her lips; suddenly aware her mouth was going dry. It wasn't Rick's crass actions that bothered her. It was the image of Sandy kissing Chris that riled her.

Chris lightly touched her elbow and led her out the back door. "You sure you're okay? You still seem upset."

"I'm fine with Rick. Whatever." Chloe shrugged. "That was not the first or probably the last time we've been asked something disgusting. And besides, I proved I can take care of myself now."

Chris reached for her shoulders to pull her closer. "You definitely did that. But what's wrong?"

Chloe swallowed. Her eyes met his. "Sandy."

Chris sighed. "What did she say?"

"She asked a lot of prying questions about you and me. Then she topped it off with telling me that you dated. Is that true?"

Chris leaned his forehead close to hers. "Well, yes." He sighed again. "But I couldn't stand her. No manners. In everyone's business all the time. And so demanding. She comes to these things with her best friend Nat, who's dating my friend Lance. Always gets in someone's way. I'm sorry I didn't get to pull you aside before she got to you … But that's no excuse. I should have warned you. And told you who she was."

Chloe pulled back. "I wish you had. It was really awkward."

"I'm sorry. I was an ass."

The corners of Chloe's mouth turned slowly into a soft smile. "You kinda were."

He shook his head. "I was a full-on ass. And I'm sorry."

Chloe let out a breath. "It's okay. Everyone has a past."

Chris rested his forehead on Chloe's. "You're sure?"

"Yeah, I'm sure," she said, blinking hard. *Or at least I think so.*

He took Chloe's hand and walked into the kitchen to see Gaby setting up the trays of cookies.

She looked up and smiled. "I thought everyone might want dessert after watching the show."

"So, you're not upset either?" Chris asked. He couldn't believe how calm the two of them seemed.

Gaby moved closer as people reached for the trays she had just uncovered. "No big deal. Don't sweat it."

Chloe nodded in agreement. "One positive that came out of it was that we got to practice our self-defense moves from class."

Chris grinned. "God, you're cute. And feisty," he said before planting a solid kiss square on her lips.

~~~~~

Chapter 16

The following morning, Chloe and Gaby called Jess on their way to dance class. "How's Oklahoma?

"Seeing Mrs. Snyder and Johnny last night was great. I've missed them. I confirmed I don't care for this place, though. It's very depressing."

"When are you going to see your mom and Marisa?"

"Lunchtime today. Daddy arranged for me to come over. I hope they don't throw food at me!"

"Wear a black shirt if it's a risky situation," Gaby snickered.

Jess laughed. "Funny! I didn't think of that. Maybe I should change—I have on light pink!"

Chloe smiled, laughing with her friends. "Well, sorry to make this short, but we just got to the studio. Call us later and tell us how it went. Stay strong. We love you!"

"Will do. Have fun, ladies!"

Gaby parked at the back of the studio. "So what's your take on Jess's trip back home?"

Chloe twisted to grab her bag from the backseat. "She's handling it well. Seems like she is excited under a case of nerves—which is completely normal given the circumstances."

Gaby turned toward Chloe. "You're right. She's one tough chick. I admire her ability to keep calm when things are spiraling out of control. Do you remember when Jackie fell down the flight of stairs in the dorm senior year? While we were all freaking out, Jess was kneeling at her side reassuring her."

Chloe nodded. "Yeah. That night I told Jess she should have been pre-med instead of computer science."

"That girl is going places. She'll probably end up going to med school and design robotic equipment for surgeons," Gaby said while she worked her way out of the car.

"You're on to something there!" Chloe chuckled. "That would be just like her."

Gaby shined a smile at Chloe and nodded toward the studio. "Let's head in. I don't want to be late."

~~~~~

After dance class, Chloe came home to shower but threw on some pajamas to sit and get some writing in before Chris arrived. Writing always calmed her, and she needed to stay calm now. Meeting Chris's parents was big, as far as she was concerned, and she wanted to make a good impression.

Chloe chose to focus on the mental health articles for work. October would be here soon and given the way Lou had been assigning more work to her lately, she knew this project needed some TLC early. Now that the plan was outlined, the next step was the research. Since researching was her thing, it would distract her well today.

The minutes ticked by, and Chloe soon lost track of time, like she often did when writing. Before she knew it, the doorbell rang. She caught a glimpse of the time. "Crap! He's here!"

She dashed for the door and opened it quickly. "Oh my God. I lost track of time!"

Chris stepped inside and looked Chloe over. "Cute."

Chloe blushed and gave him a quick kiss. "I need fifteen minutes to change. I'm so sorry. I'll be quick, I promise!"

"There's no rush. Take your time."

Chloe took note of his casual shorts and shirt. "Dress casual, huh?"

He nodded.

"Here, come upstairs." She led him to her bedroom, noting with a hint of mischief that she'd never had a man in her bedroom while she changed before. She motioned to Chris to sit down.

A devilish grin formed on his face as Chloe moved around. He couldn't help it. She was adorable. "What you have on is good for me."

"Hardy-har. Like I could wear this to meet your parents."

His mouth took the shape of a wide grin. "What? I like your little shorts!"

Chloe shook her head. She turned and grabbed the two outfits she had picked out earlier. Holding them up, she asked, "Which is better?"

He pointed to the dress. "That one looks more comfortable. My parents are laid back."

Chloe darted into the bathroom. Through the closed door, she asked, "How long will it take for us to drive to your parents' place?"

"About an hour and half. It's just a bit past Ben's place, away from

Galorston."

Chloe opened the door and moved in front of the mirror. She pulled her hair into a twist and clipped it. To top off the look, she added a pair of dangly earrings and a sparkly necklace. Moving quickly, she swept back into her room and went to her closet to pick out shoes. She grabbed sandals off the shelf. *Perfect.*

She turned to him, slinging a bag over her shoulder. "Okay, I'm 'meet the parents' ready."

"You look great."

Chris stood and reached for her upper arms with both of his hands, stilling her. "I'm sorry again about last night. Do you still think I'm an ass?"

Chloe shrugged. "I don't think you're an ass anymore."

"But you're not laughing, so it's still bothering you."

Chloe's eyes dropped. "Yeah, I guess. It was weird."

He used a finger to tilt her face upward. Her eyelashes fluttered as she met his eyes. He watched her for a moment. "Sandy shouldn't have come at you like that. Shows you how small she really is."

Chloe took a step back. "Let's just drop it." She glanced at the clock beside her bed. "We should get going so we're not late."

He followed Chloe as she made her way to the door. "Okay, but I don't really want to drop it if it still bothers you."

Chloe inwardly sighed as she started down the stairs. *I don't want to keep talking about her. She consumed enough of my thoughts last night when I tried to fall asleep, picturing you with her.*

Chris followed her to the front door, watching her profile for a hint of what she was thinking. He couldn't read her.

She turned toward the kitchen and glanced his way for only a second. "I'm fine."

She yelled to Gaby before she opened the door. "I'm heading out now with Chris. Be back tonight!"

"See ya later!" Gaby shouted back.

~~~~~

Ninety minutes later, they drove down a long stone driveway and up to a medium-sized house with a big wrap-around porch. Natural stone covered the bottom front of the house and white siding finished the look. Chloe imagined natural sunlight pouring inside through the large window on the second floor.

She glanced at Chris with wide eyes. "You grew up here? It's beautiful."

"Yup, I did. My parents like taking care of their house and yard. My dad will show you his garden. He enjoys that the most."

Chris followed the driveway that wrapped around the house and parked in front of the open garage door. He turned and studied Chloe, who was biting her lip. *Is she worrying more about my parents or last night's run-in with Sandy?*

He patted her hand, choosing his parents. "Don't worry. They'll love you. Come on. My mom's on the back porch and my dad's down in the garden."

The backyard was wide with freshly laid mulch, full flower beds, and perfectly manicured hedges. *They definitely like their plants and flowers,* Chloe said to herself. *Good thing I brought his mom a potted flower.*

Chloe waved to Chris's dad as they walked up to the porch.

Chris's mom met them at the top step. "Oh, you must be Chloe, I'm so happy to meet you. Here, come in." She held the door open for Chloe to walk through.

Chloe found herself in a large, open kitchen with a farm sink and checkered floor. "You have a beautiful home, Mrs. Sherman. Thank you for inviting me. I brought you this," she said, handing her the flowerpot. "Chris told me you like flowers."

"Like is a weak word. I *love* my flowers, and this one is beautiful. Thank you. It will look gorgeous on my porch," she said as she took the flower and set it on the table for now. "Also, you can call me Helen. No need for formality here!"

Chloe's nerves started to calm a bit now that she was here. His mom seemed like a lovely woman, so warm and welcoming. Chloe guessed she was around sixty. She kept her curly hair short, just above her shoulders. Seeing them side by side now, Chloe also noticed the resemblance between her and Chris. They shared the same blue eyes and smile.

"Can I get you anything to drink, Chloe?"

Chloe saw a pitcher of iced tea sitting on the kitchen table. "Iced tea is perfect for me."

"Excellent!" Helen bent under the counter to reach a tray. "Chris, would you grab four glasses from up there?" she asked, pointing to one of the cabinets.

"Sure, Mom."

After setting up the tray, Chris carried it out to the porch, with Chloe and his mom following. Helen motioned down the yard. "Chris's dad lives down there. The garden's been his pride and joy ever since the kids moved out."

Chloe smiled. "I heard he loves his garden."

"Oh, you don't know half of it! He'll be up soon. Until then, tell me about you."

They had a nice time talking about Chloe's work, Gaby, and Jess. She heard about his mom recently retiring and all about Briana and her family. It was a nice chat—so nice, in fact, that Chris felt okay leaving them for a while to go see his dad.

When he was gone, Chloe turned to Helen. "I want to thank you for raising such a good man. Chris is wonderful to me."

Helen chuckled. "He better treat you like a princess! I didn't raise him to be a schlub to women."

"Well he is certainly no schlub, and same for Todd. I've seen him several times. You have many reasons to be proud."

"Yes, I do."

Helen stood up and took Chloe's empty glass to set on the tray. "Why don't we head down to the garden so you can meet Chris's dad? It doesn't seem like he is making it up here any time soon."

"That would be great." Chloe followed Helen down the stone walkway. She noticed with a smile it was lined with daisies.

Chris and his dad turned as Chloe and Helen approached. Chloe noted Mr. Sherman's gloved hands covered in soil and opted to wave. "Hello, Mr. Sherman. It's wonderful to meet you."

He returned her wave. "And you, Chloe. Please, call me Mike." Mike glanced down at his dirty hand. "My wife told me I should have stopped a half hour ago to wash up, but I was close to being done … I couldn't help myself."

Chloe grinned. "It's no problem. How about a tour? I'd love to see what you have growing."

Mike smiled. "My pleasure!"

After wandering the backyard and garden, listening to Chris's dad tell her all about the things he had growing and his plans to improve it in the future, Chloe and Helen headed back to the house. Chris stayed out to look at something with his dad in the garage.

Chloe checked her phone when they got inside. One missed call from Jess. She turned to Helen. "Do you mind if I call my friend back? She's home for the first time in a few years."

"Of course, honey. Feel free to wander around the house or out front. I'll be here getting started on dinner."

Chloe walked out to the porch, where a wooden swing beckoned to her. She took a seat and swung her legs as she waited for the call to connect. Jess picked up on the second ring.

"Hey, how's it going there?" Chloe asked.

"Better than expected with my mom. We had a nice visit before Marisa came downstairs. Marisa slept past lunch because she was out late. My guess is drinking. She was bratty when she saw me."

"That sucks. How bratty?"

"She's got a sharp mouth on her. But I think it's a bunch of misplaced anger."

"Was your dad around?"

"Yeah, he was. She was loud-mouthed to him too. I hated seeing that."

"I bet. Your dad is such a sweetheart. Where are you now?"

"Back at the hotel. I'll head back in the morning to see them before I come home. How are things there? At the parents' now?"

"Yeah, we are. I stepped out on the front porch."

"So, how is it?"

"It's great. No awkwardness at all. I was a bit anxious before we got here, but it died off quick. His mom is easy to talk to and has been very welcoming."

"Aw, that's sweet."

"Yeah. Well, I'm glad things are going well enough for you. I should get back in there. Let me know if you need anything."

"Will do. Thanks, Chloe, I needed to hear a friendly voice."

"Of course, hang in there!"

Chloe stood after she hung up with Jess and cast her gaze over the front yard. It was the perfect place to relax, and to raise a family. She pictured Chris as a little boy running around chasing his brother and sister. She smiled at the thought.

From inside, Chris saw Chloe looking out. He had come in a few minutes ago with his dad. His mom stood at the stove and glanced at him. "She's returning the call of a friend. Chloe's a nice girl, Chris."

Chris nodded. "She is. It's probably Jess she called. She's really close to both of her roommates."

"I can tell." She paused. "That's a sign of good people—when they form close bonds with others and care about them."

"I agree. Women like her are hard to find."

His mom studied her son's profile. "She's a good one to fall in love with."

"Mmm-hmm."

"So, have you told her?"

He looked back at his mom. "Told her what?"

She raised her eyebrows. "That you love her."

Chris chuckled and looked back at Chloe. "Not yet. We're taking our time. I'm doing this right."

"She was right. I raised you well."

Chris came over and put his arm across his mom's shoulders. "Thank you.

I'm lucky to have you and Dad."

Chloe walked through the front door. The home's layout allowed her to see Chris and his mom in the kitchen. *Aw, that's nice. They're affectionate, like Gaby is with her mom and Jess with her dad.*

Helen looked up as Chloe neared them. "How is your friend?"

Chloe swished her hand downward. "She's managing fine." Stepping closer, she eyed the vegetables Helen had laid on counter. "May I help with anything? Chop vegetables for you?"

"Oh, that would be a huge help." Helen pulled out a chopping board from a lower cabinet and a large knife from the block. "Here you go."

She reached into another cabinet, producing a large colander and handed it to Chris. "You can wash."

He grinned. "Yes, ma'am."

Helen raised an eyebrow and cleared her throat. "Mmm-hmm." Waving her pointer finger toward Chris, she warned him. "Stay out of trouble in my kitchen. I am going to get the meat that's marinating in the spare fridge."

After his mom left, Chris moved toward Chloe with a glimmer in his eyes. She smiled and touched his arm. "You're mischievous."

He leaned down and whispered, "Yes, I am." His hands went to her waist, pulling her against him. He lightly touched his lips to hers.

Chloe raised her hand to his chest and pulled back a few inches. "Your mom is going to be right back," she playfully admonished.

"You're too cute." He gave her a quick hug and released her as his mom entered.

Helen pursed her lips. "Watch out for him, Chloe. He's a troublemaker."

A small smiled flashed across Chloe's lips. "I'm learning that."

Helen smirked. "He hasn't changed a bit since he was a boy."

"Excuse me," Chris cut in. "I am, in fact, a man now. I have a grown-up job and everything."

Helen rolled her eyes. "True that might be, but outside the office you're the same old Chris."

Chris nudged his mother.

Chloe smiled at the two of them. "I'd love to see pictures of Chris as a boy, if they're easily accessible."

Helen placed the meat in the oven. "Oh, they are. I'll get them out once we get the rest of dinner cooking."

Chris took the colander and got to work. "I can see how this is going to go. You two are going to gang up on me."

Chloe walked to the sink and stood next to Chris. He winked at her as she loaded her hands with the freshly washed potatoes. *Damn, he's a catch*, she thought. *He is playful with his mom and adores her.*

Chloe started peeling and chopping. She arranged the potatoes in a baking dish Helen had put next to her. Her mind wandered to last night again and she sighed. *I can't stay mad at him anymore. Sandy's nothing but a nosy bitch. It's clear he doesn't care about her, even though she might still be in his life in some small way.*

Chris brought the other vegetables to her and planted a kiss on her cheek.

She grinned at him. "Thank you." *I'm the only one he wants.*

Chris grabbed another board and knife, and the two of them worked side by side.

At one point, Chloe examined him through her lashes. *It's nice being in the kitchen together like this. Today is turning out great!*

~~~~~

The sun was setting as Chris and Chloe made their way back to Galorston. He reached over and rubbed his hand on her thigh. "So, you had a good time?"

"Oh, yes. Your parents are wonderful! I loved meeting them. Thank you for taking me."

She abruptly quieted then. He glanced over at her. She was on her phone reading a text. "Everything okay?"

"Oh yeah, everything is fine. It's just Mya from work. She asked me something about our project."

Chris slowly nodded. "Work is keeping you pretty busy, huh?"

She shrugged. "Sometimes it does." She turned then and twisted to see him better. "So … I was thinking maybe you'd like to stay over tonight."

Chris was a little taken aback. He wasn't thinking that was an option yet. "I-I'd love to, as long as you're sure."

"Yes, I'm sure. I'd like to have you sleep next to me."

Chris grinned, imagining their bodies next to each other. "I'd love to stay over, then." He paused. "You know I don't expect anything, though. Just sleep."

"Of course." She turned to look out the window.

Damn, he thought. *Does she think I don't want her?*

"Hey," he said softly, bringing her eyes back to him. "You know I want to, right? That I think about you all the time? But it's not just your body I think about. It's you." He pointed to her heart and mind. "It's all an amazing package that goes together, hand in hand. All three have to be ready or it won't hold the meaning I want it to for you, for us."

Chloe nodded. "You're right. Only two of the three are ready."

This made him wonder which two. *Her body is, so is it her heart or mind?*

As they entered Chloe's house, Chloe saw a light on in the living room. She popped her head in and offered a smile. "Hey, Gabs. We're back."

Gaby paused her TV show. "Oh, okay. Have a good time?"

Chloe smiled. "Yep!"

"Great." Gaby noticed the look on Chloe's face. With a grin, she said, "Goodnight," and watched them disappear upstairs.

Once in her room, Chloe turned after closing the door and moved closer to Chris. He wrapped his arms around her and pulled her to him. She leaned her head against his shoulder. "Can I get you anything?"

He looked down at her. "Do you happen to have an extra toothbrush?"

Chloe laughed. "Of course." She stepped back. Still holding one of his hands, she led him to the bathroom. Rifling through a drawer, she produced one new toothbrush. "Here you go. You can use the bathroom first."

"Thanks."

Chloe closed the door behind her and went to her dresser. She grabbed a tank and shorts to wait for her turn.

Once Chloe finished in the bathroom, she returned to find Chris sitting on her bed in his T-shirt and boxers. Her heart started to beat faster. *This is really happening.*

"Hey there," he said.

"Need anything else?" she asked, trying to calm her nerves.

"Just you snuggled up next to me." He reached for her hand and pulled her onto his lap. She smiled as he nuzzled her neck.

"Mmm," she lightly moaned. *It's going to be okay, Chloe. You can sleep in the same bed as someone without it getting out of hand.*

Her thoughts left her as Chris brought his lips to hers. The connection with him took her breath away. The faintest touch made her melt.

Chloe twisted and slid a leg over his lap to straddle him. In reply, Chris laid back against the bed, bringing her with him. His hands found her bottom; they rubbed and massaged her cheeks. His hips thrust forward too, and hers ground against his in response.

Restraint, he reminded himself. *Restraint.* He could do this—correction, he *would* do this.

Chris could tell by the way Chloe raked her fingers across his stomach and reached for the edge of his shirt that there was no pep talk going on in her head—it was all instinct now. His eyes widened as she pulled the shirt up and off in a quick motion. *She does that quite well,* he thought with a smile. *Really well.*

The amusement lasted for only for a second, though, as he found her hands running down his sides to dip into the top of his boxers. *Whoa! I have to start slowing this down or else it's really going to get out of hand.*

When her hands moved back up closer to his waist, he laced his fingers with hers and rolled with her, positioning himself on top of her.

He whispered in her ear as he found the soft skin below her ear, "Chloe, baby, you're on fire. So hot. But you have to stop."

The groan she let out made it that much harder to keep himself in check. He slowed kissing her neck and freed one hand to explore her body. Her tight tank top was sliding up, exposing her midsection and tempting him to reach for her breasts.

He whispered again in her ear, "Chloe, let's stop."

She opened her eyes.

Chris kissed her gently. "I'm sorry, but it's getting to be too much for me."

Chloe blinked, considering Chris's words. She had gone into another world; her brain was mush again. She never knew passion could be like this. It was so overwhelming, so consuming. Taking one more breath, she said, "Okay."

As they pulled away from each other, Chris smiled. "I liked what you were doing."

"I liked it too. God, I *wanted* your hands on me and your mouth all over me."

Chris got goose bumps imagining that.

"But yeah, I'm not there yet." She added quickly. "My mind just needs to catch up with the rest of me."

Holy shit, he thought as realization hit him. *Does that mean she's in love with me?*

He couldn't speak, so he kissed her instead. It was different than the kiss before—not the passionate, lustful kiss, but a gentle, loving kiss full of hope. His heart swelled in those few moments and he thought he could die of happiness. *This feels perfect.*

Smiling, he whispered, "I will wait."

Chris pulled her close to him. "Mmm, holding you is wonderful."

Chloe's lips curved and a small sigh escaped her. "Yes. I love your arms around me."

He kissed the top of her head. "Let's get some sleep, okay?"

She nodded. "Okay. Good night."

~~~~~

Chapter 17

The week before Labor Day was finally here. The girls had decided to take off that Friday to leave Thursday after work and make it a four-day weekend. However, a short week didn't mean an easier week.

At Local 9 News, Chloe and Mya scheduled several interviews with mental health professionals. Mya volunteered to do one of them, which left the other three for Chloe. The unbalanced level of work rekindled Chloe's bitter feelings toward Mya. In Chloe's mind, if they were partners on this project, they should split everything evenly when possible. To pile most of the work on Chloe but share the same credit rankled Chloe's skin.

Right or wrong, Chloe knew she was internalizing her feelings. She feared if she said anything it would result in another week—or longer—of awkwardness between them. She couldn't afford that right now in her career. Not when Lou had been complimentary toward her work. So she decided to keep her thoughts to herself and do what she could with her time.

The pinnacle point of her week came on Tuesday when Lou called her over to his office. "Chloe, the verdict for the Dunne murder trial is supposed to be decided today. I'd like you to head out with a crew to cover it at the courthouse."

"I'm on it," she said with firmness and professionalism; however, in her head she was dancing.

"Knew I could count on you. You're going with Eric and his crew. I alerted them, and they pulled the van around to meet you out front."

"Thanks, Lou. I'll get it done." Chloe dashed to her desk for her bag and headed outside.

When Chloe and the crew arrived at the courthouse, the sidewalk was already teeming with reporters and camera crews. Chloe hopped out and when her feet hit the sidewalk, she saw it in her mind. *Dunne was found not guilty and is heading through the side exit.* She motioned to Eric and the others. "Hey, let's head around to the other exit. Something tells me that's where we'll find him."

Eric looked at her with a slight frown. "Chloe, they never come out there."

"My gut is telling me Dunne is going to get off. And, with the controversy and risk of discord, they are going to bring him out that way."

Eric shook his head and sighed but followed her to the side of the building. *Come on*, Chloe thought as they waited. *Let this premonition be correct. Don't steer me wrong now.*

Eric set the camera up on his shoulder and stood next to Chloe. "Rolling." They were live.

Anxiety filled Chloe as she reported on the current status of the case. When Eric turned the camera to scan further down the side of the courthouse, Chloe let out a long breath. *God, maybe I got this wrong?*

As he filmed, Eric shot a narrowed look at her.

She mouthed, "Any minute now." She tried to exude more confidence than she felt.

Eric focused the camera back on Chloe. She continued reporting. Behind her the door opened. A security guard stepped through first, and then she saw him. Dunne.

Eric focused in on him and Chloe as she moved as close as she could; however, the security guard blocked her. Chloe raised her voice. "Chloe Larson with Local 9 News. Mr. Dunne, do you have a statement you'd like to make for the public?"

He leaned for a second around the security officer. "I'm a free man!"

Local 9 News had Dunne's words and the verdict out to the public first. *Lou is going to love this!*

~~~~~

After their last day of work before the holiday weekend, Chloe picked up Gaby and they headed home to meet Jess. Jess already had her computer shut down and her bags packed.

"No computer?" Chloe asked, noticing it not in her bag.

Jess shook her head. "No way. Labor Day weekend is a weekend off of laboring, right? I think the computer and project can stay put until we get back." She was more than ready to blow this town and get some much-needed R&R.

Chloe and Gaby smiled. They were both glad she was taking time for herself for once.

With a glint in her eye, Jess rummaged through her bag. "I am bringing this, though." Gaby and Chloe laughed as a blow horn appeared.

"Where did you get that?" Chloe asked.

Jess smiled. "From some party a while ago."

"Oh my God," Gaby chimed. "I love it. We have to blow it as we are pulling up. Momma will get a huge kick out of it."

The three girls quickly grabbed their stuff and headed to the car.

"Ah, Chloe …" Jess was all smiles as she pointed down the walkway.

Chloe turned from locking the front door and saw Chris standing there holding a small bouquet of flowers. Her heart jumped, and she walked quickly to him.

"I couldn't let you leave without seeing you," he said.

Chloe dropped the bag she was holding and gathered him in a tight hug. "Aw, I am so glad you caught us! We were just about to leave."

Chris wrapped his free arm around her and pulled her off the ground for a half twirl. Jess pulled out the blow horn and timed it just right.

When he set her down, he was laughing. Chloe laughed too, then grabbed his face with both hands and went in for a short, hard kiss. She pulled back. "Like Jess's blow horn?"

"Love it." He put his free hand up to her face and gently rubbed his thumb across her cheek. "Chloe, I'm sorry we barely saw each other this week—with your work schedule and school starting for me now it was too busy. The next few days are going to feel long."

"Yeah, I know. I'll miss you."

"I'll miss you too." He handed her a small gift bag along with the bouquet.

She looked up at him. "What's this?"

He shrugged. "Just something small."

Chloe felt a twinge of excitement as she pulled out a small box. It was the first gift he had given her. She opened the lid and found a delicate silver necklace with a small heart pendant. "Oh! It's beautiful. So pretty. Could you put it on me?"

He leaned closer as she pulled back her hair and said, "Keep Tuesday night open for me, please."

The hairs on the back of her neck prickled. "It already is."

Chris waved goodbye as they drove off. But his chest sank watching Chloe leave. He wished they could've seen each other more that week. However, he knew Chloe would have a great time with her friends. She deserved a fun weekend after all the busy workdays. And now she had a nice gift to remember him while they were apart.

He smiled as Jess stuck her arm out the window, giving the blow horn one more honk. *Crazy ladies.*

~~~~~

After driving for a while, Gaby looked in the rearview mirror. Jess's head rested against the window, and her eyes were closed. Beside her, Chloe watched the scenery pass them by, but Gaby knew she was thinking of Chris. The three of them hadn't said much after they pulled out. It was definitely a quieter car ride than Gaby imagined, but lately she preferred the quiet. It made her think.

Gaby thought a lot about Harmony, where she'd grown up. Her mom, dad, and she had lived in the same small house they were traveling to now. It rested on Main Street near the school where her mom worked as a teacher. Her dad had owned a car repair shop in town. After he died, they sold the shop to her dad's best friend, Sam. Sam was the closest father figure Gaby had growing up. He would stop by to check in on Gaby and her mom often.

Gaby sometimes missed the small-town life where everyone knew you and wanted to help you. There were, of course, some exceptions, but most people were very kind.

Living in Harmony had felt like a simple life. It was a safe town with a laidback feel. She doubted anything like the stalking or fighting she'd recently witnessed would happen there.

It had been exciting when she left after high school and moved to a city where there was always something to do and the pace of life was faster. It certainly had been fun for the first few years, at least. But over the last year or two, Gaby had been more nostalgic for home. She missed her mom and small-town living. It would be good to get back there now.

Lost in her thoughts, Gaby hadn't realized a big chunk of time had gone by. Before she knew it, she was turning into the driveway of her mom's house.

Gaby reached back and poked Jess's leg. "Jess, you have to wake up and use the blow horn."

Jess rubbed her eyes. "I'm awake. I'm awake. Grabbing it now." She had the window down and the horn going as they parked.

Momma R. came running out. "Oh dear God! Jess, you scared the crap out of me."

Jess laughed. "That's the point, Momma R."

Gaby was the first out of the car and went running around to her mom. Chloe and Jess soon joined in on the huge hug. Pointing the horn away from their ears, Jess let it go one more time. "Let the holiday weekend begin!"

Gaby's mom took the horn and gave it one short toot. "Let it begin!"

Gaby laughed hard. "I knew you'd love it!"

~~~~~

That night, Gaby's mom called them down for dinner after letting them get settled in for the afternoon. Chloe and Jess shared the spare room, and Gaby stayed in her old bedroom. For all three of them, it felt great to just lay low and relax for a while. While dinner cooked, Chloe and Jess read the books they'd brought, and Gaby paged through some photo albums from when she was little.

Gaby walked to the dining table and gasped at the array of food displayed there. "Oh my God! Mom, you went nuts cooking tonight. You shouldn't have gone to all this trouble!"

Momma R. smiled. "It's not every day I have all three of my girls in town. We need choices and leftovers. Here, each of you take a plate. Fill up, then we will sit at the table and get caught up on life."

Chloe agreed with Gaby: Momma R. had outdone herself. On the table before them sat steaming dishes of chile relleno, tostados, enchiladas, refried beans, and rice. To cap it all off were Gaby, Chloe, and Jess's favorite: margaritas.

Gaby took a little of everything since she couldn't choose between all her favorites. Chloe went after the enchiladas, and Jess claimed the chile relleno, rice, and beans.

"Jessica," Momma R. said, "you go first. Tell me all about what's new with you."

"I'm okay. I've been way too busy with work... putting in too many hours and not getting enough sleep. I at least know that my trip to California will signify the end of it all. Selfishly, I'm interested in it slowing down way before that."

"I would certainly hope so. As a mother, I must remind you that life is too short to spend all of it working. Enjoy being young and beautiful!"

Jess inclined her head and leaned forward. "I want to. It's just a matter of actually achieving it. I promise I will work on it, though."

"That's my good girl. Now, tell me all about Oklahoma."

In between bites, Gaby jumped in. "We didn't even get to hear all of it yet."

"I left on Friday after lunch time so I could make it to Oklahoma by dinnertime to meet up with Mrs. Snyder. She is, as always, doing very well. She told me about all the girls she has working and volunteering at the library. I swear that woman is a saint for what she does for the local girls."

Jess went on. "After dinner we walked to the ice cream parlor where Johnny works and had dessert. It worked out well so I could see Johnny without any issues of having Mom or Marisa around."

Chloe asked, "How is Johnny?"

"He's really good. He is doing decent enough in school and keeping that job until October when it really slows down. He has been staying out of trouble and not wasting time on girls. He plans to leave right after graduation for the marines, so getting involved in relationships wouldn't be the greatest thing for him."

"He always was a good kid," Gaby commented.

"Yeah, he has been. You can't say the same for Marisa, sadly. She had some devil in her even when she was little. Now it's worse. She stays out late, drinks, does drugs, and hangs around boys who are way too old for her. I wouldn't be surprised if she makes me an aunt sometime soon."

Gaby's mom let out a sigh. "Oh no, this is not good. Your mother and Marisa are not reliable, and your poor father cannot raise a baby."

"I know. That's why I went to visit. I am hoping that I can build some kind of relationship with Marisa. Perhaps give her some guidance and help her stop the spiral she has herself in."

"I'm proud of you, Jessica. I know this trip must not have been easy for you." Momma R. patted her forearm.

"No, it wasn't. You know the hardest part was driving over the state border. That was harder than Saturday morning when I showed up at the house to see Mom. I think it's because of what it signified. When I left and crossed into Texas, I swore I would never cross back."

"Well, Jessica honey, it is a strong person that can do something that they swore they would never do again to help family."

Jess offered a small smile. "Thanks, Momma R. I'm trying to be strong."

The woman dipped her head in agreement. "Please, go on."

"Saturday went as well as could have been expected. Mom was having a good day and was okay with seeing me. I wouldn't say she was happy to see me, but she was okay about it. Marisa, on the other hand, didn't speak very nicely to me. It's one thing to talk to me that way, but another thing to talk to my dad that way. He doesn't use that kind of language, but it's every other word out of her mouth. F this, F that, F you. It's horrible to hear a fourteen-year-old talk that way."

Jess continued her recount of last weekend. "Then Sunday wasn't good at all. Mom was having a bad day. She was confused and angry. She wasn't yelling, just snippy with everything she said. She claimed she didn't remember me being there the day before. That hurt. Johnny and Dad were there both days and tried to run interference. I was very thankful for their support. Unfortunately, it wasn't the most successful approach, because Mom became angry with them for 'tricking her.' It was all very hard to see, and still pains me to think about. I feel so yucky leaving them there to deal with it themselves. And my poor dad will be alone with them starting next summer."

Chloe had moved behind Jess to rub her shoulders. "Honey, I'm so sorry. What can we do?"

"Nothing can be done."

"Oh, come give me a hug, my little Jessy." Gaby's mom stood and waved her hands to come to her. "You're going to figure this out. I know it."

After letting Jess go, Momma R. went for the margarita pitcher. "Okay, chicas, we need a refill. Grab your second helpings too. We are going to get caught up with Gabriella next, and Chloe is for dessert." She winked.

Gaby sighed. "Well, I don't have anything as important to say as Jess or as fun as I know Chloe's updates will be. But I can tell you that I have been thinking a lot. I spent a lot of time thinking last Saturday when I was home alone. I planned a pampering night and it just ended up being a solo pity party."

Momma R.'s face softened. "Oh, honey. Why didn't you call me?"

"Because I'm an adult and I can't cry to my mommy every time I'm down. You already dropped everything and came to us that night." She didn't want to mention anything else about that, so she quickly moved on. "Besides, I needed time to think about this myself. I'm just feeling frustrated about the awkward situations I seem to have been trapped in. Obviously, you know about my 'stalker,' but in general I'm sick of the attention I get. For once I'd love for someone to see me for more than looks. You know, last Friday night we went over to Chris's house for a party and some scummy idiot asked us for a threesome."

"Eww!" Jess yelled. "It is a scummy idiot who would ask you that."

"Don't you know it! It was funny at the time, and we laughed it off. But when you start thinking about all the attention I get; it is all negative sexual attention. I'm so sick of it."

Chloe nodded and shifted in her seat.

"I know you all think I'm crazy with my *I won't date anyone for a year* pact," Gaby went on, drawing circles with her finger near her temple, "but I seriously want all men out of my way. I don't want to be objectified anymore."

"I can't blame you, Gabriella. It makes you feel like you are less than you really are." Her mom patted her hand from across the table. "Sweetie, you are so much more."

"I know. Thanks, Momma. The self-defense classes are helping some. They are improving my feelings of confidence and control. With more time, I am sure I will be fine. Until then I need to work on finding a way to either keep myself out of these situations or feel stronger when they occur."

"You will find your way," said Jess.

"We'll help you," added Chloe. Both Jess and Chloe squeezed her hands.

"Thanks, loves." Gaby let out a defeated sigh.

Chloe clapped her hands. "I know what we need! A walk and ice cream. My treat."

Jess agreed. "That sounds perfect." She pointed to Momma R. "You sit and drink every last sip of that margarita, with your feet up. We got kitchen cleanup."

"No need for that, hijas!" Momma R. tutted.

Gaby pulled out Jess's empty chair and propped up her mom's feet. "Yes, we do, Momma. Now, stay put."

Cleanup went fast with the three of them dividing it up. Gaby put away the food, Jess started on dishes, and Chloe wiped off and dried dishes. After Chloe hung up her towel, she ran upstairs to get her wallet. Returning moments later, she breathed, "Let's go!"

On the walk to the ice cream shop, Momma R. put her arm around Chloe's shoulders. "Don't think I didn't see that new heart necklace you have on. I still want to hear all about my little Chloe's life."

Chloe leaned in closer. "I know, but we needed a little break first."

"That we did."

Across the street from the ice cream store was the car repair shop Gaby's dad used to own. So close to it now, Gaby glanced over at it. She had a very faint memory as a toddler standing in the first bay watching her dad. *I miss him.* Before she could get too reminiscent, Jess directed her into the ice cream store.

At the counter they ordered their ice cream then sat down at one of the round tables. Gaby poked Chloe. "So we still have to hear about your meet-and-greet with Chris's parents. I never asked you since you seemed a little preoccupied that night and the days after."

Chloe blushed.

Jess started pounding on the table and chanted, "Now, now, now!"

Laughing hard, Chloe said, "Okay, okay, okay! It went well. His parents are sweet and fun. His mom loved the flowers I brought her. Even though I was a bit nervous in the beginning, it was easy to talk to them and the nerves wore off quickly. It wasn't awkward at all."

After a few *awes*, Chloe went on. "They live in a really beautiful place too. The house had a large wrap-around porch, very picturesque with a nice yard. They are really into outdoor work, taking care of plants, flowers, and their vegetable garden. I could picture Chris as a little boy playing in that front yard. Part of me felt a stab of jealousy—he has two kind parents, a loving house he got to grow up in, and two nice siblings. He seems to have everything. I wonder what it felt like to grow up like that."

"It does sound as though he is lucky," Momma R. agreed. "Life never seems to be quite fair, does it? The good doesn't seem to be evenly spread out. Still, you must never forget the many good fortunes that you have had along the way. What I see when I look at you now is a wonderful person who overcame challenges and is stronger because of it." Her eyes swept across all three of them. "That is what I see when I look at all of you. Wonderful people."

"I agree," Gaby chimed in, "very fortunate. Okay, but let's get to the juicy stuff!" She looked at Jess and her mom with a conspiratorial look. "You should have seen those two come running in and up to her room Saturday night, like two naughty teenagers!"

This brought a howl of laughter from them all. Chloe turned a very bright shade of red. "Oh God. I knew you noticed. How mortifying!"

"Not at all! I was jealous beyond belief. Now, out with it!"

"Well," she started with a breath, casting her gaze around the shop. They were the only customers. Still, she lowered her voice. "I guess we *were* like naughty teenagers. We did make a mad dash up to my room. I'd wanted him to stay the night, so he did."

"Oh my God. I am *so jealous!*" Gaby let out. "More, more, more!"

Chloe bit her lip. "Well, after the door was closed there might have been some really good kissing and touching."

"Dear God," Gaby's mom fanned herself. "It is getting so hot in here!"

"Geeze! Did you sleep with him?" Gaby asked.

"No. He was worried I wasn't quite ready and I'd hate it if we did. He really is very careful with me and so respectful. You know what he said?" Chloe looked around at them watching her and smiled. "He talked about my body, heart, and mind all being part of an amazing package. He said, "All three have to be ready or it won't hold the meaning I want it to for you, for us.""

This received another round of *awes*.

"Oh, honey, he sounds just wonderful." Momma R. said. "I think you're doing the right thing. You're taking your time getting to know each other and deciding together when it is right. I love that he's not pressuring you. That is certainly the sign of a very good man."

"I never knew it could be like that. That passion can be so overwhelming. So consuming!"

Momma R. patted her hand. "When you are with the right person, it is a beautiful thing."

"Momma, was it like that with Daddy?" Gaby looked at her with her big sensitive blue eyes.

"Oh yes, honey. He was a wonderful man, very loving." She leaned in. "I think you are old enough to hear this now. What I had with your daddy was so beautiful, so wonderful. It has lasted me a lifetime. I never wanted another man like I wanted him."

"Oh, that is so tragically beautiful, Momma!"

Momma R. dabbed at her eyes. "Yes, I guess it is. I miss him every day, but I'm so glad I have you to remind me of him. You are so much like him. Your personality is a carbon copy of his—always the life of the party, front and center, caring. You look like him too, with your coloring. But your height and blue eyes come from me. You got the best of both of us.

Gaby smiled.

"I know right now is hard for you and you are looking for your way," Momma R. continued, "but please don't stop being who you really are because of a rough patch. This will pass."

"I know. I won't." Gaby hugged her mom.

Momma R. looked around at the empty bowls and plates. "We certainly devoured that and probably put on a show for the employees. Let's go home, muchachas."

~~~~~

Chapter 18

On Saturday the town put on a large Labor Day weekend celebration. It took place inside the local park. There was food and desserts of all types, games for kids to enjoy, and a fireworks show to finish the evening. The townspeople prepared the food and donated it for the event. Gaby's mom helped set up the food tables. The girls had been helping her cook and bake for the past two days.

At the event, Gaby, Jess, and Chloe worked the food tables while Momma R. bounced around from vendor to vendor, tidying or socializing, or both. They loved the thrill of the atmosphere, the happy memories they could see being created around them.

Gaby was refilling the plastic utensils when she heard a "hey" come from behind her. She turned, and her eyes landed on the tall form of Brad, Sam's son. "Brad? It's been a long time! How are you?"

Brad leaned in to give her a hug. "It has been. I think a couple of years." With his hands still on her shoulders, he stood back and looked at her. "You look great, Gaby. My dad tells me you're in Galorston now, working at the hospital?"

"Yeah, that's right." She searched the crowds for Jess and Chloe, wondering what they'd think if they saw her talking to Brad. "My roommates are here somewhere. We came to visit Momma for the weekend. What are you up to?"

"I'm living back here again. I just opened the insurance place around the corner. I sell policies and do personal finance."

Gaby crossed her arms. "Wow, that's cool. Where were you before?"

"I was in Austin for a few years. I guess I was never back here at the same time as you." Brad reached for a plate and held it in Gaby's direction. "Did you eat yet?"

She smiled. "No, I was still helping out."

"Want to sit and eat with me? I'd love to hear what's new with you."

"Um …" Gaby looked around again. "Okay, sure. Let me just fill up these few things."

A few minutes later, Gaby sat across from Brad under one of the tents propped up around the grounds. Her eyes met his, and she was startled by how captivating they were. She always thought he had nice eyes but seeing them up close confirmed it. Honestly, she always thought he was very attractive. However, she didn't go near him with a ten-foot pole in high school. They were friends when they were little, since their dads had been close, but not when they were older. That was because Gaby always tried to keep her distance from him.

Brad flirted a lot with her starting when they were around thirteen, but he flirted with all the girls back then. She never thought he was authentic or felt like she could trust him. He captained their football team and could have his pick of girlfriends, and he did just that. Sometimes he had several at a time. Gaby wasn't interested in that then, and now even less so. Out of respect for Sam and her late dad, she was friendly but always maintained space.

Gaby last saw him a few years back, around Christmas when she was visiting her mom. They ran into each other at the local bar. She had just turned twenty-one, so her friends took her out for her first beer. Brad was out with guys she knew from high school, drinking and shooting pool. He had asked her to play a round with him and offered to buy her a shot, but she turned him down. About ten minutes later, he was making out with one of his many old girlfriends against the back wall. She fought another eye roll as she remembered.

Brad interrupted her thoughts then. "I'm pretty sure I know what's going through your mind right now."

She cocked an eyebrow and waited to see what he would say.

A small smile formed, showing that small dimple he had on his cheek. "I think you're wondering where your friends are so they will save you from having to sit here with me."

Both of her eyebrows went up. "Bingo."

He chuckled. "I deserve that. I've been a real jerk to you over the years."

Gaby told herself it didn't really matter, but she asked anyway, "Why were you?"

"Because you wouldn't even give me a second look."

Her face straightened. "Because you gave every girl at school a second look and third look ... including thorough looks under the hood sometimes."

He sighed. "It never occurred to you that I might have been doing that to get your attention?"

Gaby quickly countered, "Did it ever occur to you that's the reason why I didn't want anything to do with you?"

He lowered his eyes. "No, sadly. I was too dumb."

Saying with more feeling than she wanted to, "So next you're going to tell me you're different now?"

His eyes lifted and searched her face. "I want to say I'm sorry. I am different, but I don't think you'll believe it."

Narrowing her eyes, Gaby replied, "I don't."

He motioned with his head for her to look behind her. "I think your friends are here."

Gaby looked over her shoulder and then back at him. "Yeah, I better go."

As she stood to leave, he called after her, "For what it's worth, it was good seeing you, Gaby."

Gaby mumbled, "Sure," as she took her plate and left him.

When she approached Jess and Chloe, she saw the questions in their eyes. "Did he watch me walk away?"

"Yeah, with the saddest look on his face," Chloe answered. "Who is he?"

Gaby started walking to the other side of the tables. "Oh God, he's such an actor. I'll tell you about him another time. Let's go find a place to eat, away from here."

Jess and Chloe looked at each other as Gaby passed them.

Later, the girls found Momma R. and helped her lay out a blanket in the open field for the fireworks show. They all agreed it had been a fun day but were glad the night was winding down.

~~~~~

The next day, the four ladies walked home from lunch at a café following church service. Momma R. took Gaby's hand. "I'd like to stop by the auto shop."

After hearing her mom's words, Gaby's eyes grew wide and her mouth suddenly felt dry. "Why?"

Momma R. regarded her daughter with concern. She hadn't expected her to push back on the idea. "To see Sam, of course. You haven't seen him this weekend yet."

The panic left Gaby then. *Not Brad, but Sam. Whew!* "Oh, okay. Yeah, that's fine."

Chloe and Jess followed Gaby and Momma R. as they made their way to the shop, which wasn't far down the street. When they walked up to the garage, Sam came out to meet them. His eyes rested on Gaby. "Now, there's my girl. How have you been, Gabriella?"

Gaby reached up to give him a hug. "I'm good, thank you, Sam. Has business been good?"

Sam stepped to the side, revealing Brad walking up to join them. Gaby's mouth almost fell open when she saw him, dressed in dirty jeans and a smeared white T-shirt, but she caught herself and stayed still.

"Yup," Sam continued, "it has been. Especially since I have help now." He clapped Brad on the back.

Gaby looked away, suddenly annoyed. *He looks so damn hot.*

She could feel Brad's eyes on her. When she turned toward him, she noticed he wore that sexy grin again, and the tiny dimple on his cheek popped. "I help out on weekends," said Brad, "and other days when I can."

Sam nodded. "Does a mighty good job too. He fixed up your new car, Gabriella."

Gaby's face dropped. "My what?"

Her mom took her hand. "Your new old car. Come have a look."

Everyone headed around the corner of the garage. There, gleaming in the muted fall sun, sat a silver car.

Brad handed her a set of keys. "True. It's yours. Try it out."

"You knew about this?"

That dimple kept staring at her. "Yup, your ma asked about it a few weeks ago. It needed a few small things and a tune up I did this week. Runs like new now."

Swallowing some air and her pride, she took the keys. "Thank you."

"You're welcome."

Gaby looked at her mom. "Why'd you do this?"

"You don't expect to borrow Chloe's car forever, do you?"

Gaby looked at Chloe. "No, Momma."

Chloe assured her, "I never once minded, but you deserve something of your own again. Now, let's check this out. Maybe I'll take this car and you can have mine."

Gaby smirked. "No way! Hop in. Let's give her a spin."

After testing out the wheels and roads, Gaby walked into the shop to find Brad. He was sprawled under a car, his legs sticking out as he worked.

Gaby crouched down and stuck her head under. "Hey."

Brad turned his head quickly and hit it on the car. "God, you should never creep up on a guy working under a car."

She winced. "Sorry. Good news is I don't see any blood."

He wheeled out from under the car and stood up. "Thanks for the exam, Doc."

She smiled at him. "Do you know if people can still go swimming in the quarry?"

"I think so. I haven't done it since graduation night."

"Yeah, me either. It's hot out and I thought it might be fun to show my friends. Ages since I did a monster cannonball."

He laughed. "Yeah, me too."

She surprised herself with her next words. "You should join us." *Where did that come from?* "How long are you working?"

"I didn't make any plans." He shrugged. "I could leave whenever."

"We'll probably go in about an hour. Want me to stop and pick you up?"

He narrowed his eyes. "Do you really want me to go? Last night you didn't seem interested in ever seeing me again."

"Just don't try to make out with either of my friends." She laughed and started to walk away, only to turn around at the door and call out, "Be ready in an hour!"

Brad watched her walk out and shook his head. "Damn," he muttered. "What a woman."

~~~~~

Later that day, Gaby sat next to Brad at the shallow part of the quarry, dangling her feet over the edge. She watched as Chloe and Jess took turns jumping.

"So, tell me about work. Do you like what you do?" Brad asked.

Gaby turned her head and met his eyes. "Yeah, I do. It was the right career path for me. I always found it fascinating how the body works, and I like helping patients during their recovery."

"That's awesome," he said, smiling. "You always were good with people."

"Thanks." Gaby looked at her friends and waved. She returned her focus to Brad. "How is it being back?"

"It's good. It took some adjusting at first, though. I was used to a faster pace. And you know how things are around here—everyone and everything moves slower. I don't think I appreciated that enough when I was younger, but now it's what I find most appealing here."

Gaby nodded. "I can see that. You plan on sticking around for a while then?"

The corners of his mouth curved up. "I do. I like it here."

"That's awesome."

Gaby turned to look out at the water. She wondered, *Would I adjust and like it here now too if I had the chance?*

Brad slid his hand on top of Gaby's. She froze at his touch, but secretly smiled, enjoying the warmth of his hand on hers. "I saw you walk with your mom and friends Thursday night into the ice cream shop. You looked sad or something."

Gaby sighed before responding. "Things have been a bit crazy lately. Nothing that won't pass, though."

"Good. I like seeing you smile."

She turned and thought she could see sincerity there. A small smile formed on her lips.

"There it is." He paused and studied her face. He took a breath. "Next time you come to town, let me know. I'd like to see you."

Gaby slid her hand out from under his. "Sure." Her smile faded as she added, "As friends, though. I'm taking some time for myself."

Brad pulled his hand back to his thigh. "As friends would be great. I'm just glad we're talking again."

"Me too," she said softly, and again turned her attention to her giggling friends. "Let's go do some more cannonballs."

"Sounds like a plan," he said as they stood and headed to the jumping point.

~~~~~

Later that night the girls lounged in the living room at Gaby's mom's house. It was their last night there. They would leave the next day in the early afternoon. All four of them were bummed their trip was coming to an end.

Chloe was disappointed like the others, but she also had been seriously missing Chris and couldn't wait to head home tomorrow. She had texted him a few times each day and called him at night before bed. She tried to be present in the moment with her friends, but she always had him on her mind.

She could tell he missed her too. Yesterday she sent him the picture Jess took of her the night Chloe first went to his house for dinner. He recognized it and reminded her that was the night they shared their first passionate kiss. Then he sent a picture of himself back. Chloe had it open now. He was cute, but more importantly, he was good to her. She reached up and touched the necklace he bought her. She adored it and was thankful to have it this weekend while she was away.

Swimming at the quarry that afternoon had reminded her of the date at Ben's. That had been an amazing day she wanted to relive over and over. *I know I'm falling in love with him.*

On Thursday she had called to set up a doctor's appointment for birth control. She now knew she was ready for the next step in their relationship. She was hoping next weekend he would stay over again.

"Earth to Chloe." Gaby snapped her fingers, drawing Chloe's attention back to the present. "Are you okay?"

"Oh yeah, I'm fine. Just spacing out." Chloe set her phone down. She focused on Gaby. "So, what is the deal with Brad? Did you guys ever have a thing?"

She shook her head. "No, we never did. He showed interest growing up, but I turned him down every time. He was a football player and always had girls around him. That kind of guy never interested me. He told me at the Labor Day celebration yesterday that he did it to get my attention. I didn't believe him, but I have to admit I softened up some to him today."

Jess added, "I see the way he looks at you. He is still interested in having a thing with you."

Gaby admitted, "Yeah, it seemed like he is. He told me to let him know the next time I come to town. I said I would, but only to hang out as friends."

Gaby's mom squeezed her leg. "Did you explain why?"

"No, I didn't want to get into it. I gave him my number today and said maybe we can talk sometime."

"Well, honey, that was nice."

"Thanks, Momma." Gaby leaned over and hugged her mom. "I am going to miss you. Can you come see us again soon?"

Momma R. straightened in her chair. "As soon as you want me. I miss the three of you so much."

~~~~~

Chapter 19

Chris made his way down the hall to where yet another fight had taken place moments earlier. Last week, several fights had erupted, bringing the police there on two occasions and an ambulance on one. He didn't know why kids thought they had to act tough around each other and work out their aggression with their fists. Chris found it hard to believe that the changes with the school's class structure and building renovations were contributing to the rough start, as some staff claimed.

He sighed, remembering his second year of teaching. It had started out a lot like this, but there were no major changes to the school then. That had been a very long year where he had to break up several fights himself. One of them gave him a black eye.

That year he constantly wondered if he had made the right choice going into teaching. And over the past few days, he found himself wondering again.

He took a breath as he rounded the corner, preparing as best he could for the next few minutes.

Two teachers struggled to hold two kids apart as a crowd of students gathered around them. Seeing the teachers' discomfort, Chris weaved his way over to them and took one kid by the shoulder. To the crowd he said, "Get back to class. Nothing to see here now."

The class sighed and started to scatter.

Once the crowd fled, Chris released the kid. "What grade are you in?"

"Eleventh."

Chris felt a headache coming on. He knew he should have waited until they got to his office to question him, but he was pissed and wasn't holding his anger in check very well today. He gritted his teeth. "What started it?"

The kid studied the ground. "He said I was an asshole."

"Well, were you? Being one, that is?"

The kid mumbled, "Maybe."

"Either you were or you weren't. Which is it?"

He shrugged. "Yeah, I guess I was."

Chris glanced at the kid, annoyance replacing his anger. He looked like he didn't give a damn about anyone or anything. He knew he wasn't supposed to think like that, but how could he not with the way he was acting? "What did you do?" Chris asked the kid.

"I flicked him in the back of the head."

Seriously? Something so dumb to start a fight over. He motioned for both kids and teachers to follow him to his office.

As they walked, he continued questioning. "When did you do that?"

"In class."

"Today?"

"Yeah."

Chris opened the door to the office area and walked through. He let the kids walk behind him. He knew the kids should walk in first, but to hell with protocol today.

"You first." Chris pointed to the kid he'd taken out of the teacher's hands. They entered, and Chris motioned to a chair across from his desk. "Sit down." He closed the door and darted his eyes to the kid. He didn't seem familiar to him. Chris handed him a form. "Put your name on the top."

After the kid finished, Chris took the paper and looked him up in the system. He was new here this year. Moved from New Mexico. "Why did you flick his head?"

A smug grin spread across his face. "Because he looked dumb."

Chris fought an eye roll. "Write everything you told me in the first box."

"Huh? Write what?"

Chris pointed to the box. "Write here what started the fight, in the order that it happened."

While the kid did that, Chris stepped into the hall, where the two teachers waited. Whispering, he asked, "What did you see?"

One of them shrugged. "I'm sorry, Mr. Sherman. I didn't see much. I was looking down at my notes when I heard a commotion. They were already into it by then."

The other teacher said, "I was next door when I heard someone yell, 'Fight!'"

Chris took a deep breath. "Okay. Could you please write up what you know and email me? I'll attach everything to my report."

They nodded.

"And thanks for your efforts today." With that, he turned and walked back into his office.

After the kid handed the papers back to him, Chris typed up a report and told the kid to wait outside.

The other boy came sauntering in after him. *Geeze*, Chris thought. *He looks like trouble too. Do any of these kids care? Doesn't look like it. They are probably hoping to get suspended.*

He took the other kid's information and his statement and added it to his report. It was time to decide on punishments.

Neither student had any prior fights on record, so they each got off with a warning. Unfortunately, he'd still have to call their parents to report the fight and the warning they received.

Once again to himself, Chris sat back in his chair. He stared into the mug of hot coffee before him and watched the steam rise from the top. He took a drink and let it cleanse his mouth. It felt refreshing despite burning off a few taste buds. His mind once again drifted to another refreshing thought: Chloe. He picked up his cell phone. They had talked last night and made plans to go out to eat tonight but hadn't decided on where.

Hey beautiful, where do you want to go tonight? His phone made a ding moments later. *Hey you, would El Restaurante Estrella at 6:30 work? I have to be here until six. Sorry.*

It's a date, he replied.

He couldn't wait to see her tonight, but he also couldn't help looking forward to the weekend when they could spend a bigger chunk of time together. Chloe had been working a lot in the past two weeks, and their conversations had gotten shorter and shorter the more involved in her projects she became. Still, the promise of time with her encouraged him.

Taking a breath and feeling a bit calmer now, he picked up his office phone and dialed. *Parent time.*

~~~~~

That night Chloe feverishly finished the last of her work and headed to the restaurant as fast as she could. Every part of her couldn't wait to see Chris. Luckily, the restaurant was only a block from her office.

The night air felt good as Chloe walked there, her fingers absently touching the necklace by her throat. She hoped the nervous-excited feelings for him would never leave her.

Arriving just a few minutes late, she scanned the room and saw Chris seated at a booth in the back corner. He smiled when their eyes met. Chloe's body gave a little jolt of excitement as she headed his way.

"You look great," Chris said, standing when she reached the table. He took each of her hands and leaned in for a quick kiss. "A sight for sore eyes."

Chloe smiled. "So do you. I like your tie, Mr. Sherman." She reached for it and gave it a playful tug. As she slid into the booth, she pulled Chris's hand with her. "Sit next to me."

"I'd love to."

"So, how was your day? Any better than last week?"

When they had talked on the phone over the long weekend, Chris had shared some of his daily struggles with her. It made her sad knowing his days had been so stressful and she was so far away. Seeing his face now, she knew that work was wearing on him. Lines creased at the sides of his mouth, his forehead, and his eyes, revealing exhaustion.

Chris put his arm around her and shook his head. "No, worse. But I don't want to waste our time on that tonight. You've heard so much from me about it lately." He leaned in closer and paused. "Is it private enough back here for this?" His head dipped toward her.

Chloe met his lips with equal longing. She pulled back and smiled. "It is. You know ... it's private enough to do that one more time." She wove her hand through his hair just above his collar and pulled him in a little harder.

He looked at her, mischief dancing in his eyes. "I should've asked you to come over tonight, so we could do a lot more of that."

"Tonight isn't the best, but we could do a lot more this weekend." Chloe straightened then, fixing him with her gaze. "I'd like you to stay over again."

"Oh, yeah?"

Chloe nodded. "And ..."

"And?"

"I think I'm ready to do more."

Chris's eyebrows raised. "Really? You sure?"

Chloe grinned. "Yes. I'm positive I want you."

Chris felt his pulse quicken and his mouth go dry. "It's going to be a long week waiting to show you how much I want you."

Chloe's gaze sparkled. "Yes, it is. I'm already struggling."

Chris nuzzled her neck. "God, you don't know what you do to me." He gave her one more peck before he picked up a menu, trying to calm his racing thoughts. "Are you hungry?"

"Very."

After a nice relaxing meal, Chris felt exhausted. As much as he wanted to follow Chloe home, he knew his body was about to give out. Chris paid then walked Chloe to her car. It was a nice September night. Still warm, but not too stuffy.

At the car, Chris wrapped his arms around Chloe. "I really missed you."

"I missed you too. You look wiped. I'm worried about you."

Chris pulled back to look at her face. "Don't be worried. Sure, I've had a few rough days, but it'll pass." He caressed her cheek. "When do I get to see you again?"

Chloe smiled at his touch. "Whenever you want, except tomorrow. I have self-defense class."

"How many more classes do you have?"

"Just this one. We can always do drop-ins for refreshers if we want."

"I'm going to need a demonstration once more and that proper girlfriend kiss."

Chloe giggled. "Mmm, I think you're interested in wrestling. That way I can combine both defense and kissing techniques."

With a devilish look in his eyes, he asked, "Do you promise?"

"On Friday night, I'll pin you down." Chloe said, playfully punching his arm. "Calm down, Mr. Sherman. Anyway, since it is our last class, we are going to go out at the end with a couple of other women we met.

"Sounds like fun. We'll talk soon and make plans."

Chloe studied his face. "Definitely. Now go home and get some rest!"

Chris wheezed out a laugh. "Do I look that bad?"

She brushed his cheek with her fingers. "No, you look a little rough, but you're still wonderful to me. Kiss me."

"Gladly."

~~~~~

The next night after class, the girls drove through the rain to meet a couple of the friends they'd made during the self-defense sessions. Ed and his two helpers were coming too. They parked near the café and dashed into the shop. The rain was really coming down now. It had been a dry summer, but today was one of the rare times where they were getting a ground-soaking rain.

Chloe went up to the counter and ordered three teas while Jess grabbed a table. Gaby followed Chloe, volunteering to buy the desserts. Once their order was ready, Chloe picked up the tray and carried it to the table as a few of the others came in and joined them. Chloe sat across from Cher. They exchanged smiles and hellos.

Gaby slid in next to the window. As soon as she had a fork, Chloe dove into the cake. "God this is good. I wish I had the recipe. I'd put it in my cookbook."

Cher looked Chloe's way. "Are you a baker?"

"I dabble in it."

Gaby joined in. "Chloe's too modest. She's working on writing a baked goods cookbook."

Cher looked impressed. "Are you a writer then? Or a dabbler?"

"I am a journalist. I work at Local 9 News."

Realization dawned on Cher's face. "I thought your name sounded familiar. I have read your articles and seen some of your field work. You're very good. When my sister was staying with me for a few months, we would catch up on the news together every morning. I remember her commenting on your work. She is also a writer, so that is a great compliment."

Chloe lowered her eyes, trying to keep her face calm. Inside, she felt excited and a little embarrassed at the attention. "That's so kind. Thank you."

Gaby leaned across the table. "What does your sister write?"

Cher waved her hand. "Oh, all kinds of things. She's a professor, so she writes some complex works. But she also writes some fiction for fun."

"Who is she?" Jess joined in now too.

"Sylvia Burges."

Chloe's eyes lit up. "Sylvia Burges? Oh my God! I studied some of her work in a contemporary writer's class in college. She is amazing."

Cher smiled. "I'm sure she'll love to hear that. I'd be happy to put you two in touch if you like."

Chloe was ecstatic. "That would be incredible! I am a huge fan."

"Every couple of weeks a group of women I know get together to talk—a sort of support group, I guess. We started a few years back when some of us were going through personal relationship challenges. It's meant to be a safe space, a place where we help each other. We talk about all sorts of things, personal and professional. And Sylvia always comes. You should too."

"I'd love to! I'll give you my number, and you can let me know the next time you meet."

Cher looked at Gaby and Jess. "You both should come too."

After a bit more conversation, everyone finished their teas and desserts and made their goodbyes with a few handshakes and hugs.

It was still pouring out when the girls raced back to Gaby's new car. They piled in, anxious to get home and dry off. Gaby drove slowly because of the hard rain, and from her seat in the back, Chloe watched as every so often, her friend's eyes would look to the rearview mirror.

Chloe glanced behind them when they made a turn. A car's headlights dazzled the glass. As she turned back around, a vision of someone walking up to the car while parked in front of a grocery store filled her mind. "Guys, I might have just had a premonition. Nothing bad, just us in a parking lot. But maybe to be safe we should take a few extra turns rather than go straight home."

From the front passenger seat, Jess started watching the side mirror. "Do you think they're following us? Should we turn at the next light?"

Gaby made a left when she should have stayed straight. "Yeah, I'll do a few extra."

Chloe didn't want to turn around and draw attention. "Did they follow?"

"Yes," Jess said with dread.

Chloe took out her phone and pulled up Maps. "Maybe we should drive to the police station. The closest one is ten minutes away. Or I can call the non-emergency number and see what they recommend."

Gaby made a right turn and pulled into a grocery store parking lot. "Maybe stopping here will deter them."

Chloe sunk a little further down in her seat. *The grocery store!*

Jess watched in the mirror. "Damn, they turned too."

Gaby pulled up to the front of the store as if dropping someone off. The car drove by them and parked in a spot. An older woman got out and raced inside.

Gaby let out a long breath. "Thank God. I hate how paranoid I have become."

Jess rubbed her back. "It's not just you. We all have."

Chloe sighed in agreement. "Yeah, we're all still struggling with how to feel secure again."

Gaby took a deep breath and shook her head. "Thanks for warning us, though, Chloe. Okay. Everyone fine?"

They nodded.

"Then let's try driving home again."

~~~~~

On Friday night Chloe walked into the sports bar where Chris was hanging out with Todd and some friends. He'd invited her to come after work, but she'd decided to first have dinner at home with Jess and Gaby for their usual Friday night friend time. She agreed to come after since Jess had to get up early and Gaby wanted an early night.

Standing outside the bar now, Chloe saw him through the window. He was seated and completely focused on a game playing on a TV behind the counter. What caught her attention next was a tall blond woman standing a few feet away, staring at him. Next to her was Sandy. Chloe felt anger rise at the sight of her, but then she remembered Chris's words. *He's not interested in her. He only wants me.*

Still, Chloe decided to watch for a few minutes to see if anything happened.

Chris seemed totally oblivious, but Todd flickered his gaze over to the ladies. He nodded to Sandy, nudged Chris, and carried on their conversation as if Sandy and her friend didn't exist. Chloe almost burst out laughing seeing how annoyed Sandy and her friend were after that.

Time to go see my boyfriend.

She entered the restaurant and leaned down next to Chris's ear. "Hey," she murmured, glad she had on a hot new dress. She'd picked it out with the hopes of making Chris squirm, but it certainly came in handy for repelling women from her man too.

Chloe watched Sandy narrow her eyes and motion to her friend. Together, they disappeared into the crowd.

As soon as Chloe's lips touched his face, Chris turned his head with a snap. "Oh, hey! You made it." His gaze wandered over her. "Wow! Look at you. You're hot." Chris swiveled on his chair and brought her to stand between his knees.

Chloe loved that he liked her dress. It was a wrap style with a sheer ruffle along the edge. The ruffle gave it some cuteness, but the deep V neckline made it sexy.

She rested her hands on his shoulders. Without thinking, she leaned closer and whispered, "Wait until you see what's under it." Turning bright pink, Chloe looked down. *Did I just say that out loud?*

Chris quickly recovered from his surprise at her forwardness and tilted her chin with his finger, bringing her gaze back to his. He quirked his eyebrow. "I don't want to wait. This week was long enough."

She looked at the TV and back to Chris. Ignoring the flips her stomach was doing, she whispered, "This game doesn't look as good as the one I have planned for us."

Chris laughed. "You're going to have to stop that or I won't be able to walk out of here without embarrassing myself."

Chloe swallowed and bit her lip. Her lips quivered as she smiled. "Sorry. I just can't help myself."

Chris's laughter increased. "God don't be sorry. But I am going to need five minutes."

She snickered. "We'll stay for longer than five minutes. I'll stop so you can collect yourself."

"Let me get you a drink."

Chris twisted to look for the bartender. He got his attention with a wave. The bartender walked to them with a smile. Chris looked back at Chloe. "What would you like?"

192

"I'll have the same as you." She waved to his beer.

He fully turned back and tightened his hands on her waist. The way he looked at her made her feel powerful. She decided to stop teasing him for now. She'd turn it back on later.

Chloe looked around and back to Chris. "Should we mingle with your friends?"

"No, I only want to talk with you."

"Oh, really? I thought we were here to socialize. If not, you should have just come over."

Chris nodded behind Chloe. "Todd and the others are having their own conversations. I'm not fully in the mood for hanging out. It's been a long week and sitting here just staring at the TV is more appealing than talking. Well, talking to anyone but you."

Chloe smiled at that. "I'll at least go say hello."

"Okay, I'll square up here so we can leave when you're ready?"

"We'll stay just long enough for me to drink this, okay?"

Chloe brushed a light kiss across his lips and turned to the guys. Todd pulled her in for a quick hug and kept his arm around her shoulders. "Chris has been a real mess the past two weeks between work sucking and missing you. I'm gonna need you to make my life better."

"Cranky, huh?" She took a swig of her beer and saw Sandy staring them down.

Todd leaned in. "You don't have anything to worry about."

"What is the story with her? She tries way too hard."

He nodded. "Exactly."

Chris stuck his head between them. "Who's trying too hard?"

Todd lowered his voice, "Sandy."

Chloe said, "She has been giving me the evil eye since I got here. She had her eyes on you to take home tonight."

Chris twisted his face. "No way. I'm taking you home tonight."

Chloe's stomach fluttered at the thought. A mix of excitement and nervousness swirled inside.

Chris turned her toward him and whispered, "You know there is no pressure about tonight, right? I'm more than happy just to hold you while we sleep again."

"I know. I am a bit nervous, but I still want to."

Chris ran his hands down her arms. "As long as you're sure."

With more conviction in her voice she said, "I'm sure." She tilted her bottle in front of him. "Wanna help me?"

"Sure." He took a big swig and found a spot to deposit the bottle. "All right. We're out of here. See you later, bro."

Chloe gave Todd a hug and waved bye to the other guys. Chris gave a nod as they walked out.

Out on the street, Chris pointed. "I'm up there. Where are you?"

Chloe pointed in the opposite direction. "That way."

"Come with me. I'll drive you to your car."

"Okay."

Chris took her hand and they started walking. "Are we going to your house or mine?"

"Hmm, you don't have stuff with you to stay over, do you?"

"No, but I'm a guy. I don't need anything. Remember last time?"

She looked at his profile. "Yes. And mmm yes, you are definitely a guy. My guy." When he looked back, she winked.

Chris tried to keep himself in check as he opened the door for her. He touched the tie that held her dress closed. He was looking forward to pulling on that later. "You look beautiful tonight, baby."

"Thank you. I've been looking forward to seeing you all day."

"Me too."

~~~~~

While Chris drove to Chloe's house, he thought about how much he wanted tonight to be perfect for her. It would be their first time together—her first time ever—and that put a lot of pressure on him. He'd have to get outside of his head so he didn't ruin it, while trying to make it just what Chloe pictured.

Reaching the townhouse, they made their way to the door, hand in hand. Chloe rattled the keys as she put them in the lock. She looked up at him with a smile. "I might be a little nervous."

"I am too." He rubbed her arm. "I want tonight to be special."

They said nothing as they walked through the quiet house to Chloe's room. Chris closed the door and Chloe made to take off her heels. He stopped her with a light touch of her arm. "They're sexy. Leave them on."

She gave a lazy, shaky smile. "Mmm, okay."

Pins and needles shot through him. "You're so beautiful."

Chloe reached up, hooked her arms around his neck, and pulled him in for a kiss. Chris held her tight against his body and fanned his fingers across her back. Caught up in a lip-lock, they each felt need rise inside them.

Chloe moved her hands from around his neck to rest in between their bodies.

One button at a time, she slowly opened Chris's shirt and slid her hands inside. She loved the way his skin felt as she lightly moved her hands down his torso to his stomach. She pulled back for a minute to see his face. Still moving her hands along the length of him, she said, "I wanted you the first time I met you. When you shook my hand in the office that day, I felt electricity pulse through me."

"I knew I wanted you that first time too. I could see in your eyes this beauty that pulled me in and made me fall for you."

"I could tell you felt it too in how you looked at me. Your eyes were intense and bright." Chloe slid her hand to his cheek. She leaned forward and kissed him lightly.

Moving both of her hands to his shoulders, Chloe slid his open shirt off. Then she trailed her hands up his arms to his upper back and started lightly massaging and rubbing. "I love touching you," she murmured as her fingertips lightly wandered down his back and around to the front of his pants.

Still watching his face, she unbuttoned and unzipped. Pulling them open she lightly touched his hard erection through his boxers. He groaned quietly and used a hand to tilt her face to his. His kiss was more passionate now, quicker. His tongue dove deep into her mouth and explored her taste.

Chloe continued to touch him, uncovering what made him so very male. Through it all, she managed to brush her nerves aside, enjoying the newness of it all. She wanted to touch more of him, to continue to please him. She slid her hands around to his lower back, plunged them into his pants, and guided his outerwear down. She broke the lip-lock while she undid his shoes and had him step out one leg at a time.

Kneeling in front of him now and his pants off she kissed his stomach, right below the belly button. She ran her fingers up the back of his bare legs to his butt where she grabbed, kneaded, and massaged his tight muscles.

Chloe looked up at his face and saw his eyes closed. Moving one of her hands around, she hooked a finger onto his boxers, exposing his erection. *He is gorgeous.* Pulling his boxers down further, she revealed all of him and put her mouth on him. She heard a groan escape from his throat as she licked gently. She shivered and pulled away. Quietly, she said, "Is this okay?"

He opened his eyes to nod in her direction. "It's great. Are you okay with it?"

She looked at him again. "Yes." She wanted to do this.

Chloe teased him and tasted him. Soon, she felt his body stiffening against her. In a swift motion Chris pulled her to her feet. With his hands on her waist, he backed her against the door. In a low, husky voice, he whispered, "My turn. Okay?"

She nodded. Those words alone made her belly clutch, and she felt herself growing wetter.

He used his tongue to lick just below her ear while his hands skimmed her sides. He found the tie that held her dress closed. Pulling his head back so he could see her face, he tugged on the tie. He took a half-step back as her dress unraveled, revealing a light pink lace bra and panty set. "Very sexy," he commented.

He reached for her breasts and rubbed his hands gently over them, feeling her nipples perk below the lace. It sent a sharp sensation through her and reminded her just what they were going to do. With a husky voice, he mumbled, "You're stunning."

Working to keep her nerves at bay, she bit her lip. *Oh my God! It feels amazing. What if I can't make him feel this good? Stop getting inside your head, Chloe. Focus on him.*

Chris locked eyes with her. "You all right?"

Chloe nodded. "Mmm-hmm."

He pulled her into a tight embrace. "We can stop here if you want. I can hold you."

Chloe swallowed. "I'm a hundred percent sure. I'm nervous, but I am enjoying this. I want to continue."

"Okay but stop me if you change your mind." Chris dropped a kiss on the top of her head. "You're very special to me."

Releasing her from his embrace, he slid her dress off her shoulders and let it fall behind her. The simple move of it skimming her skin as it fell had heat spreading through to her core. His mouth was once again on hers, giving her deep and needy kisses. His hands were all over her, slowly trailing over her skin and giving her goose bumps.

Taking her hands in each of his, he brought her arms over her head and with one hand held them against the wall. He used his other hand to trace down her cheek and past her neck to her cleavage. He dipped his fingers under the lace of her bra to lightly touch her soft skin. He continued to her waist and around to her backside, pulling her hips into his.

Her eyelids fluttered open to see his blue eyes now dark, watching her. This felt so different from anything they'd done before. It was serious, romantic, exciting. She loved how careful he was with her too.

Chris's hand continued traveling over her body. He dipped it down her lace panties, pushing them past her hips and watching them fall to her feet. His other arm released her hands, and he stepped back to appreciate the view of her in nothing but her bra and heels. "Damn sexy, baby."

He leaned over and took off her heels and pulled her panties completely off. He slid his hands down around her until both hands held her hips into his. He ground himself up against her and a moan caught in her throat.

Chloe lifted a leg and wrapped it around his waist. He held her tightly and then picked her up. As he carried her, she slid her other leg up around his waist too. The feeling of her against him drove him crazy.

He carried her to the bed and gently fell with her onto the sheets. He stayed on top of her, pinned between the legs she still had clamped around his hips.

Their kissing had gone from deep and needy to desperate now. One thought managed to break through Chloe's trance: *This is happening.*

Unlocking her legs, Chloe let instinct take hold. She ran her hands down his back and slid down his boxers completely, using her toe to guide them past his knees and ankles. The slow rub of her legs along his was almost his undoing, but he managed to hold it together.

Chris lifted his head and stared at her beautiful face. He wanted badly to say *I love you* but couldn't find the courage. Propping himself on an elbow, he used his other hand to pull the straps of her bra over her shoulders and expose her breasts. "So beautiful." He murmured as he lowered his mouth back to hers.

Gently and slowly he traced her lips with his tongue, then moved his kisses down her neck until he licked her cleavage. Kneeling in between her knees now, he leaned over her, moving his mouth to her breasts. He used his tongue to tease her and excite her. She ground her hips to his, almost making him slip inside. He pulled his hips back and whispered, "Not yet."

She groaned, "I need you."

"Soon, I promise."

He trailed his kisses down her belly to between her legs, keeping his fingers circling and tweaking her nipples. Chloe was starting to tremor. He knew she was close, so he only took a small taste of her. She let out a small gasp. Chris smiled up at her. "You're so gorgeous, so ready."

He quickly moved off her to grab his pants. Chloe knew what he was after. "You don't need that," she said. "I started birth control this week. We're covered."

He looked up. She had rolled to her side to look at him. She took every inch of him in. "Come back and make love to me."

He moved to her. Reaching behind her, he undid her bra, making her completely and beautifully naked. He lay next to her and pulled her top leg over his hips. He ran his fingers over her hip and touched her from behind. "You're so wet. I need you."

Chloe rolled back and pulled him with her, positioning him between her legs.

He paused and met her eyes. "I'll go slow. Tell me if you need me to stop."

She nodded, then raised her hips to meet him as he slid inside her. Her eyes popped open wide and a gasp escaped her. "Oh." Chloe breathed in and out, then nodded. "Okay, I'm ready."

They started slowly moving together. Her lips found his and she greedily moved her tongue with his. Their breathing increased until Chloe let out a groan and shuddered.

Chris opened his eyes to watch her climax, resulting in his. He collapsed down on top of her. Not wanting to crush her, he rolled to one side and pulled her with him. Still breathing heavily, he asked, "Are you okay?"

Chloe was starting to catch her breath. "Yes." She fixed her eyes on him. "Oh. My. God. Wow."

He leaned in to gently brush hair from her forehead and to kiss her. "Amazing. You are incredible."

She returned his kiss with equal passion. He cradled her to him and held her tight. She murmured against his bare chest. "Thank you."

"Mmm," was all he could say. He was too emotional, too close to blurting it out. He said it quietly in his head instead. *I love you.*

~~~~~

Chapter 20

On Monday, Chloe pulled into the parking lot and dashed into the office. The first article would be published today. They planned to release it at the beginning of their team meeting and check its progress at the end of the day. After waving to Eve and heading down the hall to her desk, Chloe tried to contain her excitement. *Wow, I can't believe how this year is shaping up at work. My promotion really did come with a lot more responsibility, and I love it!*

Chloe found Mya and handed her a latte as a peace offering. Mya had helped more than Chloe anticipated last week, staying late every night developing and polishing the information with her.

"Cheers!" Chloe said as they clinked lids.

"Thank you!" Mya said after she took a sip. "I'm so excited to launch the series this week."

"Me too!"

Mya lowered her cup, her smile fading as she grew more serious. "It's been great working with you these past few weeks."

"It really has." Chloe put her arm around Mya's shoulders. "I'm sorry it started out rocky. I was being small minded."

Mya shook her head. "I was being selfish, and I pushed my way in on your idea."

"I'm glad you did. Teaming up really propelled the work and brought us together as partners."

"I think so too." They started toward the conference room. Mya smiled. "It's time we reap the fruits of our labors. I can't wait to see how today's first article is received."

"Me too," Chloe said. "I have a feeling tonight's happy hour is going to turn out to be quite the celebration."

Mya raised her eyebrows. "You know it! Any launch party Eve plans is going to be awesome!"

Lou smiled as the two walked in. He sat with his laptop in front of him. "Ready?"

Chloe slipped into the chair next to him. "We are."

"Excellent. Chloe, would you like to do the honors of clicking to post? It was your idea that put us here."

Chloe glanced at Mya beside her.

"It's all you, Chloe," Mya said.

A huge grin swept across Chloe's face as she turned back to Lou. "Before I do, I just want to say thanks for the guidance you gave us and the push to collaborate. It worked really well."

Lou nodded. "I thought it would. You two make a good team. Now, click and release!"

Chloe bit her lip and felt a spark of excitement run through her as she pressed the button. "It's done!"

The rest of the team erupted in clapping and cheers. "Woohoo!"

Chloe's insides were turning as she thought about how far she had come from that small-town girl sitting in her room alone to a woman with her news team. *This feels damn good!*

The rest of the day flew by as Chloe and Mya watched the number of views rise and read the positive comments from readers. It seemed like the week's start was a success!

As Chloe grabbed her things to head out for the launch party, she glanced at her phone. *Oops, six missed texts. When was the last time I checked it?* Two were from Gaby and Jess, congratulating her on how well the article was received. Four were from Chris.

11:07 How did the release go? It's really good! You should be proud … I am! I sent the link to my parents. They were impressed.

2:21 How's your day going? You're getting a lot of great comments … I bet you're busy with reading them and getting compliments.

4:55 I hope everything went well today. You're probably headed to the happy hour soon. Have fun!

4:58 Call me later if you can.

Guilt gripped her at the last line, and she quickly texted back. *Thanks! Crazy here, but I'll try! xoxoxo*

Mya strode up beside her as she pressed send, snatching her attention once more. "Ready?"

Chloe dropped the phone into her bag, vowing to make it up to Chris later. "Yup! Let's go!"

~~~~~

By eleven that night, Chloe felt every bit of her busy day crashing down on her. She told Jess as soon as she got home, "Don't let me sit. I may not get back up."

"That tired, huh?" Jess asked as she swiveled away from her computer to face Chloe.

"God, yes. But it was a great day."

Jess smiled. "I bet it was. How was the party?"

"Awesome. Everyone came and had a good time. It was nice to go out with my coworkers. It had been a few months since we had a launch party."

"That's great. You deserved a nice celebration. You worked hard."

Chloe nodded. "Boy, did we. The rest of this week will be busy too as we get new assignments and catch up on other work."

Jess pursed her lips. "This isn't going to interfere with the festival this weekend, will it?"

"No, I wouldn't let that happen. Of course, I have some work to do while I'm there. Lou wants me to interview as many of the bands as I can. He wants lots of pictures too. Maybe you and Gabs can help out with that?"

Gaby walked up next to Chloe. "Help out with what?"

"With the interviews I have to do at the festival on Saturday. You guys can help grab some shots so we can post them."

Gaby walked into the study and plopped on the chair. A smile spread across her face. "It will be a hardship, but I guess we will manage."

"Yeah, tough," Jess added with sarcasm.

Gaby bounced up then. "Oh, I talked to Momma earlier. She said to tell you congratulations, Chloe. You wrote an amazing article today. She is *so proud of you.*"

Chloe beamed. "Aw. Sweet."

Gaby smiled. "I think she misses us. She wants to know when we are coming back."

Jess thought about it. "Sometime after I get back from California? Definitely for the holidays."

Gaby agreed. "Yeah, definitely, but I was thinking of going before that. I might go the following weekend, since you'll be traveling and you—" she pointed to Chloe "—are going to the East Texas Fair with Mr. Sherrrrman." She laughed. "Now that you will have a weekend alone with Chris, will you finally tell him you're in love with him?"

"Oooh! Oooh! Oooh!" Jess teased.

Chloe smiled wide. "I am going to tell him soon. But 'Oooh! Oooh! Oooh!'

at you too, Gabriella! Can I guess who you are going to *run into* while you're visiting your mom?"

Gaby turned her face away. "Yeah, so what if I do?"

Jess clapped. "Oh, Gabs, I think you should! He is so dreamy."

Gaby stifled a giggle. "He really is, but I don't think I could ever tell him that. It would go to his head."

Gaby had been texting and talking with Brad for a month now. However, she wasn't sure how she felt about him. She admitted she enjoyed talking to him, but she worried if she got romantically involved, he would break her heart or end up treating her badly or changing completely on her, like all the other guys before. For now, she was leaving it at friendship and enjoying getting to know him again.

Chloe raised her eyebrows. "Maybe. Maybe not." Then she tilted her head back and yawned. "I'm going to head up. Busy day tomorrow again. Good night."

"Night."

~~~~~

Chloe's eyelids drooped as she sat on the edge of her bed thinking about how much strength it would take to pull herself up. It was finally Friday, the end of another crazy week, and she felt it in every muscle and joint in her body. She knew Chris would be there in less than an hour to have dinner, and she needed to shower the day off. She also needed to collect her thoughts. She had done a lousy job of communicating with him this week and hoped seeing him in person would smooth things over.

She took a deep breath and stood. *Come on, Chloe. You haven't seen him all week. You miss him. Go get ready.* She flopped off the bed and made a move to the bathroom.

When the doorbell rang, Chloe walked down with a bit more energy. Her stomach did a flip when she pulled the door wide and saw him. He had traded his work clothes for loose-fitting jeans and a T-shirt. *Damn! He looks fine!*

"Hey. Come on in, stranger." Chloe took one of the bags he held. The aroma that wafted out the top made her mouth water. "Gosh, I'm starving."

Chris pushed the door closed with his free hand and then pulled her close. "I am too, but not just for dinner."

"Oh? Is that right?" she whispered, melting into him. He felt so good. *Why didn't I talk to him more this week?*

He held her back to study her. "It feels like a whole year since I saw you. I missed your pretty face." He bent down then and brushed a kiss across her lips.

"I missed you too." Chloe noticed something waver in his expression and his eyes dim. "What's wrong?"

"Nothing." Chris placed his hand at her back, guiding her into the kitchen. "Let's take care of your starving belly."

He glanced into the study and living room. "When are Gaby and Jess coming home?"

"I'm not sure. Jess is staying late at work, and Gaby was meeting some friends."

Chloe studied his face while he took out the Chinese takeout from the bag. "Something's off."

Chris looked up and met her eyes. "I just missed you."

"It's more than that. I can see it on your face. Rough day?"

"It was." Chris moved around the counter to pull out forks from the drawer.

"It's something else."

Chris sighed. "I'm so proud of you for how well your work was received this week. But I've missed seeing you and talking to you." He took a breath. "Have you been avoiding me?"

Chloe's eyes grew wide. "No, it was crazy week. Why would I avoid you?"

She saw his jaw tighten. "Because maybe you're sorry we made love last weekend."

Chloe took the forks from his hand. "The food can wait." She turned him to face her. "I'm not sorry. It was amazing! I never thought anything could feel that wonderful, and you made my first time very special."

Chloe tilted her head and found herself watching his jaw. He still held it clenched. "Did you really think I could avoid you?" she asked.

"I knew you were busy but look at it from my perspective. We make love Friday night. I leave your place Saturday morning thinking it was an amazing night, unlike any night I've ever had. Then I go two days with only getting a few spotty, short texts back from you. We finally talk Monday night on the phone and it's five minutes long. And that's how it was for the rest of the week. It doesn't exactly make me feel important, or that us taking our relationship to a new level was all that special to you. Was I even on your mind?"

Chloe felt her chest tighten as panic rose inside her. "Of course you were on my mind!"

"It didn't feel like it," he countered.

"But you were! I swear! You are so good to me. Everyone can see it." Chloe's hands started to sweat, and her mouth struggled for words.

"I don't give a damn what everyone else sees. I want to know what you see."

"I see it. I do. I've never been treated so well in my life!" Chloe could feel a burning sensation in her chest. *Am I having a panic attack?*

Chris heard the gasps Chloe started to take and softened. He was letting his insecurity and anger get out of control. He reached up and took hold of her upper arms, bringing her close to him.

Tears welled in her eyes and her lower lip began to tremble. "I'm so sorry. I really am. I was insensitive. I should have made more time for you. Work has just been so crazy, with the launch and all the other articles, plus new assignments. I never meant to give you the wrong impression, especially after our first time together. I feel horrible. I'm so sorry!"

He pulled her in and wrapped his arms tight around her. He stroked her back with his hands. "No, I'm sorry. I shouldn't have gotten angry. I'm just insecure. I know work is very important to you. You're doing a great job. I have to learn how to share."

Chloe stepped back and wrapped her arms around her middle. "Are you going to break up with me now? Did I ruin everything?"

Chris's mouth dropped open. *Shit. I went too far.* "God, no! I'm not going anywhere. I'm invested in this. In us." He reached for her. "Let me hold you."

Chloe moved to his arms, sniffling. "I am really very sorry. I thought of you all week. I pictured your face throughout the day and at night when I laid in bed. It gives me goose bumps when I think about how beautiful our night together was. A few nights I looked over longingly at the pillow you slept on, wishing you were there. I even pulled the pillow close to me the first few nights before your scent wore off."

"Oh, sweetheart," Chris sighed, holding her tight against him.

"I should have told you that sooner. And that I would be so busy. I'm sorry I didn't give you the time you needed."

He pulled back and slid his hands to her face, brushing the last of the tears that fell. "I should have been more understanding and patient. And I should have told you sooner how much it bothered me."

Chloe looked up at him. "You treat me so well; it makes me feel secure. I assumed you felt as secure as I did, and you wouldn't be bothered by my busy-ness."

"I'm glad I make you feel that way. I guess you were too secure, which left me insecure." A gentle smile formed across his face. "I should have used my big boy words and told you sooner."

With his hands still on her face, he guided her mouth to his. She leaned into him as she let all the tension and worry go. Chris wrapped his arms around her again, bringing her up to her toes. She parted her lips to give his tongue access. Diving in, he relished the warmth of her mouth and the feel of her body pressed against his.

Chloe returned his kiss, licking his lips and taking her turn to plunder his mouth. She felt a fever begin to build inside her. *Ah, it was a premonition, not a panic attack. A good premonition this time.*

The imbalance of just a few minutes ago slowly started to shift. A small sigh escaped her as she repositioned herself in his arms. Exhaustion and hunger vanished, and all she could think of was him.

~~~~~

The following afternoon, Chloe pulled her car into the festival parking area. "Ready for the time of your lives?" she called to Jess and Gaby.

Her friends nodded and whooped. They'd spent the majority of the car ride singing along to the songs of the bands playing that day, and now that they were actually at the event, they let their excitement out full force.

Chloe's backstage passes also let them park close to the entrance, making it a short walk to the main gates where all the action took place. The girls had been here before, but this year the festival featured new food trucks and other vendors from the area, selling everything from hats and boots to crafts. Plus, the bands were different. *Better*, thought Chloe as she reviewed the lineup on her phone once more.

The sun was bright, but there was hardly any humidity, which made for a good day. They all knew how hot it could get pressed into the crowd, so the cooler outside the better.

Music festivals were one of their favorite things to do in the summer and fall. They loved the music, the people, and the overall good vibe they felt when they were there. And as Lou promised, this festival was one not to miss. Chloe knew how hard it was for people to get tickets. She silently thanked her boss again for getting them these exclusive passes.

After buying bottles of water, they headed to the main stage, where one of the security guards led them to a side stage the bands would use to get to and from their trailers. The first act was doing sound checks, and Chloe breathed a sigh. *No one to interview yet.*

"Picture time!" Chloe announced, turning the camera around and clicking. Jess and Gaby grinned.

Jess smiled at Chloe like a little kid at Christmas. "Now this is amazing!"

"It really is!" Chloe passed her phone to Gaby. "Could you take one of just me now?"

"Sure," said Gaby. "You look cute!"

Chloe posed. "Chris wanted to see me dressed up. Plus, I really like my braids today." She tossed her head from side to side.

Grabbing her phone back after the photo, Chloe fired the picture to Chris.

Chris: *Aw, you look great. Maybe you can wear that outfit next weekend for me? Please?*
Chloe: *You mean for the fair or the bedroom? ;)*
Chris: *Both, first at the fair, then later the bedroom??*
Chloe: *Okay. I promise then.*

A shiver ran up Chloe's spine. *Hmm. I can't wait to spend a full weekend together.*

She then focused on the band on stage. It was an up-and-coming group, the program stated. She leaned over to Gaby and Jess. "These are one of the bands Lou talked about. I'm going to see if I can catch the manager to set me up for a chat with one of the members."

"Go for it, girl," said Gaby.

Chloe wandered away from her group. When she reached the stage, she eyed the guys she thought were in charge. "Hey. I'm looking for the manager." She rattled her press pass. "I'd like to interview one or two of the group, if they have the time."

One of the guys stuck out his hand. "Hi, I'm the manager. Ray. I can set you up. A few minutes work for you?"

"Chloe. Yeah that would be perfect. Thanks."

Within moments, Chloe followed Ray onto the stage. He waved over the guitar player. "Hey Joe, can you do a short interview with Chloe?"

"Yeah, sure. No problem."

Chloe followed Joe toward the back, out of the way of the crew. "So what do you want to know?" he asked, crossing his arms.

Chloe held up her phone recorder. "Do you mind?" Joe shook his head.

After pressing record on her phone, she started, "How did Kid Cowboy start up?"

"We were just a couple of kids playing music in my buddy's garage in high school. We did some small gigs when anyone would hire us. But we got our big break when we turned eighteen and moved to Nashville. We signed with a label after they saw us play. We were lucky. We had only been there a few months when that happened."

"That's awesome. How'd you come up with the band name?" Chloe asked.

"Just a nickname for my buddy Tristen, the singer. He worked on his uncle's ranch as a kid and picked it up there."

"Nice. Is everyone in the group now original members?"

Joe nodded. "Yeah, we are. All from outside of Little Rock." Joe looked up. "Hey, sorry. I gotta run. Show is starting soon. I hope I gave ya enough."

Chloe stopped recording and shook his hand. "Yup, it'll work. Thanks a lot. Nice to meet you."

"Yeah, you too."

Chloe walked back to Gaby and Jess. "That was cool. The guitar player agreed to an interview. Good guy. The band made it in Nashville." Chloe tapped her finger on her chin. "Hmm, you know, girls? We have never been there."

Gaby bounced on her feet. "I'm in!"

"Me too!" yelled Jess. "I hear a road trip next year!"

Chloe nodded. "Oh yeah!"

The band walked by them and Joe waved. "Hey, Chloe."

"Hey!" Chloe flashed a smile and turned to Gaby and Jess. "I love my job right now!"

Gaby grinned, her eyes sweeping over Joe and the other band members. "We do too!"

After Kid Cowboy took the stage, Chloe snapped a few pictures of the group. She then stuffed her phone into her pocket so she could dance with her friends.

Several bands played next, and Chloe found at least one member to interview in each. However, not long after, she needed a break. Her stomach gave her the perfect excuse.

"I'm starving. Let's eat!"

Jess nodded. "Great idea."

They left the side stage and headed toward food trucks nearby. As she stood in line Chloe heard someone call her name. She turned in the voice's direction and saw a guy walking toward her. He wore an army T-shirt, ball cap, and shorts.

"Chloe, is that you?"

She looked harder, trying to make out the face under the brim of his cap. Then her stomach dropped as realization hit. She whispered, "Jake?"

Jake walked closer, like a ghost in a dream. But this was definitely not a dream. "Yeah, it's me," he said. "Oh my God. It really is you!"

He pulled her in for a hug, then held her back from him. His eyes swam over her face. "Wow! You grew up. How many years has it been?"

Chloe was still shocked to see him. For years she had dreamed of this happening. She'd spent months of her life pining over what could've been if he hadn't left, pouring over the emails he sent her, wishing there was something more that could develop. But then everything stopped. She didn't understand. Would he tell her why now?

Chloe found her voice. "About six years, I guess. I was nineteen when I was in that accident."

Jake smiled broadly. "Wow! Well, you look great."

"Thanks." Chloe turned to her friends. "This is Jess and Gaby."

He barely looked at them. "Nice to meet you."

Chloe pointed to his shirt. "Are you still in the army?"

He followed her gaze. "Naw. I did five years then left when a few of us wanted to start a group."

Chloe drew her brows together. "A group?"

"Yeah. I play in a band now. Part of the Rolling Thunder Band."

Chloe gasped. According to Lou's notes, the Rolling Thunder Band was her top priority tonight. A relatively new, hot band with all the promises of making it big—soon. She couldn't believe her luck. "Oh my God, really?"

Jake nodded. "Yeah, really. I play the drums."

"Wow." Chloe shook her head. "I'm here for work. I'm a reporter … interviewing the bands. The Rolling Thunder Band. I've heard so many great things. Would you be willing?"

"Yeah, of course. I'll find you in a bit. You'll be backstage?"

Chloe nodded.

After Jake walked away, Gaby pushed Chloe's jaw up. "Sweetie, you're gawking."

Chloe tilted her head. "Umm, yeah. I can't believe he is in the Rolling Thunder Band. I love their music!"

"They are good." Gaby grabbed her arm. "Come on! Let's get some grub and head back. You already have your next interview lined up."

"I guess I-I do," Chloe stuttered as she let her friends guide her.

They found a bite to eat and headed back as quickly as they could. They resumed their spot at the side stage and waited.

After a few minutes, Chloe heard voices. She turned and saw Jake walking her way. "Hey," he said. "Where do you want to go?"

"Umm, let's head over here." He followed Chloe around the back where she had done the other interviews.

Chloe turned and smiled. "Thanks for doing this."

A huge smile formed across his face. "You bet."

"So tell me how the Rolling Thunder Band got started?"

"A bunch of army guys with too much time on their hands. Sure, we were busy practicing drills and doing missions when assigned, but we were left with a lot of time to think. One night we started talking about music and next thing you know; we're planning how to start a band."

"Did everyone already play instruments and sing?"

Jake shook his head. "I don't sing. The rest of the guys do. We had all played instruments before but needed to brush up. We were all pretty rusty. It's not like we could carry guitars and a drum set around on a tour of duty."

Chloe laughed. "I guess not. So tell me about when you left the army. How did you guys get your start?" *And why didn't you write me again?*

"After we left Fort Hood that last day, we got a place together in Dallas and gave ourselves a year to see if we could make it. Tommy knew a couple of people in the business and hooked us up with some auditions. One offered us a deal, and here we are."

Chloe nodded. "Cool. So where do you guys get your inspiration for your music?"

Jake's eyes glittered. "Well, army life is rough on relationships. We've all experienced lost loves, lonely nights, and even one of us felt there was *one who got away*." Chloe thought his eyes lingered on her face a bit too long at those last words.

Trying to remain focused, she took a steadying breath. "Sounds like you four took sleepless nights and turned it into a career?"

Jake smiled. "You bet we did!"

Chloe stopped the recording on her phone. "I heard your name called. Thanks so much for doing this."

Jake leaned in for one last hug.

"Sure thing," he replied. "It was great to see you after all these years. I thought maybe you had been a figment of my imagination."

Chloe stepped back. "I know what you mean. Good to see you. Take care."

He winked as he took off.

Chloe made eye contact with Gaby and Jess as she joined them. Gaby pulled her arm, drawing her in close. "Spill it! What are you thinking?"

"All the times I thought about him over the years, and that wasn't how I pictured it'd go. He seems so different now. Established. Happy. He's definitely seen the world." She smiled. "I was sure if we ever crossed paths again I would feel something—wanted to give him my number and told him to call me or something." She hung her head low and laughed. "But I didn't."

"Nothing at all?" Gaby seemed shocked.

Chloe hesitated. "I was hurt he didn't explain what happened—why he stopped talking to me. But I actually didn't feel anything romantic." Chloe shook her head. "You know, I haven't even thought about him in months. I completely gave up the fantasy of ever seeing him after I met Chris."

Jess put her arm around her shoulders. "Aw, you know what that means? You're in love with Chris. Truly in love with him."

Chloe smiled a big smile. "Yeah, I really am. I can't wait to tell him. I'm going to do it next weekend since we'll be together for a full forty-eight hours!"

Jess squeezed her close. "Way to go, Chloe."

~~~~~

After a great night of music and fun, the girls were watching the last band play. They were winding down, but still pumped up from the music.

Chloe glanced over her shoulder while they waited their turn to pass through the gate to the parking area. "It sucks you have to leave Monday, Jess. We're going to miss you."

Jess looked at them both. "It does. I'll miss you too." She shook her head. "But what a way to send me off! I hope we always make time to do this stuff together. Even when we're old."

Gaby pulled both Chloe and Jess in so they could hear her over the crowd. "I feel like it is safe to say this was one of my favorite concerts! And thanks to Chloe, we got to see it all up close!"

"It was one of my favorites too. Once you experience the backstage there is no going back!" Chloe yelled. She glanced around again as she tried to fight the anxiety welling up inside her. During the last song, Chloe had a vision of them running. Her braids were swinging, Gaby was holding her hat on, and Jess was yelling. She tried to push her worries to the back of her mind. *Maybe it's us having fun? My last premonition was a good one.*

When the girls were nearly to the gate, they heard someone yell, "Gaby!"

They turned their heads in the voice's direction, and their stomachs dropped. Kirk slithered through the crowd, pushing people as he moved toward the trio.

"Hell no," Gaby said.

As Kirk approached, Gaby stuck out her hand, intending to stop him, but he just kept inching closer. Suddenly, his breath was on her face, and his hands fumbled for her. She shrieked, and in a blur, her knee forcefully nailed him where it counts.

Gaby and Chloe watched as Kirk doubled over.

He yelped out, "You bitch!"

Gaby growled. "Don't ever come near me again!"

Chloe had each of their hands as they fit their way through the gate. They walked quickly, weaving through the crowd to the parked cars.

Jess kept an eye out behind them. "I don't see him!"

Gaby snuck a peek next. "He was down on all fours. I don't think he'll be getting up any time soon.

Chloe knew he would be, though. They would be running soon. "Keep moving!"

Luckily, Chloe's car came into sight moments later. She dug for her keys. "Got them!" she said, holding them up.

Jess glanced behind them. "Oh shit! He's right there!"

The three raced for the car. It was just like Chloe pictured. Her hand fumbled for the lock. "Hurry!" Jess screamed.

Kirk was steps away now.

There! The locks released and they all tumbled in. Chloe clicked the door lock as the last door slammed shut and tried to calm her frantic heartbeat while starting the engine. *Just drive.*

But there was nowhere to go. Chloe watched traffic crawl over the gravel road toward the main streets around the festival. *What are we going to do?*

"Look out!" Jess gasped.

They screamed as Kirk jumped on the hood of the car and started pounding his fists. "Get out here, Gaby!"

"Don't move," Chloe ordered.

"No way," Gaby agreed. "He's crazier than before. There's no way I'm leaving this car."

Within moments, strong hands dragged Kirk off the car hood.

"Oh my God," Chloe whined, watching as one security guard and two other men wrestled Kirk to the ground. They had him face down with his hands behind his back.

"What do we do?" Jess asked.

Chloe sighed. "I guess we wait for the police."

Gaby nodded. "As much as I want you to punch it, Chloe, I agree."

Once the police arrived, two officers took Kirk away while another officer knocked on one of their car windows. "Ladies, could you step out of your car? I'd like to ask you a few questions."

"Yes, of course," Gaby responded, moving from her seat as she said the words.

With the three of them huddled together, the officer continued, "Hi, I'm Officer Nettles." His eyes passed between them. "Do you know the man who was pulled off your car hood?"

Gaby raised her hand part-way up. "I do. Well, we all do, but I'm the one who knew him first. I dated him last year. This isn't the first time he has followed us, but this was the first time he was aggressive toward us. We saw him act this way before, but he was in a fight with another guy."

Officer Nettles handed Gaby a clipboard. "Could you write down your information here? Do you have a restraining order against him?"

She breathed shakily. "No. I wanted to, but we didn't have justification. He wasn't trying to hurt any of us before. He only watched our house and followed us."

"Well, you have grounds to file one now. My report can be used. I'm collecting witness statements, which will help your case."

Gaby studied the form. The words blurred as her eyes filled with tears. She swiped them away and started writing.

Officer Nettles handed Jess his card. "I'll be in touch, but if you need something before you hear from me, give me a call."

Gaby looked up at him and handed over the clipboard. "Thanks for your help."

Once they were on the road heading home, Gaby's tears flowed freely, as did her anger. "I'm so sick of it all. I hate when people look at me with pity. I hate having to be questioned by the police. I hate the drama. I'm so tired of it all. I want all of this to go away. He's screwed up another great night."

Chloe patted Gaby's leg. "He'll get his. You'll get the restraining order this time and if he crosses it, he'll have to answer for it."

"Dammit. This is crap!" Gaby yelled. "He somehow found me again. When is it going to stop?"

Jess sighed. "It is complete bullshit. We all knew we might see him again. Guys like him don't just stop stalking." She held up her hand. "Okay, sorry to change the subject some, but let's talk about that kick you gave him! God, I was so proud of you back there. You nailed him hard."

Gaby's crying started to slow. "It did feel good to do that."

Chloe whooped. "The look on his face was priceless. Ed would be proud."

~~~~~

Chapter 21

Chloe ran to answer the doorbell. She was expecting Chris to join her and Gaby for dinner. As she opened the door and pulled him in, he wound his arms tight around her, picking her up off the ground.

She laughed as he twirled her. "I missed you!"

He put her down on her toes. Still holding onto her, he brushed a kiss across her lips. "I missed you too."

"Are you staying over tonight?"

Chris motioned to the bag hanging on his shoulder. "Yes, ma'am. Just like you asked."

Chloe leaned into his ear. "Good. I missed your body on mine."

He grinned. "Grrr, me too."

She took his hand and walked to the kitchen. "You got here at the right time. Dinner is ready."

"Hey, Chris," Gaby called from the deck. It was a beautiful night, so they lit the tiki torches and the chiminea and decided to eat on the deck.

"How are you, Gaby?"

"I've been better," she said. Chris noticed the strain in her face.

"Why, what's wrong?"

Gaby looked at Chloe.

Chris watched the two of them. "What am I missing?"

Chloe waved her hand dismissively. "Let's eat. We have a story to tell you, but it's not that big of a deal."

"Now you're still making me nervous."

Chloe started filling up his plate and passed the dish to Gaby. "Don't be. We are fine."

Chris stared at her. "What?"

"We had a little run-in with Kirk Saturday night."

"How little is *little?*"

Chloe took a bite and looked to Gaby. "Do you want to tell it? You're the one who took care of business, after all."

213

Gaby rolled her eyes. "I wish I had flattened him out like you're making it seem. It wasn't that good." She told him what happened.

Chris groaned. "Hell, not again!"

Gaby continued, "At least this time, because of his threatening actions, I was able to get a restraining order. I went down to the courthouse and filed for it today. He can't come within one hundred yards of any of us."

Chloe saw Chris's jaw tense and his eyes gaze at her with concern. "Good. I don't want him near you."

"We don't either," said Gaby. "We've had it with this crap!" To Chloe, she said, "I'm sorry I brought him into our lives."

Chloe patted Gaby's hand. "It's not your fault. He's the one to blame."

Chris wrapped his arm around Chloe. "I don't want anything to happen to you." Then his eyes fell on Gaby. "To either of you."

"We know." Chloe said, patting his knee. "We're okay."

"I'm glad." He leaned closer to Chloe. "I'm glad you told me. Thank you."

After that exchange, dinner was quiet. They talked some, but mostly about Jess, who'd left for her trip to California that morning; and the music from the concert. Chloe had left out her run-in with Jake. *It's not important. He means nothing. I felt nothing. But why do I feel bad for not telling him?* She knew sooner or later she'd have to bring up the subject.

During clean-up they discussed plans for the upcoming weekend. Gaby was taking Friday off to visit her mom and clear her head. Chloe and Chris still worked Friday but planned to stay home that night and leave early Saturday for the East Texas Fair. Chris's parents and Todd would join them.

Chris looked forward to having Chloe to himself for most of the weekend. He hadn't seen her for the past few days, and now knowing Kirk had appeared again, he was glad to have her with him.

~~~~~

They went up to Chloe's room a bit later that night. Chris sat on the chair reading while Chloe changed in the bathroom. He looked up when she walked out and found her in an oversized T-shirt, but not so big that her legs weren't completely visible. He didn't mind when she walked over to him and sat on his lap, crossing her long legs at the ankle and resting her head on his shoulder.

Chris started slowly stroking her bare leg. "Last week was a big week for you with the launch party for the mental health series. We didn't get to talk much about it. Lou must have been very happy."

"Oh, he was. He called us into his office on Friday. He was thrilled. He said we'll be getting more joint assignments after seeing what a great success this one turned out to be."

"I'm really proud of you. You're very talented."

Chloe whispered, "Thank you. I appreciate that."

Chris smiled. "You're becoming a real force to be reckoned with. Confident and talented at work, and one hell of a badass thanks to those classes."

A giggle slipped from her throat. "I try."

"You're very tough. I had a call from Rick last week. He apologized for what he did. Told me you had one hell of an arm on you. Broke his nose."

Chloe tilted her face up to look at him. "Seriously?"

"Yeah," he said, shaking his head. "Like I said, a badass."

"Wow! Is his nose going to be crooked now?"

"Naw, and if it was, he deserved it."

Chloe rested her head back on his shoulder. "Did I do better the past few days with making sure you know how important you are to me? I was sure to text you more since I couldn't call from the festival and while I caught up on work Sunday and today."

Chris cringed. "Chloe, I don't mean for you to worry now about how much you text me. I just want to know you're thinking of me. I promise I am not counting how many messages you send or how often you call or not."

"Okay," she whispered. "I thought a lot about you. I missed you."

"I missed you too," he said, feeling overcome by emotion. He brushed her cheek lightly with his fingers then pulled her in close to his chest and kissed her gently. His hand stroked her leg again. Then, drawing his hand up under her shirt, he found her breasts. Heat inside him grew when he found she wasn't wearing a bra. After cupping her and gently teasing with his fingertips, he deepened their kiss and moved his hand down between her legs.

"May I?"

She nodded, her eyes wide in anticipation.

He pulled her panties down, over her toes, and tossed them to the floor. Then slowly he brought his fingers back to her, finding the spot between her legs. He knew she wanted him when he touched her, and she shivered. He slipped a finger inside, and she groaned against his mouth, making him hard. "Take me to bed," she begged.

Chris smiled. "Not yet. I still have things I want to do to you."

In a husky, demanding whine, she protested, "But I need you now."

"I want to watch you let go with my hands, then we'll go to the bed."

In tantalizing circular motions, his fingers expertly teased her. She felt tight sensations building in her core.

He stopped to pull her T-shirt over her head.

She moaned. "Please, don't stop. I need you so bad."

"You're so beautiful." He looked at her naked body. There was something so sensual about having her exposed in front of him. Her head hung off his arm and her hair swung as she moved her head back and forth in pleasure. The beautiful way she trusted him with her body and wanted him to touch her drove him crazy, but he took quick, shallow breaths to control his deep desire.

She quivered and squirmed when his mouth closed around the nipple closest to him and his fingers played with the other. He glanced down to see her body begging for release, her legs parted and her hips grinding against his hand. He moved his mouth to hers and used both his fingers to feverishly torture her nipples. His mouth hovered over hers, promising to touch but teasing when it didn't.

He whispered, "I love watching your body build up. You're so sexy, baby."

Chloe was dying inside. She wanted him to put his fingers back inside her, but he kept playing with both of her nipples. She didn't know how much more she could take.

Chris continued his onslaught of her breasts, now palming them. Her eyes rolled into the back of her head. She was so aroused she thought she would explode.

"Please, Chloe, let go for me. Let me watch you. I want to see your body shake and quiver in my hands."

Her body gave in. She arched her back as multiple strong convulsions rocked her. She never felt anything so erotic in her life, so primal, so demanding.

Picking her up and carrying her still writhing body, he put her on the bed and quickly pulled off his clothes. As he positioned himself on top of her, she wrapped her legs around him, welcoming him inside. Unlike their first time, he drove hard and fast, building her up again. At her release, he found his own.

Still panting, he forced himself up on his elbows. "You nearly wrecked me that time."

Chloe's head rolled to the side and her arms flopped down on the bed. "You did wreck me."

~~~~~

Friday after work Chloe walked through the front lobby to head home. She had been looking forward to tonight all week. Chloe had seen Chris almost every night, sharing many beautiful nights of love making. This weekend would top off the great week by her having him mostly to herself. She was ready to say those three little words that she felt would show the growth of their relationship and commitment for the future.

She smiled, studying the flowers—a mix of daisies and small purple flowers—that had been delivered earlier in the day. They really were beautiful. When Eve had brought them to her office, Chloe had been so excited, her stomach full of butterflies. *Chris is so thoughtful.* But when she read the card that accompanied it, her stomach knotted.

Hi Chloe, it was great to see you last Saturday. Life's been busy this week, with so many shows, but I'm staying in town for a few more days and I'd love to see you again. Call me? – Jake

A few months back, this note would have been a dream come true. But now, it just felt annoying and strangely funny. *Trust me to never have a boyfriend and now suddenly to have two guys interested in me at once.* She shook her head. *Well, only one can have me. And I've made up my mind.*

She took the flowers to Eve. "Chris didn't send them. It was someone else."

Eve didn't ask questions. "Well, I'll take them off your hands, dear."

Chloe sighed. "Thank you."

Eve pursed her lips. "Aw, Chloe. I know it's disappointing that they weren't from Chris. I'm sure he'll send you flowers soon."

Chloe slipped the card into her purse. "I wanted them to be from Chris. We had such a good week together. This would have been perfect timing."

Eve stood up and came around her desk to hug Chloe. "Don't let this get you down. Young love is so wonderful. It looks good on you."

"And it feels good." *I have to remember that.*

"He'll come around. I'm sure."

Driving home, Chloe wondered if Chris thought about a future with her. Where were they headed? She believed they were in love, even though they hadn't said it yet. But would they get married someday? Have kids? Was that what she wanted? Was that what he wanted?

She wished she could talk to Chris about this, but she didn't feel ready. Four months was too soon to have the marriage and family talk. She'd have to settle for talking about love and building a relationship first. This weekend she wanted to find the right time to do just that.

Besides, before she could talk to him about a future, she had to clear up her past. She had to tell Jake where she stood and tell Chris that Jake had sent her flowers. He deserved to know. Chris had told her just a few days ago that he wanted to know things even if they made him worry. Did this count?

Chloe unpacked her things from work and settled in for the evening, choosing to wear comfy sweats over her lacy underwear. Chris was spending the night, and she fully planned on making the most of their time alone in the house.

Before any nighttime fun, however, she had a simple dinner planned, followed by a movie and dessert. Dinner was an easy casserole, and dessert was a chocolate lava cake. She knew Chris loved chocolate and wanted to surprise him with her latest cake recipe. He could help her make the final decision to include it in her baking cookbook or not.

While Chloe waited for Chris to arrive, she worked on the book. She had made a lot of progress over the past few weeks, in between navigating work and her relationship. It was exciting to see how it was coming together.

Getting lost in her thoughts, Chloe jumped when her phone buzzed. *Gaby.* She brought the phone to her ear. "Hey, Gabs. How's Harmony?"

"Good! Really good. Momma and I did some shopping today, and she taught me how to make my dad's secret mole sauce. We just finished eating it now on enchiladas."

Chloe noticed how happy her friend sounded. Being at home was just what she needed, especially after last weekend's surprise. "That's awesome. I hope you know you're teaching me now!"

"Definitely! Next Friday night! What are you up to tonight?"

Chloe looked at the time. She didn't realize how late it was. "Chris is coming over. He should be here soon." She stood up to get the casserole out of the oven. "Geeze. I think my chicken dried out. I must've left it in too long."

"Is everything okay? It's not like you to get that distracted," Gaby said with slight concern.

Chloe sighed. "Actually, no. I wanted to talk to you about something."

"Shoot," said Gaby.

Chloe felt heat rising on the back of her neck. "Well, today Jake sent flowers to my work."

"Oh my God, for real? Jake as in Jake from the festival? As in country music star Jake?"

"The one and only."

"Did he say anything?"

Chloe grabbed the card out of her purse and read it to Gaby.

Gaby gasped. "Wow! How do you feel about that?"

Chloe sighed. "Mostly disappointed. I thought Chris sent them at first."

"What did you do with them?"

"I gave them to Eve on my way out. I kept the card, though. I feel like I should call him to thank him but tell him I'm with someone. It would be rude to ignore him, right? What do you think, Gabs?"

"I think it's up to you. What does your gut say? Or have you had any premonitions that can point you in the right direction?"

Cringing a bit, Chloe said, "No helpful visions, unfortunately. But my gut says I should call, and I should tell Chris. He should know, even though he won't like it."

"Chloe, you didn't do anything wrong. You can't help if some blast from the past sent you flowers because *he wanted to.*"

"Yeah. I just hope that if I tell him this doesn't mess up our weekend."

"Well, get it over with and move forward. But don't tell him the second he walks in."

Chloe laughed. "Thanks. Point taken." She shifted the phone in her hand. "So, have you seen Brad?"

Gaby sighed. "No. He knows I'm here, though. We've talked on the phone. After he's done working tomorrow, we are going to hang out."

In a sing-song voice, Chloe asked her, "Hang out as friends or hang out as something more?"

Gaby paused. "Honestly, I'm not sure. I don't think I should let it be something more yet. I will try to keep it that way, so this stays simple and uncomplicated."

"Keep me posted."

"You know I always do. Have fun this weekend."

"Thanks, girl. Night."

When the doorbell rang, Chloe had just finished getting everything ready for dinner. She answered the door breathless with happiness and nerves. "Hey, you! Get in here!"

"Yes, ma'am! Sorry I'm late," he replied, dropping his bag on the floor and giving her a big bear hug. She let her legs dangle and gave him a big smooch.

Chloe pulled back but didn't let go. "I'm so glad you're here. Mostly because I'm starved," she teased. "Let's eat!"

Chris carried her out to the kitchen. "I don't want to let you go!" He pulled out a chair and sat them both at the table. "Can we eat like this? I can feed you."

Chloe giggled. "I don't think we'd eat much if I continue to sit on your lap."

He gave her a deep kiss. "You're right. There is already movement that tells me it's a bad idea."

Chloe slid into her own chair giggling. She served Chris and then herself, taking in his features as they sat across from each other. The same lines of tension on his face from a few weeks ago creased his forehead and his eyes. Bags from lack of sleep tugged at his lower lids. He even held himself differently, looser, more lethargic. He didn't seem like himself.

He looked up from his plate, sensing her watching him. "This is really good."

He cocked his head to one side. "What?"

"I was just thinking you look stressed. Do you want to tell me about your day?"

He shook his head. "No, I just want to forget it. Let's talk about you instead. How was your day?"

Chloe decided she would let it go for now and see if tomorrow on the car ride to the fair he would open up.

As she thought, she found herself picking at her plate. Sweat beaded on her skin. *Tell him now.* "Okay. Not too busy." She paused to bite her lip. *Just spill it, Chloe.* She sighed. "I got a delivery today from someone I ran into at the festival last weekend."

Chris stopped his fork mid-air. "Who? And what kind of delivery?"

Still biting her lip, she said, "Jake, a guy I knew a few years back, was at the festival. We ran into each other and talked for only a minute. I found out he was in one of the bands and interviewed him—Lou's orders. I kept it professional, but I guess he got a different impression. He sent me flowers today." She looked at Chris to gauge his reaction. His jaw tightened the way it always did when he was uncomfortable.

"What did he want?"

"He put his number on the card and asked me to call him."

She could see his jaw flexing now. "Are you ... going to call him?" She couldn't tell if he was mad or hurt.

Chloe paused. "Yes, I think so. But only to tell him I have a boyfriend. I feel like it would be rude to ignore him."

Chris sighed. "Why do you feel like you have to call him? Did you two have a thing?"

Chloe shook her head. "No, not really. It was only a flirting thing."

Chris was quiet then, mulling this over in his mind. Jake. She'd never brought him up. The closest thing she'd had to anything physical was Jeremy, and he was an asshole. Who was Jake? Should he be worried? He wanted to believe her, but still, the thought of another guy hitting on his girlfriend annoyed the shit out of him.

Chris saw Chloe twisting her hands in her lap. He knew she was nervous and upset. He tried to remain calm even though he was angry. Taking a breath, he said. "Thanks for telling me."

"You're not angry?"

He softened his jaw. "No. I'm not angry with you. Let's eat. It's getting cold."

Chloe took another forkful but couldn't eat much more. Her stomach was in knots. While Chris said he wasn't angry, Chloe knew he was very frustrated.

Also, he'd just dismissed her.

Unfortunately, Chris remained quiet the rest of the night. After dinner they sat on the couch and watched the movie Chloe had picked. They had cuddled, but to Chloe there wasn't that same spark. The earlier conversation had left both feeling drained and distant.

Now after midnight, Chloe laid in bed, wondering if she had made a mistake telling Chris. He rested close behind her with his arm holding her, but they hadn't been intimate. This was the first night all week they'd slept together without making love. This weekend was not starting off as she had hoped. Perhaps she put too much pressure on the idea of it being the perfect time to say *I love you.*

The flowers meant nothing to her, and it wasn't at all a big deal in her mind. She wondered why it was in his. She wanted him to talk to her about how he felt, just the way he always encouraged her to talk to him when something upset her.

Restless and wide awake with her thoughts, Chloe slipped out from under his arm and tiptoed downstairs for a glass of water. *Perhaps reading*, she thought, *would take the edge off.*

~~~~~

In the middle of the night, Chris woke up as he rolled over. He focused on the ceiling and remembered he was at Chloe's. He rolled his head over, wanting to see her. But she wasn't next to him. *Dammit*, he thought. *I am screwing this up.*

Chris was no longer young and dumb, yet that was exactly how he was acting. He was wallowing in knowing that some other guy was sending his girlfriend flowers and cards when he should've been the one doing that for her. He was angry at himself for being a slouch and worrying that some other guy would easily swoop in and take her away from him. He was deathly afraid of losing her and letting his insecurities get the best of him for the second week in a row.

He loved her and wanted to tell her, but he feared overwhelming her by saying it. But maybe it *was* time he told her how he felt. Hadn't he done that in the beginning… been upfront with her so she didn't have to guess? Now here he was leaving her guessing what he was thinking. Damn, he really was a jerk. "God, I suck," he mumbled to himself as he hauled himself up.

Chris found Chloe snuggled up on the chair in the study. A book lay against her chest, and her hair spilled over her shoulders. She looked so angelic. While he watched her slowly breathing, he felt a horrible knot develop in the pit of his stomach. He had acted like such an ass.

He reached for her book and put it on the table. Leaning over her, he pulled the blanket back. He whispered in her ear and picked her up, "It's just me, sweetheart."

Her eyelids fluttered at the sound of his voice. Dazed and confused, she asked, "Huh? What's going on?"

"You fell asleep reading."

"Oh, I did? Where am I?"

"Downstairs."

She snuggled into his arm. Gently he climbed the stairs and navigated back into bed with her next to him. He kept one arm under her shoulders and used his other arm to reach down and pull the blanket over them. Holding her tight now, he smoothed her hair back and kissed her cheek. "I'm so sorry, Chloe," he whispered. "I love you."

Chris laid there a long while, knowing she hadn't heard him but hoping she at least felt his love now. He didn't know yet how he would make the rough night up to her, but he would.

~~~~~

Chapter 22

Chris woke to the sound of the alarm. After reaching over to silence it, his eyes flickered toward Chloe, who still slept beside him. He savored the moment, watching her sleep. She meant so much to him. The desire to apologize overwhelmed him now.

He watched her gentle breaths and lightly touched her face with his fingertips. She stirred in response, slowly waking.

Rolling toward him, she blinked a few times and smiled. "Good morning."

He returned her smile, hoping this was the sign of a new start. "Good morning, beautiful." He paused. "I'm sorry about last night. I was a complete ass, and you have every right to be angry with me."

Her eyes dimmed. "I was never really angry. Annoyed, maybe."

"I shouldn't have shut down like that on you. Not when I always ask you to be open with me."

"Why did you? You just didn't like someone else sending me flowers?"

Chris wrapped a leg over hers and intertwined them to pull her close. "No, I don't. But my reaction was crappy. I wasn't fair to you. You told me what happened, and I just upset you. I'm so sorry."

"I know. It's okay. I am glad I told you still. I like being honest with you." She cupped his cheek in her palm. "He means nothing to me. Just a guy who I knew in my past. I do want to tell you how I met him, though, if you're okay with that? It ties in with something else I'd like to tell you."

He leaned into her hand. "Of course. I want to hear anything you want to tell me."

Still lying on their sides facing each other, Chloe absently traced her fingertips around his shoulder and bare chest. "After my freshman year of college, I was in a car accident. I met Jake at the hospital. He was a nurse's aide there and kept me company for a few days. It was a hard time for me—my parents never came. Gaby and Momma R. took me home with them to Harmony for the summer."

Chris sighed. "I see why you love her mom so much."

A light smile formed on Chloe's face. "She has been wonderful to me." But in her next breath her smile faded. "Jake and I stayed in touch by email for about a year, and then he stopped talking to me. Saturday was the first time I saw him since the hospital. And seeing him meant nothing to me. I'm sorry if it made you jealous, but he was a part of my past. But you ... I think you are my future."

"Aw. I think you are my future too." He thought about saying *I love you* then, but she had more yet to say. So, he kissed her instead. "I am glad he was there for you when you needed someone."

"He was." Chloe watched his jaw and saw it was clenched. Even though she knew he was jealous, she wanted to finish. "I never imagined my parents being the ones to sever the ties. I always thought it would be me. It was a real 'kick you while your down' moment in my life."

"That must have really hurt. I'm so sorry, Chloe."

"It did, but I'm okay about it now." Chloe decided that for now she would leave it at that. She would explain her premonitions another time. "We should get going, shouldn't we? The fair is more than an hour away. We can't be late for your dad's moment to revel in his glory."

Chris smirked. "We're fine on time, which is good, because you lightly tracing your finger along my chest for the past few minutes has done things to me. So now we need to make time for that. Then we can get out of bed."

He snuggled closer to her so she could feel him on her thigh. "Oh," she gasped. A big smile formed on her face. "What if I told you we could make time for that in the shower?"

It was his turn to gasp. "I'd say yes."

~~~~~

They arrived at the fair just before lunchtime. The vegetable judging didn't take place until early afternoon, so they had plenty of time until Chris's dad would find out if his colossal pumpkin had taken the blue ribbon.

Chris reached for Chloe's hand as they made their way through the crowds. "You look beautiful today." He gave her braid a flick over her shoulder. "I like your hair like this." The plaid country shirt she wore was tied at the waist, showing off her midriff. Her jeans hugged her butt perfectly. The heart necklace he'd bought her sparkled around her neck. He glanced at her ring finger and pictured a sparkly diamond there someday because she had said *yes*.

She smoldered at his words. "Why, thank you. You don't look so bad yourself in those jeans and boots." His rugged good looks made her belly turn over.

Chris led her through the crowds toward the stalls where Ben was showing

224

his animals.

As they walked, Chloe looked around. She had never been to the East Texas Fair. It was huge! Buildings spread around the open areas. Near the gate they entered through, vendors had their wares for sale in booths concentrated opposite the animals for show. In the center stood a large stadium for hosting the rodeo, races, and shows. Behind it were more vendors and tents for children's activities and exhibits. Band shells and stages sprinkled around the fairgrounds, featuring local artists throughout the day.

It was a gorgeous sunny afternoon—not too hot, as some days in October could be. A gentle breeze drifted in occasionally too, which helped keep the smell of animals from the livestock buildings to a minimum.

Chris clapped Ben on the back when they approached him. "Hey, man. How are ya?"

Ben turned and reached for Chris's hand. "Good to see you." Then he nodded to Chloe. "Hi there."

She tipped her head up. "Hi, Ben. It's nice to see you again." She scanned the immediate area. "Where's Shannon?"

"Oh, she'll be back soon. She went for some chow."

At the mention of food, Chloe noticed how hungry she was. She looked at Chris with big eyes.

"Let me guess," he said. "You're hungry?"

"Starving."

"All right. We'll go grab some food too and be back." His hand rested on the bare skin of Chloe's back as he guided her to the food stands.

She smiled at his touch. "Hi."

He smiled back. "Hi ... what?"

Chloe leaned up to his ear. "Your hand on my back reminds me of our first date. I felt my stomach drop when you first did that. The same thing happened just now."

Chris stopped and pulled her to him. "Oh, really? This is good information to have."

Chris covered her mouth with his and put his hands on her waist, pulling her up on her toes. After only a minute, he let her back down and closed the kiss.

Her eyelashes fluttered open. "Wow."

"Yeah, wow." Chris found himself breathing heavier than just a minute ago. Her kisses packed a powerful punch. "Come on. Let's get some grub too. We need to take our minds off sex."

She took his hand as they started walking again. "Who said anything about sex?"

225

"Oh, aren't you cute? Miss 'let's take care of that in the shower.' I know exactly where your mind goes!"

She squeezed his hand and put on her sweetest smile. "Fine, you're right! You've ruined me forever."

~~~~~

A few hours later, Chloe followed Chris through the crowded agricultural building where the vegetables were being judged. The pumpkin entries were toward the back, so they wound their way through a sea of people until they found Mike and Helen. When they approached, Chris's mom stretched out her arms to Chloe. "Oh, honey. It's so good to see you!"

Chloe hugged her back. "You too, Helen."

She looked to his dad then at the pumpkin before him. "Wow. That's a huge pumpkin! So impressive!"

"It is." Pride beamed across Michael Sherman's face. Then to Chloe he whispered, "I think I have a good chance this year."

She swept her gaze over the other entries nearby. "I think you do too. When do you find out?"

Chris took Chloe's hand in his. "They announce them at two."

Then from out of the crowd walked Todd, his signature smile splitting his face. "Hey, Chloe, Mom, Dad ... bro." He pointed with his thumb to the guy at his side. "This is my friend Kyle. We went to school together."

Chloe waved. "Nice to meet you."

Chris tightened his grip on her hand and pulled her close to him. He put his arm around her. She wondered if he was doing that territorially because of Kyle. Todd's friend seemed to have a glint in his eye when she waved. Given how he was acting, she was sure Chris picked up on it too.

Chloe felt her phone buzz. It was a text from Gaby. She stifled a laugh as photos of Gaby in different outfits flashed across her screen. A text went with them: *Which one says I'm sexy but off limits?*

"What are you giggling at?" Chris asked, eyeing her.

She held the text and pictures up to Chris. He didn't think long about it before answering, "There is no way any guy thinks a girl is off limits based on her clothes. You're giving us too much credit."

Chloe giggled more then texted her choice back to Gaby. In seconds, Gaby replied with an emoticon thumbs-up. Grinning and shaking her head, Chloe put her phone away and turned back to Chris. "Should I borrow one of those outfits from her sometime?"

He leaned in close to her ear. "You're killing me."

She giggled and glanced in the direction of Mike and Helen. "Do you think they heard me?"

He leaned down and gave her a quick kiss. "No, but I'm not worried about it if they did. I'm thirty-two years old. I'm sure they've figured out that I've had sex."

The announcer came on then and gave the welcome message. They went through each of the tables and rattled off the winners. When they got to the pumpkins, Chloe crossed her fingers and made eye contact with Helen. Chris smiled when he saw them exchange looks. *Mom really likes her.*

"And the blue ribbon goes to … Michael Sherman! Congratulations!"

Chloe jumped up and clapped. She gave him a congratulatory side hug. In the jumble of people, Chloe got pushed back over near Todd and Kyle.

Kyle looked down at her. "Enjoying the fair so far?"

Chloe nodded. "Oh yeah! It's awesome." Then she tugged on Chris's arm and hugged him, not caring one bit about Kyle and his shifty eyes.

~~~~~

Later in the afternoon, before the festival's main event—the rodeo—started, Chris and Chloe wandered through the vendor booths. Chris kept his eyes open for something to buy Chloe. He wanted to pick something up for her to further apologize for last night. However, nothing struck his eye.

Soon after, they met up with Ben and Shannon to watch the rodeo. They crowded close to the arena so Chloe could see everything. Chris noticed the excitement on her face as the riders took their turns in the pen. She stood on the lower rung of the outer fence to watch. Her expression reminded Chris of an excited little kid.

Chloe cheered them on with loud whoops. She had never seen anything like it. From what she could see, this was more than fun for these riders; it was a sport. Their talents were impressive and made her attempt at riding Studdly look lame. *Ah, what a wonderful day that was when we went to Ben's ranch.*

Chloe glanced behind her and caught Chris's eye as he talked with Ben and Shannon. She flashed him a big smile. *I hope he stays forever.*

After the rodeo, the four of them met Ben's parents, Chris's parents, Todd, and Kyle for dinner. Food trucks and tents lined the hill behind the hall where the home goods were on display. They found each other at the last tent closest to the stage where, Chris said, bands would play later. It was the perfect place to watch, listen, and dance whenever they wanted.

Chris marveled at Chloe throughout dinner, watching her almost effortlessly win the hearts of Ben's parents, as she seemed to do with almost everyone Chris introduced her to. Ben's mom and dad were like second parents to him since he'd spent so much time with them growing up. And as it turned out, they were dedicated fans of Chloe's journalism works with Local 9 News.

By the time the sun was setting, the first band was setting up. Shannon made plans to dance with Chloe once the music started. The dance floor was made up of thick wooden planks that sat in front of a raised stage. Flags, balloons, and flowers decorated the side stage areas, creating a fun concert feel.

Chloe admired the decorations and the natural beauty that surrounded them. Trees lined the area outside the tent, making everything feel more intimate and inviting. *A very rich autumn country feel,* she decided. The leaves of the trees here didn't look as bright as those in Pennsylvania, but they were still beautiful.

Chris handed her a beer as he sat back down beside her. "Not sure if you wanted one or not, but here you are."

"Sure, thanks," she said with a smile and took a swig. Her eyes lingered on him. "Was there a long line? You were gone for a while."

"Actually …" Chris reached into his pocket and pulled out a small bag. He handed it to her. "I got you something."

Chloe's eyes widened and her smile grew. "For me?"

"Yep!"

She untied the string that held it closed and pulled out a leather bracelet with charms. She looked up at him, then back at the gift. "You saw me looking at these?"

"Yes. I've been trying to figure out what kinds of things you like all day. When I saw you take a second look at this, I took a chance. Did I do okay?"

Chloe moved closer to give him a hug. "It's really pretty. Thank you. I love it!"

She put it on and modeled it happily. "Sparkly." She gave him a quick kiss then asked, "So, are you gonna dance with me tonight?"

"Sure, but later … probably not the second they start and you and Shannon run up there."

Chloe laughed. "Aw. Do you need liquid courage?"

He winked. "Maybe. What if I do?" He reached for her and pulled her onto his lap. "Come here. I didn't like having to share you with everyone for dinner and now I have to compete for attention with the band."

She stroked his hair. "No competition, I promise. And you get me to yourself tonight and all day tomorrow."

Chris brought his hand to the back of her head and leaned in for a kiss. "I can't wait."

He didn't get to hold her long, however. Within a few moments, the band started playing and Shannon raced toward her. "Come on!" Chloe gave a little shriek, waved to Chris, and followed Shannon to the dance floor.

The first few songs were line dances Chloe knew. She enjoyed moving to the beat with Shannon, but she wished Chris would join her. Whenever she looked his way, she either caught his eye or saw him talking with the guys.

Beside him, she noticed Helen and Ben's mom tapping their feet to the beat as they chatted. She leaned over to Shannon. "Do their moms dance?"

"I don't know about Chris's, but I've seen Ben's mom dance a few times." Shannon mimicked the devilish look on Chloe's face and took her hand. "Let's go get a drink—and them!"

Returning to the table, Chloe plopped on Chris's lap. He watched as she took another swig of her beer. "Are you done already?"

"Nope. I just needed a drink, sir." Chloe put her bottle down and stood up. Looking over her shoulder, she said, "And I needed to come get your momma."

Chris smiled as Chloe grabbed his mom's hand. "Let's go, Helen!"

Shannon took her mother-in-law's hand too and hit the dance floor once again.

Chloe watched Helen get her groove going, swaying and bobbing to the music. She wasn't half bad, Chloe admitted. In fact, she knew some great moves. Both moms held their own while the mix of old and new songs played. Chloe knew the string of songs by heart, so she sang along while she danced.

During a musical interlude, the singer jumped off stage and made his way to Shannon and Chloe. While the band kept playing, he said into the microphone, "You two seem to know all of these songs. Singers?"

He held the microphone in front of them. Shannon gave Chloe a nudge to answer. She leaned in an inch and said with a shake of her head, "Just country music lovers."

"Where you from? You ain't got a lot of twang!"

"A Yankee transplant here."

His face slackened, then he laughed. "That's fine! Real fine! All right, so I've seen you mouth the words, but can you sing?"

He turned to the crowd and yelled, "Who wants to know if the pretty little lady can sing?"

Chloe watched Chris laughing and cheering with the rest of them. *Oh God,* she thought. *What am I doing?*

The singer turned back around. "All right. They want to hear ya. Give us a line of this one, okay?"

He put the mic back in front of her. Chloe listened to the intro, waiting until the music cued her in. *Okay. No backing down now.* She took a breath and went for it. Chloe surprised herself when she heard her voice coming out of the huge speakers. *Whoa. Is that me?*

The singer started clapping with everyone else. "You've got some pipes, little lady. Didn't know they could make 'em like that up north!"

Todd leaned back over to Chris. "Looks like your girl can sing."

"Yeah." He sat there, entranced by her voice.

The singer took Chloe's hand and brought her around the side of the stage then led her up a set of stairs to the stage itself. Chris and the others moved toward the stage now.

Oh crap, Chloe thought. *This is way different than the karaoke I did with Gaby and Jess in college.* A small nervous pit began to form in her stomach. *I can do this! It's going to be fun!*

Chris came to stand just a few feet from the edge of the stage. God, Chloe looked like she belonged up there. No one else could probably tell, but he knew she was nervous. He saw the color in her cheeks and the subtle shaking of her legs. But she was really going to do this.

The singer yelled out to the crowd, "Let's see what else you got!"

The band moved onto a different tune. "You know this one?"

Chloe nodded. It was one of her favorites. *Funny,* Chloe thought. *The song is about having a real man—a cowboy—to love.* Her eyes darted to Chris then to the heavens. *This is my chance. Give me strength.*

Chloe picked up the microphone and started at just the right time. "Looking at you …" With more confidence than she knew was inside her, she took the stage like a seasoned performer. She made sure every time she sang the word "love" she made eye contact with Chris. He had to know what she was doing, and if he didn't, she would say it clearly at the end of the song.

For Chris, watching Chloe sing on stage was like seeing a whole new side of her. *How does she constantly amaze me?*

About halfway through the song, a realization hit him. Chloe looked at him every time she sang the word "love." *That means … She loves me!* He couldn't help but beam the biggest smile. *There's no doubt she is the most amazing person I've ever met.*

By the end of the song, it wasn't just Chris who had figured it out. The entire crowd too. They all whooped at the last refrain, clapping in his direction.

On the last note, she watched Chris. He had a huge smile on his face. Her heart swelled and a few tears streamed down. At the end of that last note, she said quietly but clearly, "I love you."

The singer took the microphone from her as Chris walked the few steps toward the stage. She met him near the edge and hopped into his waiting arms. The crowd went crazy.

Chris laughed and whispered in her ear, "I love you—so much." She pulled back and kissed him hard, not caring how many people watched. She was in love and the world had to know.

Chloe kept her hands framing his face and rested her forehead against his. "I love you. I love you. I love you!"

~~~~~

The drive back to Chloe's went by quickly. A weight felt lifted from her shoulders. She could now tell Chris how she felt whenever she wanted. And he could tell her the same. In fact, he told her many times on that drive alone. *He knew when I had ice cream all over my face!*

"They pulled up to the front of her place just a bit shy of midnight. Chris came around to open her door. "How tired are you?"

"I'm tired, but if you're asking if I am too tired to fool around, the answer is no!"

"Good, I was hoping you would say that." He took her hand and began walking to the front door. "I never got to ask you where you learned to sing?"

Chloe pushed the door open wide and kicked off her shoes. "Oh, I never had any training. I just like it."

"Well, you left me impressed and breathless."

She smiled.

He caught Chloe's arm as the door closed behind them, boxing her in against the entrance. "Now I'm interested in making you breathless."

"How are you going to do that?" she challenged with a smoldering smile.

"Slowly and distinctively."

"Mmm, please demonstrate."

He reached behind her back and pulled out the tie holding her braid together. Her hair fell in waves about her shoulders, making her look even more desirable. Using his fingers, he loosely combed through the waves and pulled some forward over her shoulders. Next, he reached down and focused on her shirt. There were only three buttons he had to undo before he pulled her shirt open to expose her bra. *Sexy red.*

Next, he unbuttoned her jeans and loosened them around her waist. He looked down to see a red lace thong hanging low on her hips.

Keeping her back up against the door, he reached around and grabbed her butt, pulling her hips toward his and grinding against her. After only one circling hip grind, Chris pulled her jeans the rest of the way down and off her ankles. He tugged off her shirt next, turned her around, and pushed her gently against the door so he could appreciate the view. He'd been tortured by this very picture all day long. He let his hands graze over her butt, stirring a need inside him.

She let out a moan, "Oh, Chris."

Chris took each of her hands in his and lifted them above her head. Using one hand to hold both her wrists he used his free hand to run down the length of her arm and pull her just an inch from the door so he could slide his hand between to touch her breasts. His thumb rubbed one nipple through the lace of her bra, and his pinky rubbed the other. Then he began the dizzying assault on her senses.

After several circling strokes, he moved his hand down the front of her panties to feel her. God, the excitement he aroused out of her was almost his undoing. He stopped before she let go.

"Wait," she said, lancing fear through him. *Did I do something wrong?* He watched as Chloe turned around. "Can I undress you?"

He smiled. "Of course."

With shaky hands, Chloe unbuttoned his shirt and then jeans, letting them fall to his ankles. She felt like she was making love to him again for the first time. She watched as his clothes pooled at the floor, and then marveled as he twirled her around again.

Chris delicately slid her thong string over then slipped inside her. Groans escaped from both of their throats as the heat and passion took over.

Chloe could barely think, much less move or act. Chris had her pinned against the door and what he was doing to her felt naughty, but oh so good. She couldn't do anything more than buck against him as he moved inside her. Every movement drew such a deep and primal urge from her. It took only moments for her to call out his name and let go.

Seconds later, he gave a final thrust and cried out her name through clenched teeth. Fully spent now, he released her hands and turned her around to face him once more. He found her lips with his and gave her a long, lingering kiss. "I love you, Chloe," he murmured against her lips.

"And I love you."

Feeling weak in the knees, she held onto him and balanced against the door. "Holy crap," she sighed. "That was amazing. I mean, that was the best."

"For me too, baby. Every day I'm with you, the more I see how well our chemistry matches. Let's go to bed and dream of all we have."

~~~~~

Chapter 23

On Monday morning, Chloe made her way into the office. She rounded the corner and saw a few balloons tied together and a small wrapped gift waiting for her on her desk.

Chloe looked around and saw Mya smiling. She asked, "What is all this?"

Mya put her arm around Chloe's shoulders. "Just a little something. You had a big weekend."

Chloe was touched. "Aw! You didn't have to do this!"

Lou walked over. "Go ahead."

Chloe tore off the paper and was so moved by the framed pictures her coworkers had put together. It was a rectangle-shaped frame with a spot for three photos. The first showed Chloe singing while Chris and she looked at each other, the second was him reaching for her to pick her up, and the last was the kiss. It was beautiful. She felt a few tears form as she looked at the pictures then at Mya and Lou. "Where did you get these?"

"From ones people posted online. It's quite the talk of the East Texas Fair! We thought you would like to remember it."

Chloe set the frame down. "I love it. It was very thoughtful."

Mya gushed, "So tell us about it. Did you arrange it with the band beforehand?"

"No! That is the funny part. It just came together. It was complete luck!"

Lou clapped her on the back. "Well, if you ever decide to walk away from reporting and writing, it looks like you might have success as a singer."

Chloe smiled with her eyes.

Lou turned before he left her desk. "Come see me in a bit about an assignment."

Mya stuck around a few more minutes. "Lou's right. You could make a career out of singing if you want to."

Chloe rolled her eyes. "I think I'll stick with you guys. Besides, being the center of attention like that isn't really my thing."

Mya took on a surprised look. "Well, girl, you couldn't tell. Anyway, you're lucky. It's a cool memory to have ... the video I saw posted was so sweet to watch too."

"Yeah, Shannon—the wife of Chris's friend—filmed that."

After Mya left, Chloe picked up her phone to text Chris. *Has anyone mentioned the fair to you? People here at work saw it on social media.*

She knew he had a big day at work today too, so she didn't expect a text right away. *Better go actually work now.*

Leaving the picture on her desk and her phone in her purse, she headed to Lou's office to hear about his plans.

~~~~~

By lunchtime, Chris had heard comments left and right about the fair. Everyone had seen the pictures and watched Shannon's video clip. Some teachers thought it was cute, while others gave unsolicited advice on how to be more professional. Even some of the students offered snide comments.

As much as he loved what Chloe did over the weekend, it meant Chris's personal life was now on display, something he never wanted to have at work. He knew the attention would pass, but it would likely take at least a few days, if not weeks.

After a short lunch in the teacher's lounge, Chris made his way back to his office. Marion eyed him when he walked through the door.

Chris squinted. "What now?"

Marion swallowed. "Umm ... I, um, stepped away for a few minutes and when I came back, I saw something hanging from your office door."

Chris strode to the door and saw a printed picture from the weekend taped to it. A penis was hastily drawn over his face. "Great. Just great."

Marion studied the floor and twisted her hands in front of her. "I'm real sorry that I left the office unattended, Mr. Sherman. It wouldn't have happened if I'd been here."

Chris rubbed his hands over his face and ripped the picture down. "It's okay, Marion. You shouldn't have to babysit my door."

Chris walked into his office then and closed the door behind him. He studied the picture once more before cramming it through the paper shredder. "What a bunch of little assholes this year," he muttered.

He walked to the window behind his desk and looked out at the school grounds. *Being principal is bullshit. I should have stayed a teacher.* After a few minutes of jaw clenching and cracking his knuckles, his anger passed.

Chris finally sat down to enjoy a few minutes to himself. He noticed a few texts from Chloe flashing across his phone screen. *At least one of us is getting positive comments and excitement from their coworkers.*

The framed picture had been a nice touch, and he smiled as he thought about seeing it tonight when he came over. Sleeping without her last night bothered him. He wanted to fall asleep with her every night and wake up with her every morning. Unfortunately, their lives weren't quite ready to join yet. But what a sweet time it would be when they could.

He was sure Chloe felt the same way because she already asked if he could stay over tonight. It felt good to be wanted and needed. He had to go home first to grab a few things but would then go over later in the evening. He promised Todd a workout session after work that he didn't want to miss—especially after today's annoyances.

~~~~~

Now that Gaby had her own car and didn't have to ride with Chloe, Chloe loved having a few extra minutes to herself after work to think while she drove home. Tonight her thoughts reeled with images of her confession to Chris and how happy he made her. However, her happiness soon turned to nerves as the Jake problem flooded her mind again. She had a feeling he wouldn't go away unless she acted. She also knew if she didn't call him, she'd regret it, plus maybe signal to Jake to try harder for her attention. She wanted to be straight with him: he had no place in her life now.

She walked through the front door and decided tonight was the perfect time to confront him. Gaby was at the studio, while Jess was still on her work trip, and Chris wasn't supposed to arrive for another half hour.

Well, now or never, she coached while reaching for her phone and the card.

The phone rang. And rang. Finally, a breathless "Hey!" came through.

Chloe paused, remembering how much she used to like his greetings. "Hi, Jake? It's Chloe. How are you?"

"Chloe! I'm so glad you called. I'm good. I guess you got the flowers I sent then?"

"Yes, Jake. They're beautiful. I appreciate you sending them. Thank you."

"Yeah, I couldn't stop thinking about you after the concert. You seem so accomplished. So awesome. You've been on my mind for many years now. I uh, actually wrote a song for you."

Chloe's eyebrows raised. "You did?"

He chuckled. "Yeah. 'Amaze Me' is your song."

Chloe gasped. She'd listened to that song before. It was one of the Rolling

Thunder Band's top tracks. "Wow. I don't know what to say."

"Listen, I'm sorry I stopped writing. I thought about emailing again several times, but I hesitated. I let too much time pass. Songs were how I thought I could reach you."

She wanted to be angry with him for hiding his feelings, but instead she felt flattered and a little sad. "I thought of you many times over the years too. I appreciate you writing me a song…"

"I feel like I hear a 'but' coming."

She licked her lips, steeling herself for what she'd say next. "It's because you do. It's true I have thought of you a lot. I never did any dating after we met, at least until recently. I thought about you so much I didn't want to let anyone else in. But a few months ago, I met someone and fell in love."

Jake sighed. "Dammit. I knew I was too late."

"I'm sorry. The timing is off. If we'd had this talk six months ago, everything would have gone differently. But I want you to know how flattered I am you sent the flowers and thought of me too."

"Of course. You're an incredible person. I hope your guy knows that."

Chloe smiled. "Thanks, Jake. He does. He's very good to me."

"Well, that's what matters. That you are happy." She could hear him breathing into the phone. She wanted to say something to console him, but she couldn't find the words. Finally, he managed, "Take care of yourself, Chloe. And if you need me, you know how to reach me."

Her heart pulled a little at those last words. "Take care, Jake."

"I will. Y-you too."

After hanging up, Chloe sat for a few minutes and let the silence envelope her. In her heart she had let Jake go a while ago, but this felt more permanent. Wasn't every woman entitled to a little remorse in saying a final goodbye to an old flame?

While she was completely in love with Chris, a part of her felt some sadness right now. Jake was a good person, and she didn't like hurting him. She really wanted the best for him. She hoped he'd find someone great to write more songs about someday.

She shook her head, trying to clear it as best she could. Before long the doorbell rang and her heart started to race. *I have to tell him.*

"Hey, honey," Chloe said, stepping aside for Chris to walk in. "I took care of that phone call we talked about a few days ago."

"And?"

She closed the door and pulled Chris to her. "He knows I am with you."

~~~~~

The week was a long one for Chloe and Gaby without Jess. They heard from her several times, but it wasn't the same. But she did seem surprisingly happy. Eventually, Gaby got her to confess. "I may or may not be flirting with a guy I've met here," she revealed one night while chatting. That was all Chloe and Gaby needed to drive them crazy with curiosity for the rest of the week. Saturday afternoon couldn't come quick enough.

When it did, both Chloe and Gaby rushed home for showers after dance class, then ran right back out to the airport. Jess's flight was due in at three.

The girls circled around the airport until Jess texted to say she was outside Arrivals. Finally parked, Chloe shot out the door and grabbed Jess in a tight hug. "Oh my God! We've missed you so much!"

Jess laughed. "I missed y'all too!"

Gaby came running around and joined the hug. Then she held Jess at arm's length. "Girl, California looks good on you! Did you actually work or just go to the beach?"

Jess picked up her bags. "I definitely worked—but there was some time for play. I took walks when I could, and last weekend I spent pretty much all Saturday outside."

Chloe rubbed her hands together. "You have to tell us everything. How about we switch our usual Sunday mimosa talk to tonight? Saturday night story hour with margaritas!"

Jess laughed. "Just let me unpack and shower off this travel scum and we'll do whatever you want!"

"Excellent. Saturday night story hour with margaritas it is! I'll make them!" Chloe exclaimed.

Gaby added, "And I will make chicken enchiladas with mole sauce. Momma finally taught me my dad's recipe!"

Jess grinned. "Oh yes. Sounds like an awesome welcome home party!"

~~~~~

Chris and Todd left their place around seven to meet friends for beer and wings, and to watch the game at their typical spot. Todd drove while Chris stared out the window. This week had sucked again. The kids were terrible, and Chloe's confession of talking to Jake had irked him, even though there was nothing to be upset about. That whole part of her life was finally done, and he was Chloe's one and only. But everything bothered him lately, he realized. He felt on edge constantly.

While he stared out the window, Chris ruminated over the second printout picture of him from the fair. This time an even larger penis was drawn on it. He found this one on the windshield of his car. Not sure which was gutsier of the kid—to sneak into the office like the other day, or to go near the principal's private property out in the open. Chris was confident it was the kid who recently returned from a three-day out-of-school suspension—the same kid who was in a fight a few weeks ago for flicking another student in the head. It had been a second, more violent fight that landed the kid suspension.

Do I tell Chloe? Naw, she would just worry. Besides, the kid is just being a jerk. He hasn't actually threatened me. Just annoyed the shit out of me.

Chris's phone dinged, pulling him out of deep thought.

Chloe: *Sorry, babe, but I can't hang out tonight. Jess is back and we NEED girl time! Promise to make it up to you. xoxoxo*

Before he and Todd had left the house, Chris had texted Chloe, inviting her to meet him later for a drink. He rubbed his neck and squeezed his eyes shut. He'd been looking forward to seeing her.

Todd glanced in Chris's direction. "You all right?"

"Yeah, I'm fine."

When they walked in, Chris saw Sandy and Paula, her constant shadow these days, adding to his bad mood. He rolled his eyes to Todd.

Todd smirked. "Don't worry. I'll protect you, big bro."

Sandy never took a hint. As soon as Chris's beer was in his hand, she sashayed up to him. *She's at least clever, knowing I won't go anywhere until this beer is finished.* Standing only inches from him, in her best attempt at a sultry voice, she said, "I haven't seen you here in a few weeks. How've you been?"

Chris didn't look at her. "Really good."

"Great." She started to lean closer to him, like a snake squeezing its prey. He tried to play it cool and not let on how uncomfortable she made him.

Still without looking at her, he said, "You know I'm with Chloe."

Sandy threw her head back with a smug laugh. "Oh, I know, sugar. How is the little girl?"

He stayed silent, hating the condescension in her voice. *Chloe's not some little girl. She's a woman. More woman than you'll ever be.*

After paying, he walked toward Todd without so much as a look back. *Go bother someone else.*

He handed a bottle to Todd. "If she doesn't keep her distance, I'm out of here."

"Well, get ready to run. She's on her way."

Chris muttered under his breath, "Dammit, I don't need this."

Coming up behind him, Sandy put her arm on Chris's back. "Uh oh, trouble in paradise? I always thought that girl was too young and immature for you."

Through gritted teeth he muttered, "The only trouble is you. Get your hand off me."

Her face twisted as though she was offended. "Oh now, Chris. Don't go getting all upset. I'm just saying if things aren't working out with her, I'd be happy to keep you company."

"I don't want your company." He moved to the other side of the group and started talking to Rex. She stayed where she was for now, but Chris had a feeling this wasn't the end of it.

~~~~~

Back at Chloe's house, she was enjoying spending time with her girlfriends. They stood around the counter sipping their margaritas while the enchiladas baked.

"So, tell us about where you stayed, Jess. Was the hotel gorgeous?" Chloe asked.

"Oh my God, Chloe. It was amazing. The rooms were like a palace, and the restaurant at the hotel had great food—which was a good thing, because I had a lot of late nights and didn't feel like going far for dinner. I didn't mind the long hours, though. It was satisfying to talk directly to the clients and see for myself how all the work I've done has come together.

Gaby asked, "How many people did you train?"

"It was a team of five. One woman and four men."

Gaby snickered. "So was it one of the four that was super cute?"

Jess blushed. "Yes, it was. Hunter. He was cute in a nerdy way. Tall, with short brown hair, glasses, and a great, sarcastic sense of humor. He made me laugh a lot."

Chloe dove right in. "So, did you kiss him?"

"No! I couldn't even if I wanted to because he is a client. That would be very inappropriate of me. We opted to just flirt instead."

"Can you date him now if you wanted to, since the project is over?"

Jess's shoulders slumped. "Yes, I could if the project was actually over, but unfortunately, it isn't. I really thought it would be, but there are amendments to make and upgrades that we didn't see coming. I'm going to be working on this for a while longer."

Gaby pouted. "How much longer?"

"Several months," Jess answered. "I may have to go back again when the changes are made."

Chloe pouted. "Oh no! That sucks. But at least can you flirt with him until then and maybe when the project is really done, you can kiss him."

A dreamy look came over Jess. "Yes, I'm hoping so." Her eyes regained focus and swiveled to Chloe. "So, it seems like I missed a lot here?"

Chloe laughed. "Well, you saw the video. I finally got the courage to say *I love you.*"

"It was absolutely adorable!" Jess gave Chloe's hand a squeeze. "I'm so happy for you!" She smirked. "Okay, now what was this I heard about Jake sending you flowers?"

Chloe grabbed the card out of the kitchen drawer. "I wanted to show it to you before I tossed it. Yeah, he sent them last week. Chris wasn't too happy about it. Jealous, I guess. But he got over it eventually."

"You can't blame him," said Gaby. "He loves you and wants you all to himself."

Jess added, "I can't imagine him being immature about it ... for long anyway."

"No, he wasn't. We smoothed things over within a few hours, and I got some really good make-up sex out of it!"

Gaby threw her hands up. "Okay, now you are just bragging!"

"No, no! I didn't mean it that way!" Pointing to Gaby, she said, "Besides, you have your own romance brewing!"

Gaby grabbed the enchiladas out of the oven and followed the girls to the deck. After serving each of them, she sighed. "No, not really any romance. But that's probably my fault. Correction, it *is* my fault. I've been keeping him at arm's length because I'm too afraid. Now I feel like his interest has dwindled. I don't hear from him as much as I used to. We hung out last weekend, but it really was just platonic—no flirting at all. I think I blew it."

Chloe covered Gaby's hand with hers. "Oh, honey, I don't know about that. The torch he has been holding for you for years doesn't just blow out overnight. Maybe he's just doing what he thinks you want him to do—you know, *staying friends.*"

Gaby shrugged. "You may be right, but there's nothing I can do about it. I can't string him along, asking him to wait for me while I figure out myself, and not give him any hope of a future. But I'm not ready to give anyone hope for the future."

Jess sighed. "What is meant to be will happen. We all just have to be patient."

"True," Gaby said with another sigh.

By nine, the girls had cleaned up their dinner. Jess left them to go to bed—jet lag hit her hard— while Gaby sat at the table, thinking about making chamomile tea and reading her book.

Chloe joined Gaby. "Do you want company, or do you want to be alone?"

Gaby's eyes met hers. She seemed sad. "I think I'll go up early and read." She paused. "I know I haven't been the bubbliest lately, but I'm finding comfort in some time to myself these days."

"I can't blame you. There have been times in my life where being alone to do as I please has given me a lot of comfort. You do what you need to do." Chloe gave her a side hug. "I'm going to see what Chris is up to if you both want time alone."

Gaby gave her a gentle smile. "You should go. Enjoy time with your man."

Chloe nodded. "Let me know if you need anything, though, and I'll come home."

~~~~~

Twenty minutes ago, Chris had told Chloe he was still out watching the game. She took a chance and headed there to meet him. She hoped she could seduce him into leaving with her soon after. It had been a few days since they were together, and she missed him.

Walking into the bar, Chloe smiled as she spotted Chris in the back with a few of his friends. Her keen eye also spotted Sandy watching him. *Geeze*, Chloe thought, *when will this bimbo give up?*

She wished she had spent a little more time on her outfit and makeup. She hadn't put any effort in, but now that she saw Sandy, she wanted to look hotter so she'd go away like the last time. *The black sweater and jeans and makeup from this morning will have to do.*

Chloe wove her way to Chris and instantly got pulled in by his all-consuming, comforting scent. A tingling sensation shot through her belly, adding to her excitement.

"Hi," she whispered.

Chris turned his head and looked over his shoulder.

"Hey, babe. What are you doing here?"

She whispered so only he could hear, "I'm here to take you to bed. I missed you."

He turned and flashed a smile at her. "Mmm. Whose bed?"

"I'd take either."

He rubbed his hands over her sides. "Me too." He gave her a quick kiss.

"Everything's okay, though? I thought it was girls' night?"

"It was, but it ended early. Jess was tired and Gaby wanted to call it an early one."

"Oh, well, I am the lucky one then. Come to my place then since I don't have my car here with me."

Chloe cast a glance Sandy's way and grinned. *No chance at all.* "Let's go."

~~~~~

After making love, they laid intertwined with one another. Chloe rested her head on his chest, thinking. "Why does Sandy still pursue you?"

Chris paused before answering. "I don't actually know. I've made it very clear to her I'm not interested and that you and I are together."

"She seems really insistent for someone who you only went out with a few times. Did you sleep with her?"

Chris winced. "We had some physical moments."

Jealousy stabbed so hard through Chloe's chest it took her breath away.

Chris lifted her face off his shoulder and stared into her eyes. "Please don't let that bother you. Nothing in my past means anything to me anymore."

Chloe's eyes started to water. "At least it makes sense to me now. It's why she won't let go so easily. You were a good lover to her, weren't you?"

"Being a lover would imply I loved her, and I didn't. I hope that you can accept that I have been with other women, because if I hadn't, I wouldn't be lying here with you knowing that I never experienced the real thing with them. Not with Sandy, but I believed I was in love before. When I met you that day in my office, everything I thought I once felt for anyone was eliminated. With you I am learning every day what it means to truly love someone. I may be older, and you may think I have more experience, but when it comes to love, you and I are starting from the same place."

Tears welled in her eyes. "It's so hard knowing you once laid with other women like you are laying with me right now."

"That's not true. I have never been with anyone like this before. Never in my life have I laid next to a woman and felt the swelling in my chest that I feel right now. I feel it when I'm with you, see you, or even think of you." He kissed her forehead and continued. "I do know what you mean, though. I hate when other men look at you, and you're too modest to even notice most of the time. Then there was the piercing anger that ripped through me when I heard what that boy did to you in high school. That still haunts me. One of the things I love most about you is that everything with you is new and wonderful in your eyes, and it tears me apart knowing that someone hurt you. And then the whole thing with Jake got me feeling insecure."

Chloe stilled for a minute. "Do you think Jeremy raped me?"

"I don't know what he did to you, but whatever it was, it made you fearful and for that I hurt for you."

"He did scare me, and he touched me in ways he shouldn't have, but he didn't rape me."

Chris pulled her close, burying his face in her hair. He felt tears start to sting his own eyes.

He heard her say, "You were my first and I want you to be my last. No one else matters. And Jake is nothing to me, like I said. I love you so much that I don't want to share any bit of you, even memories others have of you."

"I know, my love. I know. I want you as my only lover too."

They laid there for a long time before dozing off. Love was a complex emotion. It brought about all the good and wonderful feelings a human could possibly feel, but it also surfaced a deep fear of losing the precious and delicate love you found.

~~~~~

Chapter 24

December in Texas started out very cold. A deep trough in the jet stream ushered in a cold front that even someone from the northeast couldn't stomach. Snow threatened in Galorston for the first time in years. The cold front started the week before Thanksgiving and still raged strong as December began.

Chloe wore her thick coat and hat as she ran into the coffee shop to meet Cher and her friends. On the drive there, she thought back fondly of the weekend before, when she and Chris had split their time between Momma R.'s and his parents' house for the holiday.

They had started at Chris's parents' Wednesday night and stayed through lunchtime Thursday for a light meal of turkey sandwiches, then went to Momma R.'s for dinner. Friday morning Chris went back to his parents' house to spend more time with his sister, Briana, and her family, while Chloe went Black Friday shopping with Jess, Gaby, and her mom.

Chloe enjoyed finally meeting Briana. She loved to joke and did a great job of telling Chloe every embarrassing story starring Chris she could think of. Chloe really took to her, and they quickly became close, texting often. It had been a fun time.

Now, entering the coffee shop, Chloe found Cher and her friends in the back corner.

Cher stood up and waved. "Here, have a seat." She slid over to make room for Chloe. "Everyone, this is Chloe. We met at self-defense class." Looking back to Chloe, she asked, "Will Jess and Gaby make it?"

"Only Gaby. She should be here soon. Jess is in California for work. Unfortunately, she'll be gone for a few weeks."

One of the other ladies held out her hand. Chloe recognized her instantly. She'd seen countless photographs of her on the backs of her books. "Hi, I'm Sylvia," the woman said. "Cher's sister."

Chloe stuttered. She'd never met a celebrity author before. "N-nice to meet you."

Sylvia laughed.

"Bummer Jess couldn't make it," offered Cher.

"What does she do?" asked Sylvia.

"Jess is in software design. She has been working for a client there, developing a program."

"Impressive."

Chloe took the tea that Cher offered her and tried to treat talking to Sylvia like just another assignment for work. Her courage increased the more she spoke. "Thank you. Yes, she is very intelligent and great at what she does."

Cher waved her hand to Gaby, who'd just stepped inside. "Oh, here is Gaby now." She motioned Gaby over then gestured to the woman next to her.

"Gaby and Chloe, this is Summer. We work together." She continued to move her arm toward each woman that made up their circle. "This is Andrea, our cousin and lawyer. And Sylvia, of course. And this is Vanessa. She and I went to college together."

Gaby sat between Sylvia and Vanessa. "It's so very nice to meet y'all. It's kind of you to let us crash your party."

Vanessa waved her hand. "Oh, please. We are always looking to meet new women who are as professionally hungry as we are. Tell us about yourselves. I hear we have a journalist and author, and a dietitian and dance instructor."

Chloe and Gaby enjoyed themselves for the better part of two hours, drinking coffee and tea and sharing platters of sandwiches and desserts. Chloe was impressed with how successful each woman was and how close they all seemed, although they had very different personalities. What was most interesting to Chloe, however, was the path that each one took to get to where they currently were. Some of them, like Andrea, always knew she wanted to be a lawyer and took the most direct path to get there; however, it was Summer who had the most varied path to end up working with Cher.

She went to college for nursing and left right after graduation to join the Peace Corps. After several years of living in Africa and then South Asia, she returned to Texas to study business. Then she'd landed in the pharmaceutical industry and worked her way up through the company. Chloe found it all very inspiring.

While gathering up their things and getting ready to face the cold again, Sylvia leaned in toward Chloe. "Do you have a few extra minutes?"

"Of course." Chloe made eye contact with Gaby. "I'll see you in a bit."

Gaby gave her arm a quick squeeze. "Okay. See you at home."

Alone now, Sylvia started, "A few months ago, when Cher mentioned you to me, I looked you up and remembered reading some of your work. I have been following you professionally since, and I must admit, I am very impressed."

Chloe didn't know what to say. This was such a huge compliment, especially from such an accomplished professor and author. "I'm honored that you think so."

Sylvia smiled. "That's something I really appreciate about you too. You are extremely humble. The articles you wrote on mental illness got my attention. It's an area I have been thinking about tackling for some time in my books. Would you consider expanding on this work of yours in a collaboration with me?"

Chloe stilled. "Are you serious? With me?"

Sylvia laughed. "See, there you are, doing it again. Yes, of course *you*. You are extremely talented. I must say it isn't the writing that gets me the most—that of course is stellar—but it's your insight that intrigues me. You have a depth that I don't often see in writers, and I think we could really produce something successful together."

Chloe was still shocked but gathered herself. "I am absolutely touched with your compliments and honored you would ask to work with me. I'd love to."

"Excellent! Let's set up some time to meet soon and talk about the direction we might want to take this. I have a short proposal I can share and then we can brainstorm together."

Chloe reached out and shook her hand. "I am truly honored and excited, Sylvia."

"Well, you know so am I. You are quite accomplished and impressive. I think we can do some outstanding work together."

Chloe grabbed the rest of her things and walked out the coffee shop, holding the door for Sylvia as she followed. "This is wonderful. Thank you!"

"Of course, Chloe. Call me and we'll set it up."

Chloe waved as Sylvia walked away. She stood there for a few minutes, unable to move. *Did that just happen? Did Sylvia Burges just ask to collaborate with her?* "Geeze," she mumbled as she walked to her car. "This is awesome!"

~~~~~

Back home, Chloe found Gaby curled up on the couch with a book and decided the same sounded good to her too. She ran upstairs to change and grab her latest read, then joined Gaby.

Her friend gave her a long look, and Chloe knew she couldn't escape her easily. "Spill it."

Chloe's cheeks reddened. "What? There's nothing to spill."

That really got Gaby's attention. She shimmied into a sitting position. "Oh, yes there is. You have that look about you that says there's something on your mind. What's up?"

"God, am I that readable?"

"Just to those who know and love you," Gaby confirmed.

"It's all good. I think."

"Out with it!" Gaby insisted.

"Okay. Okay. Sylvia asked me if I would consider expanding on the mental illness articles. In collaboration with her."

Gaby's eyes grew large and her jaw dropped. "Are you messing with me? Because it's not funny."

With a slight smile, Chloe shook her head and mouthed, "No."

"Oh my God. This is huge!" Gaby jumped on the couch next to Chloe and wrapped her arms around her. "I am so happy for you!"

Chloe grinned. "Thanks."

Gaby released her, sat back, and tucked her feet under her. "When are you going to tell Chris? You are going to tell him, aren't you?"

"Yeah, I'll tell him. Tonight. When he gets here later."

Gaby applauded. "He's going to be as excited as I am for you!"

Chloe agreed. "I think so too." She pursed her lips and paused. "Sylvia also told me one of things she likes about my writing is how *insightful* it is. That made me think ... I haven't told Chris about why I'm insightful."

Gaby smirked. "Oh."

"I want to tell him. I think I'm going to soon. I have to. Right?"

Gaby tipped her head back. "Yes. He deserves to know everything about you, Chloe. And I think if you're ready, you should."

"Yes. I think it's time." Chloe dropped her head in her hands. "God, what if he thinks I'm some kind of freak and my brain should be passed off to science?"

Gaby jutted her finger at Chloe. "No way! First of all, he loves you and there is nothing you could tell him that will make him feel differently—*nothing*. I see how he looks at you. It's hardcore love, girl. The kind of love everyone wants but can't always find. He will keep loving you no matter what. And if he doesn't, get rid of him."

Chloe laughed.

"Second, this isn't elementary school where kids are mean. You're in a mature relationship. That reading-the-future stuff? It's not something I'd tell the whole world, but it's who you are and I for one know it's real. If Jess and I can handle it, he surely can too. Third, honey, you are fabulous—simply fabulous. He sees it. I see it. Sylvia sees it ..." She spread her arms wide. "Hell, the world sees it! You are unstoppable!"

Chloe laughed. "You missed your calling as a motivational speaker!"

Gaby smirked. "Maybe I did, but I didn't miss my calling as your friend. I love you, girl. You are amazing and you don't give yourself enough credit."

"Thank you. As much as all that mushy stuff made my skin crawl, I needed to hear it."

"You're welcome." Gaby patted Chloe's knee.

Chloe watched her best friend get comfy with her e-reader and blanket. "Can I ask … how many books have you read this week so far?"

Gaby let out a breath. "Guilty as charged. Say no more. I know what you're getting at. I'm hiding behind my blanket and a good book. I promise I won't do it forever."

"The Gaby I know never hid like this."

"I know, Chloe. It's a temporary situation." Gaby pulled the blanket over her head. "It's only through the holidays, I promise. *A new year and a new you* will be my motto come January!"

Chloe reached over and pulled the blanket from Gaby's face. "I'm holding you to that."

"Oh, I know you will!"

Chloe and Gaby read until early evening then stopped to have dinner. Soon after, they were back in their respective reading zones. While she read, Chloe heard Gaby's phone ding. She raised an eyebrow. "Who are you talking to over there? They seem awfully chatty. It isn't Jess, is it?"

"No, I would have told you if it was Jess. It's Brad."

Chloe sat up and put her book down. "I thought things were slowing with him."

Gaby sighed. "We still talk quite a bit, just not as much as we did in the first few weeks. I honestly think we really are just friends now."

"I'll be the judge of that," Chloe stated. "Give me some details. Does he ask what you're wearing?"

Gaby brushed it off with a roll of her eyes. "No. Trust me. There is no flirting going on. Right now, he's telling me about an annoying client who calls him every two seconds because they want a policy changed. Last week it was about him running into Momma, or something funny his dad did. Stuff like that."

"It does sound friendly, but it's what's behind the texts sometimes. Like, are you the first person he thinks of to tell when his dad does something funny?"

Gaby put her phone down and looked Chloe square in the face. "Honestly, I have no idea. I like having him to talk to, and it's all I can give anyone. Right now. What we have is perfect. It's someone to talk to when you need them. And that's just what friends do. That's what we're doing right now."

Chloe agreed. "You're absolutely right. I'm glad you have what you need right now."

No sooner after Chloe looked back at her book did the doorbell ring. She exchanged a glance with Gaby then peeled back her blanket and pulled herself up to answer it. As she shuffled to the door, she silently admitted she probably should have done more today. *But everyone is entitled to a lazy day occasionally.*

A quick look through the peephole confirmed it was Chris, and she opened the door. A cold wind blew through as he walked in.

"Oh my God. I think it got colder since I was last out," Chloe said as she closed the door.

Chris reached for her. "It did, but I'll keep you warm, baby."

From in the living room, Gaby yelled, "Save the X-rated talk for the bedroom!"

Chris grinned at Chloe and called, "How are you, Gaby?"

"I'm good. Take her off my hands. She is being too nosy and acting like my mother!" Gaby teased.

"Hey, I just care about you!" Chloe fought back.

"Yada, yada. Give your energy to your boyfriend."

"Enough fighting, ladies." Chris took Chloe's hand and started walking upstairs.

Chris closed the door behind him and threw his coat over her chair. He turned and pulled her in for a tight hug. "So, how was your time with Cher and the ladies?"

Chloe pulled back and looked up at him. "Really good." She bit her lip. "Something exciting happened."

Telling him the first part would be easy, she thought but the second part, not so much. *Stay strong.*

"Oh?" They sat on the edge of her bed. "Tell me."

"One of the women there was her sister, Sylvia Burges, a well-respected professor and author. I've studied her work. She's really amazing."

Chris nodded. "I remember you telling me about her. I looked her up and read some of her stuff."

Chloe gasped. "That was months ago!"

"Why are you surprised? I loved you then too and wanted to know about what you liked. It's simple. You said you liked her, so I learned something about her."

"That's so sweet! Thank you." Chloe beamed at him. Then she continued to tell him about Sylvia's offer to work together.

Chris's face lit up. "Wow, honey. That's an amazing offer and compliment."

"Yeah, I think so too. We're going to meet sometime soon to talk in more detail. She told me she liked the deep insight I provide when I write."

Chris agreed. "You really do. It's something I noticed right away too."

Chloe looked down as she said, "That's another thing I wanted to talk to you about."

Chris's brows narrowed. "About insight?"

She dipped her head. "Yes."

"What about it? "He squeezed her hand. "You can tell me anything."

Chloe took a deep breath. *It's okay. Just tell him. He deserves to know.* "Before the car accident, I had this uncanny ability to know when things were going to happen. I didn't realize this was uncommon until around age six or seven. I started to put it together with punishments from my dad and kids at school making me feel like a freak. I tried to hide it when I realized, but by then it was too late. I was already an outcast."

"What do you mean by 'ability to know things'?"

Chloe studied her hand in his. "Usually I see flashes or a moment in time, like a movie, right before something happens. Other times I feel afraid or taste metal or something for no reason. I call them premonitions. Whenever one happens, I know to expect it to occur soon. They disappeared after the accident and only started to come back right after I met you. I don't know why, but they're part of me and I think it's important you know about them."

Chris was quiet.

Chloe bit her lip and chanced a look his way. "Do you still love me?"

He slightly shook his head in disbelief. "Chloe, you are amazing. Every time I think I couldn't love you more, you do something or tell me something that makes me actually love you more. Chloe Larson, I might not understand everything about you, but I want to know it all. In fact, I want to spend the rest of my life showing you every day how much I love you."

Her eyes went wide.

Chris quickly added, "I'm not asking you that question right now, because you deserve that time to be special, but I *will* ask you." He grinned. "And I hope you'll say yes."

Chloe's heart swelled. *He loves me completely. And wants to be with me. I can't believe how lucky I am.* She gently nodded.

Chris pulled her onto his lap. "Tell me more about your premonitions."

~~~~~

Chapter 25

Gaby pulled into what looked like the last parking spot at the mall. "Yay for shopping the last weekend before Christmas," she said smiling to Chloe beside her.

Chloe nodded. "Happy holidays! This'll be fun." She sighed, still unsure what to pick up for anyone. Today's goal was to buy for Jess and Momma R., and to pick up anything else appealing for Chris.

Chloe texted Briana last week to see if she had any ideas for her brother. She said to get him something for fishing. He hadn't been out in years but loved it growing up. Todd had met her at a sporting goods store a few days ago at lunchtime to help her pick something out. Today she was going to look around for a new shirt and tie for him—something completely her idea.

They walked in through the mall entrance and exchanged looks as a sea of shoppers swept past them. Somewhere in the distance a bell tinkled on repeat.

Gaby consulted the list on her phone. "Do you care where we start?"

Chloe shook her head. "This year I'm so lost. I don't even have a list! I'm going to follow you and see if anything catches my eye."

"Let's start with a sweater for Mom. She expects one from me every year now since that first year when she adored the one I bought her."

Chloe cut around a few slow walkers and said over her shoulder, "What if we head to the kitchen store after that? There has to be something there she would like."

"Great idea. It's around the corner from the place with the sweaters."

While prowling through the aisles of the clothing store, Chloe came upon a winner. It was the type of sweater Momma R. loved to wear—soft, flatteringly cut, and blue. Gaby met her eye and agreed without saying a word. It was perfect.

They perused the jewelry section near the checkout. Gaby watched Chloe pick up a pair of dangly earrings. "Who are you thinking of for those?"

She laughed. "Me."

"They would look cute on you."

She shook her head and put them back. "Yeah, but I need to focus on buying for others. Here, Jess might like this." Chloe walked over to a leather jacket and slid into one Jess's size.

Gaby snapped a picture of the earrings then met Chloe at the display mirror. "Jess would love that. How much?"

Chloe took the jacket off and checked the tag. "One hundred."

Gaby looked at the rack. "It's on sale. So, it's eighty. Let's split it. I think she'll love it."

"Deal."

After hitting off a few other stores, the girls couldn't carry any more bags. "I think that's a wrap," said Gaby, waddling toward the exit.

"Yes! And what we got is great."

They'd found a new frying pan for Momma R., a few other things for Jess, and a great tie for Chris.

Not long after getting home, Gaby heard her phone ding. It was Brad. She wasn't sure what to do about him. They were still texting, but there was no flirting still. It was like the time she saw him in October. Just two friends hanging out.

Gaby needed another girl's perspective. "Chloe, what do you think about Brad and me?"

She looked up. "Hmm. He's still acting like just friends?"

"Yeah. But we've texted or talked every day since Thanksgiving. And I really like getting to know him." She sighed. "I can't decide if I want more with him. He really has changed. He's not the same guy he was in high school."

Chloe held up a finger. "I think there are three things you have to ask yourself. One, do you look forward to hearing from him?" A second finger shot up. "Two, do you feel tingles when you are near him?" She raised a third finger. "And three, did you buy him a Christmas present?"

"All three are yeses."

Chloe held both hands out and shrugged. "You know the answer. You just need to figure out the when. Talk to him face to face next week when we're at your mom's for Christmas Eve and see if he feels the same way. If he does, you two can figure it out together. If he doesn't, then you can move on."

Gaby shook her head. "Look at you. In six months you've became a relationship expert."

Chloe snickered. "Hardly, but I learned a lot from Chris."

"Well, he is a teacher."

"That he is." Chloe paused. "I wonder what he'll get me for Christmas."

"I'm sure it will be something beautiful. Maybe even sparkly." She winked.

Chloe tapped the couch arm. "You think?"

"Maybe! But I'm sure you will get other stuff too. I think he'll spoil you. And before you say, 'I should get him more,' don't. Let him spoil you if he wants to. You deserve it."

"You're not so bad on relationship advice yourself."

Gaby smirked and stuck out her tongue. Then she went back to her phone. She had the perfect gift idea for Chloe and had to tell Chris.

~~~~~

Jess did a double take as Chloe walked into the room. "Holy crap! You're a heartbreaker tonight!"

Chloe's dress hit her in all the right places, and with her makeup she looked like a model. It wasn't every day she got to attend a party, and the Christmas work party always required the most glamour.

Gaby joined them and whistled. "I knew it'd look great on you." Out of all the dresses Chloe had tried on two weeks ago, this one was the favorite.

"I'm sad I missed dress shopping with you both. I've missed a lot lately," Jess lamented.

Chloe took her hand. "Jessy, I promise you haven't missed anything major. We've kept you up on everything going on around here while you've been away. We would never let you fall out of step with us. You're part of us."

Jess squeezed Chloe's hand. "I have been homesick for you two."

"And our home has been sick for you. We've missed you so much!"

Jess fanned her face. "Okay. Enough lovey-dovey stuff for now. We can't mess up your perfect makeup. God, you look gorgeous! I'm going to grab some paper towels to clean up Chris's drool when he sees you."

"You're too much. I do like this dress a lot." Chloe did a small twirl. The short metallic silver dress made the perfect winter party attire. Its deep neckline accentuated her throat. The top of the dress had one thin shoulder strap, leaving the other shoulder bare. And best of all, the dress showed off Chloe's slender legs.

Jess held up her phone. "Let's get a picture."

Chloe posed and gave her best fashion runway face.

~~~~~

Chris waited for the door to open, surprised at how nervous he felt. He wore a black suit with a silver tie, as requested by Chloe. In his hand he held a small bouquet of red and white roses and a tiny box. He cracked his neck, and then smiled as Gaby's face peered around the door.

"Are you ready? Our girl is drop dead gorgeous tonight!"

"I feel like I'm back in high school!" he said with a chuckle. "I'm even nervous."

"Come on in." Gaby opened the door wide. There, standing in the hall, stood Chloe.

God, she is amazing. How did I ever find such a wonderful, perfect woman? "You look phenomenal!" he said.

Chris went to her and kissed the top of her hand. The way she looked at him though her thick, dark lashes made his stomach drop. "Baby, you look awesome. I love this." He fluffed at the hem of her dress, then swooped in to give her a kiss.

He handed her the box.

"What is this?" she asked.

"You have to open it."

She tore off the wrapping and pulled off the top. "Oh, wow!" She held the earrings up to her friends. "They're beautiful!" They nodded. "I'll put them on now."

As Gaby took the empty box from Chloe, Chloe pointed. "You!"

Gaby shrugged. "Maybe I helped a little."

Chloe took the flowers Chris handed her. "They're beautiful too."

He smiled.

Jess motioned for them to move closer. "How about a picture?" Chloe and Chris wrapped their arms around each other as Jess snapped away. "Okay," she continued. "And how about one more in front of the tree?"

~~~~~

At the party, Chris finally met Chloe's coworkers. Mya, Eve, and Lou obviously stood out, because she talked about them the most, but others also floated by— film crews, interns, and other journalists. He enjoyed meeting the people Chloe spent a lot of time with. He knew how hard she worked and could tell her coworkers knew it too.

He watched her through the cocktail hour, captivated by her ability to work a room. She knew just what to say to people, where to laugh, and how to leave a conversation without seeming rude. She also made a very gracious date, spending just the right amount of time socializing with her coworkers, including him in the conversations, and alone with him.

During dinner, Chris sat by the chatty Eve. She reminded him a lot of his mom with her grace, humor, and positivity. *What was Chloe's mom like? Where are her parents? Does Chloe still think about them?* He wished her childhood had been different.

Chris turned to look at Chloe and found her in a discussion with Mya. He studied her profile, enjoying the view. *One of the many incredible things about her is her resiliency*, he decided. *She's come a long way in her life.*

Chloe glanced over her shoulder and caught Chris watching her. "Hold that thought," she said to Mya. Then she turned to Chris and leaned into his ear. "Hi, sexy. How are things going?"

"Good. I like her," he said, gesturing to Eve. "She reminds me of my mom."

"Aw, yeah. She is very motherly." Chloe pointed to his plate. "You liked everything?"

He nodded.

"Dessert should be out soon. There are a few speakers and awards they do, then there's music. I'm looking forward to dancing with you." She grabbed his hand and laced her fingers with his.

"Me too. It's been a while." He looked to the stage and back to Chloe. "Have you ever received an award?"

"No, but I was part of the thank yous last year. That was nice. The awards are reserved more for the senior journalists."

Chris saw out of the corner of his eye someone walking on stage. They called out "hello" to the crowd and welcomed everyone with a few remarks. "We'll try and keep this short so tonight is more about fun. However, we have a few awards and thank yous to share."

They ran through a list of awards and names. Chloe got a mention in the thank yous, which made Chris beam with pride.

As the last of the awards wound down, Chloe peeked at her phone to read a text that beeped through. A nudge brought her attention back to the stage. "What?" she asked Chris.

"You got an award!"

"What?"

Everyone's eyes were glued to her. Chloe got to her feet, unsure what kind of award she could've possibly received. Her eyes wide, she quickly looked around. "Are you sure it's me?"

Mya leaned over. "You won! Get up there."

Chris gave her hand a quick squeeze before she walked forward. Chloe was so surprised. *Did she really win the final award?* She walked up the steps and shook hands with the company president. He leaned into the microphone. "You look surprised!"

Chloe stepped forward. "That's an understatement."

Lou, who had been handing out the awards, stepped toward her. The president handed him the microphone. "Chloe Larson, you have significantly grown this year and we wanted to recognize you for that growth. You put in extensive effort and passion into your work. The results have been magnificent. We couldn't be happier to give this to you."

Still stunned, Chloe reached for the award being offered to her, and the microphone. "Thank you! I think it's obvious that I was not expecting this." She turned her sights to the executive team. "I am honored to receive this award. It means more to me than you know. But I couldn't have been successful in my work this year if I didn't have the support from my team." She turned to Lou. "Thank you, Lou, for your tireless reviewing, editing, and suggesting. Mya, Eve, and the team, for your help and encouragement. I'm truly blessed to work with you. And Chris, thank you for your constant encouragement. Thank you all."

Before Chloe headed back to the table, Lou handed her an envelope. "Merry Christmas."

She sat back down and looked at Chris. "Oh my God. Did that seriously just happen?"

Chris hugged her. "I'm so proud of you. You deserve this. What's in the envelope?"

Chloe opened it. "Holy crap! A bonus too!"

"Holy crap is right. That is an impressive amount of money." He rubbed her back. "You had a good year."

She leaned into him. "This award surprised me, and I am grateful for it, but it wasn't what made this year good." Her eyes glittered. "That was you."

"God, you are the sweetest. And you made my year." Chris pulled into a tight hug. "I love you."

After some people stopped by to give their congratulations, Chris led Chloe to the dance floor. It had been a great night, he thought as he watched her move. He never dreamed he would find someone like her. Someone so honest and humble. Someone he could love and someone who loved him back.

Chris leaned down during a slow song. "Baby, you've been killing me in that dress all night. When are you going to let me take you home and get you out of it?"

Her eyes danced when they met his. "How about now?"

~~~~~

Christmas Eve was a big deal for the Rodriguez family. It started with an early dinner, followed by church, then closed with a large gathering of friends at home. Gaby, Jess, and Chloe looked forward to it every year. This year Chris joined them, adding to the family size and merriment.

Gaby had just finished handing out drinks when she made eye contact with Brad across the living room. She had only seen him briefly in church.

Gaby inwardly sighed. *Chloe was right. He does give me tingles every time I see him.*

She made her way to him. "Merry Christmas, Brad." She leaned in to give him a hug. As he pulled her to him, Gaby felt shivers run through her. *Why do his hugs feel so good?* She probably lingered there longer than a friend would, but he didn't complain. They may not be dating, but after all the talking and texting they did, they shared a strong connection.

"Merry Christmas, Gaby. It's good to see you." He kept his arm loose around her shoulders. *Is this like a brother-sister thing or something more?* Gaby wondered. Their small-talk conversations left her thinking the first, but every now and then the way he looked at her got her questioning. And how she felt around him didn't help either.

"Here." Gaby handed him a small gift bag.

He smiled. "I have something for you too." Brad turned and reached for his coat. He pulled a wrapped box from the pocket.

Gaby felt warmth creep into her cheeks as excitement grew. *What could he have gotten me?*

He handed her the small gift. "You go first."

She took the gift and pulled the bow and paper away from the box. Inside was a small leather journal and a dream catcher. Gaby held up the dream catcher and watched the feathers sway. "It's beautiful. Thank you."

"Sure. I thought you could use the journal to write down all of your dreams."

"It's very thoughtful. Thank you." Gaby pointed to the gift bag he held in his hand. "Your turn."

Brad pulled the tissue paper from the top and pulled out a Leatherman Tool. "Oh cool. I actually lost mine a few months ago. I left it sitting somewhere when I was out fishing. Even though I went back to look for it, I never did find it." He met her eyes and smiled. "Thanks, I needed this."

A pang shot through Gaby's stomach as she returned his smile. "Sure."

They stood talking about the town, their families, Christmas plans, but nothing more. *The gift was so thoughtful, but maybe I shouldn't read into it. It could be a gift you'd give a sister. We're still in the friend zone. Maybe I should just leave all of this alone.*

"Excuse me," Gaby said when the conversation wound down. "I'm going to see if Momma needs help." She took a shortcut through the kitchen and found her mom talking with Chris. She slowed for a second to squeeze her mom's arm. Chris and her mom were commiserating over being in the teaching profession.

Gaby moved from Chris and her mom to Chloe and Jess. Chloe watched her approach. "Why do you look so down?"

She sighed and leaned into her friends. "Possible case of holiday blues." Gaby waved her hand. "But never mind me. Does Momma look worn out to you?"

Jess put her arm around Gaby. "Momma R. is a tough lady and outspoken. She'd tell you if something were wrong. This time of year can bring out all kinds of feelings. For me, it's been a good year. I got promoted at work, grew closer to my family again, and still have the two best friends a girl could ask for—and yet I feel a bit down."

Chloe leaned in. "It cycles. Some years you're up and some years you're down. It's just a down year."

Gaby smirked. "Umm, not for you." She motioned her head to Chris.

Chloe didn't want to brag. "I am having a good holiday this year, but remember last year? I was so down in the dumps, you two had to peel me out of the house for New Year's Eve! Next year will be an up year."

Jess smirked. "Okay, nobody likes a cheerleader when they're down at the holidays."

Chloe held her hands up. "Sorry, sorry. You're right—this holiday sucks!"

Chris popped his head over. "What did I hear you say?"

Chloe shook her head. "No, no, no! You're taking that out of context!"

He wrapped his arms around her. "In what context should I take it?"

"You're not helping my cause. We were just talking about how some holidays are up and some are down. They are picking on me for having an up year."

~~~~~

After the last of their guests left, Chris and the girls helped Momma R. clean, then they all met in the living room. "Gift time!" Momma R. announced.

"Since this is the first year we've had a boy at our Christmas gathering, I say Chris goes first," Chloe said.

Chris laughed and took the present Gaby handed him. "Well, thanks! And don't hold back on your usual conversations on my account. I don't mind some girl talk here and there."

Chris opened the box and took out a framed picture of Chloe and him from the night of the Christmas party.

Jess pointed to the box. "We put a copy of each of the shots we took in there too in case you like one of the others better."

"This will look great on my desk at work. Thank you." He took out the photos and flipped through them.

Chloe peeked over his shoulder. "Hey! I haven't even seen these!" She pointed to the one of him handing her the flowers. "I think this one is my favorite."

Jess opened her gift next, which was a new pair of sunglasses from Momma R. Gaby got new cooking utensils. Chloe went last. She unwrapped several new novels.

Chloe let out a squeal of excitement. "These are great! You know me so well."

Jess and Gaby shared a look and a smile. "Yes, we do," Gaby replied.

Momma R. squeezed Chloe's shoulder. "Those look like great reads. I love this author."

Chloe paused as a flash of Momma R. in a white room and hospital gown went through Chloe's mind. "Umm, yeah. Me too." She pretended to read the back covers of her new books to get her bearings. *God, I wonder what that was about!*

Momma R. pointed at Jess and Gaby and asked, "And are you feeling any better?"

Jess rocked her hand back and forth. "So, so."

Gaby agreed. "Same here."

"Well, why don't we go to bed and see what Santa brings tomorrow?" Momma R. said with a glimmer in her eyes. "Christmas morning always brings smiles."

~~~~~

Chris and Chloe stayed behind while the others went to their bedrooms. They were sharing a room with Jess and wanted a few minutes alone.

Chloe rested her head on his shoulder. "Do you think Momma R. looked worn out tonight?"

"Maybe a little tired. She told me this year has been a busy one for her. Maybe it is that and the prep work she did for tonight."

Chloe bit her lip. "Yeah, maybe. I feel like it might be more."

"Try not to worry." Chris handed her a small present. "Maybe this will cheer you up."

"Aw! You're too cute."

Chloe pulled the ribbon loose and opened the box. Inside was a chain with a single diamond pendant. "Oh, honey! It's gorgeous. You shouldn't have gotten me something so extravagant and expensive, though."

Chris took the diamond necklace out of the box and put it around her neck. "A beautiful woman should have a beautiful necklace." He leaned back. "I love how it looks on you. Simple yet elegant, just like you."

"Oh, I love it! It's gorgeous." She wrapped her arms around his neck and pulled him to her. He leaned back with her as they laid down on the couch.

Chloe wrapped her free leg around his and locked him tight to her. She brushed her lips across his. It didn't take long before their gentle kisses became more heated and frantic.

Chris backed away. "We have to stop. Any longer and there's no going back. I'll want you too much."

"It's already too late for me. I want you now," she said with a mischievous look in her eyes. "Follow me."

Chloe grabbed his hand and pulled him into the bathroom. She locked the door and nudged him against the wall. She unbuttoned his shirt and ran her hands along his chest, over his stomach to his belt. While opening his pants, she breathed, "You must be very, very quiet. Can you do that?"

He murmured back, "Yes. But last I checked; you were louder than me."

Chloe smirked and let his pants drop to the floor. She began teasing him with her hands. "You're so hot. I want you bad."

Chris couldn't answer. Chloe had taken the breath from him with her demanding strokes. She dusted his neck with feathery kisses and then returned her lips to his mouth. The kiss was hot and heady. Still unable to talk, he grabbed her wrists and held them at her sides.

He took a few breaths so he could utter the words, "I don't want this to be over yet."

Chris pulled her sweater over her head and let it drop to the floor. He took his turn nudging her back against the opposite wall and filled his hands with her breasts. The thin lace tortured him. Instead of taking the time to take her bra off, he pulled each of the cups down and began fevered teasing, alternating between his mouth and his hand.

Chloe remembered the time he made her let go by doing just this, and she felt close to having that happen all over again. Split seconds before she did, Chris moved his hands from her breasts to her skirt. He reached to the back and pulled down the zipper, letting it fall to the floor too. Her panties were made of the same thin lace and were the only thing keeping his hands from the direct contact she craved.

He ground his hips against hers until she couldn't take it any longer. Then he helped her pull her panties down and kneeled in front of her. He put her one foot up on his shoulder and tasted her. It drove him insane to feel her shiver against his mouth. He stopped when she went weak.

Chris stood, picked her up, and pushed her against the wall. She wrapped her legs around him as he pushed into her. In only seconds, he let go, muttering something unintelligible yet full of desire.

~~~~~

That night Chris laid in bed holding Chloe while she slept. His mind was full of thoughts, preventing him from falling asleep. Momma R. had told him earlier that there was an opening for a school principal at the Harmony school where she worked. "Maybe you should apply," she'd said.

Her words stayed with him now. This year at Galorston City High was proving extremely challenging and exhausting. The angry, disrespectful students had worn him down. Between the physical demands of the job, where he broke up fights, and the disrespect, with the derogatory pictures of him, he wasn't sure he had it in him to work there for years to come. *Could it get even worse?*

A slower-paced job and a quiet life in a nice town like this interested him. The Christmas Eve church service had been beautiful and made him miss belonging to a church. He hadn't gone to a service in a long time.

The town of Harmony appealed to him too. It seemed like a great place to raise a family. He wasn't sure how much Chloe wanted a family, but he could tell she was open to the idea. She'd mentioned kids in passing to him on several occasions. Chris was positive she would be a great mom. She learned what not to do from her own parents.

What about me? he thought. *Am I ready to slow things down and be a family man?* He glanced at Chloe and smiled. *Yes. I'm more sure every time I look at her.*

During another conversation earlier in the day, he'd asked Momma R. for her blessing to marry Chloe. "Yes! Of course! Oh, how wonderful," she'd told him, all smiles and warmth. What he needed to accomplish now was buy her the perfect ring and give her the perfect proposal—and hope a premonition didn't ruin the surprise.

~~~~~

Chapter 26

Chloe sat next to Gaby, fiddling with the small sapphire ring she wore. Another Christmas present from Chris, it gave her a small bit of comfort as she stared out the window. She and Gaby sat on the fifth floor of the major medical center where they waited for the surgeon to give them an update on Momma R. She sighed. Her premonition on Christmas Eve made sense now.

Gaby and Chloe both had been feeling down since the middle of January when Jess moved to California. The client she had been working with for her company offered her an amazing opportunity, and she took it. She was now the director of a newly formed statistical department there and loving the life—and the perks.

Chloe knew it was more than the job that drew her to California, though. She was falling for Hunter, the guy she had been flirting with for months. Now that she was no longer working as a contractor in his department, they decided to take the flirting up a notch and give a relationship a try.

Gaby, on the other hand, had been in a downward spiral since the holidays. Her motto she promised Chloe of—*a new year and new you*—never came to fruition. She hardly went out to see friends, and she even cut back on teaching dance classes.

When her mom came to visit in February, it was assumed to be just another check-in on her baby girl. However, it was obvious to them first thing that something was off. The first giveaway was the dark circles under Momma R.'s eyes. The second was the lack of pep in her voice. Instead of her usual one hundred percent, she seemed less vibrant, more cautious and sadder. It may not have been noticeable to most, but to the girls who loved her it was concerning. Both of them had replayed that night in their minds many times since.

"Momma, what's wrong?" Gaby had asked as her mom moved around the kitchen after dinner, much slower than usual.

"Why does anything have to be wrong?" her mom said dismissively.

"Because you look tired. What is it?" Gaby insisted.

Her mom looked from Gaby to Chloe. "Oh dear, there is no getting past the two of you." She took their hands. "Come, let's sit."

Gaby started to worry as she followed her mom and Chloe into their living room. "Momma, you are starting to freak me out. What's going on?"

Her mom patted their hands. "It might not be much of anything. But they found a spot on my recent mammogram."

"What do you mean *spot*?" Gaby blurted.

"A dark area that looks to be a growth. They want to do a biopsy to confirm what it is."

Speaking quickly, Gaby asked, "And what do they think it could be?"

She put her arms around each of them. "A tumor."

Gaby stood up and yelled out, "Dammit, Mom. No!"

Her mom stood up and reached for a hug. "Hija, we don't know anything for sure yet. The biopsy is next week. Once we hear the results, then we can decide what or if there are next steps."

Chloe had sat quietly on that day, feeling lost and devastated, much like she sat now waiting for the surgeon. The biopsy had showed a malignant tumor, resulting in the surgery, which Momma R. had just had.

Just when they didn't think they could last another minute of the mental torture, the surgeon appeared. She took Gaby's hand to shake it. "Hi, Ms. Rodriguez."

"Hi. How is she?" Gaby asked.

"Your mom is doing well. Still coming out of the anesthesia. The surgery lasted longer than we thought. We had to take more breast tissue than planned to make sure we got it all. While we were in there, we took seven lymph nodes. We'll biopsy them for cancer cells so we have an idea of what treatment options to consider. It will take about a week to get those results. Do you have any questions?"

Gaby looked like a raccoon caught in headlights. "Not right now. Thank you."

"I know it is a lot to take in, so you let the nurses know if you think of anything you need clarification on. You should be able to see her soon. A nurse will get you when it's okay to come back."

After she left, Gaby and Chloe held on to each other, fighting the tears burning their eyes. It had been a long few weeks and an even longer day. It seemed like only a small relief to know the tumor was gone. Momma R. would likely need chemotherapy.

The sound of the nurse walking in pulled Gaby and Chloe out of their thoughts. "Hi, Ms. Rodriguez, you may come see your mom now."

Chloe lightly patted her back. "I'll be here."

She watched Gaby walk away and pulled out her phone. She promised both Jess and Chris updates.

"Jess? Hey, she's okay. Gaby just went back to see her."

"Oh, thank God," Jess breathed. "I have been on pins and needles waiting to hear something."

Chloe paced the waiting room. "Oh, I know. We have been too. It's been torture waiting."

"I'm sorry I couldn't be there. It sucks being so far from you on this day. Please give Momma R. and Gaby all my love."

"I will, Jess. I promise. And don't worry. We all understand. We'll see you soon."

After hanging up, Chloe checked the time. School was still in session. Instead of calling, she sent Chris a text with the same details she gave Jess. Within two seconds of hitting send, he called.

"Hey, you," she answered quietly, mindful of the other family and friends waiting nearby. "I happened to catch you in your office?"

"No, I was walking down the hall, but I stepped into an empty classroom. I am glad she's out of surgery now. How is Gaby doing?"

"Sad, worried, freaked out. Exactly how anyone would be waiting to get news about their mom."

"And you? You're sad, worried, and freaked out?"

"Yeah, I am. But I am holding it together for Gabs. I need to be her rock right now."

"You don't have to be steel with me, baby. I'll be your rock."

Chloe felt her tears start to fall. "Can you tell me that later when I don't have to be strong? It's making me unravel."

"Of course. Call me when you're alone. I love you."

"Love you," she whispered.

Chloe sat back down and waited for Gaby. She took out her tablet and decided to try to take her mind off the present. She opened her documents and stared at a list of open articles she had. She only had to pick one, but she couldn't even do that. She closed the list and put the tablet down. She stood. *Do something, Chloe. You'll go crazy if you don't.* She picked up her tablet again. *Okay.* This time, she opened the files for the book she was working on with Sylvia.

The book was coming along well. They had met several times since January to plan. Sylvia would research the history, causes, and treatments of mental health disorders, while Chloe would conduct interviews and testimonials with patients and their caregivers. The two of them would then work together to analyze the impact of the disorders on all parties involved. Sylvia and Chloe would also write different chapters based on their individual field work.

Chloe had already conducted a few interviews but needed to review the feedback and consult with Sylvia. Then she could start to draft her chapters.

She tried to concentrate on her work but kept getting distracted by her thoughts or movement past the window. She looked up several times, wishing she could step outside on this bright, sunny spring day and tilt her head to the sun. Anything to feel some comfort.

She jumped when Gaby joined her at the window. "How is she?" Chloe asked.

"Okay. You know, drowsy. Half in, half out of it." Gaby shrugged. "She was at least awake enough to recognize me."

Chloe saw the tears in her friend's eyes and knew the shrug she gave was one of sadness. She put her tablet away and took Gaby's hand. "So, what's next? Do they have a room for her yet?"

"They're working on it. Want some tea? I could use something."

Chloe grabbed her bag off the chair. "I could too."

~~~~~

That night was another sleepless one for Gaby. She was awake but kept her eyes closed, hoping she would fall out at some point. It was unlikely she would, though, since her mind was all over the place. She didn't know what the next few months or even years would hold for her and her mom.

Since Gaby found out about her mother being sick, she'd started thinking more seriously about moving back home to be with her. She had thoughts of missing her hometown in the past year. Galorston wasn't holding for her what she needed or wanted right now. She wanted family, safety, and peace. The only place she seemed to get all three of those things was when she visited Harmony.

She wrestled with the idea of feeling like she would be going backward if she moved home, but now with her mom sick it didn't feel backward at all. She had three months to figure out what she wanted to do while St. Mary's held her job.

Gaby rolled over and looked at Chloe, who was fast asleep. Gaby appreciated her friend being there with her, and for all the love and support she'd readily given over the past year. In less than twelve months, Gaby had somehow slipped and started spiraling. When she looked at herself or really thought about how she felt, she didn't have the same energy she once had; the light inside her felt dim. It was time she admitted to herself and her family she was depressed.

The following morning, Gaby stirred to the sound of the shower running. Miraculously, she had gotten a few hours of sleep. It must have been the exhaustion that kicked in from running on empty for weeks now. Slowly standing, she felt every muscle in her body protest. *Ugh, can people actually age twenty years in one month?*

Gaby knocked on the door to the bathroom. "Mind if I come in while you're in the shower?"

"Come in," Chloe answered. "How are you? I saw you got some sleep last night."

Gaby grumbled to herself as she looked in the mirror. "I look like shit."

Chloe yelled out, "What's that? I can't hear you."

Avoiding telling Chloe what she really said, she answered with, "I'm okay. I guess I got a few hours. You?"

"Yeah, me too. I got up early and ran down for coffee. There's a hot one sitting out there for you. I figured we'd need the hard stuff today."

The water shut off and Gaby moved toward the door. "I'll go sip some and let you get out."

Gaby sat on the end of the bed with the coffee cup in hand and stared at the wall. She might have been sleeping with her eyes open because the next thing she heard was, "Gaby?"

She shook her head to focus. "Sorry, I was out of it."

"I said you can get in."

Gaby nodded.

Chloe looked closer into Gaby's eyes. "Talk to me."

Gaby didn't hesitate. "I'm depressed. It's not just being down. I think it's actual depression."

Chloe sat next to her on the bed. "Let's get you someone to talk to. A support group could help. I'm sure there are groups for people who have family members with cancer near Harmony."

"I need something. I'm not doing well. My life is such a mess. Momma's sick. Both you and Jess are moving your lives forward, while I'm going backward. I am seriously thinking about moving home. Galorston isn't for me anymore."

Chloe reassured her. "You have time to make up your mind while you're on paid family leave. Don't worry."

Gaby leaned her head on Chloe's shoulder and started to cry. "Did you know?"

Chloe wrapped an arm around Gaby's shoulders. "I suspected you were upset but didn't realize how much you were struggling. You're going to be okay and so is your mom. You're both strong, kick-ass women. We'll find a way through all of this. I promise."

~~~~~

The two-hour drive back to Harmony felt long. Gaby watched her mom doze in and out while she drove. Chloe followed them in her car, intending to leave soon after they got to the house.

The sun was bright, and it was a beautiful spring day. Gaby knew she should be happy spring was here, but no amount of sunshine seemed to improve her mood or boost her energy level. Thoughts of her mom and sadness enveloped her.

Gaby pulled into the driveway and gently rubbed her mom's arm, waking her from a groggy state. "Momma, we're home."

Chloe opened the passenger side door, gently swung Momma R.'s legs out of the car and lifted. Her mom was still weak but could walk mostly on her own, only partially leaning on them.

They set her up in the living room with lots of pillows.

"Are you hungry, Momma?"

"Not right now. I'll rest a bit first." She put her hand up to Gaby's face. "Ah, my little Gabriella. Now taking care of me. Thank you, querida."

"Anything for you, Momma."

Gaby went into the kitchen, with Chloe following close behind. She held back the tears until she reached the sink. "It breaks my heart to see Mom so tired. And this is only the beginning. I'm going to have dig deep for strength."

Chloe rubbed her back. "You have Jess and me to lean on."

"I can't fully rely on you."

The tears started to flow, and Gaby sank to the floor. She put her forehead to the ground and let out everything. Her body wracked with sobs. When she felt it wasn't possible to shed another tear, Gaby sighed. Chloe helped her sit up.

"God, I've lost it. I'm on the floor crying. This is definitely rock bottom," Gaby moaned softly.

Chloe pulled her to a standing position. "Let's splash cold water on your face and get you lunch."

After checking to make sure her mom was good, Gaby met Chloe on the front porch.

They sat in comfortable silence taking in the warm sunshine. Gaby peeked through one eye when she heard footsteps.

Gaby waved. "Hi, Sam."

After Chloe said hello, she excused herself.

Sam took a step closer to the porch. "Hi, Gabriella. I stopped by to see how your mom was feeling."

"Surgery went well. They will check to make sure they got it all and determine what options we have next. We should hear something in about a week." Gaby started fidgeting with her hands. "She is feeling okay, just really tired. When I came out here, she was sleeping on the couch."

"You know I am here for you. You can call me anytime. Your momma is real special to me. I loved your daddy like he was my brother. I'd do anything for you two."

Gaby stood and threw her arms around his shoulders when tears welled again. Even the tiniest bit of kindness could cut at her and set her off. Against his big soft chest, a muffled "thank you" could be heard.

~~~~~

For the next week, Gaby tried to take the approach of one step at a time. Every day felt like a challenge, but she did it. She refused to let her mom see her cry. That she kept to herself behind closed doors. By the second Sunday after the surgery, her mom was feeling up to going to church. Sam offered to drive them.

On their way to her mom's favorite pew, several folks stopped them to ask how she was feeling. It was all very nice of them, but it only made Gaby feel sadder.

Just before the service started, Gaby saw Brad out of the corner of her eye sit down across the aisle from them. She turned her head and smiled at him. He returned her smile and waved.

Since Christmas, the phone calls and texts with Brad had been less frequent, but they still stayed in touch. Over the past few weeks he had reached out several times, asking how both were doing and if she needed anything.

Gaby tried to focus on the service; however, it proved difficult. She noticed Megan Price stealing looks at Brad. Her heart clenched when he returned one of them with a smile. *That's it. He likes her. Not me. And why would he after I rejected him right away? That's what I get for swearing off men. Figures. Just when I find someone good too.*

Megan seemed nice enough, although a bit younger than they were. She thought Megan might be too immature for him, but who was she to judge? She had her own problems to deal with and didn't have anything inside to give to a man right now. Brad deserved someone who could give him love and attention. *Megan is perfect.*

She looked when she felt her mom squeeze her thigh.

"Here." Her mom nodded toward the hymnal.

"Sorry," she whispered, opening her mouth to sing.

The next hymn happened to be one of her favorites, but instead of it bringing her joy or peace, she found it made her throat tighten and tears sting behind her eyes.

Although she loved the church, Gaby was glad when it was over and it was time to leave. Sam signaled to her that he would get the car. She nodded, then turned to get her purse, avoiding eye contact with Brad. She watched Megan move to him with a sexy strut and flirty smile, which only made the tears threaten more. Gaby kept her head down and scurried over to her mom. "Let's go out the side door."

"Why, Gaby?"

Her eyes followed Brad and Megan. "It's easier this way."

After she closed her mom's car door, she turned to find Brad less than a foot away. He was so close she could smell the earthy scent that was characteristically him.

He took her arm. "I'd like to talk to you when you have time."

Unable to keep eye contact as a tear slipped out, she looked to the ground. "Sure, let me know when you're free."

When he squeezed her arm, Gaby took a chance to look up at him, even with a second tear slipping down.

"I can handle crying, you know."

She shook her head in understanding and looked down again. She turned toward the car, but he beat her to the door and opened it for her. He leaned close. "Come for a walk with me today. I'll text you."

~~~~~

When Brad arrived, he came to the door dressed in an old T-shirt and track pants. How he still looked gorgeous in that was beyond Gaby's comprehension. They drove out to the river that ran around the edge of town.

There was a nice walking path that ran parallel to the river for a few miles. They called it the Little Riverwalk.

"I like that they've added the benches," said Gaby. "It's nice to take in the views."

Brad smiled. "Yep."

She sighed. "I've been here so many times. Momma used to take me when I was little. Did you go to any of the parties here after football games? I only went to a few."

Brad laughed. "Sometimes. It was a good place to talk and think too."

"Yeah."

She felt Brad's eyes on her. "You're quieter than normal," he said. "How are you doing?"

Gaby wrapped her arms around herself and shrugged. It was true. She wasn't the same talkative and bubbly girl she was just a few months ago. She studied her clothes. There was a time she wouldn't have been caught dead in these old jeans or without makeup in front of a guy. Yet here she was, doing exactly that and not having the energy to do anything about it.

"You know, that's the sign of good friends … when you don't have to say a word, you can just be."

"Yeah, you might just be the first friend I ever had."

"The first memory I have of you was here."

Gaby studied his profile. "Really? How old were we?"

"Dad told me we were two. Our dads brought us here to play in the river on a hot day. Do you remember it?"

She tried to picture it, them as little kids jumping and splashing in the water ahead. But nothing surfaced. "I don't. You remember my dad?"

"A tiny bit. They were tossing us in the deep part."

"I'm jealous. I don't remember it. I have a small memory of me standing at the garage watching him work and another of him driving with me in the front seat, which of course made Momma angry. They're just moments that flash." Gaby turned her head toward the river to watch the water flow as they walked. "Do you have any memories of your mom?"

Brad turned his head, watching her. "Like you, a few flashes. I miss her a lot. Probably how you feel about your dad, wishing she was there for the big things in life and holidays."

"So true. I'm really missing him right now." Gaby stole a glance his way to see if he was still looking at her. He was. A small flicker of light warmed her body. "I wish he was here to lean on. The one person I lean on most needs to lean on me now. I'm not sure I'm up to the challenge."

Brad stopped in front of her. "That's a hard switch to deal with. I'd love to be one of the people you lean on. I know you have your girlfriends, but I'm here in town."

Gaby found herself saying without hesitation, "I'd like that." She squinted as she tried to focus on Brad's face with the sun behind him, then blurted, "Will Megan be okay with that?"

Brad drew his brows together. "I'm not sure what you mean."

Gaby glanced toward the river. "You guys aren't dating?"

"No, Gaby. She's an okay girl, but I'm not interested in her like that."

"Oh."

His arms came up around her and she leaned into the hug. She sighed, resting her head on his chest. *His arms feel so good around me.*

He gently rubbed her back. "Is that a sigh of defeat? All these years of hating me gone?" When she didn't answer, he went on, "Or is that too hopeful?"

"I never hated you. I'm not sure I ever could. I can say with certainty that I never understood you, though."

"I'm actually quite simple. I've adored you since we were little. As teenagers, I didn't know how to act in front of you. You were so fun and pretty. So I started doing dumb stuff to get your attention and it just spiraled from there."

His use of the word "spiral" resonated with her. She knew all too well how that could happen. "How did you stop spiraling?"

"I guess I grew up ... figured out that I couldn't be an idiot for the rest of my life."

She lifted her head and stepped back. "Who knew I'd be getting life advice from you?"

"Gabriella, is that a faint smile I see?"

She punched him lightly on the arm. "Yes, congratulations. The first one in a long time."

They started walking again. Brad took her hand in his and met her eyes. "If this is too much, I'll let go."

"No, don't let go."

This is the most comfortable I have felt in a long time.

~~~~~

Chapter 27

The next few weeks felt very odd to Chloe. As she sat at the kitchen table, she thought back to last spring when her two best friends were here living with her. They spent Friday nights at home and Saturday nights out dancing. Now that Jess was in California and Gaby in Harmony, it was quiet here without them.

She had made room in her closet for Chris to hang his work clothes since he started staying there every night. Chloe loved saying goodbye to him in the mornings and coming home to him in the evenings, but she missed her friends.

Every day Chloe texted or called both. Often it was texting with Jess because of the time difference, and with Gaby it was phone calls. Jess had adjusted well to California life. It was Gaby that Chloe worried about. It was hard with her mom sick. It had already been a month since Gaby started her family leave, and Chloe knew it wasn't likely she would be going back in two months. The doctors had found cancer cells in the lymph nodes they'd extracted during Momma R.'s surgery and felt it best to start chemotherapy. It would be an eight-week treatment plan, starting later today. There was no way Gaby would leave her mom right when the treatment finished.

Chris had left an hour ago for work. He had to be in much earlier than Chloe, since school started just after seven o'clock. He usually got home before she did, but not always. Some days he would be gone for eleven or twelve hours. They both looked forward to summer when he could recharge.

Chloe hoped to take a small vacation with him—maybe the beach for a week in July. She'd love to go visit Jess for a few days too. She missed her friend and had never been to California. They could also visit Briana in Kansas City. Anything sounded good as long as they were getting away and relaxing somewhere.

She grabbed her tablet off the table and studied her notes from the project with Sylvia. She scheduled a few additional interviews to complete over the next month, and then they could really dive into the drafting.

Chloe smiled, remembering more publishing success, but this time for the cookbook she'd started last year. She had finished her manuscript a few months back and had submitted it to several literary agents. After many rejections, she had two offers to consider now. Andrea, Sylvia's cousin and lawyer, was reviewing the terms to help her decide. It was an exciting time for Chloe as well as Chris, who fully embraced his role as taste-tester and flavor manager.

In fact, just this morning he had approved the muffins she was taking into work. She hoped by people tasting and enjoying the product, she could get more interested in her baking and wanting to buy her book.

Another gorgeous day, she noted as she headed to her car, muffin tray in her arms.

Walking into work, Chloe stopped to see Eve and put a muffin on her desk. Eve waved her thanks while she was on the phone and mouthed the words "thank you."

Chloe then dropped the muffins off in the conference room, where the team would hold a meeting later, and headed to her desk.

Chloe scrolled through her list of latest assignments. She first planned to follow up on the investigation into a shooting she'd reported on yesterday. She wanted to work on that one before the meeting so Lou could review it, and then they could quickly upload the article that afternoon.

While sitting at her desk typing away, she started to feel nauseous. Her stomach lurched and bile rose a little in her throat. *What did I eat?* Thinking back, nothing she had eaten seemed like it would bother her. It also didn't feel like a premonition. *Strange.* Chloe dismissed it and continued working until the meeting.

Chloe caught Mya's attention as people started filing into the conference room. Mya had a muffin and coffee cup in each hand as she headed to the table. "Hey," Chloe said.

"Hey," replied Mya. Then she looked down. Chloe didn't have coffee or muffins. "Are you okay? Not like you to turn down a coffee."

Chloe leaned over, keeping her voice low. "I don't know. I feel a little yucky today."

Mya winced. "Maybe you should go home and work from there. I bet Lou wouldn't mind."

Chloe shrugged. "I don't feel that bad. I'll ask him if I start feeling worse."

After the meeting, Chloe finished her article and submitted it to Lou. Noting the time, she texted Gaby.

Chloe: *Hey, girl, did your mom have her appt yet?*
Gaby: *Yeah, it was earlier. She's doing okay.*
Chloe: *Good, luv you*

Chloe was happy that Momma R. was doing okay after her first chemotherapy treatment. As for her, she felt anything but good. Luckily, Lou liked what she wrote and agreed to let her do her other work from home for the rest of the afternoon.

~~~~~

The next day and the day after, Chloe continued to feel ill. Her breath hitched and her stomach rolled at the thought of food. She went into work both days, but by the afternoon she had no energy, and Lou agreed she should go home. It wasn't until the third afternoon that Chris started to really worry about her.

He called her on his way home from work. "Baby, you're home again? Still feeling sick?"

"Yeah, I am. I threw up about an hour ago."

"You should call the doctor."

Chloe hemmed. "I don't know. It's not like it's that bad. I can still eat sometimes."

"You're so stubborn, huh?" She could hear the gentle banter in his voice. "Well, if you're still sick Friday, I'm taking you."

She sighed. "Okay."

After hanging up, Chris had a thought. He made a turn instead of heading straight home.

"Chloe?" he called out as he entered through the front door.

"In here."

Chris walked into the living room and saw her lying on the couch. He handed her a bag.

She took it and peeked inside, then looked up at him. "You think I might be pregnant?"

"Well, I don't know, but your symptoms seem to be similar with that."

"I have an IUD though. They're like ninety-nine point nine percent effective."

He shrugged. "It can happen. Let's just rule it out."

"Okay." She took the pregnancy test into the bathroom and followed the directions. "All right! I peed on the stick."

Chris came in, eyebrows knit with concern. They both stared at the wand Chloe held. Within a few minutes, only one solid line appeared in the results box. Chris closed his eyes. "Well, you're not pregnant. So, you must have a virus or something. Why don't you call the doctor and make an appointment for tomorrow? I'd feel better if you got checked out. And I think you would too."

"Okay." Chloe looked at her phone. "I'll call now."

"Good idea."

"I'm going to go for a run," he called out as she put the phone to her ear.

"Okay. Love you."

"Love you."

Chris's mind raced at mach speed while he ran. He was disappointed Chloe wasn't pregnant. Once the thought had crossed his mind, he'd instantly become excited. He was more than ready to start a family. He rationalized as he ran harder that he should try to do it in the traditional order for her. She hadn't had a traditional childhood like he had. The least he could do was give her some normalcy as an adult.

So, if she isn't pregnant, what is she sick with? The question plagued him for the rest of the day. He hoped they could find the answer soon.

~~~~~

There was nothing at found Chloe's doctor's appointment and the blood work results came back normal. Chloe didn't know what to make of it. It was a full week of feeling sick and not knowing why.

On Monday, Chloe forced herself to go to work and make it through the day. When she felt sick in the morning, Lou tried to send her home, but she refused. "I need to keep busy. This will pass."

She'd carried on without much issue or discomfort for once. *Finally*, she thought. On her drive home, she called Gaby.

She answered on the second ring. "Hey, girl."

"What are you doing?" Chloe asked.

"Cooking. I invited Sam and Brad over. I'm not sure my mom is really up to it, but she said she has to keep busy, that it will pass."

Chloe bit her lip, a new idea springing to mind. "Umm, Gabs? Did your mom throw up today?"

"Yeah, why?"

"When?" Chloe asked.

"Around eleven o'clock. Where are you going with this?"

"Oh my God! I didn't see it before. When you said about your mom keeping busy and that it will pass, it hit me."

Gaby stopped stirring the sauce and stared at the wall. "What hit you? Girl, you aren't making any sense."

"You know how I haven't been feeling well? I think I'm having some sort of prolonged premonition about your mom."

"Really?"

"Yes, because I started feeling sick the same day she started her chemo treatments."

Gaby shook her head. "So, you think you're going to be sick for the remaining weeks of her treatment?"

"I don't think so, because today I am feeling better. I haven't felt this good in a week!"

"Good. I'm glad you finally figured out the mystery."

"Me too, I'm going to call Chris and tell him the good news. Catch you later!"

~~~~~

Within a few weeks, Chloe felt much better—no new "sympathy premonitions" occurred, and their typical routine resumed. Every morning, Chloe got up after Chris finished his workout and got in one of her own. She'd pass him on her way to the shower and kiss him goodbye before getting ready for work.

Today after her usual workout and goodbye, she made her lunch, got in her car, and fastened her seatbelt. As the belt clicked in place, a sharp pain pierced her shoulder. She winced as fire surged through her body and rolled off her like a wave. "What the hell?"

She shook her head to clear her mind before pulling away from the curb.

At the end of the road, the same pain hit her, and darkness blurred her vision. "What is happening!" Her mind shot to Momma R.

She pulled over to side of the road and called Gaby. "I'm so sorry for waking you, but I had a premonition about someone in pain. Is your mom okay?"

She listened as Gaby shot out of bed and ran to her mom's room. "Momma, are you okay?"

Chloe breathed a sigh as she heard Momma R.'s response. "Yes, I'm fine. I was just having a dream. What's wrong?"

"Nothing, Momma. Go back to sleep." Gaby spoke into the phone. "Momma is fine. Maybe try Jess or Chris?"

Chloe started to panic more. "I'll try Chris next."

"Chloe, call me back after and tell me everyone is okay," Gaby pleaded.

Chloe sighed. "I could be wrong. I want to be wrong. But this … this felt so real. I'll call you later."

She tapped on Chris's name and listened to the phone ring. *Dammit! Why isn't he answering?* She sent him a text: *Call or text me, tell me you are okay. I had a premonition.*

276

When thirty seconds went by and she didn't hear back from him, she texted Jess.

Chloe: *Jess, are you all good? I had a premonition, but I don't know about who.*
Jess: *Yes, I'm good. Gaby?*
Chloe: *Gaby and her mom are good.*
Jess: *Let me know.*

Chloe pulled up Mya's number. "Hey, have you heard about any news with stabbings?"

"No, but I haven't seen Lou this morning yet. Why?"

"Mmm. I must have misheard something on the radio," Chloe lied. "Can you tell Lou I'll be a little late today? I have to run an errand."

"Yeah, I can tell him when I see him."

"Thanks."

Chloe threw her phone to the side and pulled away from the curb. *Think about this a little. When other premonitions have happened lately, if they have to do with me they happen a little while after the vision. So maybe something will happen to me while I drive?* At that, she locked her car doors, imagining a carjacking or a reappearance of Kirk. *I really don't think that's it. This feels different.*

Something told her to drive to the high school. Chris was the only one unaccounted for. A pit of fear built in her stomach.

As she drove, she argued with herself. "He rarely answers his phone when I call. Especially at this time of the morning. There are lots of things that need to be done right after school starts." She glanced at her phone. Still no text. "He usually can't even text me back until lunchtime. I'm sure he's fine. The pain could have been a muscle spasm. And the darkness was just from closing my eyes with the spasm."

She drove faster as she got on the highway. "Maybe it's all just a coincidence, or I'm having some kind of psychotic breakdown. God, what if I'm wrong? What if I'm *right?* Shit! Shit! Shit!"

Chloe pulled onto the side of the road before the parking lot and gasped. Her head screamed and her stomach convulsed. Ambulances and police cars swarmed the high school. Teachers had corralled their kids on patches of grass outside. *Chris!*

She parked the car, grabbed her press pass, and raced to the scene. Caution tape prevented her from entering the building itself and attempts at getting a police officer's attention failed. She groaned and frantically scanned the people around her. *What the hell did Chris wear to work today?*

The ambulances didn't seem used at the moment, which calmed Chloe slightly. She prayed they were only there as a precaution.

She dialed Lou. "Lou, I'm at the high school. There is something major going on. Have you sent a crew yet? I'll get what I can, but I'm freaking out. I don't see Chris anywhere."

"Chloe don't worry about work. I already sent a crew."

She ran over to where it looked like some teachers had congregated. They had grim looks on their faces.

She interrupted their conversation to say, "I'm looking for Chris Sherman. Have you seen him?"

One woman shook her head. "No, sorry."

"What happened?" Chloe still looked around for him or anyone else she recognized.

"I don't know exactly; the word is a kid brought a knife with him and tried to stab another student."

Chloe moved on to another group, and another, asking the same thing. She got the same answer every time. No one knew where Chris was.

She made her way to the ambulances and waited there. *Anyone who is injured or in shock will go there*, she reasoned. As she stood, she filmed the police entering the front doors and scanned the crowd, then fired it off to Lou to use as breaking news.

She kept searching the crowds, but the more she looked, the more certain she was of what had happened. The pain she'd felt was Chris being sliced with a knife. She didn't think it was deep, but she didn't have a detailed vision, just the feeling, so she couldn't be sure. All she could do was wait until he appeared.

When she saw her station truck pull up, she waved them down. Marcia and Frank hopped out and started covering the scene. Chloe walked along the edge of the taped area to see if she could get a view of anything from a different angle but turned up empty. Now she settled for simply pacing. Every second felt like an eternity.

Chloe felt a small bit of relief when she finally saw the police walk out with someone—a kid, a student, a suspect? His head hung low, shielding his face. A pack of reporters, including Marcia, pounced on him, but the officers shouldered them away. On a different day, in a different town, Chloe would've been one of the reporters tailing him. But today everything was about finding Chris. She craned her neck to see if anyone else was coming out. *Will the injured be next?*

Then Chloe saw him. He was on the first stretcher brought out from the building. Even from a distance Chloe could see that blood stained his shirt, pooling at his right shoulder. She winced, remembering the bite of pain from earlier.

When he got closer, she breathed a sigh. *His eyes are open! He's conscious!*

She called his name, just loud enough for him to hear her. He turned his head and focused on her. "Wait!" he yelled to the paramedics. "She's with me."

One of the paramedics waved her over. She dashed toward them, not taking her eyes off Chris. After they loaded him into the vehicle, Chloe climbed in and sat near his head.

He whispered, "You knew, didn't you?"

Chloe leaned close. "I felt it."

"That's amazing."

Chloe felt her heart swell. The love she had for him was like nothing she'd ever experienced. It took her breath away. And now that she'd found it, she would never let it go. "You're everything to me."

~~~~~

Chapter 28

"Are you sure you're okay to drive? It does take a little over an hour to get to Harmony." Chloe emphasized as they pulled away from the curb.

"Yes, I'm positive. The doctor said everything was fine when he took the stitches out the other day. They were in for three weeks and it's all healing great. I promise." Chris patted her thigh.

"Your arm might get tired, though?"

"Okay, now you're just making up stuff. It's not that long of a drive. I can handle it."

Chloe snapped her head toward him as a chuckle escaped her throat. "Tough guy, huh? Let's imagine for a minute the roles were reversed, and I had been stabbed. You'd be treating me like glass!"

"First of all, I was not stabbed. I was cut. Second, the roles aren't reversed." Chris poked his finger into her arm. "And third, I'm the man who has to protect you."

"You did not just say that!" Chloe jabbed back at him, laughing. "God, you're impossible!" She picked up her phone. "I'm going to call Gaby and tell her we are on our way."

Gaby's voice breezed on the other end. "Hey, are you guys on the road now?"

"Yup, we left about ten minutes ago. We should be there a little after one o'clock. How's your mom today?"

"She's really good, actually. Looking forward to seeing you for your birthday."

"Me too." Chloe continued, "I am sad about Jess, though. This is the first time in what—seven or eight years? —where we aren't all together on one of our birthdays."

"Yeah, I know. It sucks. It's been weird not being at the townhouse for almost three months now. Oh, by the way, I told work yesterday that I won't be back. I have no idea what I'm going to do. I just know I can't go back to Galorston."

"You'll figure something out," Chloe reassured.

"Okay, let's change the topic to something more fun. How was your fancy birthday dinner last night?"

Chloe gazed at Chris. "Our dinner was beautiful. Wait until you see the new fabulous shoes he bought me."

"Oh man, I'm so jealous. You have them on?" Gaby asked.

"Of course. They're too gorgeous not to be shown off at my birthday party. He also got me a beautiful bracelet and a new bikini for our trip to the beach this summer."

"Okay, now you're just trying to make me furious," Gaby teased.

Chloe took a breath. "Hey, Gabs? In all seriousness, you sound good."

Gaby paused. "Yeah, I mean, it's all still really hard, but it doesn't feel as suffocating as it did in the beginning."

"I'm glad." She paused. "I'm so excited today. I keep having visions of everyone together. Can't wait to see you!"

"Hurry up!" Gaby insisted.

"We are. Chatting with you is making the ride go by fast. We'll be there soon."

As they approached the edge of the town, Chris made a turn. Chloe looked at him. "What are you doing? Gaby's place is in town," she said, pointing to her left.

"I know. I was just thinking about something and want to see if it's still here."

Chloe's eyebrows knitted together. "Huh? What do you want to see?"

Chris didn't answer. He hoped those visions she had of everyone together stayed glimpses and didn't tell her what else he had planned.

"Tell me?" Chloe pouted.

He smirked. "This place I remember from when I was a kid. You know my parents aren't that far from here." He pointed to his right. "And Ben's over that way."

Chloe's shoulders dropped a bit. "Okay, but we won't be here long, right?"

Chris risked a glance at her. "Don't pout," he said, squeezing her thigh. "We won't be late. It's just down here—another minute."

Chloe strained her neck and squinted in the sun. "I don't see anything. Is this near the river? It's some view or something?"

"Geeze, Miss Twenty Questions. Have patience."

They headed down a gravel driveway. Up ahead, Chloe could see a house. *Who does Chris know here?* Chloe wondered.

Placing the car in park, he reached over and patted her thigh. "Come on."

Chloe looked out the window. "Does a friend of yours live here?"

He smiled. "Let's go for a walk."

She held his hand as they walked up a small path leading to the farmhouse's entry.

"Do you like the porch?" Chris asked.

Chloe shot him a questioning look. "Yeah. Big porches are beautiful. Why?"

Chris made his way up the porch steps and reached for the front door. Chloe grabbed his arm. "You're not going to knock?"

"No," he said, and continued walking.

She followed him into the empty house. "Uh, Chris? It looks like nobody lives here. What are we doing here?"

"Baby, we need to talk."

She whirled around to face him. "What's wrong?"

His grin widened. "Why does anything have to be wrong?"

"I don't know! Because this is so weird."

He took her by her shoulders and pulled her into a hug. He started smoothing her hair. "The thing is, honey, I've been giving this a lot of thought."

When she took a step backward and opened her mouth as if to speak, he put a finger to her lips. "No more questions, okay? Let me get this out."

Chloe sighed, but nodded.

Still holding her one hand, he gazed into her eyes and spoke softly. "Having you in my life has made it wonderful, but it makes me greedy and want even more for us. I want to come home happy at the end of my day, not just because I am coming home to you, but because I liked at least one thing I did during the day. Otherwise I don't have anything good to tell you when I walk in the door. I need less stress so I can enjoy life with you more. I want us to slow down, spend more time together, to be closer to our family and friends. Most of all, what I want is to build a family with you.

"So, I've asked myself, how do we get all of that? For months last fall, I tossed around the idea of going back to teaching instead of administration, but then Momma R. told me that Harmony School District was looking for a principal. That got my attention, yet I hesitated. I've worked hard to become a principal in a large district. It's a prestigious position and an opportunity many want. Then a few weeks ago, a student turned a knife on me after I tried to break up a fight. I thought of only one thing while I was in that debacle."

Chris brought one hand up to cradle Chloe's face and rubbed his thumb along her cheek. "It was you, Chloe. I worried I'd never see you again, that I'd never have a chance to build a family with you. My so-called prestigious job no longer felt prestigious. I called the Harmony School District and interviewed for the principal job."

He watched her eyes scan his face. He forged on. "I called a realtor and asked them to send me a list of houses for sale in the area. This one caught my attention immediately. I remembered seeing it once years ago. Plus, the drive is still manageable for you to get to the office. I think it could work for both of us. I picture you standing on the front porch taking in the sun. I see you sitting under that tree, writing. And I see us happy here.

"I haven't said yes to any of it, though. We can walk out that door and keep things exactly the way they are. I'd still love that because I am with you. But saying yes could mean living in a place like this down the road from our families and friends. It could mean taking the next step forward.

"I know I am springing a lot on you all at once. Don't worry. We don't have to have all the answers today. There is one answer, however, I am looking for today …"

Still holding her one hand, Chris kneeled in front of her, not losing eye contact for even a second. He heard Chloe gasp, and watched her bring a hand to her face. "Chloe Larson, from the second I saw you and shook your hand, I knew I wanted it all with you. Your innocence captivates me. Your inner and outer beauty leaves me breathless. I can't imagine even one day without you. I need you every day, forever. You are my future. Baby, will you marry me?"

Tears started to burn Chloe's eyes, her heart hammered in her chest, and her mouth went dry. Everything in her screamed yes, but no words would form. She could only nod.

Chris took a ring out of his pocket, stood up, and held it over her finger. "Is that a yes?"

Chloe kept nodding as he slid the ring on her hand. Then she took his face in both hands and kissed him hard. Pulling back, she said breathlessly, "That's a yes to all of it."

He swung her around and when he put her down, the kiss, they shared said all the other words that were in between the lines.

~~~~~

Out in the backyard, Gaby held her mom and Jess's hands while they waited under a large tree. They'd been there for a while now, having parked the cars behind a hill down the road. Now they watched for Chris and Chloe to come out. Chris's parents, Todd, and Briana were there too.

Todd leaned forward and whispered to Gaby and Jess, "She is going to say yes, isn't she?"

They both turned and narrowed their eyes at him. He put up his hands and leaned back. "Okay then. That's a yes."

Helen stood on her tiptoes and craned her neck. "Ooo! I see them! They're coming!"

Chris flung open the back door and watched Chloe's face as she took in the scene. Then he yelled, "She said yes!" Clapping and cheers erupted from where their friends and family stood.

Chloe looked up at him and shook her head in disbelief. Tears started falling, but she found her voice. Although quiet, she was able to get out the words she felt in her heart. "I had nothing when I came to Texas but a few bags of clothes. No friends. No family. I didn't know I'd ever be able to find it all … all of you. I say yes to it all!"

~~~~~

Acknowledgments

Thank you to Madeline and Anna Bigert for your patience while listening to me talk endlessly about writing this book. It was a guarantee that you would hear something about my trials and tribulations on every walk we took. I appreciate all of the advice and encouragement you provided. You are the best daughters and girlfriends a mom could have.

Thank you to my husband Teddy for encouraging me to keep going and nudging me when I let insecurity get the best of me. It is your kind and patient love that inspired me while writing this book. Meeting and falling in love with you made me feel as though I was the one who had found it all.

A big thank you also to my editor, Kristen Susienka, for all your help, advice, encouragement, and belief in Chloe and Chris's story.

To Lynn Pilewski, my dear friend, thank you for sacrificing your time and your willingness to be my first beta reader. Without your support and faith I may not have continued past the first draft.

And finally, thank you to my readers for picking up this novel and welcoming it into your home.

About the Author

Stacey Komosinski blends her love for romance novels and Texas with the opinion that you can find it all in this debut novel. She was inspired by her own love story and a visit to San Antonio in 2016.

Stacey grew up strongly influenced by her mother's love for reading and belief in library access for all. She holds a master's degree in molecular biology and is employed as a supply chain product leader within the pharmaceutical industry.

She makes Pennsylvania her home with her husband, Teddy, and two daughters, Madeline and Anna.

~~~~~

To connect with Stacey, find her links at https://msha.ke/staceyakomosinski/ or visit her website, https://staceyakomosinski.wixsite.com/books to sign up for her newsletter. Stacey genuinely enjoys hearing from readers. Please reach out!

~~~~~

If you enjoyed reading Finding It All, then watch out for Book #2 in the Finding Happiness In Harmony Series, coming out in 2021.

Reviews are appreciated. Thank you!

Made in the USA
Middletown, DE
24 May 2021

40352020R00175